Characters of
Lust

Characters of Lust

A novel by

LeBlanc

URBAN Renaissance
www.urbanbooks.net

Urban Books, LLC
78 East Industry Court
Deer Park, NY 11729

ISBN-13: 978-1-60162-308-9
ISBN-10: 1-60162-308-9

First Mass Market Printing July 2011
First Trade Paperback Printing March 2008
Printed in the United States of America

10 9 8 7 6 5 4 3 2 1

Distributed by Kensington Publishing Corp.
Submit Wholesale Orders to:
Kensington Publishing Corp.
C/O Penguin Group (USA) Inc.
Attention: Order Processing
405 Murray Hill Parkway
East Rutherford, NJ 07073-2316
Phone: 1-800-526-0275
Fax: 1-800-227-9604

LUST TWENTY-EIGHT

I woke up at six in the morning. Megan was meeting Blair and me at the hospital for Kelly's surgery at eight.

I called Kelly. "Are you ready?"

"As ready as I can be," Kelly voiced softly.

"You'll be fine. There is power in prayer," I said, finally realizing that I needed to turn my life around too.

"I know. I've prayed repeatedly. God has plans for me. He told me in order to be set free I must turn my life over to Him," Kelly preached.

"If the Lord said that to you, then you need to listen. Be obedient," I lectured to Kelly. "And I need to so the same."

"By the way, thank you for letting me stay with you. My mom was high last night. I don't think she can care for me, and I don't want to be bothered with Kevin," Kelly confessed.

"Well, sweets, that's what friends are for," I said, wondering if she got the picture.

Kelly poured out her heart. "Shelby, I love you. I

LUST ONE

It was Friday night and I was bored again. I was sitting on the fluffy pink carpet in my bedroom, wearing only my bra and panties, looking at a box of letters. Again, I was thinking about him, Sebastian LaCroix. I was unsure if it was the lonely weekend feeling or the breeze of spring that made me think of him more than usual, but I was. I hadn't felt his touch in a year and my body was yearning for his loving. My panties became moist as I massaged the tender spot between my firm thighs and my mind consumed itself with thoughts of the man I gave my virginity to.

Sebastian traced my body with small, intimate kisses. He licked my earlobes melodiously. The low suckling sounds made my vagina drip with sweet cum. As I stood facing him he lifted my skirt and pulled my panties down with his teeth. He sat on the park swing and I implanted myself on his deep tan-colored baton. I bounced up and down his slippery penis while I moaned his name, "Sebastian," continuously. The faster the swing moved, the more enmeshed our aroused bodies became. I clutched his

back tightly as I slid to the bottom of his shaft and rose back up to the tip in a matter of seconds. Sebastian's lips locked my neck and he mumbled, "That's what I'm talking about. Baby, take all of this. Show me how much you love me."

My muscles clinched his girth and I held him tight within my succulent walls. "I love you, Sebastian," I cried aloud as I buried my face in his chest.

He pulled my head back and kissed away my tears. "Don't cry. I love you, Shelby Tate. You are my life. My everything . . . I will always love you."

The more I rubbed my hot, pulsating flesh, the madder I became. I rolled my eyes and shook my head.

How much longer can I do this saved thing? One year is too long to go without sex. I want to be fulfilled. Sebastian, you were supposed to be my husband. We should be married and making love right now. Why did you have to leave me? Why did I waste five years of my life with you?

I moved my hands from between my legs and rolled on my knees as tears flowed freely down my red cheeks. The last time I masturbated I was in high school. Two years before I gave myself to Sebastian. Oh, how I would do anything to have my virginity back.

I thought back to the day when we first met in Latin class. It was my senior year in high school. He approached me; we exchanged numbers, and began talking on the phone daily. I felt that he was intriguing; however, my intentions weren't on dating Mr. LaCroix. Although he was very desirable, I couldn't fathom the thought of dating outside of

my race. Nevertheless, there was nothing wrong with having an attractive close friend.

Sebastian wasn't down with the friend crap. He was very adamant and persistent about wanting me.

"Come on, Shelby. Be my girl," he begged daily.

I rejected him each day with a bold "No."

After a month of being friends, I decided to fix Sebastian up with Liberty, a girl in our Latin class who was crazy about him. The connection was made and the two were an item. I could have choked when I saw them walking down the halls holding hands. Liberty was so proud. She wasn't concerned about the gaping stares and the whispering; she was happy to be holding the hand of Sebastian LaCroix.

Jealousy hit me fast, like a flying baseball smacked by a bat. I said I didn't want Sebastian, but my heart interpreted things differently. I couldn't wait to get home to express my love and to tell him how wrong I had been.

"Sebastian, I want to be with you now," I whispered through the phone.

No questions were asked. Poor Liberty was dumped that night. The next day at school, I was walking down the hall holding the hand of my new man, Sebastian LaCroix, aka, the sexiest man at Christian Hills High. Liberty never spoke to me again.

Our relationship was wonderful, at first. Sebastian met me at my locker with a kiss between classes, showered me with romantic love letters, and escorted me home daily. If it rained, he was at

my part-time job with an umbrella to walk me to
my car.

We spent every spare moment together. The
world revolved around Sebastian. The boy had my
head spinning.

"Shelby, 'Mahal Kita,' means I love you in Tagalog."
"Shelby, I'll never leave you."
"Shelby, I want you to be my wife."
"Shelby, I want a family with you."

When we graduated from high school, our relationship escalated. I went to college at University
of Illinois in Chicago, not far from home, and Sebastian found a full-time job as a manager of a de-
partment store. That's when the pampering
began. He wined and dined me daily. Bought me
expensive clothing from classy boutiques and
draped my body with diamonds and fine gems.

I dreamed of becoming Mrs. LaCroix. The
thought of being his wife and the mother of his Fil-
ipino children brought me hysterical joy because
he was my first and I just knew he would be my last.
We wanted two kids, a boy named Caleb and a girl
named Amber, and a four-bedroom home with a
swimming pool. He promised me the world and
our happy life in the suburbs was planned. The
two of us were young and in love with big dreams.

It was a cold autumn day when things came to a
complete halt. The wind was blowing dried tree
leaves and snow fiercely through the air in a circular motion. It reminded me of the swirling confusion in my head the day I let my heart take control.
Blair called me out of the blue, informing me that

Sebastian was messing around. She picked me up minutes later and escorted me to the front door of Persia Smith's home. We made it there just in time. Sebastian was walking out, leaving his faint footprints on her steps. A shocked Sebastian looked at me in disbelief as Blair and I approached him.

I remember the tragic cursing event like it was yesterday.

"Did you fuck her?"

"No, no, Shelby. It's not even like that. She likes my cousin, Talmar. I was over here trying to fix them up."

"Well, let's see what she has to say."

I stomped into her home. He hurried to catch up with me. She was standing at the end of her staircase in her black satin lingerie.

"Bitch, did you fuck him?" I said, watching her watch me intrude on her and her premises.

He quickly answered for her, "No."

She opened her mouth and began to speak. "He wanted—"

I swiftly interrupted, "You filthy bitch."

I also remember saying, "ho" and "slut" amongst other rude and hurtful things.

She spoke again, "I ain't no—"

In rage, I intercepted, "Shut the fuck up, bitch."

By this time, Blair grabbed me and carried me out of Persia's home.

Blair drilled me. "Look, you've called her every bitch in the book. It's time to go."

Blair gave Sebastian a cold look like she wanted to slap his slanted eyes straight.

She whispered, "Shelby, they aren't worth it. You're better than this."

I ignored Blair's words of encouragement.

I kept screaming like a wild woman and fighting my tears. "Get the fuck out of her house, Sebastian. Now."

He was moving slowly, entranced. "I love you, Shelby, just you . . ." was the last thing I remember him saying to me that day.

I couldn't believe my man cheated on me with Persia Smith. The girl was nice and quiet, practically a nerd in high school. She was sweet, and well, she wasn't ugly, but she was homely and plain. The girl wore the same hairstyle all the time, loose-fitting, dull clothes, glasses, and braces. She was somewhat shy, always carried a stack of books close to her chest and kept to herself. If Persia had curves or a great personality, only she and those books knew it. Now, Miss Smith was a grown woman, screwing my man and just another whore in my book. Sweet or not, she had earned a permanent place on my shit list.

LUST TWO

The noise from the phone invaded my memories. I'm not sure how long the phone was ringing or which ring made me snap out of my daydream. I answered hurriedly. It was Blair and Kelly on three-way.

"Hermit bitch," screamed Kelly.

"Let's go out tonight," they said simultaneously.

"Blair, cut her off of three-way," I moaned dryly.

"My girl isn't going to hang up on me. You need to stop being a nun," Kelly joked.

Blair yelled into the phone, "You've sat in the house almost a whole year now. We rarely see you. Let's roll out in the *Chi* tonight."

I hesitated, wanting to hang up. "You two know I'm saved and in medical school. I have homework . . . Since I've changed, I don't do the club thing anymore."

"Damn, bitch. Live a little," Kelly shouted.

"I'm a Christian woman now. I go to church three times a week and Bible study every Wednes-

day night. I'm trying to get my life together," I said slowly.

"You have to come, Shelby. I got a promotion today, girl. It's better than I thought," Blair exclaimed.

"Yeah, girl, big money is going to treat us tonight. Plus, your church members will never find out you went to the club, unless they are there. Come on, God doesn't care if you go to the club. And you know the homework can wait," Kelly chimed.

I knew I had to celebrate with Blair. She was my girl. She stood by my side through the whole ordeal with Sebastian, checking on me all the time, begging me to get out of the house, but didn't judge me when I didn't. I was proud of her too. She had worked so hard. However, I still didn't say anything. My mind drifted. I started thinking about Sebastian again.

"You are so indecisive. We'll be there at nine o'clock. Good-bye, Shelby," Blair shouted.

I whined. "Wait, I'll pass. I'm not burning in hell at the club and I can't afford to flunk out of medical—"

"Just get ready," Blair interrupted.

"Yeah, and wear something hoochie," Kelly shouted before the phone clicked off in my face.

I smiled. My girl was moving up in corporate America. I needed to go out and have fun, and Blair knew it.

I guess I could miss Bible study. The church doesn't control me. I can go to the club if I want to. I'm having impure thoughts anyway. Anytime I'm thinking about screwing Sebastian again, I know it's time to get out and

clear my mind. Fool, don't you remember how messed up it was when he dumped you?

Breaking up with Sebastian left me distraught and unfulfilled. I mourned over Sebastian as if he had been murdered in front of my face. I cried every day. I was addicted to him the same way a dope fiend is addicted to crack cocaine. I needed to wear a sign that said, "Don't put Sebastian in front of me or I will chase him."

After our relationship ended, I promised myself and my friends that I wouldn't call him anymore. Some days I couldn't fight the temptation, so I'd pick up the phone and call him anyway. Most of the time, I just wanted to hear his voice. Other times I wanted to feel him inside of me because my aching womanhood craved his masculine stroke, and he never turned down my free loving.

When my best friend Joel was with me, he would hold me back from running and jumping into Sebastian's arms. Joel would always tell me not to make a fool out of myself.

"Shelby, don't chase him," he'd warn. "There is a fine line between love and stalking."

However, when Joel wasn't around, I would almost break my neck rushing to Sebastian to tell him how much I loved and missed him. I made Joel my hero, spending many nights crying on his shoulder, wishing he was Sebastian and wanting him to make the pain go away.

After months of begging and trying to get Sebastian back, I realized it was a lost cause, because he started dating other women. I ran into him in the mall one day with his latest friend. I was flaring with envy as they passed me holding hands.

"Look at you with your bitch," I mumbled.

I wanted to snatch the weave out of the girl's head, as if she had something to do with my broken heart. I finally gave up after "stalking" Sebastian for three months.

The time I spent separated from him eventually made me stronger. I didn't talk to him or see him. I stayed in the house because I couldn't face bumping into him. I went to class and I came back home. I dedicated my life to school, determined to become a psychiatrist in a short period of time. I increased my workload, studied, and kept busy. I made the dean's list too.

I changed my religion and started going to church and Bible study, faithfully. I also joined water aerobics during the week, trying to keep my mind free and my inner voice clear. My desire to curse decreased also. I thought I would never get over the loss of our relationship; but with time, focus, and extreme amounts of prayer, things brightened up.

The doorbell rang. I looked at my watch.

I know they can't be here already, I thought to myself.

I looked out the front window. It was only Joel, so I didn't bother putting any clothes on. I felt comfortable around him, so relaxed that I would bathe and dress in front of him. He was like a brother to me; he was always there, emotionally and financially. Who would've ever imagined Joel, who was Sebastian's best friend in high school, would turn into one of my closest friends?

Joel was a respectable young man, and we never crossed our friendship boundaries. Don't get me wrong, the brother wasn't gay or anything. In fact, he was very attractive. Sometimes women told him he looked like the model, Tyson. He ate that garbage up, and I would tease him that those girls were blind or crazy.

"Come in, Joel," I said quickly with a Chester Cheetah grin.

I glared at Joel's dark chocolate baldhead, tight chest, and his bulging blessing.

"The devil is too busy tonight," I mumbled to myself.

"I'm going out with my girls tonight," I said, twirling my hips and shoulders, as if I was already in the club.

After I told Joel my plans, happiness overtook me. The spell of boredom was being broken, and I was finally getting out of the house. My goal was to go out, have fun, and maybe meet a man.

Joel looked like the dog in the RCA ads, as his head twisted in amazement. I thought my announcement confused him, but I was wearing a pair of pink cotton candy fury thongs that must have caught his attention instead.

He reached for my butt. "Girl, your booty is getting plump."

"You think so?" I said, feeling myself up, looking over my shoulder to my backside. "Look, dog, Let me hit the shower before you nut all over yourself."

Or before I do again. I have to wash these lustful thoughts out of my head. Jesus, what am I doing? Please forgive me. Give me strength. Lord, remove the sexual urges from my spirit.

* * *

It was the end of March, so I could still wear leather. I smiled as my firm body glided into the black leather booty shorts, black leather halter, and black leather Steve Madden high heels. I was looking and starting to feel like a dominatrix—bold, sexy, and in complete control. I was almost hoping we'd run into Sebastian that night. He needed to get a good, long look at what he was missing. Why not? I owed my new physique to him. All those days I stayed in the house eating my tears away and sweating away my hurt with exercise had paid off.

Joel watched me from the time I exited the shower until I had every piece of clothing on, as if he had to see me leave to believe I was really going out.

"What color lipstick should I wear?" I asked, poking out my lips.

Joel didn't answer.

"Does red go with this outfit?"

He still didn't reply.

"Hello," I yelled, as I turned to him, waving my hand in his face.

Joel was gazing at my butt, as if it was filet mignon. "Damn, girl. You are finally starting to bubble up." Joel pulled his bottom lip. "It's getting hard to ignore how fine you're getting. Now, if only we could do something about that attitude."

We laughed, but I noticed Joel still gawking at my legs.

"Legs trying to get fine too," he said, becoming more serious. "You look good," he said, looking straight into my eyes.

"Thank you," I replied, feeling a little ashamed for being dressed so seductively.

"I sure hope you have fun tonight. For a while, I thought you were going to become a nun, always in the house reading your Bible and shit."

"Are you high?"

"Where did that question come from? I'm sober," Joel answered slowly, still staring me down.

Joel's cell phone rang, interrupting our awkward moment. He had never looked at me so intensely before. I blew it off, realizing I had picked up some weight in the right places, and he was a man.

Joel pointed to the phone. "Someone wants to talk to you."

We looked at each other as I grasped the phone. Joel's expression didn't change.

"Hello," I said slowly. I couldn't believe the voice I was hearing. My temples throbbed as my heartbeat quickened.

"How's my wife to be?"

"Bitch, what the fuck do you want?" I yelled, breathing very hard.

Joel looked at me, shocked by the evolution of my old habit, my dirty mouth.

"Shelby, I miss you," Sebastian expressed tenderly.

"I can't tell. You had no problem leaving me," I snapped.

"Baby, I was young. I'm sorry. Can I come over?"

"No," I yelled.

"Let me make love to you. I know you miss this. You will always belong to me. I was your first," he said in an exaggerated way.

"Look, Sebastian, I belong to God. I have repented for giving you my precious virginity. I don't have time for your games anymore," I stated, as my mouth inched away from the phone.

"You don't sound like you belong to God."

"What?" I yelled obnoxiously.

In a pitiful voice he reported, "Wait, Shelby. I apologize for everything I ever did to you. I've been accused of rape."

"And you probably did it," I replied, thinking he couldn't be serious.

Joel was standing beside me mouthing, "He just bailed out of jail."

I looked at Joel in disbelief.

"I need you to testify for me," Sebastian pleaded.

I answered him quickly and coldly. "No."

"Come on, Shelby, I love you. I need you. You know my true character."

"I'm sure your rich family can get you off."

I knew the single life would catch up with him eventually, but rape?

Sebastian wouldn't . . . I cut off my own thoughts by shaking my head from side to side. I didn't want to continue caring about him.

"No, I can't help you," I said softly.

He paused. "How can you act like this after all we've been through?"

"I don't know anything about you anymore," I said with conviction.

He tried to sound sexy and alluring. "Baby, you know you still love me."

I pressed *end* and handed Joel his cell phone.

LUST THREE

The loud horn of Blair's red Honda Prelude alerted me that she was waiting outside. My palms began to sweat.

Lord, protect us tonight. Keep us safe as we journey out.

The night air slapped me in the face as Joel and I exited my home. I found the sting refreshing. It was a cool, dry breeze; just right for a light leather jacket.

Joel spoke to Blair, Megan, and Kelly, and then he jumped into his black Impala. I made myself comfortable next to Megan in the backseat.

"Don't sit on the Gucci," Megan teased as she moved her purse.

"Blair, please put your cigarette out. I don't know why you continue to smoke anyway. You're harming your son. He can develop asthma from that secondhand smoke."

"Just for you, Shelby Pooh," Blair cheerfully replied, as she tossed her cigarette out of the window.

A smile crept across my face.

I was so happy my girls hadn't thrown me away. Kelly and Blair had gone to Christian Hill High with me, but Megan and I grew up together in the same neighborhood, so we were the closest. I acted as if I didn't know anyone when I was with Sebastian. When we broke up, I felt as if I was alone. They didn't give up on me though. However, I always felt Kelly did. I rarely heard from her during my year of depression.

We rode down I-57 at seventy miles per hour, zipping in and out of the lanes. It was Friday night and the interstate was packed. Nevertheless, the traffic was flowing at a high speed.

Kelly turned down the radio. "Now that I have the three of you together, I have a proposition. I have my own new business. I'm selling local, long-distance, and cell phone service. You tricks need to help me, so I can make some money."

I looked at Kelly as if she was crazy. She was always getting tricked into selling garbage. Always trying the get-rich-overnight gimmicks that usually ended in her being broke.

"Kelly, get a real job. You are always doing those quick scams for money. Nobody gets rich selling that shit but the owner. You need to go back to college and get a degree so you can get a real job," Blair said.

"Blair, college isn't for everyone. I know plenty of people with degrees who don't make any money. I'll make more money selling phone service than working with a useless degree."

Megan placed her hands in the air, trying to get Kelly's attention. "Just marry a rich man. Get you

an old sugar daddy with some cash and sell your little phone cards if that's what makes you happy."

"Kelly, I'll change my service. I'll call my mom too. You can do anything if you have faith. I'm just happy to hear you aren't selling your ass for cash," I said.

"Did Sister Shelby just curse?" Blair said jokingly.

I rolled my eyes. "Shit, Sister Shelby is full of sin tonight. The devil has been busy. I just got off the phone with Sebastian the rapist."

"Yeah, we heard about that. They said it was four of them. They supposedly ran a train on a girl from Maywood. The rumor is, she let them hit it at a party and then called rape after everyone found out. Charges have already been dropped on two of the guys," Blair reported, always knowing the scoop before anyone else.

"Anyway, I was sitting in my room reading love letters from that fool and I started to get horny. I got to rubbing. Hell, I started to break out my Barbie doll."

"Yeah, y'all know that whore used to masturbate with her Barbie's foot," Kelly snickered.

They all laughed.

"Back then I had to do me, and Barbie was the closest thing I could find at the time." I chuckled a little myself. "Kelly, don't hate. What about you and the television remote control?"

"Shit, I ain't ashamed. I used to throw a rubber on the remote and go to town. Hell, those flicks used to have me hornier than a motherfucka. I'd grab the remote and anything else I could find."

"Barbie, remote control." Blair giggled profusely.

"Shit, I used a cucumber too," Kelly said, fanning her head.

"Have you cheap tricks heard of vibrators?"

"Megan, you know no one had access to a vibrator at thirteen."

"Well, we do now, and I'll buy each of you one with the cleaning spray," Megan told us, as she rubbed hand sanitizer into her palms.

"What did your glamorous vagina utilize for self-pleasure?" Kelly asked properly.

"I didn't masturbate. I utilized the real thing," Megan said, turning away from her small make up mirror.

I crossed my legs. "Yeah right, we are just like men. We have all explored our bodies. It's a normal stage of life. Babies go though it too."

"Well, I used my toothbrush," Blair said gleefully.

"Toothbrush?" We chanted simultaneously.

"I bet your pussy was fresh and clean," Kelly blurted out with a loud giggle, finishing off a half pint of Seagram's Gin and juice.

I closed my eyes and laughed until tears streamed down my face.

Kelly turned the volume up on the radio. "Hey," she blurted out, responding to the song on the radio. "I can't wait to get my drank on." She started to groove to the music and I joined in. I started snapping my fingers and swaying my arms to the song.

Jaheim knew what he was talking about. "*You*

better put that woman first. " I loved that song. It explained how I felt.

I know Sebastian wishes he had put me first in his life. He wouldn't be in trouble today if he had. It is too late now. I am out of his life, and I don't plan to return. Stop thinking about him, Shelby, not tonight.

I was out to celebrate with my girls, seeing what the big Windy City had to offer.

Soon we were on the Dan Ryan Expressway, with the subway train nestled in the middle, and I could see the Sears Tower building standing tall, reminding me that I should do the same. The Dan Ryan Expressway gave us a quick glimpse of the south side of Chicago, the good and bad. Prominent, large black corporations lined the expressway. There were also small business developments, including food joints and strip malls. We passed chicken shacks, seafood markets, rib joints, hoagie shops, pizza parlors, and Polish stands.

We exited the Dan Ryan shortly after passing US Cellular Field, the home of the White Sox. The scenery changed every time we traveled down Lake Shore Drive at night. I felt like a tourist, gazing at Soldier Field, the home of the Chicago Bears, the aquarium, and the art and science museums.

My eyes admired the lights of over a hundred tall buildings and beautiful Lake Michigan. The view was mesmerizing and soothing to the soul.

As we passed the Buckingham fountain, I thought about Sebastian again. Talmar told me Sebastian

had planned to propose to me next to the huge, hundred-foot water fountain. I thought about all our lost dreams as the clear water shot up in the air, displaying its spectrum in the midst of red, blue, green, and yellow. The fountain was certainly one of the most beautiful artifacts in Chicago, one that Sebastian and I treasured.

Acknowledgments

I would like to give thanks to God, my husband (greatest man alive), my children, mother, father, brother, nieces, nephews, cousins, friends, co-workers, book clubs, reviewers, fellow authors, my editor, and readers for your support during the writing of this book. Your encouragement and faith in me was greatly appreciated and will be cherished forever. May the blessings of our Savior Jesus Christ rain upon all of you.

Dedications

Dear Mother,
I love you for making me the woman I am today.
Thank you for investing in my future, putting my
needs before yours, teaching me the fundamentals
of life, and reminding me to always carry myself
like a respectable Christian woman.

You are my hero, right next to God. Keep on
being you and helping the world, no matter how
much flack you get from others. You have a heart
made of rare gems, and sometimes it's hard to
share you with others. Just know I love you and you
are the best mom in the universe.

Dear Grandmother,
Thank you for reminding me to always carry myself like a Christian woman. Thank you for telling
me not to hang with the wrong crowd. Thank you
for expressing the negative in the men I dated.

As I reflect, I appreciate your boldness and your
words of encouragement. I am glad I made things
right before you left this earth. You didn't get to
meet my children, but you made sure I married
the greatest man alive; *we hooked him with your biscuits*. I love you, Grandma, and you will always be
the best cook in the world.

Love Always,
LeBlanc

LUST FOUR

"Keys and name please." The valet attendant, who was wearing a black top hat, summoned us over.

We stepped out of the car like celebrities, as if Blair's old Honda Prelude was a stretch Hummer or something. Blair fired up a cigarette right away. The four of us knew we were looking good. I held my head up high in the air as I bounced with pride. My mind felt rejuvenated. This was the step I needed. I was finally out of hibernation, and I decided at that moment that this was my last thought of Sebastian. My mourning period was over.

"Wait, Little Red Riding Hood, I need to finish smoking before we go in, and I don't want to hear your mouth," Blair preached to me.

The Club, Lake Rivera, was lit up like a Broadway show. There were lights shining everywhere on the name of the club, which was flashing constantly. The red carpet and twisted gold ropes led the crowd to the entrance. The outside of the newly built club reminded me of the buildings you

would see on the music award shows. It was glamorous.

The line wrapped around the corner, almost near Lake Michigan, which was just four blocks away. My mouth dropped.

I'm looking too good to stand in that long line with these high heels on.

"Pick up your face." Megan laughed.

She opened her purse. "*Voila.* There's no waiting tonight. We have VIP passes."

We all smiled in relief.

"I used to screw one of the owners." She waved the passes in the air as we marched to the front of the line. "I guess you ladies forgot that I am Megan Cole. I get anything I want," she boasted, checking her face again in her cosmetic mirror.

We walked in. The club's trimmings were gold, and the floors were covered with black carpet that resembled suede. The place was very enchanting. It looked like the Apollo Theatre. There were three levels with side stages. The first floor had both male and female staff and played hip-hop music. The second floor had glass floors with an all-male staff and played slow jams and oldies. The third floor had a female-only staff and played R&B music.

Goodness. Men were plentiful in the club. They were dressed to kill; clothed in their fine designer suits, name-brand shoes, and top-of-the-line cologne. We decided to chill on the second floor where all the distinguished men were. I couldn't stop staring. I had been off the scene for so long; I had forgotten Chicago had so many fine men.

"Let's get a table in the front to see all the booty walk by," Blair said frantically.

"No, let's get something to drink," Kelly stressed.

We found a cocktail table near the bar. As soon as we sat down, Megan was ready to go her own way. She popped up real fast and swung her shoulder-length, flipped hair. "Girls, I'll meet y'all at the end of the night. Watch my expensive purse, and don't let anyone rub their dirty hands on it." She waved her hand and started walking away. "A girl has to get her bills paid. Being a registered nurse just doesn't do it."

Megan was dressed in a Versace black spaghetti-strapped dress that hugged her hips. She had to keep up with her "Gucci lifestyle." The girl was glamorous. She was petite and well proportioned. The men loved her small waist and huge behind.

Glamour girl loved the best of everything, a diamond and pearls kind of woman. She also kept up with the latest clothing fashions and hairstyles. Megan lived in a high-rise condominium located on the Gold Coast, which was very ornate, and she only dated men with deep pockets. If your boss made more money than you, you were good as gone. Being with Megan meant you had to pay, because her loving had a high price.

I heard a different beat of music, and it sounded like it was coming from the bottom level. I looked down. Through the glass floor, I could see people dancing. The area was dark, sparkling lights rotating around the dance floor. I was certainly feeling the ambiance of this place.

Our eyes focused on the specimen walking our

way. A fine shirtless male waiter greeted us, wearing a black top hat, bow tie, and black slacks.

"He looks delicious," Blair mumbled.

We slapped each other's hands under the table.

"Gin and lime juice, with two extra shots of gin," Kelly yelled over the music.

I shouldn't be at this club. Should I have a drink too? I'm here. What will a little drink hurt?

This was my first night out in a long time, so I ordered something sweet and tasty, instead of strong.

I put my hand on my chin and stated, "I'll have a fuzzy navel."

Blair was driving, so she ordered a coke. She was always the responsible one, even on her big night.

The waiter returned with our drinks. He pointed to the bar. "The two guys at the bar paid for your drinks."

The men approached our table and asked us to dance.

"First, buy us more drinks," Kelly demanded.

"Don't listen to her. Thank you for the drinks," Blair and I replied.

One of the guys walked away and Kelly began to flirt with his friend. Minutes later, the guy returned with three glasses filled with gin and juice.

"Thank you, baby. You can have my number now," Kelly stated.

She opened her purse, took out a piece of paper, wrote her number on two separate pieces of paper, and gave both men her number. She winked at us. They smiled and placed the number in their wallets. Kelly turned to Blair, "Two to your zero."

I whispered in Blair's ear, "Kelly is out to find a new home. You know she's lived with her mother, 'Estelle the hellion,' for too long."

Blair replied, "Yeah, my baby is out to find a new address. She'll move in with any ol' Joe who lets her."

"I really can't blame her. I couldn't live with a parent like Estelle either," I responded.

Blair just smiled and puffed on her cigarette.

Kelly finished her second drink and shouted loudly over the music, "I'm ready to dance." She snatched my hand, and we scattered out to the dance floor with the two guys.

Kellyanna Swanson was wild and daringly bold. She believed her breasts were her greatest asset; though it was her long black hair, courtesty of her white mother. Kelly dashed out on the dance floor and began her escapade. She danced so sensually. Her hair and breasts swung to the beat of the music. Kelly licked her full lips and caressed her chest.

"What's your name, sexy?"

"My name is Kevin."

"I love men named Kevin. Do you have any kids? Are you married? Do you have your own place? Is your dick big?" She flirted.

"You're inquisitive," Kevin stated.

"I have to be. I think you're someone I really need to know," she replied. "Let me find out what you're working with," Kelly whispered low, but not low enough for me not to hear.

Her fingertips rubbed up and down Kevin's crotch, feeling up his manhood, exploring every

vein. The Perry Ellis suit he was wearing made her journey a breeze.

Kelly and Kevin exited the steamy dance floor. Blair and I followed closely behind the two, not wanting to be bothered with the guys on the dance floor.

"Go, girl," Blair shouted, as she blew cigarette smoke into Kelly's face. "I saw you on the dance floor stroking that man's chicken. I taught you well," she said, laughing and slapping Kelly's hand. "Little boy, if you can't go down on my girl, you need to step off. You need to eat cat like barbecued ribs to be with my girl."

Kevin blushed. "Oh! Big girl, you ain't said nothing. My long, thick, strong tongue can reach her ovaries and ass too."

"Ooow, I'll find out soon," Kelly stated eagerly.

Blair's facial expression was flat. She looked at Kevin. "I want to know who in the fuck you were calling *big girl!*"

"Damn, Blair. He was only joking."

"No, fuck that," Blair yelled as she pushed Kelly out of the way.

"I was talking to you. You know you look just like the big black fat lady on Tom & Jerry. The one with the red house shoes who always says, 'Thomas, oh Thomas.'"

Blair's hazel contacts turned red. She leaped toward Kevin. Her thick arms wrapped around Kevin's neck. "Nigga, I will kill you. Who do I look like, now?" Blair bellowed.

I was so embarrassed by Blair and Kelly's actions. This was the main reason I didn't want to go

out with them. Association meant everything, and
I was definitely not acting like I was saved.

Kelly placed her hands on top of her head.
"Blair, you are always beating up my men. Shit . . .
and he had a big dick."

Blair rolled her eyes and then stuck her middle
finger up at Kelly.

She threw Kevin into Kelly. "Here, take this—
little punk."

Kevin straightened his suit out with his hands.
Kelly grabbed his free hand and escorted him to
the lobby. I followed closely behind them in search
of the bathroom. I could hear them chatting.
"Baby, I'm so sorry. Blair is such a bitch. Let's go to
the restroom so you can fix yourself up."

"She's lucky I don't fight women."

"I know, sweet baby," Kelly murmured as she
pushed Kevin in the ladies' restroom:

"Kelly, he can't come in here. Are you trying to
get him arrested?"

Kelly ignored me as she pulled Kevin into an
empty stall.

"Let me show you how sorry I am," she slurred.
"I'm going to put my branding on you. A cute little
heart on your *d-i-c-k*."

I could hear her yanking at his pants, telling
him how she was going to make him feel good.

"Baby, we just met. I don't want you to—".

"Shut up and let me taste this big dick."

"Can you close the door?"

"No, I want the other women to see me devour
you."

I looked down and saw Kevin's pants and boxers

on the floor. I couldn't believe they were carrying on as if I wasn't in the restroom.

"I'm gonna twist that penis like a servant making fresh squeezed lemonade. Oh yeah! You are nice and hard. I want you to fuck me in my mouth."

"Kelly, what are you doing?" I cried aloud, making my presence known as I crept out of the stall after urinating.

"Shelby, get out of here. Go to Bible study if you can't hang."

I looked at the two in the dirty stall with toilet paper all over the concrete stained floor. Kelly was sitting on the toilet, and Kevin was standing facing her with his pants down, his buttocks facing me.

"Look, I said fuck me in my mouth."

Kevin didn't budge.

"Shelby, if you want to watch, so be it, 'cause I'm not stopping what I'm doing." She continued in a drunken tone, tugging at Kevin's penis. "I said fuck me in the mouth," Kelly yelled desperately.

Kevin plunged into Kelly's mouth.

"Faster!" she garbled.

I stood there like a freak watching the two. I found the act repulsive, but I wasn't moving. My curious eyes were glued to them, focusing in on the blow job, studying Kelly's movement every step of the way. She swallowed relentlessly. Saliva dripped from the sides of her mouth as she consumed his long, thick being.

"Darn, girl, I want to marry you."

Kelly grabbed his butt cheeks and shoved his penis into her mouth deeper and faster. Then she glided her fingers into his butt.

He sighed freely, enjoying every stroke she presented him with. His mouth flew open. "I'm about to ejaculate."

"Go ahead. I swallow."

The ladies' restroom door opened, and I scurried toward the sink. Two girls walked in.

"I had to check my make up. Megan Cole has to look good if she wants to leave with the wealthiest man in the club."

"Girl, stop referring to yourself in the third person. You act like you have an alter ego."

"Look here, Blair, don't diagnose Megan Cole."

"Oh my goodness! Oh my goodness!" Kevin screamed.

Megan lowered her voice. "Girl, what is that noise? It sounds like someone is getting screwed."

I placed my finger to my mouth and whispered that Kelly was in a stall giving a blow job.

"Let's peep. I have always wanted to see someone doing the nasty," Megan said eagerly.

"Girl, I've been spying on them already. I don't want to see any more. My saintly eyes have seen enough." I grabbed Megan's hand. "See, that's why I don't come to the club. Let's get out of here."

"Oh, hell no, Kelly. I know you ain't in here being nasty," Blair called out, walking toward the open stall. "Goddamn, you are a freak, nasty ho," Blair hollered out, rushing toward me and Megan, who were halfway out of the restroom. "She is sitting on the toilet swallowing that punk-ass Negro's cum. Girl, that shit was flying all in her hair." Blair sighed. "That drunk bitch needs to get some help."

*   *   *

The club was dim with flashing lights, and the music was drowning out my thoughts. How could I sit on the bathroom and watch Kelly? Who was I kidding? I was no different than my girlfriends. All of my pent-up sexual frustrations were coming out. My soul was too weak to be in the club. The drinks, the men, and the fame were just too much temptation for me.

I sat at the table, shaking my leg nervously, praying no one would talk to me.

I'm ready to go . . . I'm ready to go. Why am I here anyway? I am so pathetic. This club is full of sexy men, and I haven't had sex in a year. This is too much temptation for me. I can't miss Bible study this week.

I was really anxious about meeting someone new, but I found myself uneasy around men. It was like I didn't know what to say or do without sounding corny or mean. Didn't want to be alone either; however, the thought of starting over again gave me chills. The whole idea of getting to know someone else made me sick. How could I let another man touch what belonged to Sebastian?

I sipped on my drink.

"Would you like to dance?" a brother about the size of the Keebler Elf asked.

I was nervous, but I had no trouble turning him away. "No, I'm waiting on my husband," I lied in a sharp tone. His little legs trotted off real quick. I didn't find short men attractive.

Maybe I am as mean and shallow as some people think.

As I sat at the cocktail table having a lonely conversation with my drink, I decided to call Sebast-

ian. I had been hard on him that day. When I turned around to get my cell phone out of my purse on the back of my chair, I locked eyes with a fine brother across the room. He was eye-catching. My senses told me he was my soul mate. I rubbed my eyes to pretend I wasn't staring, not wanting to seem overly eager. He caught my intense gaze and strolled toward me. I turned back around quickly, trying to play things cool.

My conscience whispered, "*Saved by the fine brother.*"

Suddenly, I heard footsteps. It felt like someone was standing behind me. I felt a tap on my shoulder. "Can I buy you another drink?" The voice sounded familiar.

I twisted my hips around to greet the mystery man. "Hey. How are you?" I said gleefully. It was Max, my ex-boyfriend. I wasn't sure what to do. He still looked good. He was a cross between Tupac Shakur and Brian McKnight, if you know what I mean. He was somewhere between dangerous thug and quiet choirboy.

"Shelby, I know I get a hug," Max said in a sexy, yet demanding tone.

I stood and we hugged. His strong grip shocked me. The touch of his robust body made my small nipples hard and perky. I hadn't felt the touch of a man in a long time. I looked at Max from head to toe. He was dressed in a navy blue tailored suit, and his small feet were covered in Prada dress shoes. His hands were beautiful like Godiva candy; dark, tasty, and came in expensive wrapping. He wore two platinum diamond rings, a diamond earring, and an expensive diamond designer watch.

I couldn't believe it was Maxtin Brooks. I had often wondered about his whereabouts and new career. I hadn't seen him in a year.

He whispered in my ear, "When did you get all that ass?"

I answered back slyly, "I'm a woman now."

Max glimpsed at me quickly. "I can tell. You are definitely all woman. And I like the way that black leather hugs your body. I see your man is treating you to nice things. Are you still in love? You know I got tired of waiting for you and Mr. Kung Fu to break up."

"Funny, Max. I see you're still a comedian. Sebastian and I broke up last year. Right after the last time I saw you."

He became silent, like he was calculating the time in his mind.

I paused. "Are you still dating three women at a time?"

"Nah. I'm not with anyone," he said slowly. Max put his hand on his chest. "I've changed."

The truth was I always wanted Max. We had dated on and off when we were younger. He was a true playboy, and I loved the dog in him. I guess I wanted to see if I could tame him. His games started back in elementary school. This man even dated my friend and me at the same time when we were thirteen years old, so I knew I couldn't trust him. I was young and very proud to be a virgin, and Mr. Max wasn't getting any of my innocence, but I liked to get him all hot and bothered anyway.

Kelly's mom would always tell us, "These little boys with big dicks are out to steal your virginity.

You girls better be careful. That coochie is some powerful stuff."

I remember being curious, scared, and proud all at the same time, and I didn't know why. I just knew that I had something he wanted. I often wondered if things would've been different between us if he hadn't moved off our block when he did. His aunt, who raised him, was addicted to crack cocaine by the time we entered junior high. She had men in and out their apartment all the time. His aunt would move their family around, trying to keep a job, and a front.

Max never disclosed her habit to anyone and went through a lot of pain as a child. We could relate because I also had issues. Max teased me about my grandfather being an alcoholic.

When we were nine years old, he would laugh and say, "I saw your drunk granddaddy walking down the street."

I wouldn't say anything back to him; instead I'd laugh with him, trying to hide my pain. I guess that's because I knew he was trying to hide his too. Maybe he actually thought it was a secret, but everybody in the neighborhood knew his aunt was addicted to crack.

Max and I sat together all night drinking and getting reacquainted. He enlightened me about his new business, "A Gentlemen's Touch," a full-service barbershop with a lounge in it.

"My best friend and I decided to try entrepreneurship, and our setup is real nice. We have four barber stations lined up against one wall, and the bar is directly in front of the barber chairs. The

men get a good view of the bar and the three tele-
visions. Our business is a huge success, and we
plan to franchise it."

"That's wonderful," I replied in a bubbly manner like a frantic teenager.

The Courvoisier was definitely kicking in, because Max couldn't stop talking about himself. He
talked about not living on the south side any
longer, and that he relocated to the north side on
Lake Shore Drive. I was impressed. My childhood
sweetie moved on up like the Jeffersons to a high-
rise condominium.

Max was always smart. I knew he would make it
big one day, once he decided he wanted to. I didn't
want to tell him about my boring life after hearing
about his rags-to-riches excitement, but I did. I
told him that I was in medical school to become a
psychiatrist. He appeared to be very happy for me.
Max was always supportive of my education and he
said he wanted to go back to college himself to
pursue his dream of becoming an attorney. Our
conversation went on well into the night.

My familiarity with Max, and the drinks, made
me at ease. We started to reminisce.

"Why didn't you ever French-kiss me?" Max
asked.

"I didn't know how." I giggled.

"I remember our first kiss. It was in your apartment hallway, and you wanted it pitch dark."

Max took another shot of cognac and reflected.
I was a little embarrassed listening to him because
I was tipsy.

A thought crossed my mind. *What would my pas-
tor and church members think if they saw me like this?*

The thought faded quickly as Max laughed. "Those were the good old days."

"Remember the first time I touched 'it' during an episode of *Good Times,* J J's eighteenth birthday?"

Max replied, "Yeah, I remember you were a big tease back then. I kept blue balls."

We sipped again from our drinks. Max had already downed three double shots of cognac.

I crossed my legs under the table, feeling a slightly warm sensation between my legs. "I know I was too slow for you, but I loved me some Max."

"I loved me some Shelby too."

"It's funny how we always seem to bump into each other. I see you almost every year. And every time I see you, you talk about hooking back up again," I stated.

Max clutched my hand very gently. "Shelby, I'm not letting you slip away this time."

"Really? I remember giving you chance after chance, waiting for a relationship to blossom, but it didn't," I said softly.

"I've always loved you. I didn't want to hurt you back in the day. Hell, I knew I couldn't be faithful," Max admitted. He looked at the drink in his hand. "We were just kids," he added, lifting his head.

"I know," I sighed.

"Now, I'm ready for a serious relationship with you, Shelby."

Maybe he has changed. Is he still the same dog that has to have every woman he sees? Am I ready to be with him, or anybody, right now? Would this time be different

since we are adults now? Can I remain saved, with a boyfriend like Max? The thoughts kept coming.

Kelly and Blair returned to the table one hour later, thicker than thieves. Kelly was loaded, leaning on Blair for support.

"Where is Kevin?" I asked Kelly.

"Let's go. I don't want to be interrogated by this backsliding nun. Look, she's drinking and talking to a man," Kelly stammered, pointing to Max and sipping on a glass filled with gin and juice. "Kevin went home to his very own place. He'll be picking me up later. I think I found me a sucker to move in with."

Blair winked her eye at me as I introduced them to Max, who reached to shake Kelly's hand and then Blair's. "Nice meeting you ladies." Max excused himself and walked toward the bar.

The girls took a seat at the table and watched him strut off. "Girl, he is definitely a pimp," Blair murmured. "That's a cat daddy. He is too sly for you."

Max returned with four shots of cognac. "I want all of you to take a shot."

I looked at Max as if had lost his mind. Cognac was really pushing it.

"Come on, Shelby. Don't look like that. Let's drink to old times."

My head shook from side to side.

Kelly snatched the shot glass off the table. She guzzled it down in seconds. "Finished," she shouted as she flipped the empty glass over and banged it on the table. "Come on, girls, drink up." When Kelly noticed the expression on my face and Blair's she stole our shots and placed them in front of her.

Seconds later both drinks were devoured. "So what do you do for a living?"

Max told Kelly about his business; she couldn't stop smiling as she listened intensely. When Kelly was finished interviewing Max, I pulled out my cell phone and punched his number in. He had already placed mine in his Palm Pilot. I reached for my purse and Megan's. Max pulled my chair out and walked us to the entrance of the club.

"Where is Megan?" Blair asked, scanning the club with her eyes.

"She probably has that big ass bouncing around here somewhere," Sapphire said, approaching us.

Sapphire was a girl that Blair, Kelly, and I went to high school with. However, she was much younger than us. Sapphire was what the men called a "brick house," and her outfits were always very skimpy and usually made of spandex. She was dressed in a blue sequin bra top that only covered her nipples and a short black spandex skirt with slits on both sides. Her lips were painted with red lipstick, eyes with blue eye shadow, and her earrings were huge silver hoops. She had a diamond stud in her nose.

The three of us couldn't stop eyeing Sapphire. She had her navel pierced with a long, dangling rhinestone belly ring, and on her left breast she had a huge, colored tattoo of two nude women kissing.

Kelly walked unsteadily. "Are you a dyke?"

Sapphire licked her lips. "That depends. Who wants to know?"

Kelly giggled and blushed softly. "I want to know."

"Lift your skirt up and let me show you."

Kelly blinked profusely. "Girl, don't play. I have always wanted to experience sex with a woman."

"Today's your lucky day. I aim to please."

"Blair, give me the keys to your car," Kelly slurred.

"Kelly, you need to leave that gin alone. You can't handle Sapphire."

"One lick and I'll have Sapphire in love with this pussy."

Sapphire smacked her lips, ignoring Kelly's last comment. She turned toward Blair. "Hey, my Blair, may I have a ride home?" Sapphire asked in a sneaky little voice.

"Sure, baby," Blair replied nonchalantly, puffing on her cancer stick.

Max interrupted, "Y'all wild. Would you ladies like to go to breakfast with me and my boys? My friend Bryan owns a nice soul food joint on Cottage Grove. They have great breakfast."

"I would definitely like to go," Sapphire intercepted.

"We are down for breakfast," Blair spoke up for all of us.

Max peeped around. "Dexter and Bryan were here earlier." He glimpsed down at his sparkling watch. "You ladies will have to meet my boys when we get to the restaurant. Let's roll out."

Max turned to Kelly. "I want you to meet my best friend, Dexter. He could have some fun with you."

We spotted Megan outside of the club near valet parking. Max squinted in Megan's direction. "Is that little Megan Cole from the old neighborhood?"

"Yes," I replied.

"I can't believe you two have kept in touch all these years."

I knew Max liked Megan when we were little, but she never gave him the time of day. Megan hated Max. He was a cruel little boy at the age of nine, who teased all of us, especially Megan, and she never got over it. I guess Max and I remained friends because I never took him serious, and we dated on and off for several years.

Megan yelled out, "I have a ride home. Give me my purse."

I met Megan halfway and handed her the purse. And, boy, did she have a ride home. She was standing next to a dark, tall, handsome man. He was fine. She waved good-bye to all of us as the attendant opened the passenger side of the car. They jumped into a fire-red Mercedes SLK.

Guess her bills will be paid tonight after all.

Max seized my hand and guided me to his brand-new silver Cadillac Escalade with chrome twenty-four-inch spinners. I saw the truck when the valet attendant pulled it up and parked it, but I had no idea he was "flossing" like that, as Joel would say. He opened the door and escorted me into his truck. Before he jumped into his truck he pulled a huge gun from his back and placed it in his glove compartment. The sounds of hip-hop blasted through the sound system.

"Still a thug, I see," I said as if I was all that. It was evident. Some things never change, like men and their love for hip-hop. I sat on the heated black leather seats, trying not to look unhappy or tense as I crossed my legs.

We drove down Michigan Avenue, and the beats

of the music polluted the air. Cars fled past us with rumbling sounds gyrating from their trunks. Blair, Sapphire, and Kelly followed us.

The avenue had clubs on every block. I looked to my right at the Cotton Club. I noticed all the people standing in the long line in front of the club. The other clubs on Michigan Avenue had people gathered outside as well. I looked back. Kelly must have been loaded, because she was hanging out of Blair's sunroof, shaking her breasts. The men were beeping their horns in response. My girls were acting as if they were eighteen, and I thought I would vomit from embarrassment.

LUST FIVE

We arrived at the quaint restaurant, which was located near Beverly Hills, a mid to upper-class section of a south side neighborhood. The restaurant, which resembled a drug store, was lodged in a small building on a corner.

I looked into the cozy little place. The windows were decorated with red-and-white-checkered curtains. White linen dressed the small round tables with clear vases holding three daisies each.

As we piled into the tiny lobby, two of Max's friends greeted us.

"Shelby, Sapphire, Blair, and Kelly, this is Dexter and Bryan."

"I am pleased to meet you guys. Would you like to change your phone service?" Kelly chuckled.

"Please ignore her. Nice meeting you," Blair said as she gazed into Bryan's eyes.

I stood there, wanting to be polite to Max and his friends, but I couldn't. My eyes wouldn't move away from his friend Dexter, who stood over six feet tall. A bolt from the blue hit me. Was I having

flashbacks? He was Mr. Stunning, my soul mate, the man who locked eyes with me in the club. He shook my hand firmly and returned my *it-is-you* look.

Hesitantly, I spoke. "It's a pleasure to finally meet the two of you."

Dexter was well built and very pleasing to the eye. I found him sophisticated and more attractive up close. I couldn't keep my eyes off him. He had the sexiest face you could just fall in love with. Not to mention his beautiful, shiny, black, wavy, low-cut hair.

Kelly nudged me, and I snapped out of my daydream. "Can I borrow twenty dollars?"

I pulled the money out of my purse and handed it to her. At that point, she could have had one hundred dollars if she wanted it. "You can have it. I don't loan out money."

Kelly tucked the money in her bra. "Thank you, darling. I love you. When I become rich selling my phone service, I'll pay you back."

I looked at Bryan, who was holding a biscuit in his hand. He was tall and thick with curly brown locks. His stomach hung over his waist.

Kelly mumbled, "I'd love to have a threesome with you guys. I'd fuck the shit out of y'all."

The men didn't hear her comment, but I did. She could be so tacky at times, and I was starting to lose respect for her.

I am tired of Kelly's lusts for gin and threesomes. But it is not right to judge others. Lord, forgive me for judging others and for that drink I had in the club. Oh, yeah, and for lusting over this fine man before me.

"Follow me," Bryan stated. He sat us at a large

round table, pulled out Blair's chair, and sat down right beside her.

Immediately, Kelly turned to Dexter and began to converse. She looked down at the bulge in his pants.

"Very well hung," Kelly whispered to me.

Max sniffed. "What's that smell? Man, something sure smells good."

"Look under the table." Sapphire giggled.

Everyone looked under the table. Sapphire's legs were wide open, and she wasn't wearing panties. "That's my pussy you smell," Sapphire replied, barely containing her laughter.

Kelly and I quickly raised our heads. Dexter, Max, and Bryan moved much more slowly than we did.

Bryan sat up. "Girl, did that clit-piercing hurt?"

Sapphire licked her lips. Then she stuck her tongue out and wiggled her tongue ring. "No, this one didn't either."

"Dexter and Bryan, you better get on that," Max snickered.

"No, you get on this," Sapphire said boldly.

"Baby, you ain't my type. I date respectable women," he said, while reaching his arm behind my back.

"Shelby, respectable, yeah, right," Sapphire said slyly, inching toward Blair.

The waitress appeared with biscuits, and everyone quieted down and quickly grabbed one. They were fluffy and light as a feather. I put one in my mouth and began to chew. The biscuits were scrumptious. They tasted just like my grandmother's.

"Can I take your order?" the waitress asked.

Max, Dexter, Bryan, and I ordered smothered pork chops and grits with gravy. Kelly ordered pancakes covered with fresh strawberries and whipped cream. Blair and Sapphire requested cheese and onion hash browns, ham, and two eggs.

Kelly grazed Dexter's hand with her fingernail. "So Dexter, I hear you and Max own a top-of-the-line barbershop with a bar inside of it. Do you need a bartender? I can walk around that bitch butt naked if you're paying."

Dexter paused. "As a matter of fact, we can use a female bartender. I been filling in, but I'm sure the boys would rather look at you. Let me know what hours you're available and you got yourself a job. Are you cool with that, Max?"

Max put his thumbs up. "Most definitely, just because you're Shelby's girl."

Kelly stood up and tightly hugged Dexter and Max.

Bryan rubbed his forehead as if he was dying of starvation. Then he yelled across the room, "Grandma Pinkie, give me an order of fried chicken too."

A heavy woman with the most gorgeous smile walked to our table. "Well, how y'all doin'?"

"Fine, ma'am," we replied.

Bryan looked up at the woman and grinned. "This is my lovely grandmother. She is the best cook in the world. Wait until y'all taste her cooking."

His grandmother waved her hand. "Boy, stop bragging. I'll fry you some chicken, but I swear you're going to eat us out of business."

"I'm really impressed with your place," Blair re-acted shyly.

Bryan said he opened the restaurant with his grandmother. "People come from everywhere to get her cooking," Bryan boasted, with biscuits in his mouth.

"I bet they do," Blair replied calmly, not her usual obnoxious, intimidating self.

"She brings the southern taste of Mississippi to the city," he explained, as he licked the maple syrup off his fingers.

"What part of Mississippi?" I asked.

"A small town called Crosby, a few miles from Natchez."

The waitress brought our breakfast out, and Dexter blessed the food. Our table looked like a scene from the movie, *Soul Food*. There was no talking going on, only smacking.

"Well, breakfast was delicious. Your grandmother can burn way better than mine can." Kelly flirted.

I smiled at Bryan. "The breakfast was good. I'll have to bring my parents back."

Every single one of us sat at the table looking like stuffed potatoes after breakfast, except Blair. Blair only ate half of her food. She was on her best behavior. I couldn't believe it. She was being polite and very well-mannered. Blair didn't bust out with one good joke and surprisingly not even a ciga-rette. She had her eye on Bryan. I guess she was really trying to impress him with her lady-like atti-tude. They talked the whole time, focused on each other as if we weren't sitting there.

Bryan looked at Blair as if he was going to give her bad news. "I love a woman who takes care of her fingernails." He picked up her hand. "I got to have you, Blair."

"Please," Kelly yelled out. "You could have come up with a better line than that. Bryan, just tell Blair you like her. 'Cause those long-ass, decorated nails are ghetto. I'm surprised she didn't break them when she was beating my friend down in the club."

Bryan ignored Kelly and kept his eyes on Blair. "I have tickets to Keith Sweat's concert next month. Would you like to go?"

"Keith Sweat? Is he still living?" Sapphire said.

I intercepted quickly. "Bryan, I think that's nice. Blair, you should go."

Blair covered her eyes and said, "I can't if it's on a Saturday." Then she brought her fist down to her chin and frowned. "I have to work every weekend after this week."

"Call off. We are talking about Keith Sweat," Kelly shouted. "See, you don't deserve the nice guys."

Bryan started singing Keith Sweat's lyrics to "I'll Give All My Love to You."

Kelly looked shocked. "Damn. Boy, you can sing your ass off."

Sapphire and I clapped. "Bryan, you have a beautiful voice," I whispered softly.

"She's hooked, man," Dexter shouted.

Blair sighed. "I'm sorry, Bryan. I would love to go, but I just got a new position."

"Bryan, fuck Blair. I'm free. I can go," Sapphire muttered. "And I'll give you a little something extra if I'm feeling *bi* that day."

I yawned, knowing I had no business being out that late. "My medical school colleagues are going to kill me," I mumbled.

"There she go. My medical colleagues are going to kill me. Everyone doesn't need to know you're in medical school. You act worse than Megan sometimes, with yo' wanna-be-saved ass," Kelly ranted. "If you were so saved you wouldn't be out clubbing with us."

I wanted to slap Kelly. She was the one who begged me to come. Instead I ignored her dumb statement and decided not to reply. The devil had a way of using your friends to attack you.

"Sleepy head, can I take you home?" Max asked, noticing the stressed look on my face.

I exhaled deeply. "That would be great. I have a lot of studying to do . . . It was nice meeting all of you," I said, standing firmly and beating myself up inside for letting them persuade me into coming out.

LUST SIX

The phone rang loudly. My eyes darted to the clock.

Who could this be at seven in the morning? I thought, while fumbling for the phone.

"Hello," I managed to verbalize, still half asleep.

"Good morning, beautiful," a man whispered over the phone. "I thought about you all night," he said, sounding wide-awake and full of energy. "I want to see you tonight. How about a movie?"

"Ahh . . . I'll think about it."

The truth was, I was elated that Max took the time to call me and wanted to take me out. I was so tired of being alone. Being a Christian woman took so much out of me, and I just wanted to be normal again.

"Well, you think about it. Dexter and I are going to shoot some hoops at the *Y.*"

I yawned. "I will. Call me back around five o'clock and I'll have an answer for you."

Rolling out of the bed took no effort, because I was feeling good. My daily ritual began the minute

I rushed downstairs to clean my townhouse. I turned on my gospel CD, and began praising God for another day and repenting at the same time. I washed clothes, dusted furniture, and put all the dishes in the dishwasher. Then I called my mom. She was already up, of course.

"How was your night? I called you five times last night, but I didn't get an answer."

"Oh, Momma, I went out to the club."

"I know you didn't go out to a nightclub. I thought you were saved. You've been going to Bible study twice a week?"

I exhaled noisily. "I needed to get out. I hadn't been out since Sebastian and I broke up."

She grunted, "I worry. It's so dangerous out in those streets. If you're going to be a Christian woman, stay out of the club."

"Mom, I don't plan on doing the club thing again."

"I bet you had on that red nail polish and lipstick. I told you, little girls don't wear nail polish or lipstick."

"Mom, I'm grown."

"Oh yeah, I keep forgetting. Well, I hope you didn't stay out late. I've never heard of anyone going out to the club while in medical school . . . Shelby, I don't want you to flunk out."

"I was in by midnight," I lied, not wanting to hear her speech. "No, I didn't drink anything," I lied again to avoid her tongue-lashing on alcoholism running in the family.

"Mama, let me call you back later," I said, not giving her a chance to reply.

Lord, please forgive me for lying to my mother. Damn,

if you tell one lie, you have to tell twenty more. Oops. Sorry about the cursing too.

The doorbell rang.

"Flowers for Shelby Tate," a delivery guy announced from behind the door.

I looked at the door as if I had never seen it before. The door opened, and twelve white calla lilies greeted me. They were beautiful. I loved the long sleekness of the calla lilies. The flower had an elegant and sophisticated look about it. I preferred them to a bouquet of roses, but only one person knew that. I guess Sebastian really needed my help.

He must really be in trouble. Did he really rape someone?

The flower trick wasn't going to work this time. I tried to shake memories of him from my head again. I looked in the kitchen cabinet and located a crystal vase, filled it halfway with water, and placed the flowers in it. I picked up the card.

"Why is he doing this to me?" I whimpered, feeling a little weak. I closed my eyelids and fantasized about the first time Sebastian and I made love.

He arranged my naked body on the calla lily-covered bed, gently tracing my delicate, virgin body with the fresh flower, kissing each spot the divine lily landed on. I rested freely with my legs opened wide as he placed soft kisses on and around my pulsating vagina. My natural liquids covered my clit as I welcomed him with tears.

A tear rolled down my face as I forced myself to snap out of my daydream. Opening the card hurriedly, I began to read. A sweet melody of love covered my spirit.

Shelby,

    I have always loved you. I believe God brought us together again. We have been in and out of each other's lives for years. I am a man now, not that foolish boy you remember. I was young and didn't know how to treat a sweet goddess like you. I know what I want now, and that's someone pure like you. I should've been your first. Well darling, it's on you because I'm ready to give you all of me. I want a serious relationship this time, just you and I.

    Please say you'll be my lady.

Love Always,
Max

The words of the card touched my heart. *"Love Always, Max."*

I couldn't believe my eyes. Just when my body and mind were ready for Sebastian, Max appears. Was Max capable of being romantic? Was he turning into my new Casanova? Could I use him to finally get over Sebastian once and for all?

A knock at the door startled me. Through the peephole, I saw Joel. I flung open the door excitedly. "Look what Max sent me," I said, showing Joel my flowers before he could get all the way in the house.

"Calm down, Shelby. They're nice," he said walking to the sofa, not sharing my enthusiasm.

I sat on the couch next to him and bounced in my seat. "Max is my old boyfriend, and he wants to take me out tonight."

Joel looked at the television then he glanced at me. "Go for it. You need a man right about now to calm your ass down."

Joel was right about one thing. I did need to feel the touch of a man again.

We sat there for a while until the house phone rang. I beckoned for Joel to answer. He picked up on the second ring. "Hold on," he said, nonchalantly passing the cordless phone to me. "Shelby, it's for you."

Joel didn't move. He continued lying on the sofa, pretending to watch television. I knew he was listening to my conversation.

"Are you trying to pay me back for all the times I sat eavesdropping on you and your women?" I whispered to Joel with my mouth away from the phone.

"I didn't interrupt anything, did I?" Max asked assertively.

"No, no. That's my boy, Joel. He always answers my phone."

"How are you doing this morning?"

"I'm fine. Thank you for the beautiful flowers."

"I'm glad you liked them, beautiful."

"Oh, by the way, I'd love to go out with you, tonight," I gloated, full of anticipation. I winked at Joel, trying to signal for him to go away, but he didn't budge.

"Then I'll be there around seven, after I drop off Dex."

"Okay," I replied.

"Bye for now," Max said in a love-making voice.

"Bye," I voiced ecstatically and started thinking back about how weak I was for Max when I was younger. He was aggressive, yet caring. And I can't forget how cool he was. Max knew everyone and was well respected and desired by all the girls.

I slammed the phone down and started smiling like a geek. "Well, Joel, it's official; I have my first date for the year."

"Good. You need to get out. You've been locked up too long. Are you gonna let a nigga borrow the car?"

I handed Joel my car keys, figuring he was on a creep mission. Whenever he asked to borrow my car it was for that reason or something shady. "Don't go to that casino in Joliet."

"Baby, I have a date with a dime piece. I'm not going to gamble."

"I hope that crazy baby mama of yours doesn't bust your ass. You know that big yellow bitch is crazy."

Joel smiled and gave me a kiss on the cheek. "Don't worry about Chloe. I got this. As for you, I want you to chill with the curse words. I don't know what has come over you. You went out with them hot-ass girls last night, now look at you."

I put my hands over my ears. "Just fill my car up and use condoms."

Max arrived at seven on the dot, and I was ready. He didn't have to come in for me because I ran out of the house before he could open the door to his truck.

"Hey, baby. That was quick. You didn't give me time to get out and open your door for you," Max said adoringly.

I gave him a sexy look and said a sweet, "How are you this evening?"

Max's eyes surveyed my entire body. He leaned

over and kissed my peachy-colored cheeks. "I'm doing fine, just fine." He glided his hands through the layers of my long, sandy brown hair, then slid back slowly, checked the mirrors, and put the truck in gear all in one motion.

The sunroof was open in his shiny clean ride, and my hair swayed to the rhythm of the wind. Alicia Keys sang "You Don't Know My Name" on his radio. He grabbed my hand and kissed it. Max was being the perfect gentleman.

"You know your girl Kelly looks like Alicia Keys. Dexter and I were discussing that today as we talked about you resembling Beyoncé, especially your body," he said deviously, but swiftly changed his expression to a soft, relaxing, innocent gaze. "Yo, you know what's up for real. I can't believe we found each other again."

"I told Megan we hooked up again too, but you know how she feels about you," I replied as we shared a smirk, remembering our childhood and the time he threw rocks at Megan and I, then smashed her face in the mud.

We arrived at River Oaks twenty minutes later. Before we made it to the door, a man dressed in a gray Sean John outfit approached us.

"Hey, man. What's up?" Max said as they shook hands.

I looked at Max and blushed. He was still popular and well known all over the south side of Chicago. They both turned my way as Max introduced me. "This is my lady, Shelby."

Max was standing up straight, looking very proud, as his friend freaked me with his eyes. The man licked his lips quickly and reached for my

hand. His eyes were fixated on my thighs. "Damn. Do you have a sister?"

He mumbled in Max's ear, "Damn, bro, I like that dime piece on your arm. Don't let me catch you slipping."

"Peace," Max exclaimed, abruptly dismissing his friend's foolish behavior.

"Two for *Barbershop 2*," Max informed the cashier, pulling out a fifty-dollar bill.

"Burrr," I mumbled, wrapping my arms together tightly the minute we walked into the theater's lobby.

"Are you cold?" Max asked with a surprised look.

Before I could answer him, he was halfway to the door.

Max returned minutes later with his jacket. "Put this on since you're so cold. I had to get my gun out the car too. Can't get caught without it."

We found seats in the back of the theater where no one was sitting. The movie had been out a couple of weeks, so the theater wasn't crowded. Max and I made ourselves comfortable in the dark, secluded area.

Twenty minutes into the movie, Max wrapped his arm around me and gently bit my ear, which sent chills down my spine. His tongue glided in and out of the center of my ear. Arousal struck me. My nipples were stiff, and the element that made me a woman was pulsating with excitement. Max reached down, lifted my dress up, shifted my lace panties to the side and dipped his finger into my wet innocence.

"Stop," I whispered faintly, liking the way it felt. I smacked his hand lightly, but he didn't stop.

Max moved his finger in a slow, circular motion, touching all the right spots inside of me. His finger was saturated with my syrupy substance.

"Please stop," I said lightly, enjoying every stroke of his finger. I wanted to explode, so I exhaled slowly to hide my happiness as my eyes rolled back and my muscles contracted. I bit my bottom lip in an effort to stay quiet. I felt energized. He revived feelings in me that I no longer knew I had. I desired Max in a naughty way, but I knew I had to wait. I wanted to drown the lustful flame that was searing within me.

My conscience said, *"No, you can't have sex in a movie theater. Maybe you two should've gone to the Holiday Inn on your first date. Your behavior is very whorish tonight, not Christian-like at all. Say no to lust."*

The audience was laughing at the humor on the screen. I blinked very fast, thinking, *What the hell am I doing?* "We're missing the movie," I said hurriedly as I moved Max's hand from between my legs.

"Come on, Shelby. Live a little. There aren't many people in here."

"No. I don't know what came over me anyway. I shouldn't have let you do what you did," I said firmly, sitting up straight and ready to battle the temptation.

Max continued to try to get me to see things his way, but there was no convincing me. We came to watch a movie, and that's what we did.

On the way back to my house, Max drove down 159th Street in silence. I was speechless and a little

embarrassed about my behavior. I couldn't believe I let him feel me up in a public theater. A cheap Forty-seventh Street hooker is what I felt like; nothing like the quiet, innocent, Bible study-going girl that I was.

Max saw the repulsive expression on my face. "What's wrong?" he asked, poking me in my arm.

"I'm tired," I replied with no explanation.

He didn't ask any more questions, so we remained silent the rest of the ride.

When we arrived at my place, Max walked me to the door and kissed my hand. "We'll have to rent the movie when it comes out." He chuckled.

"Will we?" I asked, wondering if I'd date him again.

LUST SEVEN

The sparks from the high-speed, eight o'clock subway train glared to the right of me, letting me know that I was running late for class.

This will be my fifth time in two months being late because of Max. I can't continue to be late. This is my hardest year of medical school, and I can't fail. I guess I'll have to cut some of the time I spend with Max.

Things were going well between Max and me. No more lonely, boring days for me. I finally had a companion to talk to again. He filled a void that Sebastian left behind. He took me to dinner three times during the week. Occasionally, we'd go to the movies, skating, or dancing. And our downtime was incredible. Quite often, we spent late hours conversing and debating about political matters. Other nights, we'd analyze our behavior and the people around us. Our relationship was deep. It didn't revolve around sex, because we weren't having any. It was composed of deep conversations and honest communication.

Don't get me wrong, sometimes I found it hard

to believe Max was with me, especially after our first date. Because it was apparent he wanted sex and I wasn't ready for that. But after we discussed my religious beliefs and my uneasiness with his sexual advances, he agreed to wait until I was ready. It seemed unbelievable, but after several weeks I realized he was genuine. Some days he'd even read the Bible with me.

I was twenty minutes late for class. Dr. Myru didn't say a word when I slipped into my desk. As a matter of fact, he didn't look my way.

After class, he marched up to me and whispered in my ear, "Megan is moving in with me."

I was thankful. I just knew he was coming to give me bad news about being late, and to tell me he was planning to fail me for missing so many days.

"Oh." I smiled, overjoyed, that my tardiness and absences weren't the issue. But why hadn't Megan told me about her plans to shack up with my professor? I was the one who introduced her to Dr. Myru four months ago. She saw him in his pearl Mercedes SL500 and insisted I introduce her. I'll never forget that conversation:

"Shelby, that nigga got money. That car cost eighty-five thousand dollars, and those platinum cufflinks he is wearing are worth three thousand dollars or more. Not to mention the man's finely manicured hands. He shows all the signs of a wealthy man. Dr. Myru will be mine. So get ready for A's in all of his classes."

* * *

Dr. Myru lifted my hand. "Shelby. Shelby. That's all you have to say is *Oh*?"

I stood up and paused. "Well . . . I'm happy for you two. I just thought you were getting on me about my attendance."

Dr. Myru directed me to the classroom door. "You have an *A* in my class. Now, go home and get some rest."

LUST EIGHT

Joel sauntered up to my car in his short brown UPS shorts. His dark, well-defined legs were gleaming with sex appeal, and I couldn't keep my eyes off of him.

"What you staring at, girl?" Joel asked, rubbing his chin.

I grinned mischievously. "My best friend is looking good. I have never noticed how cute your legs are."

"That ain't all that's cute," Joel said in a flirtatious manner, gripping his penis.

I snapped out of my lustful moment real quick. "Stop playing with me, little boy. I really have something to tell you."

"What, Shelby?"

"I haven't heard from Max yet. He usually calls or meets me after class." I sighed.

"Shelby, stop sweating the pimp. The man has other bitches to see about."

I hit Joel's arm. "Shut up. We are together almost every day. He can't be with anyone else."

He pinched my cheek. "Little sister, you are so naïve."

I sighed. "That's why Chloe's giving it up as we speak."

"She can share the wealth," Joel clowned, pointing west. "Stop over Preston's house."

"Preston from high school? The one who used to hang out with you and Sebastian?"

"Yeah, nigga, don't sound so damn happy."

"Cool, he always has a nice variety of men in his house, plenty of eye candy," I said, blinking my eyes like Betty Boop.

Joel covered my face with his hand. "You are so silly."

When we arrived at Preston's, I was shocked. His house was filled with men gambling and drinking. The obscenities of the street game were being yelled out, "seven," "back doe little Joe," "six and eight running mates."

I surveyed the huddle and the pile of money in the middle of the floor. The guys were shooting dice for a hundred dollars a roll. I never knew Preston's house served as a gambling shack. I thought all the men just hung out at his place, watching basketball on television.

I pointed my finger at Joel. "You better not play. This is where your five hundred dollars went last week."

Joel pouted, looking around to see if anyone heard me. "Shelby, calm down. I just came to pick up some money from my boy Steve. Don't try to embarrass me up in here."

Preston strolled up sucking his teeth. He looked at me and smiled. "Shelby, when can I get with you?"

I stepped away from Preston. "You're too late. I got a man."

"I let you chill with my boy Sebastian, but I was supposed to be next." Preston chuckled, moving closer to me.

Before I could respond, a short, petite, middle-aged woman walked into the room scratching her head.

The group of guys said, "Good evening, Miss Brown," almost in unison without lifting their heads.

Preston's mother was wearing a thin red night-shirt, quite noticeably, with no bra. She called Preston's name and started to walk toward him. The noise ceased. Heads turned. It looked like every guy in the house had a wet dream. She sashayed past the dice game, now having everyone's attention, and approached me. "Honey, I like your belt," Miss Brown stated, reading the name on the buckle. "Who's Maxtin?"

Her question surprised me, and before I could answer her, Joel told her that I was dating Maxtin Brooks, the owner of Gentleman's Touch barbershop.

"Oh, really," Miss Brown snapped. "Well, tell Maxtin you met Lola Brown." She articulated clearly, rolling her eyes and walking away in a rushed manner.

"What was that about?" I asked Joel, not believing how immature the older woman was behaving.

"She's probably cold. I bet she rushed away to

put some clothes on." He laughed, still gawking at the older woman, who was half-dressed.

"I know you're lying. Did that old hag date Max?"

Joel didn't answer. He just gave me a silly smirk and hunched his shoulders.

I frowned. "I'm going to ask Max. He'll tell me the truth. I know women. She didn't roll her eyes for nothing."

"That's on you. I'll be back," Joel volunteered to tell me as he glided away smoothly toward the dice game.

The secondhand smoke was clouding the room, and my eyes burned.

I can't take this anymore. It feels like someone threw hot sauce in each pupil. Where is the door? I got to get out of here . . . Joel, your butt is going to get left. That's why I don't frequent spots like this.

While rubbing my eyes, I staggered to the door. Right before I reached the doorway, a group of guys busted through the door. One familiar face seized my stare. My stomach dropped. I never expected to see him here. Thought he'd be back in jail. Didn't know what kind of rape case he had. The whole story sounded so flaky.

"Hey, Shelby, how are you?" he asked gleefully, reaching his arms to embrace me for a hug.

"Excuse me. I don't know you," I said curtly, with plenty of attitude.

The guys chuckled in the background. "Damn, dog. She played your ass."

Sebastian touched my arm. "Shelby, what's wrong with you? How you going to play me? We have history."

"Fuck you, rapist. Shouldn't you be somewhere

in jail?" I raced through the door, trying to escape his presence.

"Those charges were dropped," he yelled to the back of my head.

It was so hard seeing him again. I thought I'd forgiven him and moved on, but the animosity was still there. I hated him for taking my virginity—or, shall I say, talking me out of it. My faith was dissipating fast.

"There was no way I should've let Sebastian get to me," I uttered aloud on my way to my car, not seeing Preston outside.

"Shelby, I didn't know Sebastian was coming over here," he interjected, overhearing my whole conversation with myself.

"Oh. It's cool. I'm fine. I'm over him," I countered hurriedly, immediately turning off my irrational emotions.

"Good. I wouldn't want to upset someone I'm interested in."

"Preston, what did you say?"

"I would really like a chance to get to know you better, Shelby."

"What?"

"You know, intimately, sexually." He caressed my arm and wrapped his other hand around my waist.

"Preston, my man wouldn't like this scene," I replied, appalled by his behavior, yanking his hand off of me.

"Well, what he doesn't see can't hurt him," Preston said deviously. Preston folded his hands together around my waist again. "You and Joel stick together like glue. Why can't you and I be close too?"

I moved Preston's hands for the second time. "Joel and I are just friends. He's like a brother to me," I said, getting a little annoyed with his crazy talk and wandering hands.

"Yeah right, that nigga sleeps at yo' house sometimes." He touched my waist again.

I smacked his hand.

"Joel must be eating the hell out of that pussy."

"Are you crazy? That's nasty. We are just friends," I yelled, shocked by his accusation.

"Well, the ladies tell me your boy Joel eats pussy very well."

"I don't believe that. But if he does, he's not eating mine," I stated, defensively moving to the driver side of my car.

Joel snuck up behind Preston and I and pinched me on my butt. "Come on here, old hot-ass girl."

"Joel, get in the car before I bust you in your head. You know I don't allow butt-pinching."

"Yeah, Joel, that's my ass," Preston said assertively.

"Kiss my ass," I blurted out and stuck up my middle finger.

"I'm trying to. You won't let me."

I was ready to see my man after hanging with Joel all day. I gave in and called Max. No one answered, so I left a message. As soon as I hung up, my cell phone rang, perking me up instantly. "Hello."

"Hey, may I speak with Kelly?" a timid male voice asked.

"Sweetheart, this isn't Kelly's number."

"Shelby, this is Kevin. She said she was staying with you this weekend." I forgot all about Kevin,

the guy Kelly met at the club. One minute she was giving him a blow job in the bathroom, and the next day she was moving in with him. Kelly had a way of getting what she wanted from guys who were naïve and weak.

"Oh, yeah, she's on her way," I lied, trying to cover for her.

My line clicked. I looked down, and it was Max's number. "Look, I'll tell Kelly you called," I said suddenly, trying to rush Kevin off the phone.

"Hello," I answered sharply, a little pissed that he hadn't called all day.

"Hey, baby, I'm at Dexter's," Max replied, sounding glad to hear my voice.

The first emotion that hit me was jealousy. I was used to Max spending his time with me, but lately it seemed like we were drifting apart. The last two days he'd been at Dexter's house or the shop, and I didn't know what to think. I had told him I needed a little space so I could study.

"Baby, you just found time to call me? Damn, is Dexter replacing me?" I asked jokingly, not wanting to give the impression that I was a spoiled brat.

"What? Girl, you better watch your mouth. Saved women don't curse. And you know Dexter is my boy."

"Okay, I hope you two aren't on the 'down low.'"

"Shelby, don't play. All this big, long, black dick I have over here is for you, whenever you decide to stop fronting."

I let out a sigh without delay, dismissing Max's statement. "On the serious tip, today is my sister's birthday. I spent the day with her. And, besides, I was just trying to give your little butt some time to

yourself. You said you needed to catch up on your studying, and I don't want you to flunk out of school. We have a future to build together. I want to be able to retire and sit at home while you make that cheese."

I gave a phony laugh. "You are such a funny guy."

"So what's up for tonight? If you're not too busy I have something special planned for you. It's our anniversary. Today is the date I met you seventeen years ago. We met in front of the neighborhood church when we were eight years old on my older sister's birthday."

"Max, are you serious?" I asked frantically, not believing he kept up with how many months we'd known each other.

"Girl, just pack your bags," he ordered. "You need a break from all that studying."

"Wait," I shouted, a little ill at ease. "Do you know Preston Brown? Or his mother, an older woman named Lola Brown?"

Max giggled. "Why?"

"Just answer me."

"Yeah, she's someone I used to mess around with occasionally."

My eyes widened. "What? That woman is old enough to be your mother."

"Baby, old women need thug-loving too," Max said, holding in his laughs.

"You are so full of it, Max. I knew something was up by the crazy way Miss Brown looked at me when she found out I was dating you. Do you still go over there?"

Max rushed off the phone. "Hell no. That was in my pimping days. I belong to you now. Just be ready in twenty minutes."

As soon as Max and I hung up, Joel intercepted. "Was that Kelly's boyfriend you were talking to before Max called?"

I nodded my head up and down, nonchalantly.

"Doesn't that nigga treat your girl good?"

"Yes, Kelly should settle down with Kevin. He treats her real nice."

Joel took his hand and gestured as if he was cutting his throat. "Dude is a fool. He know Kelly ain't spending the weekend with you. Damn. You shouldn't lie for her. Let that ass get busted."

"I try not to lie. My girl needed me," I snapped.

Joel laughed. "Well, she's involving you in her lies. You're starting to slip back to your old ways. I keep on telling you that one night out has really changed you. If you're trying to be saved, you need to go to church every Sunday, like you used to, and don't miss. You ain't even been to Bible study, have you?"

I jiggled my hands as if I was throwing dice. "Don't lecture me, Reverend Magic Casino. I thought you were going to stop gambling. How much money did you lose this time? Gambling is a big lust."

Joel waved his hand at me. "Girl, I came up. I always get my dough."

"You can't talk about anyone. Just leave me and my girl alone."

"You and your girl? I'll tell ol' boy how Kelly has all of those pimps in and out his crib. And you

don't want me to call your mom. I'm sure she would love to know how her little Shelby has fallen back into the worldly way of life," Joel teased.

"Don't hate." I snickered but became serious when I reflected on my recent behavior. I had cut back on my prayer time, Bible study, and church activities.

"Drop me off at the corner," Joel said frantically as we approached his baby mama's neighborhood.

He did not want her to see me. She hated me for some unknown reason. I think she was a little jealous of our relationship, and the fact that I was fine as wine didn't help the matter. "Cool. I have an overnight date, anyway," I said excitedly.

Joel ignored me, concentrating on removing the gold link chain from his neck. "Here, keep this for me. You know how these folk niggas are around here. A "nigga in red" ain't welcome on this block."

I didn't hesitate. I quickly snatched the chain from Joel and placed it on my neck. "I'm surprised you haven't lost this shooting dice."

"Very funny. How many times do I have to tell you? I don't have a gambling problem."

"Yeah right," I said squirming, trying to rush Joel out of my car. "The secret is out. Now I know why you're always at Preston's house."

He pointed to the door. "Just hurry up and let me out. I don't want Chloe to see me. Don't feel like explaining for the umpteenth time that we are only friends, that big-booty Shelby is just my girl."

I stopped at the corner of Oglesby Street for a brief second. The car door opened, immediately.

"Be careful tonight. I don't like that Max dude you're messing with. He's too slick for you. Things were cool when you were sitting at home, being a good girl."

"Just be careful in the hood. I hope you're packing," I replied earnestly.

"All is well. I'm a real gangsta," Joel retorted, throwing up gang signs then patting his waist where his gun was hidden. "Here, take these Magnum condoms in case you get to itching for a little something-something on your date," he teased, throwing two gold packets to me before closing the car door.

I caught the items and placed them in my purse then I rolled down the window and smiled. "Thanks!"

"You better not fuck that scrub. I was only kidding," he stated in brotherly way.

"See ya," I called out and pressed my foot on the accelerator.

LUST NINE

Tensely, I stood, awaiting Max's arrival. The minute the doorbell rang, my heart fluttered. I didn't know what this night would bring. As the door opened I was greeted with soft, passionate kisses and tight hugs as Max covered my eyes with a red satin blindfold. Unable to contain ourselves, our bodies became intertwined as we drifted to the car.

R. Kelly's "Twelve Play" vibrated throughout the vehicle, and the aroma of Burberry cologne filled the truck. The atmosphere was hypnotizing me as Max sat me down on the heated seats and traced my neck with soft suckle-kisses. To my surprise I became relaxed.

"Max, where are we going?" I asked seductively, shocked by my own actions.

"Shush . . . no talking." Max placed my fingers in his mouth, one at a time, in a slow, mesmerizing manner.

The more he licked and rolled, the wetter I became. My panties were saturated with liquid nec-

tar. "Max, the foreplay is unbearable. We shouldn't. I'm saving myself."

"Hush . . ."

My hands would no longer obey as they crept between Max's legs to his pulsating member. He took control of my fingers and toured my hand up and down his shaft.

"Oh my God, Max. It's so big. I really want to feel you inside of me."

Max seized my lips with his tongue then he pulled away. "Shelby, you don't know how long I've waited to hear those words from you. I'll make love to you in a few seconds. We are almost there," he said as he turned in front of the hotel.

I wanted to scream, "What? I was only playing." But Max was serious. He was a grown man, and I knew what he expected.

"Valet," the gentleman yelled out.

My fake smile widened, nervously. I couldn't believe what was happening. Anxiety bubbled inside of me. Seconds later, I was swept out of the car and escorted into the hotel.

The elevator door opened, and Max grabbed my hand and led me inside. The door slid open again, and Max removed my blindfold. We were standing in front of ten-foot windows, overlooking Lake Michigan, on the 32nd floor of the Ritz Carlton. The curtains were wide open, and the view was beautiful. Chicago's city lights sparkled brightly. The bed was covered with fresh calla lilies in white, pink, and lilac. A chilled bottle of champagne was also sitting next to the bed in a silver ice bucket. A note card on the nightstand read: EXCLUSIVELY FOR OUR PRESIDENTIAL SUITE GUESTS.

"This is so nice," I replied apprehensively, still uncomfortable about spending the night with him.

Max kissed my lips delicately. "I want to make this moment extraordinary." He moved my body to the side of the bed, poured me a glass of champagne in a beautiful crystal flute, and handed it to me.

I sipped slowly, savoring its taste and the ambiance of the night.

He poured another glass. "A toast to the new us," Max announced, breaking the silence.

We drank. A few minutes later he pulled out a bottle of Courvoisier and poured a couple of shots in his glass. "Would you like some? This will help with the pain I bring."

"You know I don't drink that stuff," I answered, aware that Max was trying to get me toasted so he could have his way with me.

Max fell to one knee and took off my shoe. He tilted his flute and positioned my toes to touch his glass. Then Max situated my toes in his juicy mouth. I squirmed. He sucked harder. I squirmed more. He repeated the act with each toe, making me moan and squirm more intensely.

"Wait," I cried out, stopping him dead in his tracks, to prolong things.

I grabbed my bag and dashed to the bathroom. There were his-and-hers white robes hanging near the Jacuzzi. I sat on the sofa in the bathroom and searched for my bed clothes. I covered my body with the chemise, and then I opened the bathroom door.

The lights were off and candles lit a path to the bed. The view was more evident in the huge win-

dows behind the bed. I was speechless. Max had really gone out of his way to please me. He must have spent over six hundred dollars easily for the room, champagne, flowers, and candles.

Max crept up behind me, lifted me effortlessly, and carried me to the bed. Our eyes locked as he positioned my head on the pillow.

"What are you doing?" I asked as his head lowered. "Why don't we just hold each other tight?"

"Don't start with your mixed signals. I'm going to suck on these sweet creamy thighs," he stated as his tongue landed on my thighs.

The moist device between my legs had a mind of its own. I was saying no, and she was saying yes, trembling and pulsating like a broke-down Chevy. His kissing and intense sucking increased. I squirmed and she rocked, taking pleasure in the heated moment.

"Wait one second," Max said as he stopped to remove his shirt and jeans.

Things were happening so fast. The next second, his finger was inserted inside of my wet device. That made her happy. She released instantly; juices rained down his finger. He snatched his boxers down fast and directed his manhood toward my vagina.

I opened my eyes in disbelief and placed my hand on his tight stomach. I couldn't do it. "Where is your condom?" I whispered, trying to save my grace. I prayed he didn't have one.

"Baby, I've known you half my life," Max replied, agitated by my attempts.

I looked down in disappointment at Max's igno-

rance. I looked down again in amazement at what I saw. He was the size of a Twix candy bar. I had the condom Joel gave me, but I wasn't going to pull it out for that.

"Baby, come on. I've waited too long for this moment," he pleaded.

"I only have safe sex," I argued, still trying to act like I was cool.

Max's eyes glared at me with anger. He bit down on his lips, but didn't say anything.

"I will not get an STD, HIV, or pregnant," I yelled angrily because, evidently, Max thought I was a fool. I didn't play when it came to having safe sex. People were dropping dead from AIDS every day, and I wasn't going to be one of them.

"Okay, Miss Safe Sex, why don't you have any condoms?" he said, sounding aggravated.

I lied. "I . . . I . . . I . . . forgot. I've been celibate for over a year."

"Did you use condoms with Casanova?" he said, moving to the side of the bed where his bottle of cognac was.

"Yes, I did, asshole. Every single time," I shouted, craving to say, "I have a condom, but a Magnum will fall off your little-ass dick." Instead, I said, "Let's just go to sleep since you aren't prepared."

That comment made Max livid. He rolled over in silence, reached on the table, and took possession of the almost empty bottle of cognac. My eyes bulged as he downed the liquor like it was water, leaving none remaining.

"You know what?" he asked but gave me no time to reply. "I should've never messed around with yo' stuck-up ass. You have always thought you were

better than everyone else. I spend all this money on you and you can't give me some of that sanctified, baptized-in-the-name-of-Jesus pussy?" he slurred. "You ain't shit."

Wow. Max came out of a bag on me. I felt like we were nine again. His immaturity was ringing loud; a toddler temper tantrum at its best.

"Won't be getting any of this tonight or ever," I said silently as I inched to the edge of the bed and closed my eyes.

Max's vibrating cell phone woke us both up at four in the morning. He seized his phone and traveled to the balcony like a private detective, which didn't bother me one bit. It gave me the opportunity to escape to the shower.

The hot water felt good beating down on my body. I smiled as I remembered the look on Max's face after finding out I wasn't having unprotected sex. I almost laughed aloud when my thoughts crept to the little Twix bar I saw.

After I showered, dressed, curled my hair, applied make-up, and perfumed my body down, one hour had gone by.

I stepped out of the bathroom. "Max, I'm finished. I had to get ready for school. I'm wearing that Ann Taylor dress you bought me."

No one responded.

I peered over at the bed, but it was empty. I looked on the balcony. There was no Max. I checked the lounge area. There was no Max.

Guess he went to the car.

I placed my purse on the nightstand right next to a note.

Shelby,
    *I had to leave. I have an emergency to handle
with my barbershop. Dexter will pick you up.*

What kind of man leaves a note? I was steaming
mad. That was probably his woman calling this
morning. He suddenly had to rush out. Yeah right,
emergency.

*Calm down, Shelby. Now you know Max is immature.
Nothing good happens when you're sinning. You had no
business leading him on. Don't go back to your old ways.*

Before I could complete my thoughts, the elevator opened and Dexter walked in. "Good morning, Shelby." He looked me up and down. "I see
you're ready for school."

I walked toward Dexter, trying to look emotionless. "Good morning." Our eyes met. We couldn't
stop staring at one another. I turned my head because I didn't want my eyes to tell what my mind
was thinking. The truth was, I wanted Dexter. Not
for just one night, but eternity. It sounded weird
and shallow, but what I felt was real—a spiritual
connection. Each time I saw his face I smiled. I tried
to deny the feelings because he was Max's best
friend, but today there was no ignoring my emotions. Good girl or not, I had a major crush on my
boyfriend's best friend.

He spoke, "I guess you two had a hell of a night?"

I laughed nervously. "Nothing happened, Dexter, but I know Max told you that already."

"No, lovely. Max doesn't reveal anything about
his sweet Shelby," Dexter joked, laughing at his
own lie.

"I'm so sure. Men gossip more than women."

"All I know is, I'm here to pick you up. So get on my back," he urged, motioning for me to get on his back.

I dismissed his silliness and gathered my belongings.

"Are you hungry?" Dexter asked.

"No," I replied, checking the bathroom to see if I left anything.

"Well, looks like you're ready."

I nodded in agreement, and Dexter grabbed my bag and escorted me to the elevator.

The valet attendant drove his white Acura 3.5 RL to the front of the hotel. I slid into the seat slowly. Dexter turned the CD on immediately. The rap music blared loudly. I didn't know what artist was rapping, but the noise was getting on my nerves. "Can you turn that down please?" I yelled over the music.

"You don't like rap?"

"Not today," I said snobbishly.

Dexter laughed. "You're not black." He ejected the CD. "What do you like? I have all kinds of music. I'm a music lover."

I hunched my shoulders. "Something slow, quiet, and relaxing; it's too early for that loud rap music."

"What about Luther?" he asked, reaching for his CD.

I smiled. "That's better."

Dexter inserted the CD.

"Thank you," I said softly.

I thought about Max and I got mad all over again. I closed my eyes to hide my emotions and remained quiet. The Lord was chastising me, and I

was feeling really guilty for the way my life was
going. How could I go back to church or Bible
study? I wouldn't know how to explain that I'd
been clubbing, cursing, damn near getting booty,
and now lusting over my boyfriend's best friend.

Dexter kept his eyes on the road, but asked.
"What's wrong? Max will be back next week. Cheer
up, girl. My boy loves you."

I didn't respond.

He continued, "You guys grew up together on
the south side, right?"

"Yes," I told Dexter, trying to end the conversation.

The truth was, I didn't know what to think of
Max. His drama last night was out of order. He
showed me his true colors, an ugly side I didn't
like. Oh, how I wished I hadn't wasted months
with him. He was definitely not husband material.

"Dexter, would you drop me off at the County
Hospital? I have to be at school at seven," I said,
still trying to appear emotionless.

"Sure. What do you do at the hospital?"

"I'm in medical school."

"You'll make one sexy-ass doctor."

*Is this brotha trying to flirt with me? Or am I tooting
my own horn? I'll just pretend like I didn't hear him because he is off limits . . .*

A silent ten minutes later, we pulled into the
hospital parking lot. I was sorry I'd been so distant. Dexter hadn't done anything wrong. It wasn't
his fault I had a crush on him.

"Thank you for the ride. Max is lucky to have a
best friend like you," I said, grinning now.

"No, Shelby, he's lucky to have someone as special as you."

My smile widened.

"Have a good day, sexy," Dexter said flirtatiously.

I waved seductively, wanting to say something, but my mouth wouldn't let me speak. I was afraid of what this could lead to.

"You too, delicious," I mumbled under my breath.

LUST TEN

I walked up to the giant public hospital. The building was historic. However, it had been disrespected by graffiti artists and had become the shelter of many homeless people. It was old and run-down, but some parts were under reconstruction.

Several people were huddled in the front of the hospital waiting for the CTA bus to come. I rushed past the crowd and entered the building looking for Megan, who also worked at the county as a registered nurse. I needed to ask her for a ride home and tell her about Max's disappearing act.

I walked to pediatrics. "Is Megan in?"

"Yes, follow me. She's in with a patient," the nurse answered.

We walked through the halls and located Megan. She was standing in a baby's room. The baby was in a caged baby bed with a clear plastic bubble over his bed.

"Hey, Nurse Megan," I called out.

Megan waved her hand while taking the little boy's temperature.

"Can I get a ride home?" I uttered.

"Yes, meet me in the garage at three o'clock. I was stopping by Blair's anyway."

I thanked her and headed to the stairs. There was only a few minutes left before my class began. We were observing a group for "Suicidal Women."

When I made it to the conference room, everyone was sitting in chairs formatted in a circle.

"Good morning, Dr. Ziger," the group greeted.

"Good morning. Don't be alarmed, but some of my students will be observing today," he announced.

"Wait . . . I see we have a new member. Please introduce yourself to the group."

A young girl who looked about seventeen replied, "My name is Sydney."

"Hi, Sydney," the group replied.

"Why are you here, Sydney? Take as much time as you need. We are here to listen," Dr. Ziger stated.

Sydney replied, "I'm here because I tried to kill myself. I'm having problems with the father of my child. We dated in high school, and I got pregnant at the age of fifteen. We were engaged three years ago, and he still hasn't married me. Each year the date changes. Now, I'm pregnant again and I want to die." She paused. "I can't sleep. I stay up all night. I have to take NyQuil or prescribed sleep medications just to get a wink of sleep. If I don't have that, I take a hit of cognac. I don't even eat. I've lost twenty pounds in two weeks. Ohhh. Ohhh.

I had dreams of going to college. A second child will ruin all of that.

Sometimes he stays out late drinking and, I'm sure, screwing because he doesn't come home. He spends his money on women. Hell, they call my house all times of the night. The other night a woman drove up to our house and rung the bell for him. I don't understand."

She started to ramble fast. "I make love to him every single night, and when he stays out all night I have sex with him when he returns. I perform any sexual task he demands. However, he has never satisfied me; the man is afraid of oral sex. He'll nibble on my thigh, but that's it."

One of the group members laughed.

"I have never had an orgasm. I just give, give, and give more, catering to his every need."

"Girl, you don't know what you are missing. I can see why you wanted to kill yourself," one of the group members blurted out.

"Can we refrain from making any comments until Sydney is finished?" Dr. Ziger announced.

"Well, I guess it's not that bad. He does take good care of me financially. He pays all the bills. He bought me a new Jeep. He purchases all of our clothes. My daughter and I only wear designer clothing. Don't get me wrong. I like the expensive clothes. I just don't have the joy of picking out what I like or want. He even buys groceries and tells me what to cook. I just don't know what's wrong with him. I guess he's just a little controlling. What's funny is that his friends are the complete opposite. They give their women freedom and respect. Why can't he respect me?"

Sydney was rambling rapidly and jumping subjects like a schizophrenic. The group was patient with her, but very antsy to make comments.

"It sounds like you're frustrated," Dr. Ziger intercepted.

"You need to get yours," another member shouted out.

"Leave that man if you want respect," an older lady yelled.

"One at a time please," Dr. Ziger interrupted.

Sydney replied, "Have you guys ever been in love? He was my first. We've been together since high school. It's like he has a spell over me. I let him control me. I let him . . . I let him . . ." Sydney cried uncontrollably.

My heart ached for her, and I wanted to cry too. I hated to see young black women in this situation, and for what? A no-good man. I empathized with her because I too felt like this when Sebastian left me. I thought the world would end and I honestly wanted to die.

By the end of the session, Sydney had perked up. She was smiling and looked a little hopeful.

"Group, we'll continue this session next week," Dr. Ziger advised the group and ended the meeting.

I exited the room and headed toward Megan's nursing station to finish my documentation from the group session. My thoughts journeyed to Sydney. She was a pretty woman who appeared to be intelligent. How could she let a man intimidate and control her? Why did she want to die?

I could partially relate to Sydney. *Never again*, I repeated to myself, thinking about my relationship

with Max. Emergency, my butt. Something was up with him, and I was determined to find out what.

Max, you're playing games with the wrong woman.

I went to a payphone and dialed Max's home number. A man answered the phone.

"Hello."

I didn't say anything. I was too shocked to speak.

"Hello," the man said, much louder this time.

I remained speechless. It was Max's voice.

What is he doing at home? Out of town, my ass.

"Hello, hello," he repeated again.

I hung up. I thought he had to rush out of town so fast. Something was mysterious about Mr. Max, and our whole relationship was turning into one big joke.

After work I walked through the parking garage until I spotted Megan's green 1999 BMW.

"Trick, I was just getting ready to leave you. Get in," she yelled out.

I opened the door and sat down. Megan's car was outdated, but it was very clean.

Megan opened her ashtray and took out her tennis bracelets. "Help me put these on."

She had two six-carat tennis bracelets.

"Cute," I said as I placed the bracelets on her wrist.

Megan grinned. "Thank you. The owner of Lake Rivera bought these for me."

"First, congratulations. Dr. Myru told me you were moving in with him," I said.

"Thank you, Shelby. I was meaning to tell you, but I didn't want to hear your lecture on living in sin," she replied, putting hand-sanitizer on.

"Un-uhh. You don't have to worry about me.

I'm not here to judge you. Victor is a minister. He knows all about living in sin," I muttered, worrying about my own soul going to hell with all my latest sins.

She laughed. "If it weren't for you, I would've never met Victor, my African prince with all the jobs. Now what did you have to tell me?"

I laid my head back. "Girl, Max took me to the Ritz Carlton last night, and we stayed in the Presidential suite. It was really nice."

Megan stuck her wrist out, admiring her diamond bracelets.

"I'm glad you got a taste of that, Shelby. I see Max knows how to treat a lady because the little black boy had no manners when we were younger. Well, what happened?"

I turned my head. "Nothing . . . well, Max isn't packing," I confessed unexpectedly.

Megan looked stunned. "He was coming up short? The same bastard that called me bald headed and teased me about my big booty when we were nine?"

"All these years I thought Max was packing."

Megan started laughing. "No, you didn't leave my homeboy hanging after he spent all that money on you?"

I rolled my eyes. "I wasn't about to commit half a sin. I didn't wait a year to get a Twix candy bar. Give me a Snickers bar or something."

Megan giggled more. "Shelby, I'll sleep with a little brother any day if he has the cash. Think about that before you dismiss Max. He has money and owns his own business. You can always find a big one. Like my grandma always said, 'A woman

should never be broke as long as she has her money-maker.' "

"Megan, you are so crazy."

"Remember it's the size of the wallet, not the size of the penis," Megan teased. "But that's good for the little bastard, pushing my face in the mud."

I reflected about myself. I had changed. Each day I seemed to be moving further and further away from the Lord. I laughed nervously to stop myself from crying. "I really think Max is cheating on me . . . Megan, Max was furious. He cursed me out then left me at the hotel this morning." I swayed my finger. "I'm not done with him. He will pay for acting a fool with me, having me break my religion. I may have to step out of these Christian shoes for a minute. I didn't want to play games, but I'm going to show him. I was honest with Max. I told him I was looking for a man who was husband material . . . I wanted to be good and live right. Get married."

Megan giggled faintly. "You're right. I feel the same way. Victor is not the best-looking man, but he is rich, he respects me, treats me like a queen, and loves me more than I love him. He is absolutely, positively husband material." Megan snapped her fingers and started chattering about moving in with Victor and living in his big house in Highland Park. She went on and on, and I stopped listening when she went berserk about the housekeeper not ironing her white underwear and putting them up in the wrong drawer with her black panties.

I gazed out the window, staring at the splash of mud planted on the passenger glass, hoping Megan didn't see it. She was such a drama queen at times.

She had this obsessive-compulsive disorder going on. Everything had to be clean. She got her car washed every day, and if a spot appeared on it, she paid for it to be rewashed. Not to mention her hair; it was crucial for her to shampoo her hair every day, which was unheard of for a black woman.

"Why are you so quiet? Are you assessing me again?" Megan asked, tapping her red fingernails on the steering wheel, waiting for a reply I was not willing to give. "Or is it Max? Remember, never love a man more than he loves you."

She pulled in front of Blair's apartment building, nearly scaring the crap out of me when she let out a piercing cry. "Oh my God, there's a spot on my car window. Why didn't you say anything? I just got this car washed on my lunch break." She hurried out of the car and popped her trunk to get Windex and paper towel.

I pressed the numbers on my cell, watching Megan wipe on the passenger-side window diligently. "Megan and I are sitting in front of your place. Are you decent?"

"Yes, Blairson and I are home alone. Come up."

"We'll be up when this nut finishes washing this car."

When we finally made it up the stairs to Blair's apartment I was tired. Not only was I not going to Bible study and church anymore, but I was also missing in action from the gym.

"This is ridiculous. When are you going to move in an updated apartment building with an elevator?" Megan asked, barely audible from her heavy panting.

Blair just stood at her door laughing at me and

Megan. "You skinny bitches need to get in shape. You make me sick with all that complaining. If my big ass can trek up and down these stairs three to four times a day, I know you two whores can." She looked at us and pouted. "I hate skinny bitches."

Megan pushed right past Blair and pulled her shoes off. "Shelby, don't come in here with your shoes on. This baby is crawling on the carpet," she stated as she scooped Blair's crawling son off the floor. "Blair, you need to keep this carpet cleaned and keep shoes off of it. Germs are not your friend. Oh, look how big you are. Aunty Meg hasn't seen you in so long. Your mom never brings you around anymore."

Blair exhaled noisily. "Excuse me, miss lady. You act like you're too good to come on the south side."

"Blair, you need to stop. I come on the south side all the time. I am not bourgeois."

I ignored their normal tirade and went straight to the closet to hang up my purse. I could barely get in the closet, which was crowded with blue-sequined suitcases on the floor. As I reached to place my bag on the brass hook, a strap-on, dark chocolate-colored dildo fell on my head from a box on the top shelf labeled, FIRE. I hurriedly grabbed the long floppy toy by the leather straps with the tips of my finger and stuffed it back into the box, which was filled with other erotic adult toys.

Blair smacked her lips, still fussing with Megan. "Anyway, have a seat Miss Megan Cole, ma'am. Can I'z get anything for ya, madam? I'z here to serve you. Fix you bourgeois ladies a margarita?"

"You know I don't drink," I replied promptly.

They both looked at me.

"Well, I don't."

"Shelby, I don't know what to say about you. I think you are trying to be too virtuous. Live a little. You did the saved thing to get over Sebastian, but now it's time to enjoy life. You are much too young to be acting like a saint," Blair verbalized in her most serious stance.

I knew I was straddling the fence. A part of me wanted to hang my leg on the righteous side of the fence, and the other one wanted to swing in and out of the world.

Blair turned to Megan. "Now that you're messing around with that psychiatrist professor slash part-time preacher, can you drink?"

"Sure, but no cheap stuff," Megan answered firmly.

Blair rolled her eyes at Megan. "Rich bitch. I don't drink cheap shit either. Bryan just bought me a Cuervo Margarita set. Is that good enough?"

Megan laughed. "It will do. I prefer Patrón."

I flashed a smile at Blair. "How are things between you and Bryan?"

"Great, girl. He's on his way over. He went to that Keith Sweat concert last night."

The doorbell rang.

"Speaking of the devil. That must be him."

Blair buzzed Bryan up and opened the door.

A few minutes later he greeted Blair with a huge, sweaty kiss. He was huffing and puffing like the big bad wolf from the story, "The Three Little Pigs." He handed her a bag of Harold's Chicken and a McDonald's Happy Meal for Blairson. Then

he pulled his shoes off, and Blair took the bags and placed them in the kitchen.

Bryan poked his head in the living room, perspiration covering his face. "What's up, girls?"

Megan looked at Bryan, waved, and smiled. "I told her she needs an elevator. That poor man is about to have a heart attack." Then she turned to me and whispered, "He is cute for Blair. I'm impressed. He looks like a plump version of that pretty-eyed boy that played in the movie *Barbershop*."

"Bryan, come here. I want you to meet Megan. You didn't get to meet her the first night you and Blair met."

Bryan eased over at a snail's pace, his shirt drenched with wet brown spots under his armpits. I introduced the two, and Bryan took a seat on the floor.

Megan wasn't shy when it came to fashion. "Why do you have on a tight turtleneck?" She shook her head and looked at Bryan. "That isn't in season. You should be wearing spring attire, not winter."

Blair walked in and wondered the same thing herself. It was much too warm outside for winter attire. "Yeah, Bryan, why do you have on a turtleneck? Are you trying to hide something? How was the concert?"

Megan shook her finger. "Girl, the boy just needs some good fashion tips. Bryan, I'll be glad to help you."

Blair yanked on Bryan's turtleneck. "You must think I'm a fool. What is this?" She stabbed her long fingernail into a huge ugly red mark on the left side of his neck shaped into a disfigured heart.

Bryan stood up and covered the mark with his hand, pretending to not know what Blair was talking about. Blair was no fool. She wouldn't let off of him. "I know exactly what that is. Kelly gives passion marks like that all the time. Women brand their men."

After that statement he had no choice but to tell the truth. "Baby, I'm sorry. The girl means nothing to me."

Blair wrapped her hands around Bryan's big neck. "You wait months into our relationship to cheat. I told you I wasn't for games, when I met you, but you insisted on being with me."

Bryan gently removed Blair's hands from his neck and kissed her on the cheek. Then he embraced her body with his arms and led her into the kitchen. That's when more yelling started. They were so loud, Megan and I could hear every word they spoke clearly.

"That bitch must have had some big-ass lips. Look at your damn neck. We don't have to play games; you can be honest with me. That's all I want. If we don't have trust, we have nothing."

"The girl was nobody to me. I didn't even know she was going to suck on my neck."

"Are you still messing around with her? Did you sleep with her after the concert?"

"No, I just took her to the concert with me because you had to work. I wouldn't lie to you."

"This shit better not happen again if you want to be with me. I need a man, not a boy. I will never play the fool again. I let you in my life because you said you wanted to be a father to my child. I don't let men around my son. You should feel privileged

to be standing in my home. If you're in our lives to stay, do that. If not, you can leave."

"I'm not going anywhere. I love you and Blairson. Baby, I promise you this will never happen again. I'll never mess up. I'll always be honest, no matter what. I'm here to stay."

"From this point on, the matter is dropped. We are in a serious relationship, and I don't expect this to happen again . . . I forgive you."

We didn't hear anything else. Minutes later, Blair and Bryan returned with the bag of chicken and fries and a pitcher of margaritas. "Let's eat."

LUST ELEVEN

I opened the door, stepped in, and flopped down on the couch to check my messages. Nothing from Max. He hadn't called since he left the hotel this morning, and I knew he was still in town.

Should I call or shouldn't I?

I dialed his home number. "Hello," a female voice answered.

My heart began to beat fast. "Hi, may I speak to Max?"

"Who's calling?"

"This is Shelby, his girlfriend."

"His who?" she asked loudly.

"His woman," I repeated even louder.

"I'll tell him you called." Then the phone went dead.

The woman's voice sounded familiar. Maybe she was his sister. I knew I heard her voice before somewhere. Before I could complete my thoughts, the phone rang again. "Hello," I said angrily.

"This is Preston. Joel was stabbed."

"Where is he?" I shouted.

"He's at South Suburban Hospital."

"I'm on my way," I said hysterically. I hung up the phone, snatched my purse and keys, and ran out the door. I drove my car as fast as it would go. My best friend needed me.

How could this happen?

I rushed to the emergency room. Joel wasn't anywhere. I walked to the front desk and asked the volunteer if she had admitted Joel Cullen.

"Room 332."

"Thank you."

I pressed the elevator button, and the doors opened with a beeping sound.

Chloe, Joel's girlfriend, walked off the elevator and approached me immediately. "What are you doing here, Shelby?"

"My best friend is here. What do you think?"

"Stuck-up-ass bitch, my man doesn't need you," Chloe screamed.

"Chloe, can we not argue for once?" I asked calmly.

Chloe rolled her eyes as if she wanted to fight me. "I'm not arguing with you. I'm telling you I don't want you around my man. I'm speaking facts."

I jumped into the elevator and looked back at Chloe. "Joel needs to get rid of your welfare ass. You are so ignorant."

The doors closed. Chloe banged her tattooed fist on the elevator, trying to reopen the doors. "I'm gonna whip your ass when I see you again," she yelled.

I entered Joel's room. He was lying in the bed with an IV hooked to his arm.

"Baby, I was so worried about you. Are you okay?" I asked as I kissed him on his forehead, happy to see him breathing.

"I'll live, Shelby. I was stabbed in my leg," he said and kicked back the sheets. "See, I got eighteen stitches."

"What happened?"

"I was leaving Preston's house and three dudes robbed me."

I became upset and raised my voice. "I told you about gambling."

"They weren't shooting dice with us." Joel pouted.

"You really scared me. I don't know what I would do if something happened to you. You have to stop that gambling before you end up dead," I pleaded.

"Okay, okay," Joel sulked.

"I just ran into that lunatic woman of yours. She didn't want me to see you."

"I told her to leave. She was working my nerves," Joel said with exhaustion in his voice.

"What do you see in her? You never bring her around, and I kind of wish you would because she hates me with a passion. If she were around me more she'd know there's nothing going on between us and I'm really a nice person. We've had parties, cookouts, and other gatherings, and I always invite her and your son, but you never bring them. You don't even bring them to my house when you visit. Why?"

Joel started to speak, but he hesitated.

"Why? You make things hard on me. That big girl wants to fight me now. This shit has to stop."

"Shelby, she's ghetto, okay? I don't bring her around because she's a hood rat. I'm embarrassed. You and your girls act sophisticated."

"What? No, we don't. We act ghetto too."

"No, y'all suburban, private school girls try to act ghetto to be cool. Chloe is straight-up ghetto; she was raised in the Robert Taylor housing projects. You have class, and Chloe doesn't. She'd never like your crowd. Y'all different kind of folks."

Joel's hospital phone rang, bringing our conversation to a halt. "Hello," I answered.

"Bitch, put my man on the phone."

I hung up immediately, being that bitch was not my name. The phone rang a second time. I answered again. It was Chloe. "Look, nut. Don't call here anymore. Joel is resting."

"Shelby, I will slap yo' ass purple and blue if you don't put Joel on this damn phone." She exhaled noisily. "Tell you what, be a good bitch, and just tell Joel I'll be there in the morning."

"Chloe, see a shrink before you come," I yelled out and hung up again.

"You need to get some rest. Oh yeah, Chloe said she'd be here in the morning. That woman has a serious problem. You really need to shake her loose. She probably set you up anyway, or those raw boys you gamble with. Living wrong will catch up with you."

"Shelby, don't start preaching," Joel sneered.

"When are you going home?" I asked in an attempt to stop my nagging.

Joel took the sheet off his leg. "The doctor said I might be able to leave tomorrow." He rubbed his leg. "I'm glad this injury was a minor scrape."

I covered his leg up. "You may not be so lucky next time. Just leave psycho diva, before you end up dead."

Joel didn't hear a word I said. I looked at him and his eyes were shut. I guess the pain medication started kicking in.

I sat quietly, watching Joel sleep.

Why is my friend so naïve?

My instincts told me either Chloe or his gambling buddies had something to do with this incident.

The phone rang again. "Yes," I said loudly.

"Pooky, calm down. Is Joel okay?"

"He's fine, Blair. I thought you were his crazy-ass girlfriend."

"I'm glad he's okay. You know word gets around fast. Sapphire told me someone stabbed him for one thousand dollars. That boy needs to stop gambling before someone kills him," Blair huffed. She didn't miss any gossip she knew everything about everybody.

"You're right. I just got through fussing at him," I confessed.

"Well, make sure you tell him I called." She cleared her throat. "I have something to tell you before you hear it from someone else." She paused. "Sapphire is staying with me until she finds a place because her folks put her out. And you know what? It's cool having her here because she helps me out with Blairson."

"That's nice. Just be careful about what kind of spirits you let in your house. Because Joel said Sapphire goes both ways," I warned.

"I'll be careful, Mother Shelby," Blair groaned.

We hung up the phone. Thoughts flashed back to Max. What kind of spirits had I let in my own home? I hadn't exactly been an angel myself. I looked down at my cell phone. Still no missed calls or messages, which was out of the ordinary for Max, being that we spoke to one another three to four times a day. Not wanting to play the waiting game anymore, I gave in and dialed his cell phone number, but no one answered.

Kelly popped into my head. She worked for Max and Dexter at the bar, so she had to know something about Max whereabouts, since it was an emergency with the business.

"Hey, girly," Kelly answered gleefully, like she was waiting for my call.

"Have you spoken with Max today?" I asked immediately, not wanting to have girl talk about anything else.

"No, isn't that your man? 'Cause he's surely not mine."

"I just thought you heard from him, being that he's your boss. And they had an emergency with the bar today."

"Girl, no. Call and ask Dexter. They talk twenty times a day. Those two are like Siamese twins."

"How is Dexter? I thought you two were feeling each other?" I found myself wanting to know. The question just slipped out of mouth with no warning.

"That is my boss, nothing more or less. But I think he's feeling you. Girl, I saw the way he looked at you when we first met. Hmmm . . . Boss man doesn't want any of this. I sure hate it too because he looks like a good ride. I know he's mak-

ing some poor woman happy. Naw, on the real, Dexter is cool as hell. I love working for him. He's real polite and easygoing, yet thuggish when he has to be. Why, Shelby? Did he tell Max something about me?"

"No, I'm just trying to reach Max."

"Well, call Dexter," she ordered as she rattled off his cell phone number to me. "And, ahh, do me a favor."

I sighed. "Kelly, I told you I would switch my phone service. I got your nagging email."

"No, not that. I'm trying to get away from Kevin because I have a date tomorrow. A gorgeous friend of mine is going to take me out for an overnight date. We're going to the Four Seasons. It's a five-star hotel," she bragged. "He's supposed to pick me up from the shop. Can you give me a ride there tomorrow?"

"Sure, as long as you don't need money."

"Naw, the money has been coming. Those tricksters at the barbershop be hooking a sister up. I get mad tips. You should see the sexy-ass men that come in that place. I've been on five dates already. I got several of them to sign up with my phone service too. Your girl is going to be rich."

"Kelly, I wish you'd be good. Kevin pays all the bills and lets you use his car. He appears crazy about you," I reasoned with her.

Kelly blew air from her full lips. "So? One man can't fulfill me."

Realizing I had done enough judging for the day, I rushed Kelly off the phone. "I'll talk to you later. I need to get in touch with Max. Bye," I said, before hanging up and dialing Dexter.

"Hello, Dexter. This is Shelby. I'm trying to reach Max. Have you heard from him?"

"No, sexy, he's in Oakland. I dropped him off at the airport earlier."

"Well, tell Max to call me if you hear from him."

"Bet. Call me if you need anything else, kid." Dexter made a noise like he wanted to say more, but he didn't.

The bright sun glared through the hospital window. I rolled out of the bed quietly, trying not to wake up Joel.

"Boy, you woke up before my feet touched the floor."

"Shelby, I didn't know you stayed here all night. You are sweet, when you want to be."

"I had to make sure Chloe didn't send those guys back to finish you off," I said, smiling and laughing at the same time.

"Did she call anymore?" Joel asked.

"No, thank God. That girl was making me step out of my Christian shoes."

"What? You've been out of those shoes for a minute, ever since Max. I bet you stayed on the phone with him all night."

"No, actually I spoke with Blair and Kelly for a second, and then I called Dexter."

"What's up with that, Shelby?"

"No, Joel, Dexter is Max's best friend. I was looking for Max."

"That was out of order. You shouldn't have called Dexter."

"I'm going home," I said abruptly, not wanting to hear Joel's sermon this time.

"Can I come with you?" Joel announced unexpectedly. "I'll be discharged today, and I don't really feel like being bothered with Chloe."

"You want to stay with me?" I asked with a little uncertainty in my voice.

Joel had stayed the night a few times, but moving in was a big step. Not that I had any objections. My thoughts kept going from one extreme to the next. Joel could help pay the mortgage and help around the house. Plus, it was always good to have a man around for protection.

"Yeah, I just want to kick it at your place for a month or two, you know, until I get my shit together."

"Cool. You are always at my crib anyway. A few months won't hurt."

The moment I entered my home, a ringing phone greeted me.

"Shelby, where the fuck you been all night? I called you at eleven last night and four this morning."

"Max, I was at the hospital with Joel. He was stabbed yesterday."

"I expect more out of you."

"Max, did you hear what I just said about Joel?" I said calmly.

Max was so angry. He said I should have left a message on his cell phone if I wasn't coming home. I was unsure if he heard me, or if he just didn't care.

He proceeded, "My sister said you called my house yesterday. Why didn't you call me on my cell phone?"

I gasped. "Look, I thought you were at home, since you had an emergency. Remember, you left me at the Ritz?"

"Shelby, don't start this shit. Dexter picked you up right after I left, didn't he?"

"Yes, but—" I tried to explain, but was cut off.

"Look, baby, I have a business to run and emergencies evolve," he said firmly.

"Max, I was worried about you."

"Dexter told me you called and he told you where I was . . . Look, Shelby Denise Tate, you need to let your guard down. I've changed. You can trust me. I will not hurt you like that bitch-ass eggroll did. I love you," he chanted, sounding incredibly convincing. "I'll be home in a few days to make it up to you. I'll be flying in at Midway Airport." Max gave me his flight information and told me he loved me again before I could reply.

Just because Sebastian hurt you doesn't mean every man will.

LUST TWELVE

The wind was blowing, and various thoughts were going through my mind, like, why was I driving down Cicero toward Midway Airport when I should have been at home studying?

Two days had passed and I still didn't feel at ease about Max. I wasn't too sure if I wanted any more drama in my life. Max told me he loved me. But Sebastian also told me he loved me too. I'd been hurt once and I damn sure wasn't going to be hurt twice. Not by Maxtin Brooks. I liked him, but love was not an option. There were just too many unanswered questions.

First, I picked up Kelly from Kevin's house. I made her ride with me, since she needed a ride to meet another fling.

Why she cheated, I didn't understand. Kelly had a good thing with Kevin. She didn't have to pay any rent, he cooked, cleaned, she drove his car, and he put money in her pocket, but that wasn't good enough for her. Kelly loved men and she had to have more than one. It was almost as if she was

searching for something, always jumping from man to man. How could she be happy with so much turmoil in her life?

Then again, who am I to judge her with my confused life? I haven't been to church or Bible study in forever. I curse, drink, have impure thoughts about men, and judge others. Lord, I have fallen out of Your arms. How do I come back home?

While roaming the airport, I visited a gift shop. I wanted to make sure my breath was fresh for Max's welcome-home kiss. As I reached for a pack of cinnamon gum, someone else reached for the same pack, and his hand was on top of mine. I looked up. My cheeks turned red and my heart raced. I couldn't stop my eyes from staring at him.

He gazed at me. "I didn't know you were coming to pick up Max."

"I was coming to surprise him," I stuttered, wondering why Max told both of us to come.

He murmured, "That's very nice of you."

I realized I was still holding Dexter's finely manicured hand when he reached to try to pay for my gum. I released my hand nervously and thanked him for the pack of Big Red.

We strolled to the gate, joking the entire way about our weird encounter at the airport gift shop. Dexter was fun to be around, and I could see why he and Max were best friends. They both had outgoing, exciting personalities, yet Dexter had something extra. He appeared more genuine and seemed to have a mellow, witty, humorous character. We playfully grabbed at each other, laughed aloud, and eventually our hands reconnected again. Kelly

followed behind us, bored I'm sure, because our entertaining conversation and acts didn't include her. It was like no one else existed.

The speaker announced, "Delta flight 3200 has just arrived at gate B8."

The three of us stood at the security gate waiting for Max to walk up. People rushed off the terminal, seeking their loved ones. As we peered over the crowd looking for Max, I heard someone yell out. Immediately, I dropped Dexter's hand. Playfully, Dexter tried to retouch my soft skin. This time he rubbed against my bare arm.

I fled from his spell into Max's arms. "I'm glad you're back. I missed you," I said as we kissed.

"Damn, I must be pretty important. Three escorts?"

We walked to the baggage claim area. Dexter and Kelly were walking side by side behind us. She was all in his face, rubbing on his soft, caramel-colored skin. Then she hugged his waist playfully.

I looked into Dexter's sexy, light-brown eyes. He was stunning. Hell, the man was luscious. His lips were succulent, full, and inviting. I wanted to turn around and wrap my tongue around his, but that would've been out of character for me. Instead, I gazed intently. He returned the gaze with lust in his eyes. Suddenly, nothing else mattered. Speech and movement eluded me. I remained transfixed as Max went off to retrieve his luggage from the carousel.

When Max returned, I was in the same spot. His grip on my butt disrupted the looks exchanged between Dexter and me.

"So, Shelby, what time are we making love tonight?" Max asked, sucking his teeth and staring at my butt.

"Max," I said, embarrassed by his question. *This fool is showing his ass in front of Dexter and Kelly.* "We aren't."

"Then I won't be riding with you."

"Fine," I exclaimed. "Kelly and I are going out anyway."

Max ignored my last statement. "Look, Shelby, I have to go to my shop now. I'll meet you at your place at ten."

"Un-huh," I mocked, pissed off that he had me drive all the way to the airport to pick him up, but happy that I had a chance to see Dexter again.

"We are going to finish what we started at the Ritz," Max said in a serious tone.

"Bye, Dexter. I'll see you at work tomorrow," Kelly said as she waved and blew kisses.

I said nothing as we watched them walk to their car.

Kelly and I jumped in my car and we cruised down Cicero. Dexter and Max sped past us. I was livid. It was unbelievable how cocky Max was acting in front of his boy.

Kelly turned down the radio. "Girl, I guess I haven't told you about Kevin. Brace yourself. I like Kevin, but he has some serious issues. Ahh . . . the sex is slamming, but the boy wets the bed. And I ain't talking 'bout cum either. The grown man pees *in the bed*. I caught him changing the sheets at four in the morning."

"Not that fine, dressed-to-impress brother?" I said in disbelief.

"Yeah, girl. I smelled the sheets."

Kelly preached, "The sex is good, but I have to find a new home."

Trying to sound professional, I said, "The man just needs your patience and some therapy. Enuresis is common. There has to be some underlying issues he has not dealt with. It might stem from his childhood."

"Fuck that. I don't have patience. I'm freaky, but not that freaky. Hell, the next thing you know he'll be asking to pee on me."

We pulled into White Castle's drive-thru and ordered ten cheeseburgers. It was Friday night and people were hanging out for the car and motorcycle show.

"Shelby, pull next to that purple Corvette," Kelly pleaded.

I looked at Kelly. "Girl, this is Seventy-ninth and Stoney Island. Do you see all of these thuggish-ass niggas and naked girls dressed like hookers?" I had other things on my mind besides flirting with some young punk driving a purple Corvette. "Don't you have a date?"

Kelly peeped at her watch. "Yes, but I have time. He's not meeting me until I call him."

Like a fool, I pulled next to the car.

Kelly rolled down the window and started conversing. Then she got out of the car and sat on his hood. She was so immature. Kelly acted like a sex-crazed teenager.

My mind wandered back to Max. I decided to give him a call while Kelly was doing her thing.

"Hello," his sister answered before I could hang

up, realizing I dialed the home number instead of his cell.

"Sorry. I meant to call Max on his cell phone."

"Who is this?"

"This is Shelby."

"Well, Shelby, I'm Sydney, Max's fiancée."

"His what?" I said in shock.

"I think you heard me. I'm also the mother of his child," she said calmly.

"That's nice. Keep your man at your house and not at mine and I won't call," I said slowly, then hung up quickly, wanting to scream.

"Get his number, Kelly. It's time to go," I yelled out the window.

Kelly ignored me and continued her conversation with Mr. Corvette. They both looked at me as she leaned back on his car, getting more comfortable.

"No, she didn't," I muttered.

I remembered how unconcerned Kelly seemed when Sebastian and I broke up.

She didn't call me one time. I hadn't heard from her in over six months, before Blair's promotion. Kelly is selfish. She doesn't care about anyone else. The only times she calls now is if she needs something.

I was becoming angry just thinking about it, so I did what any black woman from the south side of Chicago would. I rolled down my window and threw her purse out.

"Bye, bitch," I shouted, as I pulled off without glancing back. The good-girl shit was getting me nowhere. Besides, I hadn't hit the church doors in months. Blair was right. I was too young for this saved, trying-to-live-right garbage. It was just too

much to keep up with because one minute I tried to do right and the next minute I was scheming and lusting, indecisive in everything I did and said.

I was on a mission, racing toward Eighty-seventh Street. My little silver car was in rare form.

The words *"I'm Max's fiancée. I'm the mother of his child"* kept ringing in my ear.

Suddenly, I realized where I had heard Sydney's name and voice. She was the same girl in the suicidal group I was observing. The new girl . . . It seemed incredible that my Max was the same man she had depicted as a devil. I made a mental note to inform Dr. Ziger about the incident so that I could be removed from that group.

It all made sense and I wanted Mr. Max to come clean about everything. Hell, take the guilt off of me so I could pursue better opportunities.

I drove down Cottage Grove swiftly. I instantly spotted Max in front of his business, his arms embracing a female.

Who in the fuck is he with now? Is he about to kiss her?

I pulled up close to the old white Ford Escort and rolled my window down, looking Max and his friend straight in their eyes.

His arms dropped. "Shelby, what are you doing on this side of town?" Max ranted.

My voice echoed, "I spoke with Sydney."

"Go home right now," he commanded, waving me off.

I started to drive off, but changed my mind. I backed my car up and parked.

"I'm going to kick your ass," Max said, marching to my car.

The girl in the white Escort followed him very slowly.

I swung the car door open and I stepped out. "Kick my ass?"

"I don't want to hurt you," Max pleaded.

"Max, I'm sick of your lies," I shouted. "I thought we were better than this."

"Go home. We'll talk later," he tried to reason.

"We'll talk now," I hollered. "Yo' little sawed-off ass been lying to me for months."

The girl stood behind Max, not mumbling a word.

I interrogated Max. "Now how many women do you have?"

Max didn't answer.

"Let's see, this young fool standing here, your crying baby mama at home. Who else, Max?"

Dexter walked out of the barbershop, strolling toward us.

"Shelby, you are being so immature," Max snapped.

The girl grabbed Max's hand. She appeared to be seventeen or eighteen years old. Max moved his hand away from hers. She looked worried and hurt, but continued to follow him as he moved toward me.

"I have an obligation to Sydney. We have a daughter."

"You what? Just take your two-dollar whore to her raggedy-ass car, and stay out of my life," I said in rage.

"Shelby, you can't have me all to yourself. You are so selfish. I have to spend time with my child."

"So is this your child?" I said, pointing to Max's date.

Max was silent and stunned by my boldness. He abruptly turned his back on me and started walking in the opposite direction, with his date scurrying after him.

Dexter stopped Max. "I'll walk Shelby to her car."

"I don't care what you do with her," Max replied loud enough for me to hear.

"Shelby, are you okay?" Dexter asked, seeming concerned.

"I'm fine. I'm not sleeping with Max, so I don't care what he does," I muttered under my breath. "Now I see why he was so patient with me. Hell, he was getting pussy from several sources."

A few minutes later Max approached us. "Dexter, let's roll, man. Shelby is a spoiled brat."

Dexter turned to Max. "You need to chill. I think you've had too much to drink. Let Nakia take you home."

The girl drove her car to the spot where the three of us were standing.

"Max, are you coming over tonight?" the young girl, who Dexter referred to as Nakia, cried from her car, which was still rolling.

"Shelby, call me when you get your mind right. Dexter, I'll meet you in the shop," Max replied before sprinting off to catch up with the young girl's car.

Dexter touched my hand. "Don't pay any attention to Max. He has that 'Yack' in him."

"I knew his breath smelled like liquor," I replied.

"On the serious tip, I thought you knew about

Sydney and the kid. Max said he was open about everything," Dexter disclosed.

"I knew Max had a daughter. I didn't know the child's mother was still in the picture." I paused. "You know, Dexter, I just wanted Max to be honest this time."

"I don't blame you."

"Well, thank you for everything," I said, as I reached to shake Dexter's hand. He moved my hand and reached his arms around me, lightly. I hugged him back, being free, allowing my emotions to rule my body. I wanted to grasp him tighter, but I wanted to be appropriate. The latter won.

Dexter apprehensively released his clasp from around me and whispered in my ear, "I think you needed that hug . . . and a kiss," tenderly pecking my cheek with so much respect. Then he opened my door and closed it after I was in, leaving me hot, bothered, and wanting him even more.

Something powerful was drawing me to this man—a divine intervention that I could not explain.

LUST THIRTEEN

My long drive home was strangely relaxing. I rolled down the window, and the brisk, cool wind whipped my hair around my forehead. I took a deep breath, filling my lungs with the serenity of the night air. I listened to the waves from Lake Michigan as they swept across the rocks and sang a pleasant, soothing song. I glanced at the lake and found peace in the tranquil view. The boats reflected on the glass-like water, and people were taking pleasure in their late-night sails. Others were walking along the shore. I smiled as the wind filled the walkers' shirts with air. Chicago was absolutely beautiful at night. The astounding scenery and my talk with Dexter made my drive home pleasurable. I couldn't believe I had created such a scene with Max, but, hey, I was doing me.

"No more good girl," I said aloud, placing my hand on my lips and kissing it, then throwing my imaginary kiss out of the window. A long sigh signaled the end of that chapter of my life.

* * *

I entered my home. The sounds from the television came from my room. I dashed upstairs. Joel was getting ready for work, just days after being hospitalized. I toddled in my room, leaned on the bedpost, and stared Joel down. I thought about what Preston asked me. *Is Joel eating your pussy?*

"Why don't you eat me?" I asked jokingly.

Joel looked at me as if I had just lost my mind. "I don't eat pussy," he replied quickly.

I laughed. Had Preston lied to me? I just wanted to make sure. As badly as I missed the love of a man, it was worth asking.

Joel laughed. "Girl, you are so crazy. Where is your Bible? Please find it. You need to carry it at all times. You say anything," he declared before charging off to work.

I giggled, knowing just what to say to get Joel out of the house in a hurry when I wanted to be alone. He closed the front door and there was complete silence. The atmosphere was tranquil. The taupe-colored walls were different this time. The monotony of the neutral walls relaxed me. I stripped down to nothing and sashayed around in my birthday suit, not wanting the weight of clothes on my back, being free, liberated, and boundless.

I checked my messages. Kevin left a message for Kelly, who he thought was at my house again. No messages from Max. At first, I was a tad bit upset because I felt he had more explaining to do, but suddenly a feeling of peace covered my soul. Happiness was attainable; I hadn't slept with Max, so that made things much easier. It was all about me.

I walked to the door of my balcony and looked out at the stillness of the night. This would've been the perfect night to make love on the balcony. If only I had the right man. However, since I didn't, I sat down on the couch to watch television.

This was definitely a *Waiting to Exhale* night. I started the movie, looked in the fridge and noticed Joel had bottles of champagne. I pulled a bottle out and clutched a crystal flute, filling my glass to the rim. I smiled. *Yes, this is a special occasion, isn't it, Shelby?*

I took a sip. The champagne warmed my insides. The tart taste tantalized my lonely tongue. I wrapped myself in a blanket and sat on the edge of my sofa with my feet folded under me. I watched the movie intensely, as if I hadn't seen it before. The effect of the alcohol made the movie more hilarious, yet very depressing.

I heard knocks, and the doorbell rang several times. I took my time to drape the blanket around me and I walked to the door very slowly. I just knew it was Max coming to apologize. I decided to make him wait a while, so I dragged. The knocking and ringing ceased. The door opened at last, but no one was there, so I closed the door and resumed watching my movie.

Another series of knocks on the window began only minutes later. The fool was back. I looked out the window and saw a Cadillac Escalade. It was definitely Max. I thought for a minute about what I should do. I went to the door and unlocked it. Then I walked back to the sofa. The blanket fell loosely, barely covering my body. I wanted Max to

feel more foolish for screwing things up with me. Get a good look at the pussy he was never going to get.

"Come in," I hollered.

The door closed. Heavy footsteps echoed in the hallway. I was lying on the couch, with my legs open and my breasts totally exposed. I glanced up, licking my lips, putting on my sexy look. Pink roses and a bottle of champagne with masculine hands wrapped around them appeared in front of me. I looked up. My eyes widened. My heart sank. I was stunned.

Eyes were gawking at my naked body. "Were you expecting someone else?"

I looked away. "No. This is how I relax when I'm alone."

My hands trembled as I tried to gather the rest of my blanket to cover up. "Where is Max? Did he send you? Why are you in his car?"

Dexter smirked at me. "What's with the series of questions?" He handed me the roses and champagne. "First, I don't know where Max is, I came on my own. Second, Max isn't the only brother who owns an Escalade."

I grinned at Dexter. "You two must really like the same things."

Dexter glared down at me. "I guess we do, because I definitely want you."

I blushed as I smelled the roses, trying to ignore his comment. "Thank you," I said shyly, standing up and casually walking to the stairway. He didn't need to know how mortified I was. I handed the champagne back to him and pointed to the

kitchen. "Put this in the freezer, please. I already have some open."

His eyes followed my every step. I smiled at his expression. "Is something on my butt?" I asked, wrapping the blanket over my body tighter.

"My eyes," he replied smoothly.

I ran upstairs quickly without looking back. I grabbed my chest.

I can't believe he's here. I can't believe I was damn near naked.

I grabbed the first thing I found in the closet, a red rayon halter dress. I slipped it on, took five deep breaths, and joined Dexter downstairs.

He was sitting on my sofa looking at the television. He glared at me. His eyes moved slowly across my body from head to toe. He smirked when our eyes met and said, "You could've kept your other outfit on."

"Very funny," I said, humiliated.

"*Waiting to Exhale?* Baby, I'm here now. You can breathe easily with me," he said, patting down on the space next to him.

"Wait." I took the flowers Max had given me weeks ago out of the vase on my coffee table and replaced them with my roses. I sat next to Dexter, and he put his arm around my shoulders as we continued watching the movie.

"It's a gorgeous night out. Would you like to sit on the balcony?"

Dexter grinned. "Sure."

I stopped in the kitchen for another crystal flute, and Dexter followed me with the green bottle.

We sat at the table, just as a strong breeze came off the man-made lake, which was shooting waterfalls in the air.

"Shelby, can I tell you something?"

"Of course."

Dexter caressed my hand. "I'm feeling you. You're an intelligent, attractive young lady. I was drawn toward you the first day I saw you at the club. Ummm . . . Woman, you were wearing the hell out of those black leather shorts, sitting, shaking your ravishing legs. I should have never pointed you out to Max because that's when he realized it was you. Just wanted you to know I saw you first." Dexter shook his head. "Shelby, if you were my woman, I'd cherish every moment with you."

I wasn't sure how to respond. I wanted to say, "Dexter, I was checking you out also." Instead, I said nothing. I was too shocked.

I spoke after a moment of silence. "Tell me about yourself."

"I was born in New Orleans," Dexter said.

"Really?" I replied, very excited. "I have always wanted to visit New Orleans."

He sat back in the chair and told me after the divorce of his parents, he moved to Chicago when he was fourteen to live with his father. Dexter revealed that he wanted to be a pharmacist and the service was his stepping-stone. He said that he and Max joined the Air Force together after high school, but Max was expelled after a year because of his conduct.

He tried not to mention Max, but he couldn't converse about himself without talking about his close friend.

"I'll be transferring to California this fall." He looked into my eyes and noticed that I wasn't excited about his statement. "I won't be there long. I'll complete my time with the Air Force, open up our new franchise in Oakland, and hopefully start pharmacy school here or at Xavier in New Orleans. You told me you were in medical school. What type of MD do you want to be?"

"I'm going to school to be a psychiatrist."

"How much time do you have left?"

"I'll be finished before I'm thirty."

He poured more champagne in my glass. I lifted my flute and drank the entire glass of bubbly in a matter of seconds. He raised an eyebrow at me and emptied the rest of the bottle in his glass.

"I'll go get more champagne."

I took a few more deep breaths while in the kitchen alone. Dexter had no idea the commotion he was creating just sitting there. I was wet and tingly, wanting to jump on his lap and kiss every word that came from his lips. My conscience kicked in.

Shelby, good girls don't date their boyfriend's best friend. You're not following the rules. You can't have feelings for Max's best friend. Why can't I? I made a mistake by getting back with Max. I was just lonely and confused at the time. Plus, he has too much drama. I don't want a man with kids and other women. I think Dexter is my soul mate. There is something about his spirit. A feeling I can't fight. Some rules are just meant to be broken.

I retrieved the bottle and placed it in a crystal bucket filled with ice. I slowly placed the bucket on the patio table. I filled Dexter's glass and then

mine. I took a sip. The bubbles were burning inside of me. The champagne was fuel to an already rustling fire. I was losing more inhibition with every sip, dumping all morals and restraints.

Lust consumed me. I continued to sip, heightening the feeling.

Dexter took a sip from his glass. He turned and fixed his eyes on me. His strong hands lifted my chin. Dexter moved closer and his lips touched mine.

My eyes closed and I relinquished all rights to him. His luscious tongue entered my mouth. It was intoxicating, every move expertly calculated. My heartbeat quickened. My tongue began to run laps around his. I felt as if I were descending.

Dexter lifted me from my chair. We stood, tongues still enthralled in battle. He wrapped his strong, tattooed biceps around me. His hands slid down to my bottom, feeling every curve of my body.

I couldn't control myself. Juices trickled down my leg.

Dexter transported me to the lounge chair. He lifted my dress slowly as he stared down at my naked body. His face moved closer. The hot steam from his mouth made me gasp for breath. The juices reactivated, surging freely down my leg.

Dexter fell down to his knees. "I want to taste you," he murmured.

Our eyes locked as he placed his hands between my thighs and began to kiss my sweetness. My eyes closed in ecstasy. I felt hands opening my inner lips. His long, thick, luscious tongue danced inside of me. I moaned uncontrollably as I rocked in his

rhythm. My body shivered under his control while he devoured every drop of my sweet juices.

Before I could open my eyes, I felt the night breeze on my exposed area. He grabbed the empty bottle and poured the remnants on my flaming fire. His famished mouth consumed each drop. I let out a cry and bit down on my lip hard. I could hardly hold back my screams. He took the empty bottle and fondled my wetness.

I was ready to feel him inside me. My eyes flew open, and I reached down to move the bottle. I grasped for the huge bulge in his pants. "Dexter, please make love to me," I cried, thinking about how it would feel to be with a real black, man being that Sebastian, an Asian, was my first and only lover.

Dexter ignored my demands. Instead, he tightened the suction and held me down with the weight of his body. His mouth was wide, and its power was electrifying.

"You taste so good," Dexter moaned.

He drank intently, and each time my body released. I pulled him closer with each forceful spasm until I collapsed in ecstasy. Dexter smiled contently as if he had just won a prize.

When my eyes opened, I was floating. We reached for each other's hand as I led him inside my home. "Please stay the night, Dexter. You've had a lot to drink. You really shouldn't be driving."

Dexter agreed as we strolled to my bedroom. He sat on my bed as I walked in the bathroom and ran hot water into the garden tub. Then, I poured strawberries-and-champagne bubble bath in the water. Next, I lit all the candles surrounding the

tub and placed a few more around the bathroom. After that, I undressed and glided into the hot, steamy water.

Dexter entered the bathroom wearing nothing. He was beautiful. His chest was bursting with muscles that contoured into a chiseled six-pack stomach. His soft, black, silky hair continued on his chest and down to his gorgeous crotch. There were no marks on his body, besides the ones put on there by a tattoo artist. I smiled as I read the one on his bicep which read, PRECIOUS LORD, but the joy was short-lived, replaced with guilt. I reflected on my sinful act, but jiggled it off swiftly when my eyes met Dexter's striking gaze.

Dexter took the washcloth and massaged my back. The touch of his hand on my back left me helpless. I wanted to melt. He caressed my body with every stroke.

When we finished bathing one another, he picked me up and carried me to the bed. He lowered my body. "Shelby, I want to make love to you, but I'll wait until you're all mine."

God, this man has to be the one.

We held each other's naked bodies until we fell asleep.

The rays from the sun shined beautifully through my pink curtains. It was a gorgeous day, and I felt wonderful. I loved the way Dexter made me feel. I thought my night with him was a dream, until I saw that gorgeous baby face lying on the pillow next to me fast asleep, a moment I had lusted for since the night I met him. I had no regrets.

I tiptoed out of bed, threw on my robe, and headed to the kitchen. This man had every right to be served breakfast. He did things to me no other man had done before. I had never experienced oral sex. I felt addicted. It was a breathtaking sensation that I had missed out on with Sebastian and Max.

I reached in my cabinet and pulled out my frying pan. I prepared him a Creole omelet with tomatoes, onions, cheese, shrimp, and bell peppers. I knew he would love the taste of my recipe, being from New Orleans and everything. My friend Ursula, from Baton Rouge, Louisiana, gave me the recipe during our freshman year of college. She called it her catch a man voodoo omelet. I sautéed the onions and bell pepper and I added the shrimp; I was flying around like a cooking show host.

The aroma filled the whole place. I knew Dexter would be up soon. Before I could finish cooking, he was walking into the kitchen, fully clothed.

"Girl, it smells like my mother's house in here," he said excitedly.

I usually hated when men compared cooking to their mama's, but today that rule was forgotten. No words exited my mouth. A smile covered my face. I was just thrilled to be with Dexter. I finished his omelet and served it on my best china.

My phone rang right after we blessed our food. "Hello," I yelled, aggravated that we were being disturbed.

"Are you done tripping yet?" Max asked.

"Excuse me. I think you have a woman and

child to be concerned with," I whispered, knowing Dexter could still hear me.

Max was speaking in a gentle tone. "Sydney is just the mother of my child. I take care of her because she has nowhere to go."

"That's nice. Whatever. Look, I have company."

"Is Dexter over there?"

I was flabbergasted. My head swung around to look at Dexter, as if he could hear Max's question. I lowered my voice. "No. Why would you think that?"

"Well, you two were still talking when I walked off, and he isn't at home," Max said, falling out laughing.

"You have jokes early in the morning," I said in a friendlier tone.

"Yes, I can joke sometimes." He chuckled.

"Yes, I know. You were the comedian of our block when we were kids."

"I'll pick you up tonight. I have a lot of explaining to do."

"Okay," I responded, wanting to know exactly what the truth was.

"Shelby, I love you."

"I gotta go," I stated and hung up the phone quickly.

Dexter looked up at me. "Shelby, this is really good."

"Thank you," I replied, fidgety, worried if Max really thought Dexter was at my house.

"Dexter, call Max. I think he knows."

"Girl, Max was pulling your leg."

"I guess he was trying to see where my mind

was," I said, nervously taking a seat at the kitchen table.

"I'm not afraid to tell Max how I feel about you," Dexter said in a serious tone.

"I think we should chill awhile," I said, not looking at Dexter. "I need time to end things with Max and I don't want to come in between the two of you. You guys are best friends." I sighed, feeling a little uncomfortable, like the cream stuffed between two cookies.

Although, a part of me wanted Max to know that I too could be a player, that I wasn't as dumb as he thought I was. He'd pissed me off by being a lying, cheating dog, running game on me, Sydney, and the young girl from last night. And I'm sure there was another woman in Oakland. No one travels all the way to California for an emergency with a barbershop. Mr. Max thought he had a naïve, church-going, good, pure girl in me. But that person no longer existed.

Dexter stood up and placed his dish in the sink. "Shelby, I know you'll never leave Max. You act as if you enjoy his verbal abuse. What control does he have over you?"

On the contrary, I had no intentions on staying with Max. He had no control over me, but I wanted him to think he did. Craved for him to hurt and be belittled, like he had done so many other women. I just needed to teach him a lesson about playing with the word *love*, especially when it came to me. Nothing came from my mouth. Silence dominated the room.

Dexter looked impatient with the non-reply. He

glanced down at his watch. "Shelby, I'm outta here. Call me when you're ready to be my woman."

The old Shelby evolved into the one who stalked after her man. "Wait, Dexter. Don't leave like this. I want to be with you so bad, but I just need time," I cried, pulling on his arm, gesturing for one last kiss.

Dexter turned around gradually and kissed me passionately. He rolled his succulent tongue in and around my mouth. The sensual touch of his lips were invigorating and arousing to my soul—a mind-blowing moment I didn't want to end.

"Don't leave, Dexter," I begged, when he stopped kissing me and turned away.

"You are right. I can't do this to my boy. Either you're with me or not. You can't have us both," he said calmly, as he walked out the door.

LUST FOURTEEN

Six long weeks had gone by since I'd seen Dexter. School was getting tougher and occupying all my time. Surprisingly, my grades were good. A day didn't pass that I didn't think about him, reminiscing about our intimate moment. I missed Dexter so much and wanted to call, but pride wouldn't let me, especially since I hadn't broken up with Max yet, which was another story. He confessed that Sydney was staying with him because her parents put her out, but they were not engaged or involved intimately anymore. Never did he explain who the young girl named Nakia was, and I didn't push it, still wanting him to think that I was naïve. It was all a part of the plan.

"Shelby, I'm so glad you and Kelly agreed to help me plan this surprise birthday party for Bryan," Blair stated as we pulled onto Lawrence Street.

"Anytime, Blair. You know I love you. Almost more than Bryan does, but I think he wins. Look at you, driving in his brand-new black Yukon. It has to be love."

"We'll see. Time will tell if his love is real." Blair parked the huge truck in front of Kevin's apartment building and sounded her horn.

"Kelly needs to bring her butt down. I'll go in," I volunteered, leaping out of the truck.

I walked into the lobby of the three-story brick building and pressed the button with the name KEVIN GREEN underneath it. I heard a buzzing sound, so I ran up the three stairs to get to the door before the buzzer stopped. Kelly was in the hallway of the building, hanging over the banister on the third floor with a wine cooler in her hand.

"Are you ready?" I yelled up to her.

She looked at me with disgust. "I'll be down in a minute. My bodyguard has to check me out first."

I trotted out of the hallway and headed back to the truck. Kelly and Kevin were behind me. Kevin had Kelly's hand in one hand and her luggage in the other.

"Blair, those rims are glowing," Kevin said, admiring the truck.

Blair didn't look up. She had a Virginia Slim in her mouth, with no care in the world.

"Blair, unlock the trunk."

She pressed the button that unlocked the trunk, and Kevin placed Kelly's luggage in.

Then he opened the door for Kelly. "I love you," he said in a soft tone.

Kelly kissed him and closed the door, never acknowledging his statement.

"I have a sucker." Kelly laughed aloud, before we made it to the corner.

"Girl, he's real sweet."

"I still think he's a pussy," Blair said, turning her

nose up. "Every time I see him, I think about him wetting the bed.

"Kelly, he treats you real good. You need to settle down with him."

Kelly turned her hand down and rolled her eyes at me this time. "Blair, I agree. He's weak, but he hasn't urinated in the bed lately. I think his doctor put him on a pill." Kelly made a popping sound with her lips. "I am not talking to you, Shelby."

"You two need to stop—Damn, I forgot my luggage. I need to go back to my house," Blair yelled in the middle of her conversation.

While driving down Blair's street, we saw Sapphire smoking on a joint and walking Blair's son in a stroller. She flagged us down and walked to the passenger side of the car. She was dressed in a short white halter spandex dress with red lipstick as usual.

"Don't let him see me," Blair stated, trying to dodge her son.

"You are a big silly something. This boy ain't thinking about you now," Sapphire replied in an aggravated manner.

"Can I have a puff?" Blair asked.

Sapphire rolled her eyes and passed Blair the illegal cigarette. "Look. Why didn't you come home last night?" she asked, sounding pissed off.

She handed the half-smoked joint back to Sapphire. "I, I, I was at Bryan's house," Blair stuttered.

Sapphire pointed the joint at Blair. "Well, your child cried all night. I am not a live-in babysitter." She poked her head in the car. "Shelby and Kelly, what are you two doing with Blair? Don't y'all know she's a dyke?"

"I'll dyke your ass right out on the street," Blair said playfully.

Sapphire took a puff of her joint and passed it back to Blair. "I'll see you whores tonight." Sapphire laughed.

Moments later, she twisted her hips and walked off with the baby.

"Huhh. That bitch is going to babysit as long as she's living with me for free," Blair said, opening the truck door.

The minute Blair jumped out of the truck and went inside, I looked at Kelly. "Kelly, do you think something sexual is going on between Sapphire and Blair?"

Kelly didn't reply. I detected she had a little attitude.

"You are a dirty bitch. Why did you leave me at White Castle? I missed my date."

I held my hand out. "Why are you tripping? That happened almost two months ago. Anyway, you knew I was ready to go."

Kelly smiled with a phony expression. "Haven't you noticed I haven't spoken with you?"

I felt a little embarrassed. With school kicking my ass and all the drama with Max, I really hadn't noticed.

Kelly rolled her eyes. "I just thought you had turned back into a nun again and wasn't talking to any of us heathens." She smacked her lips.

"Thanks to you, Mr. Purple Vette gave me a ride home that night, and I almost got busted. I had to tell Kevin the guy was my cousin."

"You knew I was ready to go," I said calmly.

Kelly smirked. "It's all good. Mr. Vette and I went to Gino's East for some deep-dish pizza, and after that, we broke in his new Corvette. I've been seeing him ever since."

"You are going to catch something if you keep on having sex with all these different men."

"I have to die of something. Why not die of a dick overdose?" Kelly joked.

"Kelly, what happened to us? We were so close. You changed when I was dating Sebastian. Why didn't you call me after we broke up?"

"I don't know. Why are you asking about old shit? I've blocked out all of those years. I can't remember anything from my past."

I rolled my eyes. "That's okay. Blair and Megan checked on me."

Kelly looked off as if she was in deep thought.

"You don't love anyone, not even yourself," I scolded.

"Fuck you, Shelby. Don't talk to me the rest of the night."

"Cool. I won't," I exclaimed as I peered out of the window.

We arrived at the Embassy Suites hotel near Navy Pier.

"Since I'm a sales manager now, my entire birthday party receives a group rate. I blocked half of the tenth floor," Blair gloated. "And you and Shelby are sharing a room."

"What?" Kelly and I asked at the same time.

"Kelly makes my blood boil. She is so noncha-

lant about everything. Her ass doesn't even know how to be a friend. Her problems stem from her not dealing with the death of her father, and her mother being crazy."

"What? Bitch, don't act like I'm not in this car. I'm not one of your damn patients. Don't analyze me or my crazy family."

"Did someone say something? I could have sworn she wasn't talking to me," I said to Blair.

"Hey, Blair, what ya got?" the guy in valet asked.

Blair pointed to the boxes in the truck. The guy opened the trunk and carried the items inside and into the ballroom.

Kelly and I went to our room, and Blair went to her suite. Our rooms adjoined, so we kept the door open.

"Girls, the party starts in one hour," Blair said, walking in circles from our room to hers, puffing on her cigarette. "Dexter and Max are bringing Bryan to the party. They told Bryan their friend Kenneth is having a bachelor party. Perfect lie? It goes well with my whole Wild Kingdom theme because everyone is supposed to wear animal-print pajamas."

"Blair, you got it mapped out," Kelly egged her on.

"And did you all hear what Sapphire said? That spandex queen loves to joke around, calling me a dyke," Blair stated nervously.

"You should kick her ass," Kelly cursed, kicking her leg out.

"Blair, I told you Joel said that girl goes both ways," I commented, wanting to say I told you so.

"If she does, she wouldn't like someone like me." Blair snickered. "She'd like someone like you two, short and sexy."

Kelly raved, "I love big dicks. Sapphire will get her feelings hurt, and you too." Kelly punched at Blair, pretending to hit her.

The three of us fell out laughing.

I took a deep breath. "Kelly, I'm sorry for leaving you."

Kelly sighed. "I'm just tired of you acting like my mother."

"You two kiss and make up," Blair announced, clapping her hands all the way back to her room.

Kelly looked at me, but didn't say a word. She wasn't giving in that quick. I turned away and buried my face in my overnight bag. Kelly strutted into the bathroom.

I decided to dress sexy for the Wild Kingdom Pajama Jam. I bought a silk tiger-print babydoll chemise with tiger slippers. My outfit was cute and very revealing. The front of my chemise had a split from my breasts to my belly button, with matching bottoms. I wanted to get the prize for best dressed.

Kelly stepped out of the bathroom in her fuzzy zebra-print camisole. The front was furry, and the back was sheer. She wore white thigh-highs, a garter belt, and furry slippers to match.

Blair strutted on our side of the room with her black fishnet lingerie on. The front was fishnet, and the back was leather. She wore black riding boots with her ensemble.

"What guy did you invite, Kelly?" Blair asked.

"No one. I'm hoping to hook up with Dexter," Kelly slurred and licked her lips then she poked her tongue out at me.

"I'll snatch it out of your mouth," I threatened.

Blair glimpsed at the two of us. "You two really need to stop."

"No. What she needs to do is stop being a selfish brat. My life doesn't revolve around her. She wanted me to sit in the car and wait for her while she got her freak on, sitting on the top of a man's car hood."

When Kelly heard those words, she rushed toward me. "I should knock you out. You didn't have to pull off and dump my shit out of the car."

I stared Kelly down, without blinking. "You aren't a queen, and I am not your chauffeur. By the way, I wish you would hit me."

Kelly turned away. "You make me sick." As she walked into the bathroom she mumbled, "I ought to sleep with Max and Dexter. 'Cause I know you like both of them."

"Well, Kelly, if you sleep with Max and Dexter, I'll never speak to you again. Why do you always want something that isn't yours?"

Kelly walked back into the bedroom. She laughed with her mouth and eyes closed. "Boy, are we ironic tonight? I knew you had a crush on Dexter when we were at the airport. You dirty slut, you're supposed to be with Max. I knew you had whorish tendencies in you. Sorry, Shelby, you can't have Max and Dexter all to yourself. You need to share the wealth." She licked her lips. "You can't handle that dick on Dexter anyway. So don't even

try to go there. He needs a freak like me to ride him backwards."

I let out a heavy sigh and refused to argue with Kelly. Nothing mattered but me seeing Dexter again. Just thinking of him made me smile. I couldn't wait to inhale him. Steal a touch of his skin. I tingled inside and became wet as thoughts of him clouded my mind.

LUST FIFTEEN

Huge tropical plants were draping the food table. A large leopard-print candle rested on the mirror centerpieces, and the cake table displayed animal print balloons around the leopard-shaped cake.

Blair assigned each table a theme: leopard-, zebra-, tiger-, cheetah-, cow-print, or leather. We began tying animal-print bows on every single chair, to match the theme of the table. Gift bags, which were imprinted with the table's designated theme and filled with sexual goodies, adorned each place setting. There were also door prizes for the twenty-fifth guest, the best-dressed, and the best dancer. After we finished tying bows on the table, we placed jungle vines around the mirror on each table. Miniature bottles of champagne with a customized HAPPY BIRTHDAY, BRYAN emblazoned on them decorated each table. Animal-print cloth napkins shaped like fans also accented each table.

"It looks good, girls. I think we're finished," Blair said ecstatically.

The three of us looked like high-class hookers in the jungle. "I'll greet the guests since I'm wearing a robe," I said.

"That's a good job for you, Miss Goodie," Kelly uttered as she nudged Blair.

I sat at the table with the leopard-print sign-in book and the animal-print nametags. The lighting in the room was dim; candles on each table were the only illumination. The ambiance of the jungle was present.

No guests had arrived yet, just the bartender and DJ. The DJ was dressed to impress; however, his pants were pulled up to his chest. He was wearing a tight black shirt, brown pants, and a leopard-print hat.

Kelly rushed over to chat with him. "I'm Kelly, and where are your pajamas?"

"I'm Shawn, and I'll have to show you later."

"You do that, sweetie. I'm in room 1008," she snickered. Then she walked to the bartender and ordered a glass of gin and juice with three shots.

Five guys walked in wearing all black. I was wondering why they weren't wearing pajamas.

Didn't they read their invitations?

"Hello, sexy cheetah. We're Bryan's cousins from Mississippi."

"*Mane*, that's leopard print."

"Is that your real hair?" his cousin named T-Red asked, while touching my hair.

I reached to shake their hands. "What's up? I'm Shelby, and yes, this is my hair."

"I'm Patrick."

"Big George."

"Smitty, what's up, what's up?"

"T-Red, and give me them digits."

"I'm . . . Kojack, baby."

I pointed to Blair. "There's Bryan's girlfriend."

"That big, thick, tall, fine one with that short blond hair there and them leopard-print finger-nails?" George asked.

I nodded. "Yes. I see you have an eye for detail."

"Boo, I have an eye for you," Patrick mumbled in his Southern accent.

"Where the food at?" George asked.

I pointed to the two Latino waiters dressed in black suits with leopard bow ties, walking around with appetizer trays in their hands.

"Thank ya, boo. Brothas from that Dirty South like to eat," Patrick replied.

The boys walked near Blair.

"Dang, *mane.* She's sexier up close. Bryan got him a brown suga," Smitty stated.

"Hey, I'm glad you guys came." Blair gave each one of them a hug and sat them at a round table.

T-Red passed Blair a huge tray. "Here, our Aunt MaeBell sent Bryan and Aunt Pank three sour cream pound cakes and two lemon pound cakes."

"Thank you."

"*RRRRuff,*" Smitty barked as Blair walked away. "I'm gonna have to take that one there away from cuz."

"Man, stop acting like a juvenile," Patrick said.

"Man, I don't look nothing like that rapper," Smitty replied.

"What?" George and T-Red asked, as they laughed.

"Not the rapper, fool. Stop acting like a juvenile, meaning child, in front of these classy folks." Patrick laughed.

"You showing off. I'm gonna take your ass out in them woods," Smitty replied slowly.

"What woods? There ain't no woods around here," Patrick remarked.

Kojack interrupted. "Y'all act like y'all ain't never been out of Mississippi. Let the Jack show ya how it's done."

Megan arrived next with Victor. She was wearing a long hot pink leopard satin nightgown with a huge split in the back that almost reached her butt. Victor wasn't dressed in pajamas either. He was wearing a black Kenneth Cole suit with a pink leopard-print tie.

"Professor Myru, you and Megan look great together," I said as Kelly grabbed Victor's hand.

She sat Megan and Victor at the leopard round table and quickly rushed to greet the other guests. There were eight guys walking in, five with women on their arms.

Kelly ran to the three single guys. "Follow me."

"Blair, why aren't the men in pajamas?" I asked, sounding annoyed.

She shrieked, "Got ya. Only the women were told to wear pajamas."

"I can't believe your Amazon ass, exploiting women like strippers. Shit. I just knew I'd get a chance to gawk at Dexter in his boxers. That's fucked up, bitch."

"Now, now. I thought you were working on your cursing," Blair teased.

In fact, I was working on my cursing, but it was such a hard habit to break.

Blair snickered and walked to the podium. "The bar is open. Order whatever you want."

The jewel named Sapphire swayed in. She wore a leopard-print mask and a leopard-print spandex lace crotchless teddy, with six-inch leopard boots. When she turned around, I noticed the back of her outfit had a tail attached to her butt and hoops were hanging from her clit. The men gazed intently and some jealous women rolled their eyes.

"*Mane*, that girl pussy hanging out. I oughta sneak up on her ass and lick it a little," T-Red said.

"Sapphire, who are your friends?" a horny Kelly inquired.

"These are my boys," Sapphire hummed, pointing to them. "This is Martin and Percy."

I made them nametags and placed them on their chests.

Kelly turned to Percy. "You resemble the Coca-Cola boy."

Percy was tall, dark, bald, and his hazel-colored eyes were mesmerizing. She couldn't stop looking at him. Hell, I had to tear away from him. He had the prettiest white teeth that sparkled like diamonds. The boy was handsome and movie-star sexy. He needed to be on someone's magazine cover. Kelly grabbed Percy's hand tightly and guided him to her table.

Joel showed up with Chloe. She was dressed in a chiffon black-and-white cow-print thong teddy with a matching sheer robe.

She exhaled. "Where's your man, Shelby?"

"I'll let you meet him when he arrives." I reached to hug Joel as if we didn't live together.

Before I could let my arm down, Sapphire darted over to hug him. "Hey, darling. Are you okay?" she asked, kissing Joel's ear.

"Who is this cat-bitch?" Chloe bawled to an astonished Joel, who put his head down and looked away.

"I'm Sapphire. Call me for a threesome." Sapphire turned around and kissed Chloe on the cheek. "Oh, she's cute and feisty. I like her, Joel."

"Joel, where is my motherfucking gat? I'm 'bout to kill that dyke bitch."

"Calm down, Chloe. Joel and I are just friends now. I fucked him in high school, but I prefer women, and you are too hood for me," Sapphire said nonchalantly, before strutting off.

Joel's mouth was wide open. He took his hand and covered Chloe's mouth. "Baby, Sapphire is gay and crazy. Come on, let's have a good time." Joel pulled Chloe toward an empty table.

Two young girls walked in and signed the book.

"Joy and Nakia." Nakia looked at me, rolled her eyes, and then whispered in Joy's ear.

I recognized Nakia too. She was the young girl that was in front of the barbershop clinging to Max. I smiled. "Ladies, please find a seat at an empty table."

Joy was wearing a two-piece jungle-print set, with the nipples out. Nakia wore a black sheer furry shirt with the matching bottoms. She had a terrible shape. The girl was big at the top and small at the bottom. Her breasts were huge and sloppy, just like her chubby arms. The bottom half of her body wasn't much to talk about either. Her butt was flat, and her legs were skinny. She looked like a huge red lobster. I giggled to myself, wondering what in the hell Max saw in that sad girl.

Blair's cell phone rang. "Everybody, he's on his way in."

When he entered, everyone shouted, "SUR-PRISE! HAPPY BIRTHDAY!"

Dexter and Max screamed, "Happy Birthday, man."

Bryan was shocked. A huge grin covered his face. He gazed around in search for Blair. When he found her, he tongue-kissed her in front of everybody.

"Oohh," we teased.

"Were you surprised?" Blair asked loudly.

"I sure was. Thank you so much. I love you, girl," Bryan exclaimed.

Blair grinned. "Wait until you see the three cakes your Aunt MaeBell sent you and your grand-mother."

Bryan blushed. "Now that's what I'm talking about. Where my folks at?"

Max walked to our table and sat next to me. Dexter followed, sitting next to Kelly and Percy. Kelly was busy touching Percy's face and sipping on her fourth drink.

I twirled around to look at Dexter. He looked so appealing. I wanted to jump across the table and tell him how much I missed him. Instead, I teased him by pulling off my robe. Dexter fixed his eyes on me; I returned the stare. He winked at me, and I childishly licked my tongue out when Max wasn't looking.

Seeing Dexter really set my heart ablaze. Long-ing for kisses we shared, searching for the love that was almost there, not believing I let him go. I

should have found a way to escape from Max. I should've broken all those rigid rules. I couldn't fight the strong feelings anymore. I had to have him, best friend or not. It wasn't too late. To hell with my plan.

Max elbowed me. "I'm going to get a drink. Do you want anything, Shelby?"

"No," I replied. I wasn't in the mood for drinking. I was in the mood for Dexter.

"Max, please bring me back a glass of gin and juice," Kelly stuttered.

Joy's long ebony legs hiked over to our table and whispered in Dexter's ear. A smile beamed across his face. He turned around and stood up. They embraced one another and walked out to the dance floor. Dexter draped his arms around Joy's small waist. She placed her head on his chest as they danced slowly.

I was fuming mad, with beet-colored cheeks. My eyes followed every movement they made.

When the song ended, they walked hand in hand out of the banquet room, and my eyes followed every movement. I looked back at the bar and noticed that Max was in a deep conversation with Nakia. Both of my men were out of the box tonight. Max didn't matter, but Dexter did. I cared about him and wanted desperately to be with him.

I stood up. "Excuse me, everyone," I said politely, jealousy settling in.

"Shelby, can you go to the room to get Bryan's birthday crown?" Blair asked. "The adjoining doors are open."

"Sure," I replied as I rushed away from the table.

Dexter had really got the best of me. Seeing him with another woman made me realize I had no time to waste. I stood outside the banquet door, trying to calm down, not wanting to act too irrational or make an ass out of myself.

The relationship with Max is ending tonight, no questions, no explanations, no more games.

A big surprise greeted me when I glanced to the right. Joy was in the lobby sitting on Dexter's lap, nibbling on his left ear. My expression displayed amusement as I laughed at the two, slowly walking near them. I stood in front of them with my hands on my hip. "Excuse me, honey," I said with plenty of attitude.

Joy looked at me as if I was crazy. "What?"

"Dexter, I need to speak with you about a very important matter," I demanded, like I was his wife.

Dexter nudged Joy. "Beautiful, let me see what Max's ol' lady needs."

Joy stood up and caressed Dexter's hand. He tried to hide the swelling in his pants with his arm.

"Okay, my love. I'll be waiting for you," she said, softly planting a kiss on his cheek and then prancing off to the ballroom.

He turned to me impatiently. "Look, I don't have time for your games. You are too indecisive and shallow. Didn't you make a choice? Don't come busting up my action. I'm single," he said, pointing to his chest. "Shelby, you need to grow up. You said you needed time to end things with Max. It's been weeks and you are still here with him." He rubbed his chest. "You had your chance with *D-E-X*."

"Is it too late?" I looked up and questioned Dexter, who peered over me.

A stunned Dexter towered over me, unable to speak. He glanced over at Bryan's cousin, Smitty, who was in the lobby smoking a cigarette and listening to our entire conversation.

"I said, Is it too late for me to be with Dex?" I repeated softly. "I don't care what anyone thinks. All I know is I want you."

People in the lobby were beginning to look at us, which didn't bother me. I had already waited too long, putting my happiness off to prove a point and deliberately trying to hurt Max. Yet, I was denying myself from something that could be true love.

Kelly walked past with Sapphire's guest, shaking her head at me. I looked her in the eye and mouthed, "Whore."

She grinned and strolled toward the elevator.

Dexter touched my hair and turned my face back toward him. "I like you, but—"

My heart dropped, not wanting to feel rejected. "So it's like that, Dex?" I murmured with tears in my eyes.

Dexter nodded his head. "No, it's like this."

He looked into my light brown eyes with sincerity. My body ached. I wanted to collapse in his arms.

Suddenly, he reached down, and our lips locked together passionately. Dexter's tongue sped into my mouth erotically. My arms draped around his neck, while his arms wrapped tightly around my waist. Dexter's hands moved down to my butt slowly. He massaged each cheek tenderly. It didn't

matter who saw us. We were connected, not willing to stop our wild, untamed, hungry, sensual kissing and fondling.

Our embrace unlocked after several minutes. I was left feeling feeble and nervous. "Dexter, I've missed you so much," I cried out. I stroked his hand. "I'll do anything to keep you in my life. This feels so right. I made a big mistake by staying with Max. You're the one that my heart yearns for. I can't stand to see you with anyone else."

"I was just going to tell you, I like you but . . . you can't be my woman with all that ass hanging out." He reached too close my robe, playfully rubbing my breast.

Smitty walked up and interrupted, "Y'all two needs to get a room for all that there. Big city folk don't know how to act in public . . . Dog, I'm just playing. It's bootiful. Just bootiful, to see two people in love."

Smitty walked away mumbling, "That there is nice."

"Yes, it is . . . Oh, goodness. I forgot to get the birthday crown for Bryan," I said, dragging Dexter with me to the elevator.

"Girl, what's the rush?"

"Just get on this elevator with me and press number ten."

"Little lady, you sure are bossy."

I turned to him and rubbed his shoulders in an apologetic way. "What room are you staying in tonight?"

"Wherever you're staying," he said boldly.

"What about Max?" I asked.

"Didn't you say you were ending things?"

"Yes, but I haven't yet. And I still don't want to tell him about us. You know his little ignorant ass will cause a scene," I said, trying to make Dexter see things my way.

"Yeah, you're right. We'll lay low for a while."

The elevator doors opened slowly, and we walked out and headed to my hotel room hand in hand, enjoying the company of one another.

I opened the door quickly. Within seconds I closed the door faster than it was opened. My face became flushed with embarrassment.

"What's wrong?" Dexter sighed.

I was speechless. My heart was pulsating, and tears were forming in the corner of my eyes.

"What is it?" Dexter questioned, stunned by my emotional state.

"N-O-T-H-I-N-G," I replied slowly.

The birthday crown can wait.

"I can't believe what I just saw. Well, yes, I could."

"What did you see, Shelby?" Dexter repeated.

I ignored his question.

"Shelby."

I didn't respond.

"Shelby," he yelled louder.

"It . . . was . . . Kelly . . . and . . ." I slurred.

"Is she okay?" Dexter asked, frantically.

I stood like a zombie, shaking my head left to right.

Dexter took the key from my hand and rushed to the door. He inserted the plastic card into the door and swung it open. His eyes bucked open. He

turned to me, bewildered by what he saw. The door closed slowly, as Dexter inched away to join me at the elevator. "Your girl is off the chain. That's why those men at the shop keep taking her out. She looked up at me and kept on sucking. I knew I should've got with her." Dexter walked back toward the room in a jolly state. "I'm going to get in line."

"I would kill you and her," I said scornfully.

Dexter turned back around teasingly. "That's okay. I saw the jealous side of you when I was with Joy."

The ballroom was hopping, and the crowd appeared pleased, as Dexter and I walked in and went our separate ways. The second Joy spotted Dexter she ran up behind him and wrapped her arms around his waist.

I wanted to turn around and yank her hands off of my man, but I decided to proceed toward Blair. "Get your own crown," I stated angrily, looking back at Joy.

Blair looked at me astonished by my comment and facial appearance.

I shook my head. "I'll tell you about it later."

She screamed over the music, "Forget about the crown, let's do the door prizes."

I went to the podium and announced, "Best dressed is Sapphire Tillman, Twenty-fifth guest is Percy Young, and best dancer is Joy Smith."

Blair and Bryan were standing next to me as Joy glided up to the podium. I wanted to knock her in the head with her gift bag.

Instead, I smiled and handed it to her. "Congratulations."

Sapphire sauntered to the podium to claim her prize. She did a little dance move then she licked the side of Bryan's face.

"Congratulations," I repeated to her. "Percy Young." I knew where he was—upstairs with Kelly, receiving a better prize.

Martin walked up and claimed Percy's prize, and I took a seat.

Max walked up to me holding a glass of cognac. "Where the hell have you been all night?"

"Why? Are you worried? You were talking to the 'big red lobster.'"

"Are you ever going to stop being so insecure?"

"Do what you want to do, Max. It doesn't matter anymore."

Max finished his drink. "I don't want to fight. Let's dance."

I didn't want to dance with him, but did anyway, to keep down confusion. At that moment, I was willing to do anything to keep him quiet.

I shook my butt hard, hoping Dexter was looking. And he was. I was wild and nasty as "Little Red Corvette" projected through the speakers.

"I don't want everybody looking at my ass," Max slurred, becoming annoyed with my wild antics and undomesticated behavior.

I didn't listen but continued the butt-shaking, hoping to tick him off even more.

A "Soul Train" line was started the moment Percy and Kelly returned to the ballroom.

Max stopped dancing and whispered in my ear, "Look, I'm going to get a drink with Smitty. I don't do the Soul Train thing."

"Whatever." I continued to dance freely.

For once, it didn't matter what society thought. I was following my heart. If Bryan's cousin, Smitty, wanted to tell Max about Dexter and I, that was fine too. Nothing mattered anymore, because in my mind it was over between Max and me.

Michael Jackson's song, "Beat It," played. Blair and Bryan, Dexter and Joy, Joel and Chloe, Sapphire, Martin, Nakia, Big George, T-Red, Kojack, and Patrick joined in on the Soul Train line.

"They need to play some of that there Johnnie Taylor around here, so we can really set things off," Big George yelled out.

I strutted down the Soul Train line as if I was Janet Jackson at the Super Bowl. The crowd's growing excitement was intoxicating.

And Joy was too nasty as she pranced down the line. However, the girl had rhythm. She turned around, caressed her exposed dark nipples, dropped low to the ground then jiggled her booty. George dropped to his knees and crawled behind Joy down the line. Kojack followed behind Big George, doing the moonwalk.

"See, that's how we do it in the country. Them country boys are on the rise."

Patrick shocked everyone when he dropped to the ground and did a James Brown split and popped up a second later. We couldn't stop laughing. Bryan's cousins had taken over the party.

"Yeah, *mane.* That's that there R. Kelly 'Move Your Body like a Snake Mama,' " Kojack announced loudly.

Joy bent over and backed her ass into Dexter's crotch. Then he grabbed her waist and grinded hard.

Within seconds I intercepted, dancing right behind Dexter. The two of us had Dexter in a sandwich. I whispered, "I want you."

Dexter turned around and rubbed my bottom. He smacked my butt as I twisted like a snake.

Kojack and George swept Joy away. Nobody paid any attention to us because Sapphire was entertaining everyone else. She plummeted to the dance floor and spread her legs wide open, displaying her clit piercing. She stood up and shocked all of us when she glided her body like a snake on Blair's butt. Her hands were reaching for Blair's chest, but Bryan and Blair ignored her presence and kept on dancing together.

The music slowed down, and the volume decreased when Blair walked up to the DJ stand. "I would like to dedicate 'I'll Give All My Love to You' by Keith Sweat to Bryan, the love of my life."

My eyes turned to Joel. He was a Keith Sweat fan too. "I'll Give All My Love to You" was played twenty times a day, every day in his car and mine. It was our song. Joel extended his hand. "Would you like to dance with your best friend?"

"Yes, this is our song," I said quietly.

Bryan and Blair and Sapphire and Martin followed us to the dance floor. George and Kojack led Chloe and Joy to the dance floor as well. I looked back admiring Victor and Megan. They were really in love. I could see it in their eyes as they embraced one another while swaying to the beat.

"Wait, Shelby. He is getting too comfortable with Chloe. I'm cutting in," Joel said abruptly as he walked away hastily.

A second later, Dexter tapped my shoulder and swung me around. His strong biceps supported my back during our delicate glide across the dance floor. I had no cares in the world. My eyes were closed, and my head was resting on his chest.

Blair muttered in my ear, "You look too comfortable in Dexter's arms. Don't get your ass kicked. You know Max is full of that Yack."

"I'm not worried."

That didn't stop me from peeking back to see where Max was. Just like I figured, he was busy lurking around Nakia, which didn't bother me one bit, since I was in the arms of the man I adored.

When the song ended, Dexter and I remained enveloped in each other's arms.

Blair pinched my arm. "Go sit down before Max sees you two. I don't want any fighting in here tonight."

When I spotted Max I scurried to the table where we were sitting earlier. Dexter followed behind me slowly.

"Does anyone need a room?" Blair broadcasted.

Max approached me. "Baby, I can't stay."

"That's cool. I'll be fine," I said, unconcerned.

Max spoke to Dexter, who was standing near our table. "Joy was all over you, man. Are you guys staying the night?"

"We might," Dexter replied with a huge grin.

"Not if I have anything to do with it," I mumbled under my breath.

"I'm about to bounce," Max said, dapping Dexter and Bryan. He reached over and gave me a hug. "Come on, baby, walk me to the lobby."

I remained calm and serene as we exited the room. "Max, I don't think things are working out. I don't want to be with you anymore. Let's just be friends," I blurted out.

"Baby, you don't mean that. Let's talk about it tomorrow. I gotta roll out now."

"Max, I'm serious. I'm through with you. It's over," I repeated assertively as I left him standing alone.

On the way to the room, I caught a glimpse of Dexter; he was talking to a girl I hadn't met.

I guess he likes young girls too.

They stepped toward me. "Shelby, this is Kandace, my sister."

We shook hands.

"I just stopped by to wish Bryan a happy birthday," she said. "Nice meeting you, Shelby."

"Come on, baby," T-Red begged Kandace.

"Boy, I don't want to dance with you. What have you been drinking?" Kandace asked.

"That Hpnotiq," he slurred.

Kandace brushed him off and walked away to chat with Bryan.

"Your sister is cute. She looks just like you."

Dexter smirked. "We all look alike. Wait until you meet my other siblings."

I yawned. "Dexter, I'm going to retire. I really enjoyed our two-minute dance."

"That doesn't have to be our last one."

"Oh, it doesn't? Why don't you accompany me to my room then?" I requested, surprised by my own boldness.

*   *   *

When Dexter opened the door to my hotel room, I was surprised to find two dozen pink roses lying on my bed and a huge balloon bouquet on the nightstand, with a card attached.

Max is really trying to win me over, I reasoned with myself.

Dexter didn't say a word. He looked more surprised than I did. "Somebody really cares about you," Dexter responded.

I read the card.

Shelby,
I really like you. You're amazing and I'm not letting you walk away this time. Will you be my girlfriend? Yes or No?

Love, Dexter

I spun around and squeezed Dexter tightly. "When did you do this?

"I never gave you the key back when we busted in on Kelly. Naw, Kelly helped me."

"Kelly took the time to do something special for me?"

"Yes, she did."

I gazed into Dexter's eyes. "Thank you so much. And, yes, I'll be yours. I broke up with Max tonight."

He hushed me up as his lips touched mine. Our bodies fell to the bed, and we began to caress one another. Within minutes we drifted off, cuddled up together without a care in the world.

* * *

"Oh, baby. That feels so good, yes, Percy."

I thought I was dreaming, so I didn't open my eyes. Then I heard another scream.

"Ohh . . . ahh . . . umm . . . put it in deeper."

I opened my eyes and rotated my body to the right. It was Kelly. She was in the room next to me, butt naked, riding up and down on Percy with her back toward him. Percy's friend Martin was also in their bed asleep.

I shook Dexter. "Wake up. Don't look to your right. . . . Let's go."

Dexter rubbed his eyes. "What's wrong now?"

"Can you hear?"

Dexter looked to his right. "Damn, kid. Not again. I got with the wrong girl."

I pinched his butt. "Let's go. Get my flowers, balloons, and suitcase."

Dexter stared at me. "I told you about trying to boss me."

"I'll meet you at the door," I said, rushing to get out of the hotel room.

Dexter sat up, looked over at Kelly, and shook his head. Then he leaped up, clutched my suitcase, and darted out of the room. Kelly never looked up.

Dexter shook his head. "Damn. Your girl is on the whorish side. She's buck-wild. I'm going to make her bartend topless."

"What? Don't talk about my girl. It's not what it looks like."

Dexter looked at me as if I was a fool in denial.

"You have to understand Kelly. She's searching for love wherever she can find it. Her father, who

she adored, died of cancer when she was seventeen, and she never got over his death. In fact, she didn't shed one tear at his funeral and didn't go to the burial. She has never mentioned his death again. Kelly was a daddy's girl. Whatever she wanted, he gave to her. I remember for her sixteenth birthday, her dad brought her a brand-new red Ford Mustang convertible. The rest of us had used cars, but not Kelly. Her father worshiped the ground she walked on. She only received the best. He worked three jobs to cater to her needs, supporting her financially and emotionally. Her dad attended all of our volleyball games, while her mother was at home high. When he died, Kelly's life changed. She began turning to men for happiness, recycling her virginity time after time. She's looking for a man to give her the unconditional love her father gave to her."

"Man, that's deep. I guess I was wrong for judging her." Dexter sighed.

Tearfully I said, "I try not to judge her, but it's hard. I just hate seeing her ruin her life."

"Shelby, just keep on praying and being a friend to her. I'll continue to let her work at the shop, topless." He laughed.

As we were leaving the hotel, I caught a glimpse of Max's car. He turned on Randolph Street. I ducked, not wanting him to see me in the car with Dexter. He didn't see me, but who I saw him with gave me all the closure I needed.

LUST SIXTEEN

Dexter lived on the south side of Chicago in a distinguished brick house. It was his father's old place, which he and Kandace shared.

He held the door open for me to come in to his neat, well-organized house. The carpet was white, and the furniture was bronze; African art decorated the walls.

"My dad bought a new house up North, and he left us this place fully furnished."

"That was nice of him. Your dad has good taste."

He motioned for me to follow him upstairs. "Kandace isn't coming home tonight."

"Really?" I said enthusiastically, as I walked into his huge bedroom. *This man has exceptional taste in furniture too.* My hand glided across his hand-carved mahogany rice bed. "I like that piece," I said, glancing above his bed to an extraordinary oil painting of a couple making love.

"Thank you. I love nudity, especially that sculpture you had at your place."

I hit Dexter's arm. "You are so crazy. I like nu-

dity too. I have a similar piece hanging over my Jacuzzi by the famous artist, Karshieka Graves."

Dexter moved closer to me. "That's her piece too. I didn't notice your painting when I was at your place. I see we have a lot in common."

"Speaking of Jacuzzis, can I wash up?"

He gave me towels and directed me to the bathroom. "I'll go in my sister's bathroom to shower."

When I finished, he gave me a T-shirt. I stretched out my arms, breathed deeply, and exhaled, feeling refreshed.

"Good. Get under the covers with me."

I rolled under Dexter's fluffy down comforter. "Dexter, did you know Max and I have never had sex?"

"Shelby, Max is my best friend. He tells me everything. Of course I know. Believe it or not, Max respects you. He really thinks a lot of you."

"You know what? I don't want to talk about him anymore. He's old news. I'm moving on to bigger and better," I said in a flirtatious way as I rolled on top of Dexter, grinding my body close to his.

Dexter took control and reversed our positions. His strong, muscular body towered over me, his tasty lips sucked my neck passionately, and I welcomed his seductive advances. Pleasure hit me rapidly as he lifted my shirt and placed my breasts into his mouth. My insides were blazing; I had to release my desire onto him. I situated my lips on his neck and sucked uncontrollably. Our bodies created heated friction as they grated together. My vagina lips expanded freely, throbbing and longing to be pleased. I was hungry for the oversized

treat pounding between my thighs, and Dexter was eager to feed me.

He placed his hand in my panties, massaging my wet, creamy clit. "I wanna make love to you so bad. Baby, I know you're ready."

I nestled my head into his chest, not wanting to admit that I was screaming inside to make love to him. "Not now," I whispered faintly as I gyrated to the movement of his touch.

"Shelby, let me taste it again then. I have to please you. You are about to explode. You're dripping wet."

Yes! Yes! I'm addicted to your tongue between my thighs, I screamed internally. I pushed his shoulders down. His PRECIOUS LORD tattoo didn't faze me this time.

He placed his thumbs on my outer lips and dipped his face in. A shower of wetness invaded my exotic delicacy as his crafty tongue lashed about.

Oh! His tongue feels so good. This is one lust I can't do without. My eyes swayed back. Serenity overpowered my body. I was left helpless and weak, longing and wanting the night to never end.

Morning came quickly. When I opened my eyes and glanced at the clock in Dexter's bedroom it was nine o'clock. I expected to see Dexter asleep next to me, but his side of the bed was empty. I heard voices coming from downstairs. I put my clothes on and walked to the edge of the stairs, listening intensely.

It can't be . . .

A nervous feeling covered me. My stomach tingled. I didn't move, fumble, or speak as I paced back to Dexter's room. I didn't want Max to find out like this.

What have I gotten myself into?

"Man, I left the hotel last night with Nakia. We went back to her place, and I tore that pussy up. When we finished we came back to the hotel, but I didn't see you or Bryan. I saw that freaky-ass lesbian, Sapphire. She was giving Nakia the eye. I told that bitch she had to do me too. So the three of us hooked that shit up right in Sapphire's hotel room. I fucked both of them. . . . Damn! It was off the chain. That ho Sapphire can really do wonders with that tongue ring. She had Nakia screaming for mercy. I started to call you for a foursome."

"Man, you know I don't roll like that. It's too much shit out here, like HIV. I want one woman, that's it."

"Whatever."

"Max, you can *whatever* me. But you know I'm telling the truth. You have two good women and look at you."

"Man, you right. When I got home last night, Sydney was fired up. She was lying in the bed with two butcher knives. Her eyes were scarlet red and full of rage. I have never seen her so mad before. Sydney has lost her mind. I don't know what's up. Maybe it's the pregnancy. Hell, she told me to leave if I didn't want to be cut from head to toe. I just left to avoid any conflict, 'cause you know you gotta watch those quiet ones. Shit! I was already fucked, so I slept in the car."

"I feel bad about Sydney and Shelby. Shelby is really pissed off at me. She called herself breaking up with me last night. I wasn't trying to hear that shit. She knows we belong together. I'm going to marry that phat ass. Shit, she's going to be a doctor too. We're going to be set."

Dexter rubbed his chin. "Man, you got some serious drama going on."

"You know, man. I'm going to iron that shit out with both of them. I guess it's time for me to step my game up, you know, do something special for my ladies again. I'm going to take Sydney to dinner tonight. There is a real exquisite restaurant on Lake Shore Drive, the Top of the Rock, located on the fiftieth floor. It's nice. The floor rotates around as you view Lake Michigan. Sydney will love that, and afterward we'll get a room at the Drake hotel. She'll forget about everything I've done. Tomorrow night I'll take Shelby. I'll keep you posted. If you don't hear from me, call the police 'cause Sydney has sliced my ass," Max snickered.

Dexter stood up, returning the laugh. "Well, I'm leaving for New Orleans tonight."

Max faced Dexter. "I wish I could go. I need to get away from this madness with these broads. Well, be safe, bro, and tell mama and my boys hello. And your fine-ass sisters, especially Katelyn."

"I'm not telling Katelyn anything. She'll be up here on the first plane. Just hold the business down until I get back."

"I don't know what I'm going to do when you move to Cali," Max said.

"You'll be straight," Dexter reassured Max, walking him outside.

I watched from the window as the two men pounded each other's back and embraced.

My cell phone rang as Max leaped into his car. I answered on the third ring.

It was Kelly. "Sorry about that peep show last night. I just couldn't stop in the middle of that shit. I thought you would have stayed and watched longer like you did when I was doing Kevin in the bathroom stall," Kelly joked.

"Ha! Ha! You a funny bitch," I whispered so Dexter wouldn't hear me.

"Yes, my threesome is complete. Girl, it was the bomb. That was my first time with two men. After you left, I rose off of Percy's big black dick and bent over that bed. He dipped his fingers in a jar of "lubrication" then he spread my cheeks open and inserted his fingers. He moved them in and out three times. Then threw a condom on and jabbed that dick inside my ass. Girl, I was screaming. That ass-fucking ain't no joke. Don't know how the faggots do it on a regular basis. It felt good, though. A feeling you can't"—Kelly clapped five times—"explain. My mouth was wide open. A smile was blasted all over my face."

I remained silent, wanting to hear every single detail. I too had wondered about threesomes. "Girl, what else happened?" I said eagerly.

"Percy was unmerciful. He was working that dick, moving it fast, back and forth with ease. Them hands were rubbing my tits, while his mouth sucked down on my back. That bed was

doing some shaking." She laughed aloud. "That's when Martin woke up with his drunk ass. He saw my pussy in his face. He blinked his eyes twice. They bulged out and then that dick did. Martin inched toward me, foaming at the mouth. His lips met with mine, and that tongue explored my wet insides. Shelby, I was screaming and howling . . . OOHHH . . . OOHHH . . . AWWW . . ."

I giggled into my hands and kept on listening to Kelly, like I was watching a movie.

"My body was quivering, and I couldn't stop drooling. Shit, I grabbed that hook-shaped dick and swallowed it whole. The faster Percy drove that rod into my ass, the harder I sucked on Martin. And you know I put a heart-shaped passion mark on the side of his dick." Kelly clapped five times. "Then Percy start yelling to Martin that he was about to cum, asking him to finish me off while he jerked and fluttered, pulling his dick out of my ass.

The minute Percy fell to the bed, Martin took his tongue out of my pussy and removed his dick out of my mouth and stuck it inside of me. Shit, his crooked-shaped dick was jabbing my G-spot and making me scream like a lunatic. I came after the third hit and told him to stick that dick back in my mouth.

Soon afterward, Martin's tangy cream poured down my throat," Kelly happily screamed through the phone.

I heard Dexter dashing up the stairs. "Bye, girl. You wild. Yo' ass is going to hell." I chuckled.

"Right with you, bitch," Kelly teased before ending the call.

Dexter looked at me and rubbed his chin. "I guess you heard your boy."

"Yeah, I heard his dog ass. It's all good." I smiled, not really caring too much about Max or his dilemma.

Then out of nowhere, Dexter asked, "Would you come with me to New Orleans, tonight? I'm going to see my mother, and I need to handle some business. I can also show you around, since you've never been to The Big Easy."

Without thinking, I replied, "Sure, I'd love to," forgetting about medical school. I was pulling strong A's, so a few days absent wouldn't hurt my average.

"Don't worry about any expenses because I'm handling everything."

"One problem, Dex. I'm not flying," I said, shaking my head.

"Cool. We'll take the train. Be ready at seven."

"How long are we staying?"

"Three days," he answered.

Dexter was being daringly spontaneous, and I was following my heart, being beautifully bold, distinctive, and classically satisfying.

"Let's go out to eat lunch," Dexter said as he rubbed his stomach.

Not waiting for a response, he escorted me out of the house and into his car. We headed north to a New Orleans-style restaurant on Rush Street called Heaven on Seven.

Kanye West's "Through the Wire" was pumping through the speakers as Dexter and I rode down Grand Avenue, a few blocks from the restaurant. I

thought about Chaka Khan's lyrics, which were playing in the background.

Dexter gazed at me and said, "Kanye, ain't no joke. He's flowing." He paused. "The lyrics in the song remind me of us. For a chance to be with you I'd gladly risk all—my best friend, business, and respect."

I blushed. "You won't believe it, but I was just thinking the same thing. How we love so dangerously."

We shared smiles, sat back, and enjoyed the rest of the song.

LUST SEVENTEEN

The obnoxious sound of the train horn blared through the city as the fumes from the huge locomotive befouled the air. The silver streak pulled in and I grew excited. At last, I was sneaking away with Dexter. I hurriedly kissed Joel's cheek and advanced toward Dexter as Joel handed him my suitcase.

An attractive, middle-aged black man greeted us. "What city?"

"New Orleans," Dexter replied assertively.

His eyes reverted to me. "Upstairs to the right."

We located two seats nestled in the back of the train.

A white conductor approached us. "Tickets, please."

Dexter passed him our tickets. "We'd like to upgrade to a sleeping car."

"Sure. Follow me," the conductor said.

The train was operating at full force. We bounced and jiggled through each train car. Dexter grabbed

my waist occasionally, when the turbulence was extreme.

"I'm not going to fall," I reassured him, feeling like I'd had a full workout. When we reached the sleeping car I was relieved.

Our sleeping room was the size of a small walk-in closet with bunk beds and a toilet. Dexter sprawled out on the top bunk and I took a seat on the bottom.

I pulled out my book and began to read. My body became warm. Novels always lit the fuel in me, especially hot, steamy ones. I looked up, Dexter was asleep, and I wanted to play around. Oooh. My soul was grieving for the stroke of a man. I turned back to my book and continued to read. My fuel was ignited. The more I read, the hotter I became.

A long freight train whistled past us, causing our sleeping car to sway uncontrollably. Our car vibrated. My body felt the fluttering, which stimulated me. A sexual rage covered my soul. I tore my clothes off, down to my bra and panties. I snatched a condom out of my purse and climbed to the top bunk and straddled Dexter as if he were a Clydesdale horse. I fiercely massaged my searing flame against the gigantic bulge in his jeans.

Dexter's eyes opened and he rubbed them in disbelief. Then without warning, he flipped me underneath his masculine body. He captured my mouth with his sensational, sumptuous tongue.

Before long, his greedy jaws were swallowing my naked breasts, and his powerful body was nuzzling

against my tender frame. Dexter propelled his body in a hypnotic motion.

My head was flipping left and right. I couldn't wait to explore his vast nature. "Make love to me," I yelped, feeling lively, adventurous, and tantalized.

"Are you all mine?" Dexter asked, breathing very hard.

"Yes, I love you." I was surprised when the word *love* popped out of my mouth. I had never confessed my feelings for a man that quick before.

My words didn't surprise Dexter. He kept on moving, as if I hadn't said anything.

I thought about Megan's words, "Never love a man more than he loves you." He hadn't confessed his love for me yet. So I decided not to worry about it. Instead, I turned back to Dexter, enjoying our moment.

Dexter inched down to my stomach. He grazed my belly with his luscious lips, holding my wrist to the bed. Soon afterward, he dipped his juicy tongue into my meticulous blend of sweetness.

"Ohhh. Ohhh. Ummm. Ummm," I cried aloud, loving the beautiful, amazing, sophisticated man between my luscious thighs.

I put the condom in Dexter's hand, as he ripped down his pants and underwear. Immediately, he placed the condom on his eager friend.

The moment of lust was ending, and I was definitely getting ready for a whole sin, a big milk chocolate one.

Lord, I know I said not until marriage, but do You see the size of this man's penis? Please forgive me. This is a sin I have to commit.

His moistened mouth saturated the crotch of my panties as he wrestled them to the floor. He lifted his head up and guided himself to my vagina. I shivered at the thought of his robust penis entering me.

"I'll take it nice and slow," Dexter assured me when he saw the terrified expression on my face.

My head rotated, my eyes closed gently, and my legs separated freely, inviting him in. His delicious, mouth-watering thickness met my creamy, succulent clit.

Upon entrance, I felt intense pain. I gasped for breath as his enormous penis sent electrifying, passionate shocks to my tight, luscious opening. Gradually the discomfort dissipated as pleasure overtook my body. He cautiously shifted his body on top of mine, inching more of his big, long dick inside of me.

The topsy-turvy movement of the train heightened our moment. My voluptuous hips gravitated to the rhythm of our exotically blended lovemaking. I extended my legs and straddled them around his back. He was pushing and thrusting inside of me, not forcefully, but tenderly and soothingly.

"Baby, you can put more in," I whispered in his ear, thankful for every smooth, affectionate, caring stroke.

Dexter lifted his body off me. "Baby, are you sure? I don't want to hurt you. That's why I only have the head in."

"Put it back in," I shouted impatiently, while grabbing and reaching.

"I don't want to hurt you."

"You won't hurt me," I said softly.

Inch by inch he inserted his aroused friend back inside of me. He picked up speed as I rubbed his smooth, tight, muscular butt cheeks. Dexter started plunging and sliding his dick further in. The sweet juices of my pussy covered him, gripping his girth with each thrusting force, driving me insane. For the first time in my life, I was making love to a real man.

The branches and leaves of the tall trees scattered as the train glided through. We were sitting at the white linen table enjoying our breakfast and the view of nature. Our hands stayed entwined, and the touch of his skin reminded me of last night. I gazed into his eyes in disbelief. We were finally together; no longer did I have to fantasize about our destiny. I was in love with Dexter and everything about him.

After breakfast, we sat enveloped in each other's arms in the movie lounge watching *Finding Nemo*. I looked away for a second and thought about Max; however, my mind quickly turned back to Dexter. I realized Max and I would've never lasted; the feelings weren't there. He didn't make me feel the way Dexter did. Dexter was always very loving, caring, and compassionate, and it wasn't an act. Max and I could have been good friends, but we were never meant to be intimate.

Oh, how I wish Dexter had approached me in the club. That would've made things less complicated. Now I have to figure out how I am going to tell Max about Dexter and me.

* * *

The hot, humid climate of Louisiana slapped me in the face the moment I exited the train. My hair was going to hate this city. It was nearly ninety-eight degrees outside. A wet, clammy texture masked my face, leaving me feeling unclean.

Dexter took a deep breath. "Nothing like that Dirty South," he announced as we strolled along the railroad tracks and into the small train station.

"Hey, little brother," two ladies shouted and waved when they saw Dexter and me.

He beamed with excitement. It had been a couple of years since he'd last seen his sisters.

They ran to us immediately, hugging their brother tight and showering him with kisses on the cheek.

He gestured to me. "This is Shelby."

The ladies hugged me before I could speak. "I'm Dexter's oldest and prettiest sister, Karrington."

"I'm Kincaid, the wild one. Pleased to meet you." Kincaid turned to Dexter and asked about their younger sister Kandace. "Why didn't Kandace come?"

Dexter shrugged his shoulders. "I don't know. I guess she wanted the house to herself." He held out his hand out. "Give me the keys so I can go get the car."

"My little sister doesn't want to associate with us poor Southerners anymore," Karrington joked, in a sarcastic, poor-slave voice and then gave Dexter the keys to her car.

A homeless man sat near the exit door with a

harmonica in his mouth and an empty coffee can in front of him. I looked in the Café DuMonde can. He had three one-dollar bills, two quarters, and six dimes in it. The sisters walked past him as if the man didn't exist. I straggled behind, slipping the smiling man twenty dollars.

The muggy atmosphere went well with the soiled city. I gazed intensely at the trash in the streets. There was a housing project and a liquor store on every corner. There wasn't an attractive sight around. I turned my nose up as I looked out of the window, wondering what kind of neighborhood his mother lived in.

Dexter snapped his fingers. "I got to stop for a daiquiri. You don't know nothing about that, do you, Shelby?"

I glared at him as if he was crazy. "We have daiquiris up North."

"Duh," Karrington said. "You guys don't have drive-thru daiquiri shops."

"What? That's too neat."

"Turn on Napoleon. There's a new daiquiri shop on Claiborne," Kincaid stated.

Dexter pulled up to the daiquiri shop window. "Would you ladies like anything? I'm treating."

Kincaid sat up and leaned on the front seat. "Give me the strongest thing they have."

"I'll have a hurricane daiquiri," Karrington replied.

Dexter looked at me impatiently. "Do you know what you want yet?"

"I can't decide between piña colada and strawberry."

"Get half and half," Kincaid suggested.

"That sounds good. Thank you, girl. I'm so indecisive."

"I figured that out. You are a little bourgeois too. I see how you're turning your nose up at our city," Kincaid said when I passed her the daiquiri in the white Styrofoam cup with a straw.

"Chill out, Kincaid. Let's hit it, Dexter. The quickest way to my new place is to go down Magazine Street. I'm going by Kincaid's, so you guys can keep the car," Karrington yelled to the front.

Minutes later, we were pulling in front of his sister's home. "We'll see the two of you at Momma's tomorrow. It was nice meeting you, Shelby. Call us after you guys get some rest."

We traveled down Canal Street viewing the sights, and my opinion changed drastically. The Big Easy was beautiful and overflowing with tourists. It was the middle of the day, and people were walking down the streets drinking daiquiris and beers. Some of the people were sloppy drunk. I was amazed at how free everyone was at three in the afternoon. I couldn't talk, though. I had been in the city twenty minutes, and I was already sipping on a daiquiri.

We arrived at our French Quarter hotel, Royal Sonesta. It was located right on Bourbon Street. Its aura reflected a distinctive, sophisticated, royal blend of European elegance and Southern charisma. The hotel surrounded a lush tropical courtyard, a world-class art collection, and secluded pool and serene gardens.

I was impressed because the hotel was pleasing to the eye, not to mention the Southern hospitality the staff displayed. I had never met so many

friendly people in my life. The people looked very similar to the folks up north, with the exception of a gold-tooth epidemic. Nevertheless, I was already loving the city of New Orleans' freedom, culture, and class.

The minute we opened our hotel door I fell to the soft, fluffy, feather-top comforter. My body ached, especially between my legs. I felt like I had been riding a bike in a two-hundred-mile marathon. Dexter wore me out. My "little treasure" was sore, and I wanted to soak in the giant hot tub.

"Let's take a dip in the Jacuzzi," I said softly.

We undressed each other and snuggled up in the Jacuzzi. Dexter caressed my lips with his. I shut my eyes and took pleasure in our moment.

Later on that evening, after relaxing in the Jacuzzi and resting, we took a journey to a restaurant called Jack Dempsey's. We had to travel through several bad areas to get there; however, the restaurant's location wasn't any better. I looked at the simple white building, which resembled a house, and figured they couldn't possibly have anything good.

A lady with a long ponytail, which reached her bottom, seated us. The inside of the restaurant was full of people. It was very small and cluttered, yet the atmosphere was jovial. I couldn't get over how friendly the staff was. At that moment, I realized Southern hospitality wasn't just a phrase. The people in the South were overly friendly, polite, and caring, nothing I was used to in the big Windy City.

When the waitress served our food, I understood why Dexter brought me to this place. The

seafood platter looked like it could feed four. I had fried shrimp, fried oysters, fried red fish, fried catfish, fried crawfish, fried crab fingers, seafood gumbo, boiled crab legs, and macaroni and cheese.

"How are you going to eat all of that, little mama?"

"I have no idea."

Dexter grabbed my hand. "Father, God, I thank You for blessing us with a safe trip. Lord, bless this food for the nourishment of our bodies. In Christ's name. Amen"

I took pleasure in eating my food. Every single morsel was divine. I had never tasted seafood so fresh, and the macaroni and cheese deserved a trophy.

"We need a 'to-go' box."

"That will be fifty cents," the waitress said.

"They charge fifty cents? That's different. I know they get paid well with that extra perk because I don't know who'd be able to finish all of this food."

"I love this place. I come here every time I come home."

"I see why. I was a little worried when I saw the outside."

Dexter looked at me and smirked. "Never judge a book by its cover. The holes in the walls have the best food."

And he was right about that.

The next day we ate breakfast in the French Quarter at The Court of Two Sisters. The atmos-

phere, food, and live jazz were breathtaking. The ambiance of the place was unforgettable. I had never seen an all-you-can-eat brunch as elegant as this one. By now, I wanted to move to New Orleans; the people were pleasant, and the food was to die for.

Dexter placed his arm behind my waist as we leisurely walked down Royal Street. I situated my arm around him and exhaled, loving every moment of our voyage. We peeped at all the specialty stores our feet carried us to, stopping every second, admiring the art galleries and other showcases. The sites were overwhelming. The city of New Orleans had so much culture and class. I understood why it was voted the best place for adults to tour.

When we made it to the French Market there were artists painting pictures freestyle. I stopped and stared at the talent that lined in the street. It reminded me of the vendors in New York City in Central Park.

"Let him draw your beauty," Dexter said as he sat me down in the gentleman's chair.

I glowed with happiness as I sat down.

The gentleman glanced up at Dexter. "You two are a lovely couple. Let her sit on your lap. I'll draw the two of you. I want to capture the sparkle in your eyes. You must be newlyweds?"

Neither one of us replied. We just smiled.

"You two don't have to say a word. I can tell. Is this your first visit to The Big Easy?"

"Yes! And I love it."

"Make sure you go get some pralines from Aunt

Sally's Praline Shop," the gentleman urged as he stroked his pencil.

After our portrait was drawn we walked down to Aunt Sally's, where we watched the lady make candy with pecans and sugar.

"This is delicious," I mumbled while sampling a taste.

"Cool. I'll buy you, your mom, and your girls some, and remind me to get Kelly something special. She has really boosted up our sales at the shop."

"Kelly is easy to please. She likes everything and is always appreciative, no matter what you give her."

The two of us journeyed deeper into the French market. Dexter bought five bags of garlic pistachios. "Wait until you taste these."

"I have money. You don't have to spend your cash on me."

Dexter covered my mouth with his. "You always try to be so independent. Let me spoil you. I want to spend my money on you."

"Okay, but look at the time." I glimpsed down at my watch. "We better head over to your mother's. I don't want your family to think I'm taking you away from them."

I could tell when we entered Dexter's neighborhood, because he appeared to be very acquainted with the area, which was nowhere from Canal Street. The mostly wood houses were very close together.

"What up, Dexta?" A man with three gold teeth approached the moving car.

Dexter let the window down and shook the boy's hand. "Butterball, my nigga. I ain't seen you in a minute."

"I heard you in the Chi, doin' it. Ya heard me. Got ya own gig and everythang. Brang that shit to the N.O. We can have bitches servin' dranks butt-ass naked and cutting hair." Butterball laughed.

"Nigga, you still a fool, but that's a good thought. Come by my mom's and we can try to hook somethang up."

"A'ight, bro, I'ma holla at ya a li'l later."

I giggled. "Boy, how we change. Look at you."

"You didn't know I had a little gangsta in me? I used to be ruthless."

"I can tell. I see all the tattoos. I like the one with the cross," I said, rubbing his arm. "You can keep the pitch fork."

"Oh, you love the thug in me. Every woman wants a gangsta."

We parked in front of a gray wooden house with green French shutters. There were cars everywhere. I was so nervous because of Dexter's huge family. His mother was sitting on the porch with about five children. I remembered her face from the pictures at Dexter's house. Her home was directly across the street from a housing project.

"That's where Master P used to live," Dexter said, pointing to the row of housing projects.

They looked like vandalized townhouses to me. "They aren't as hideous as Chicago's housing projects," I said.

"Yeah, right. The N.O. ain't no joke."

Dexter opened the car door. He grabbed my hand, and we strolled up to his mother. "Hey, old girl,"

Dexter said to his mother. He kissed her cheek and hugged her so long and tight that her feet lifted off the ground. "Mama, this is Shelby."

"Hello, Miss JeanPierre. It's a pleasure to finally meet you."

"Hey, sweetie," she responded with a vibrant expression.

She was a beautiful woman. Her cinnamon-colored skin was flawless, and her silky, curly hair was black as coal. She could definitely pass for a Cuban or Puerto Rican.

Dexter's mother looked me up and down. Then she focused in on my chest. Looking at Dexter she stated, "That little girl has some big ol' titties." Then she mumbled something in French.

I turned my head to laugh. *Yes, my wonder bra is working.*

She reached to hug me. "I've heard so much about you, I think a hug is more appropriate."

I hugged her back. "Pleased to meet you."

Has Dexter told his mom about me?

We walked into the kitchen and all eyes turned to me. "This is Dexter's Chicago lady, Shelby," Kincaid announced to the large family.

I waved my hand at the crowd shyly. It looked like thirty hands waved back. The kitchen was full of people. I silently counted forty.

Dexter personally introduced me to his eight siblings. The girls were all in the kitchen helping his mother cook, and the men were outside at a table playing spades. Dexter's siblings varied in age. His oldest sister was fifty, and the rest of them were two years apart. His elderly grandmother, great-aunt, and uncle were also over for dinner.

They were the only civilized people in the joint.
The other folks were obnoxious. I felt like I was at a
club. You couldn't hear anything, not to mention
the dense smoke.

Dexter's teenage niece walked in with a friend. I
couldn't believe she was wearing a one-piece
"Daisy Duke" bodysuit. The top part of the bodysuit was halter, which was too low-cut for a twelve-
year-old, and the shorts were too low; half of her
butt cheeks were hanging out.

"Hey, Uncle Dexter," the young girl said with a
loud country accent. She gave him a big hug and a
kiss on the cheek. She waved at me and approached her father.

Damon was Dexter's thirty-two-year-old brother.
He turned around immediately; his eyes gawked
at the young girl. The girl was fair-skinned with
slanted eyes.

"Hello, Connie Chung," he said.

The girl cackled and kept on walking.

Then he stared at his daughter. "Lateka, is your
ass working on Bourbon Street? Damn, bitch got
mo' titties than her mama," Damon rambled.

She hit his leg. "Shut up, Daddy." After saying
that, she strutted right past him.

I sat at the table hoping he wouldn't come my
way.

Damon wasn't sexy like Dexter. He was much
shorter and he appeared to be losing his hair. He
grabbed his wife by the butt. "I was fucking the shit
out of this bitch last night. I had her raggedy ass
tied to the bed post," he boasted.

His wife, whose name was Spring Honey, didn't

say a word. She just laughed, while her husband made an ass out of both of them.

Where is Dexter?

He must have slipped out when I was being nosy. I looked outside and noticed him standing near a cooler, pouring salt into it.

Damon held my hand. "So, Shelby, how are ya? I'm so glad my little brother finally brought you over to meet us." Damon's tone was calm, and for once he sounded like he had some sense. "I love visiting my dad in Chicago. That Harold's Chicken is the bomb," he said, shaking his head.

"Yeah, it is pretty good," I said in agreement.

"I can tell you like that chicken. Yo' ass is phat."

"Excuse me?"

"Girl, calm down. I was trying to give you a compliment. That's why I could never date women from Chicago. Y'all have too much attitude. Big-ass mouth."

I didn't respond. I was hoping he would end his conversation with me.

He looked into my eyes. "Do you suck my brother's dick?"

I couldn't believe my ears. I looked into his red eyes and answered quickly, "No."

"Why not? You need to do something with that big-ass mouth. Spring Honey sucks my dick."

I couldn't respond. I was stunned, speechless, and humiliated. Hell, I was livid. I stood up and faced the ignorant little man. Then out of nowhere, I slapped his cinnamon brown face.

His sister Katelyn came to my rescue. "That's right, girl. Damon deserved that."

Damon grasped his cheek. "That little mother-fucka is crazy. Get her the fuck out of my face before I get it crunk up in here."

Katelyn walked me outside to Dexter. She turned to Dexter. "Why did you leave her in there with crazy-ass Damon?"

Dexter approached me with open arms. He placed a delicate kiss on my lips. "What's wrong, sweetheart?"

I turned my head away from his sweet face. "Nothing," I told Dexter, trying to downplay the incident.

"She slapped your stupid brother," Katelyn blurted out, pulling Dexter and I back in the house.

Damon was still standing in the kitchen with a look of bewilderment on his face when I reappeared. "Them Chicago bitches have no sense of humor." Damon held onto Spring's hips. "That girl is crazy."

Spring pointed her bottle of Mickey's beer at Damon. "I'll stab your ass. Fuck around and get killed if you want to. You had no business saying what you said to that girl. You must want her."

"Stop showing yo' ass, motherfucka. You ain't the only one that can stab and shoot."

"Damon, just apologize to that girl. You act so silly," Dexter's mom stated.

"Mama, yo' ass is silly if you think I'm gonna to apologize for being me."

"Shit," Damon mumbled as he walked up to me. "Chicago, I'm sorry."

"That's okay. I know how obnoxious little short men can be sometimes," I replied.

Damon turned to Dexter. "Take her smart-

mouth ass back to the Big Windy before I dump her in the bayou." He chuckled on our way to the backyard.

Dexter hugged his brother from the side. "You better leave my woman alone. I plan on marrying her, so you need to get to know her real good."

We all laughed, but I rejoiced. I was ecstatic. He hadn't told me he loved me yet, but he was already telling his family he wanted to marry me.

I looked into the large cooler. There must have been a million little red lobsters crawling around. "What are those?" I asked.

"Shelby, those are crawfish," Dexter replied, as if I had asked a dumb question.

"You never ate crawfish before?" Dexter's older brother Derek asked with a puzzled look on his face.

"You a dumb motherfucka. You've never seen a goddamn crawfish before? Where did you find this stupid-ass girl?" Damon laughed.

I laughed back at Damon's stupid butt. "I've read about crawfish and I've seen them on The Food Network. I was born and raised in Chicago, and I've never eaten crawfish."

"That bitch got proper on me. I watch The Food Network."

Dexter tapped Damon. "You got one more time to call my woman a bitch, and it's going to be you and me."

Damon laughed. "Bitch, you may be taller than me, but I can rumble."

"Well, baby. We're about to show you how the Creoles throw down," Derek replied, ignoring Damon.

That seemed to be the norm around the house. He ranted, raved, cursed, and acted a nut and no one reacted. I guess everyone knew him and just accepted him for the ass that he was.

There was a huge pot of boiling water sitting on an outside butane burner. I could smell the cayenne pepper. Derek poured lemons, onions, celery, corn, potatoes, and hot smoked sausage in the water. Dexter drained the water from the cooler and started pouring the crawfish into the boiling water. I looked into the pot, and the water was orange from Louisiana crawfish boil seasoning. Damon was at another burner frying catfish and potato logs.

"Wait until you taste my catfish. Yo' man can't cook. Shit, us Southern boys can burn," Damon said excitedly.

Then Damon and Derek slapped hands. "That proper little titty-sucker likes to play golf. He's a re-tarded son of a bitch."

"Man, skip y'all," Dexter replied.

"Where is punk-ass Max?" Damon questioned Dexter.

"I just knew he was coming," Derek commented.

"Somebody had to stay and manage the busi-ness," Dexter answered.

"How does that little runt get all them fine-ass bitches? He's one ugly motherfucka. That bitch is black as the crack of my ass," Damon yelled.

"He's a trick," Katelyn replied.

"Women like men with money," Derek retorted.

Damon blurted out, "That black-ass prick wasn't a trick when you were trying to fuck his brains out

at Mardi Gras last year. Yo' ho ass was hunting that
dick down."

"Shut up, fool." Katelyn laughed nervously.

"I was going to whip Katelyn and Max's ass for
messing around," Dexter said, hugging Katelyn.

*What have I got myself into? Max and Dexter are
closer than I thought. There is no way I am telling Max
about Dexter and me.*

When the crawfish finished cooking, we sat at
the picnic table in the yard. The guys poured some
of them into an empty cooler and dumped the
others on the table, on top of newspaper. Dexter's
family gathered at the table, gobbling down the
"baby lobsters." The only thing I heard was gross
sucking and slurping.

Dexter broke the head off and sucked all of the
juices out of the carcass. Then he pinched the tail
and pulled the meat out quickly. "Here, Shelby,
taste this," he said, damn near shoving the tail in
my mouth.

I chewed the crawfish tail slowly. I could taste
the spiciness the minute the tail touched my lips. I
was amazed. The crawfish was delicious.

Dexter peeled more and fed them to me. Derek
was feeding his girlfriend too.

"Thank you, my baby," she replied each time
Derek put a crawfish in her mouth.

She was very quiet and appeared to be nice. He
was definitely treating her like a queen because he
pulled out her chair and caressed her every free
second. Derek looked just like Dexter too; however, he was taller, darker, and older.

Twenty minutes later Dexter's mom brought

out red beans and rice, turnip greens, potato salad, and macaroni and cheese to go with the fish Damon fried. Dexter followed Derek's lead as he fixed my plate.

"What do you want, baby?" Dexter asked.

"Everything," I said proudly, anticipating the home-cooked Southern meal.

LUST EIGHTEEN

The night air was hot like a sauna. Jazz music blared through the street. After leaving Dexter's mom's house in Karrington's car, we decided to spend a night out on the town before retiring to our room. We walked down Bourbon Street, observing the exquisite sights.

"Hey, Mister. Throw me some beads," a white lady, around fifty-five years old screamed up at the hotel balcony.

The guy on the balcony was drinking beer with about five other people.

"Show your tits."

She pulled her breasts out, and he threw down three beaded necklaces.

"Damn! You have perkier breasts than mine," a young girl from the balcony yelled.

Dexter and I laughed as we walked by. I really chuckled because hers looked better than mine too.

It was one in the morning, and the party was just beginning. With the entire street shut down, peo-

ple roamed freely. We barely had enough room to walk side by side. The peddlers were out: fortune-tellers, artists, dancers, musicians, puppets, drag queens, and mimes were all doing their thing.

"Look at the five kids tap dancing for change. The youngest one looks no older than five. And there isn't a parent in sight."

"Chicago girl, these children are surviving the best way possible, so is the silver-painted tin man mime."

"Now I find him very amazing, standing still on a box crate without making a move. We don't have tin men in Chicago."

"You are so silly," Dexter said playfully as he planted a kiss on my cheek.

We passed a club with two fake legs swinging out of the building. Women were standing in front of the club soliciting business. They were dressed in bikinis and stiletto heels. The sign read NUDE TRANSSEXUALS.

"Dexter, can we go in?" I begged. I was so curious. I wanted to see the transsexuals.

"I'm not interested in seeing any of that," Dexter said firmly.

I kissed Dexter on the cheek. "I'll protect you."

"You better," he hissed as we entered the club. It was very dark and smoky. To our surprise, there was nothing but heterosexuals inside. I guess the other couples were inquisitive like me.

We sat at a cocktail table in the middle of the room.

"There's a two-drink minimum," a waiter dressed in drag informed us.

Dexter pulled out two twenty-dollar bills, handed them to the waitress, and ordered four hurricanes.

When the show started, I was amazed at how much the men looked like real women. They were petite with real breasts. One of them let the couple next to us touch his breast.

"Oooh . . . they feel so real and soft," the lady stated as she massaged the transsexual's chest.

I wanted to know how they felt too, but I was scared and I didn't want Dexter to think I was a freak.

"Here are ya dranks," the waitress announced. She put the drinks down and Dexter gave her a five-dollar tip.

I guzzled the hurricane down fast. "This is good."

"Shelby, wait. Those drinks are strong. They sneak up on you."

"It tastes like 7UP and cherry juice. I don't taste any liquor."

Dexter grinned at me. "Okay, slow down. I'm warning you."

I ignored Dexter and continued to slurp the drink like it was soda pop.

The next transsexual that came out on the stage was gorgeous. I was jealous. He had the perfect shape. His skin was flawless and creamy like French vanilla ice cream. I just knew this drag was a real woman, until he pulled out his penis. It was the size of a cigarette. "Don't you bitches hate on me. I took pills to shrink my penis, and eventually it will be gone. And I'm gonna take all of your men."

The show was hilarious and so entertaining. The guys were so friendly; however, Dexter didn't think so. When we were leaving, the biggest queen in there, who looked like a football player, slapped Dexter on the butt.

"I can't believe this shit. I'm going to bust that nasty punk in his mouth, violating me up in this bitch."

I grabbed his waist and moved him out of the club rapidly. "This is New Orleans; let's not end up in jail over fun."

I felt good. My body was light and tickly. Dexter was right. The hurricanes were delicious, and I was buzzing.

Dexter grabbed my waist. "Shelby, are you okay? You're wobbling."

"I'm fine," I said, stuttering and giggling over my words. I turned to Dexter and stuck my tongue in his mouth as we stood in the middle of the street. "You know your boy's dick was the size of that transsexual's?"

"Who?" Dexter replied with a look of worry on his face.

"Max, your best friend with the little dick," I cackled.

Dexter cracked up in my face. "Well, it's a good thing you got with me."

My facial expression turned conservative. "Dexter, I really like you a lot."

He looked into my hazel eyes. "Shelby, I've liked you since the moment I laid eyes on you in the club."

I thought he was going to tell me he loved me,

but he didn't. My ego was a little bruised, but I knew confessions like that took time. Although, I felt in my heart he did.

I pointed to a club with people falling out of the doors. "Let's go in there."

Dexter looked perplexed. "Baby, Razoo's is packed. They stay crowded."

From the outside, I could see two girls on the stage, tongue-kissing as if they weren't in a crowded room. I pulled his hand, and we squeezed our way into the club. The music was bumping.

"This is unquestionably the place to be," I said as Dexter and I found our way to the dance floor.

"Slow down, Shelby. You're stepping on my feet."

"I know I dance fast, but bear with me," I said, almost out of breath.

A man with an Australian accent came up to us, while we were sitting at the bar resting. "Would you dance with my wife, sir?" he asked.

I swiveled my chair in the man's direction and answered no for Dexter. "These people are freaky down here," I chanted in Dexter's ear and turned back to the Australian man. "I guess you want a threesome with my man too."

He perked up. "No, a foursome; it would be nice if you could join us."

"Sure. Meet us in room 767 at four. We are staying at the Royal Sonesta," I replied boldly, giving him our neighbor's room number.

"Cool. See you guys later," the guy said happily and trotted off to tell his wife.

A dark-skinned black female wearing white

bunny ears and a white fluffy bunny tail in the middle of her bottom approached Dexter. "Would you buy me a drink?"

Dexter eyeballed her, noticed the pad of paper in her hand and the bunny pen. "Sure," he replied and beckoned for the bartender.

The girl bounced up and down. "Thank you," she screamed and licked her tongue out at the other playgirl bunnies that were with her.

I wasn't too pleased with the whole situation, but I didn't want to appear jealous and insecure.

Dexter stared at his watch. "You ready to go? I'm hungry."

"I am too. I would sure like some more of your mother's cooking. We should have fixed some plates to go."

"Mama asked. You were too cute to take a plate."

"I regret that," I replied as we walked down Bourbon Street.

"You gotta try a New Orleans' famous Po' Boy."

I had a puzzled look on my face. "What's a Poor Boy?"

Dexter gazed at me as if I was silly. "It's a *Po' Boy*, not a Poor Boy. It's a sandwich on French bread. I usually get shrimp or catfish. They taste the best," Dexter said, trying to convince me.

We stopped at a restaurant named Desiree. Dexter looked at the menu and ordered one shrimp and one fried soft-shell crab.

"I ordered you a crab Po' Boy, since you love crabs."

I grinned, showing all of my teeth. "Thank you, sweetie."

When our food arrived I bit into my Po' Boy quickly. It was fantastic. I had pickles, mayonnaise, tomatoes, lettuce, and two fried crabs on my sandwich. I was impressed with the soft-shell crab, and boy, was it seasoned well. I didn't have to crack open anything. I just ate the crab whole since the shell was edible. "Dexter, I'm glad you ordered for me."

"See, I know all about New Orleans cuisine. You are too indecisive anyway," Dexter said, smacking on his sandwich.

An electric pink sign blinked every second KITTY KATS ADULT TOYS. This was the fourth novelty shop we passed on Bourbon Street. I wanted to go in so badly and I did. Dexter followed me in, shaking his head. This store had every sexual novelty you could name. There was a vibrator called the "Ultimate Eager Beaver." It had a rotating head and a tongue to tickle the clit. They even had a vibrator for men called a "Warm Cherry Pie" for the man to stick his penis in. I was flabbergasted.

Ultimately, I did find something I could use. It was flavored lubricated climax gel. I needed something to ease the pain this time because tonight I wanted to feel all of Dexter inside of me without the throbbing sting. Just reminiscing about the night before made my panties moist. I planned to enjoy tonight even more, showing him a part of my wild side.

Another young black lady in her early twenties wearing white furry bunny ears and a white puffy bunny tail in the middle of her butt approached Dexter. She was a few shades lighter than the other girl, and her hair was longer. "Would you dance

like Beyoncé?" she asked Dexter as she looked down at her list.

Dexter's eyebrows arched. "Naw, I don't think so."

She appeared down, but not discouraged. "Are you sure?"

Dexter shook his head side to side.

"Ahh . . ." she sighed and wiggled off toward her bunny clan.

"I'm ready to go back to the room," Dexter announced excitedly, stroking my hair.

"No, I want to go to the casino. Hopefully, we won't run into any more of your playgirl bunnies," I teased, moving my hand to his bottom and smacking it.

Dexter glared at me. "Those girls were on a scavenger hunt. Evidently they were playing a game for a bridal party. There were about twenty of them." Then he smacked my butt. "And what do you know about gambling?"

"My boy Joel is a professional gambler. He showed me all the tricks of the game."

Dexter held my hand tight, and we journeyed down Canal Street, toward Harrah's Casino.

"I ain't cool with that you-and-Joel shit either."

"What? We are just friends and roommates. He helps me out with the bills."

Dexter kissed my lips. "I'll help you with your bills."

I smirked. "I'm sure you will."

He raised his eyebrows. "I trust you, kid. I was only kidding about the Joel statement."

*   *   *

"ID please?" the security guard at the entrance of the casino asked.

The sounds of the slot machines rang loudly as we walked into the place. "Let's go where there's less smoke."

Dexter swung my hand side to side. "This is a casino. There isn't a place with less smoke. Let's go listen to the band."

"Boring. I want to play roulette."

Dexter handed me fifty dollars and strutted off to see the band.

I handed the dealer my money. He gave me fifty pink one-dollar chips. I grabbed a stool near the middle of the game board, placing one chip on numbers 1, 7, 10, and 9. Then I put five chips on number 28, the date Dexter and I made love. I also placed ten chips on the odds section.

The dealer held his hand across the wheel. "No more bets."

The ball rolled around the wheel.

"Number thirty-one," the dealer announced. He gathered all my pink chips that were inside the board. He placed two stacks of chips next to my ten chips on the odds section.

"At least you won twenty dollars," the guy next to me said.

The cocktail waitress approached our game table. "Drinks? What would you like to drink, ma'am?"

"Water is fine," I stated.

An Asian guy walked up. He gave the dealer five hundred-dollar bills.

"Check change."

The guy in the suit came by. "Mr. Pham Wu, do you have your player's card?"

The guy handed the man his card. The dealer gave the gentleman twenty-five green twenty-five-dollar chips.

"Place your bets."

Mr. Wu placed $50 on number 14, $100 on 27, $25 on 6, $25 on 32 and $25 on 21.

I reached over the lady next to me. "Can you put this on number three for me?" I placed ten chips on 28, five chips on 27, and two chips on double zero.

"No more bets."

Dexter walked up and whispered in my ear, "Did you play twenty-seven for the date you became my lady?"

I hugged his waist. "I sure did. How was the band?"

Dexter smirked. "It was exceptional. You know jazz originated in New Orleans."

"Number 28," the dealer announced.

I jumped up and down. "I won, I won. Three hundred and fifty dollars."

Dexter rubbed my hips. "Let's go cash all those chips in."

"Cashing in pink. Three hundred and ninety-four dollars," the dealer announced.

I handed Dexter the chips to cash in. He returned with the money and handed it to me. "Baby, take your $394 and spend it on whatever you want. We can go to Canal Place and visit the Gucci store."

"No, I won with your money. I want to buy you those Gucci shoes you wanted," I said.

Dexter clutched my hand as we walked down the steps of the casino.

"You are so sweet, but I can't let you spend your winnings on me. Now, what was significant about number 28?"

I spoke softly in his ear. "That was the day we made love."

We returned to our room early in the morning. I was tired, but I knew some hot, passionate, wild sex would rejuvenate me.

Dexter turned the radio on and found a jazz station when he returned from his shower.

"Let me go take a quick shower now," I stated anxiously as I rushed in the bathroom to wash up. After I was finished, I slipped on a sheer black nightgown and stroked a teaspoon of the climax lubrication on my wet mound.

Dexter was resting on the bed with his face in the pillow. "Are you ready for this dick?" he asked as he turned over and sat me on top of him.

"Yes, I guess," I whispered nervously. "But let's role-play."

"I'll do whatever you want me to do. Role-play it is. Who do you want me to be?"

"Never mind." I nodded. "Okay, bring a couple with you. The Australians we saw today," I said playfully.

"You look so sexy when you're indecisive," Dexter teased as he exited the bed and walked toward the door and knocked on it, pretending to let the Australian couple in.

The night I caught Kelly with the two men rang in my head as my body was spread out on the bed, awaiting my turn. Soft kisses were deposited on the

side of my neck and hands stroked my body. Juicy lips moved to my chest, nibbling lightly on each nipple. My waist was clutched, while hands moved down to the sensitive part of my body. A finger was introduced, which caused me to quiver. This sinful act made me nervous and embarrassed at the same time. Though, you couldn't tell her that. She purred and poured with wetness, welcoming the show.

I opened my eyes, which were partially shut, ready to face reality. Silky black boxers greeted me as they slid to the carpet. I looked the big hairy vessel in the face, knowing one day I'd have to return the favor.

"Have you ever sucked a man's penis before?"

"No, all of this is new to me."

"Put the condom on and let me insert this wrath."

"Sorry I don't do oral sex. I only receive it."

"Aren't you a special Shelia? Scoot to the end of the bed and open your legs wide. My wife would love to please you orally."

"No, you lay down on your back. Let sweet Shelby please you." My juicy pussy welcomed the aroused, long, thick dick while strong hands massaged my bottom.

"Play with my hard nipples while I travel up and down your cock." The sound of my butt clapping down on his torso echoed throughout the room as I rode him expeditiously like a professional bull rider, feeling every bump on the traveled road.

"Oh, this is some good dick," I chanted as I clinched his cock tightly with my vaginal muscles.

"How do you like this tight American pussy?" No one replied. "I said how do you like this tight pussy?"

"I love it. Just slow down, I'm going to ejaculate prematurely."

"No, let me go. Ladies should be first. Where are your manners?"

All of a sudden, our bodies let go simultaneously, and I felt an adrenaline rush.

"Ahh . . . ahh . . . sssh . . ." he yelled, gripping my waist and pinning me down.

My orgasm had me paralyzed. I couldn't move as I felt warm liquid shooting up like an erupting volcano.

"Ohh . . . shit," I cried.

LUST NINETEEN

"Hello, I would like to make an appointment with Dr. Benson ASAP."

"Are you having any problems?"

I took a deep breath. "I need some tests run, HIV, STDs, and a pregnancy test."

"The doctor can see you next Monday at eight o' clock."

How am I going to function until next week without knowing my destination? Why did I have sex? That one sin may cost me my life. Lord, what am I going to do? I really need You. I know I haven't prayed to You or visited with You at church in a while, but . . .

One night of pleasure had brought so much joy, yet so much uncertainty. I was paranoid and scared shitless. I sat at the table with my eyes closed and my hand over my mouth and nose.

I hadn't even told Dexter that I thought the condom broke. Maybe I should call. I went to the phone and noticed I had six messages. I pressed the button on the answering machine. The first call was from Max. The recorder beeped again

with a second message. "Shelby, where are you?" The call ended and the machine beeped again with message number three. "I'm gonna kick your ass if you're fucking around." The fourth message was a hang-up. The next message was from Max again. "I'm leaving you for Nakia." And the sixth message was from Max stating, "Girl, I miss you. Call me."

I didn't bother calling that fool back. Instead, I telephoned Dexter.

"Hi, love. I enjoyed our weekend together," I said in a seductive voice.

"I did too. I want to see you again tonight."

I could hear men in the background. "Is that the mystery girl on the phone who placed that huge passion mark on your neck?" The voice in the background was Max.

I said quickly, "I see you have company. I'll call you back."

"No, sweetheart. What's wrong?"

I exhaled noisily. "We'll talk when you get here."

By the time Dexter arrived, I was in shambles. My hair was unruly. My eyes were puffy. And I was just having a huge pity party. I could be so paranoid and anxious at times. "What took you so long?" I whined.

Dexter kissed each tear with his soft lips. "I went to play golf."

He passed me three boxes wrapped in pink iridescent paper with neon pink bows. I opened the boxes. A purse, sandals, and sunglasses were enclosed, the items I wanted from the Gucci store in New Orleans.

"Thank you. I didn't see you buy all of this. I

only saw you buy Kelly's purse," I said dryly without smiling.

"What's wrong? Are you having regrets about us?" he asked in a serious tone.

"No, I thought *you* were. I was a bit of a freak in New Orleans."

"We were both freaks in New Orleans. Now, is something else bothering you? You look a mess."

I closed my eyes tight and folded my hands together as if I was praying, as we walked to the bedroom.

"We may have a problem. The condom must have broken the other night. I think I might be pregnant. What am I going to do about school?" I blurted out, tears streaming down my face.

Dexter appeared shocked. There was a moment of silence. "What?" he finally replied, looking at me like I was the silliest creature living. "You wouldn't know this soon anyway. It's only been a few days."

I started to cry. "A woman knows her body. I feel different. Plus, that damn sperm was inside of me; some came out when I went to the bathroom that night."

"Shelby, just relax. I love you and I'll take care of our child, but I seriously doubt you're pregnant. You worry too much."

I can't believe it. He finally said the three words I have been waiting to hear. A tingling sensation tickled my insides. I was elated, and I wanted to jump up and down and scream, but I remained calm. Didn't want to appear too frantic.

He winked at me and laughed. "Wild Bill. Your rodeo lubrication probably punctured the condom. You were riding the hell out of this Aus-

tralian man," Dexter replied, rubbing his chest. His penis inched down his jeans.

I rolled my eyes. "His wife enjoyed your big black dick too. By the way, she wanted to know if you have anything."

Dexter gnashed his teeth. "I only have protected sex, and this is the first time a condom has broken."

I switched subjects quickly. "I don't know if I can continue to do this."

"Do what? We had fun, pretending to be Australians. It was only role-playing. I would never have a real threesome. I have morals," Dexter stated firmly.

"Not that, silly. I meant, date you and Max."

Dexter expression turned serious. "Shelby, I thought you said you weren't seeing Max anymore?"

"No, I'm not. I mean, sneak around. How long do you think we can go on like this?" I said, fidgeting around with my hands.

Dexter asked in an authoritative manner. "I was waiting on you. Do you want me to tell Max?"

"No, not yet. I'm just confused about all this drama we have going on," I answered.

He turned his head to the side, focusing on me with a steady gaze. "Shelby, what's really wrong?"

"Are you involved with someone?"

A smile stroked his face slowly. "Let me tell you something," Dexter preached. "One thing you don't have to worry about with me is cheating. I know you've been hurt before, but I'm not the one. I will always keep it one hundred." He explained that he had just ended a relationship with

Joy two months ago because he wanted space. "We only saw each other for sex. We hardly ever went out." He put it in plain words. Joy was a lazy brat, who lived at home with her parents, wasn't in college, was unemployed, and club-hopped three times a week.

"I appreciate your honesty."

Then I told him more about my sexual habits. I conveyed to Dexter that I was very conservative and he was only the second man I had slept with in my life. I made it clear that I had nothing against him. I was just mad at myself for having wild, irresponsible sex, and annoyed because the condom broke. I was also hurt because he was leaving. When I finished pouring out my heart to Dexter, he closed his eyes and rested for the night. I stayed up worrying what I would do with a baby. And how would I finish medical school.

LUST TWENTY

My pocket vibrated. I answered my cell phone. It was Joel. "Where are you?"

"I'm in my car," I answered.

"Pick me up from Chloe's."

"I'm on my way."

I closed the phone and drove toward Jeffrey Street. When I made it to Oglesby Street, Joel was standing on the corner. I unlocked the door. "Did your girl put you out after sex?" I asked as he hopped down on my leather seats.

"Naw, I just didn't want to hear her complain about you picking me up, so I walked to the corner." He paused. "Stop at the auto store. I need to get a part for my car."

"Sure." I headed toward the nearest automobile parts store.

We both exited the car and walked into the store. Joel went to the back, and I wandered down the aisle where the air fresheners were located. The minute Joel yelled out my name, I ran to meet

him in aisle four, where all the car mats were located. I snuck up behind him and put my hands over his eyes. "You looking for me? I ran to you as fast as I could to avoid your embarrassing screaming. I guess everyone in here knows my name now."

"Do you like these?" he asked, pointing at mats with a pair of dice on them.

"Of course not. I thought you had to buy a part for your car?"

Joel gave me the finger and kept looking at the mats.

"I'm going to pay for my merchandise." I stepped to the register, placed the coconut-scented car air freshener down on the counter, and looked up at the clerk.

Why did I have to run into her, out of all people? I've always wanted to see her again after that shit she pulled in high school. Hell, I'm doing me. Why not act an ass?

"Hello. Is that all for you today?" she asked.

I rolled my eyes and said nothing.

She sighed. "One dollar twenty-five."

I threw a dollar down and tossed two dimes and a nickel at her. The change scattered everywhere. "Bitch, can you catch?" I mumbled under my breath.

She huffed, "You threw the money at me."

I raised my voice. "No, Miss Minimum Wage. You must have holes in your hands."

Joel rushed to the register. "What's going on, Shelby?"

She replied quickly, "I think she's still mad

about something that happened years ago. How immature."

I intercepted, "Two-dollar whore! I will jump over this counter and whip your ass."

Joel attempted to cover my mouth. "Don't pay any attention to her. She has a problem when it comes to cursing. Go sit in the car."

I moved Joel's hand. "I'm not going any damn where. And you have a problem when it comes to gambling."

Joel looked the girl up and down. "You look so familiar." He grabbed her hand. "Baby, what's your name?"

She blushed. "My name is Persia Smith."

I was thinking, *Duh, Joel. It's the funky little whore whose house I caught Sebastian at back in the day.*

"Let's go. Leave this tramp alone," I said, angrily.

Joel released Persia's hand. "I'll be back to holla at you."

We walked out of the store. "What's wrong with you? You're starting to act like your old self, with all that cursing and shit."

"I am my old self. You haven't noticed. It's too hard to live right."

"Well, I want that little timid, sweet, mild-mannered, church-going Shelby back. She would've never fucked up my chances with Miss Persia. I could've got some pussy from that ho," Joel lectured as we walked out of the store.

I pouted, "I have a lot on my mind."

When I reached to open the car door, I started

gagging. Before my hand touched the handle, vomit poured out of my mouth onto the ground.

Joel held me up. "Are you okay? Did that girl upset you that much?"

"No, I'm fine. I guess I ate something that didn't agree with my stomach, or it may be a virus."

Joel helped me into the passenger side of the car and he drove the rest of the way.

Police sirens blared before he pulled into the driveway. It was like they were waiting on us. Three police cars surrounded my house. The officers moved quickly as they approached the car. "Step out of the car slowly."

Damn. I hope this boy didn't steal anything from the auto store.

"Where is that nine millimeter?" I yelled in a panic.

"The gun is under the seat," Joel mumbled under his breath.

We stepped out gradually, not wanting one of the cops to make a mistake.

The officer spoke, "Miss, we're looking for Joel Cullen."

I pointed to Joel like I was just hit by a hammer on my knee, a natural reflex.

They told him they had a warrant for his arrest. Then they slapped handcuffs on his wrist. "You have the right to remain silent. Anything you say or do may be held against you in a court of law."

Joel didn't flinch as the officers escorted him to the police car.

"Call me," I yelled, feeling a little guilty for turning him in so quick. But I didn't want them to find

his gun under my seat either. That would've been another charge.

What has he gotten himself into? Did he steal something? Did he pay his child support? Is he selling drugs again? Does it have something to do with his gambling addiction?

LUST TWENTY-ONE

Joel knocked on my door. I wondered where his keys were. Then I remembered he left all of his personal items in my car when the police arrested him eight hours ago.

"What happened?" I shouted, glad to see he was okay and out of police custody.

"Kayla, a little seventeen-year-old I was fucking with, said I raped her."

"Oh my God. I told you about those young whores."

"Man, chill out. Her cranky-ass daddy came home while we were screwing the other night, and I ran out the house before he saw my face. She told that motherfucka I raped her."

"You shouldn't put yourself in those kinds of predicaments."

"It's all good. They let me go when Kayla told her father the truth." He put his thumbs up. "All the charges were dropped, and I'm free."

"You are so careless with women. The point is, the little girl was too young for you and you knew

that. You're lucky they didn't file statutory rape charges."

"Shit, I want a woman who's going to make me feel young."

"I've told you time and time again about those young girls," I shouted, as if I was his mama.

Joel tilted his head up. "The booty was tight, though."

I replied, "The booty is going to get you in a lot of trouble."

The phone rang, interrupting our shouting match. "Hello, may I speak with Joel?"

"Who's calling?" I asked.

"This is Kayla."

"Bitch, haven't you done enough? You are bold, after the stunt you pulled."

"I didn't want to, but my daddy threatened to put me out. I finally told the truth," Kayla said in a childish voice.

"Little girl, leave Joel alone. He is too old for you anyway."

She hung up the phone without saying goodbye.

Joel looked at me and laughed. "That was some good, young, tight pussy you just threw away. And you love to use that word *bitch*. You want to be a gangsta girl so bad. But you ain't cool."

"Humph. That booty almost put you away for ten years."

I sat on the other end of my bed watching television. Joel was on the phone with another bimbo. I was thinking about my trip with Dexter—the fun we had together, and especially the passionate love we made.

I was feeling so horny. I went to the bathroom and noticed my panties were wet with a clear jelly discharge. I was in need of some loving, even if I was pregnant. Once you get a taste of some good sex, you can't stop.

I reached for my cell and called Dexter. "Baby, can I come over?" I whispered, not wanting Joel to hear me. "I want to be near you. I miss you."

"Shelby, it's one in the morning. Don't you have class this morning?" he said in a sleepy voice.

"Yes, class can wait. Dexter, I have to see you tonight."

"I'll be here."

I hit Joel's foot. "Drop me off at Dexter's. I don't feel like driving."

"What?" a surprised Joel asked. He hung up the phone. "That brotha must have some chronic dick. I thought you were sick."

I grabbed my purse. "Shut up. I am sick, that's why I want to be with my man. So he can take care of me."

Joel made small talk in the car. "Do you want me to pick you up in the morning? I know you have class."

I cut him off. "No, Dexter will take me to school before he goes to work." I had my mind on one thing and that was Dexter. I wanted to feel his strong arms holding me, and the stimulation of his tongue and loving inside of me.

When we made it to Dexter's house, I ran out of the car without saying good-bye or thank you. Dexter's sister Kandace must have heard the car pull up because she opened the door before I could knock.

"Hey, Shelby, go upstairs. He's in there asleep."

I peeled my clothing off and jumped in the bed with Dexter. He didn't acknowledge my presence. His body was still and he was sound asleep.

My mind was saying, *Please wake up. I have to be fulfilled tonight.* I rubbed my body against Dexter delicately.

He opened his eyes, surprised to see me in his bed. "Shelby, I didn't know you were serious about coming over," he said, wiping his eyes. "You are going to flunk out of medical school if you keep this up."

"Shut up and make love to me."

Without warning, he flipped me to the side and swiftly entered my erogenous zone. His testicles brushed against my healthy booty. I rejoiced at the occasion, as my body released joy juices.

"Damn! You are so wet. This pussy has never been this juicy before," Dexter moaned, sticking his penis into me deeper and deeper.

"Baby, don't talk. Just make love to me." I groaned with pleasure.

"Shit, it's just so good." He placed his mouth on the back of my neck, moaning and sucking uncontrollably as he gyrated inside of me.

My mouth was hanging on the bedroom floor. I was enjoying every second of our sinful act as he glided in and out with ease, hitting all the right spots.

"Baby, this side position is a fool," I murmured lightly.

Our lovemaking continued throughout the night. When our bodies released, his hot liquid potion ex-

ploded down my leg. An exhausted Dexter never withdrew. Instead, he drifted off inside of me.

When the television alarm flashed on at six in the morning, Dexter removed his flaccid organ. I repositioned my body.

Then he put his finger to my lips. "Shelby, don't go crazy. I was tired and I forgot to put on a condom."

I kissed his lips. "I know," I said calmly, already accepting that I was pregnant. "The damage was already done in New Orleans when that condom broke." I glanced up at our picture on the wall. "Dexter, it's beautiful. When did you get it framed?" It was the portrait of us kissing that the man painted in New Orleans.

"I don't mean to change the subject, but do you want me to go to the doctor with you?" he asked, rubbing my shoulders. "If it will make you feel better, we can get tested together."

Walking to the shower, I stated, "No, you can go to your own doctor and bring me back the results."

When I returned home from class I opened my bedroom door. Joel was still asleep with his head under the pillow. I was mad about him always sleeping in my bed when I wasn't home, but I was too sick to complain. I wrapped my arms around my waist to ease the stomach pain. I rushed to the toilet and released.

Joel lifted his head from under the pillow. "Are you throwing up again?"

"Yes, my stomach hurts. I think I have a virus. I feel fatigued and dizzy at times, and then other

times I'm fine." I rubbed my stomach. "I think I have to shit," I shouted.

"Thanks for sharing. I really wanted to know about you having to shit. By the way, Max called."

"So . . . Did he ask where I was?"

"No."

"FYI, I broke up with Max. I haven't been talking to him, and I don't plan to. I will not be returning any of his phone calls," I said defensively.

"Whatever. That's what women always say."

I sat on the toilet. "Come sit in front of the bathroom door, so we can finish talking."

"I am not Sebastian. He told me he used to sit on your bathroom floor. Girl, you crazy. I'm not the one. I don't want to watch you shit."

"I'm not defecating yet. I'm just sitting here relaxing, waiting for something to happen."

Joel sat on the floor in front of the bathroom. Indeed, he did exactly what he said he wasn't going to do.

"I told Max you'd be home around eight tonight."

"You what?"

"I didn't know you kicked him to the curb for ol' boy."

I started clapping. "Good performance. You knew exactly what was going on. You know how I feel about Dexter. I talk about him all the time. You drop me off at his house. Do I ever mention Max anymore?"

"I thought you were being a player," Joel said sarcastically.

I rolled my eyes. "I can't be a player. I can only handle one man at a time. That's why I ended things with Max."

Joel sighed. "Max is going to kick your ass about his best friend."

"Why do you think that?" I said, still sitting on the toilet.

"Cuz you're disrespecting the brother," Joel said, pointing his finger at me.

"You don't understand; I couldn't help it. I really like Dexter. He is the man of my dreams." I screamed, "The sex is good too. He is very blessed."

"I don't wanna hear about another man's dick," Joel shouted back. Then he mumbled under his breath, "I know Dexter shit ain't bigger than mine."

The doorbell rang several times, and we heard a loud thump. "Sounds like someone's at the door," Joel said, rushing to see where the noise was coming from. "You have a box at the door," he added, looking out of the window.

"I'll go get it," I bellowed, running down the stairs.

Max was standing in front of my door with the box. "The parcel people just dropped this off," Max said, handing me the package. "What's up, Shelby? I've called you several times, and you haven't returned any of my calls."

"Max, I thought I told you it was over."

"Just like that?" Max asked.

I saluted with my hand. "Yes. I told you that shit at Bryan's party. Don't act like you didn't understand."

"Stop playing games," Max yelled.

"I've been through drama with one man, and I will not go through it again."

"That boy wasn't a nigga," Max taunted.

"The definition of nigger is *a trifling person,* and that doesn't have a color," I hissed.

Max touched my waist. "Baby, let's talk about this."

I snapped, "Don't touch me. You talk about it with Nakia, Sapphire, and Sydney."

Max squinted. "Who have you been talking to?"

"It's not important. It just won't work," I said, swinging my head away from Max.

Max grabbed my hair, swung it to the side, and gazed at my neck. "What the hell is that on your neck?"

I rolled my eyes at Max. "What does it look like?"

Max came closer to me. "It looks like a motha-fuckin' passion mark. You doin' some ho-ass shit." His eyes bugged out. "Yo' ass been busy."

"Yes, very busy," I said assertively.

Max pointed his finger in my face. "Huh? Thought you were so saved? Living for the Lord? You been cheating?"

I slapped Max's hand. "Bitch, you never quit Sydney," I shouted.

The porch light came on, and Joel walked out-side. "What's up? Is everything cool?"

Max stared up at Joel. Then he rubbed his mus-tache. "Yeah, we straight."

Joel looked at me. "Shelby, are you two chill-ing?"

Max stepped up to me and mumbled. "You sleeping with him?"

Joel approached Max. His vast chest was bulging out. I could see the vehemence in his eyes. He was ready to kick Max's ass.

He was looking down at Max. "Scrub, please. If she was my woman, she wouldn't be out here with you."

I pushed on Joel's massive chest, trying to force him back in the door. "I'm fine."

Joel hesitated, but twenty seconds later, he walked back in the house.

I glared at Max. "I'm seeing someone else and it's not Joel."

Max repositioned the Twix bar in his pants. "I hope you aren't out there being a slut."

I licked my tongue out quickly. "Maybe." My tone became serious. "Things didn't work out between us, but we go way back. I still want to be your friend." I extended my hand.

Max pushed my hand away. "A handshake? I should be getting some pussy."

I extended my hand again, trying to be polite. He pushed it away.

"You are so ignorant and rude. My hand is the only pussy you'll get from me." I turned away and slammed the door in his face.

LUST TWENTY-TWO

The trees swayed from left to right as the breeze attacked their leaves and branches. It was a beautiful day to spend on the Gold Coast at the spa with girlfriends. I drove up to the cream-colored marble building in the circular driveway. I searched in the parking lot and spotted Megan's candy apple red convertible BMW with red leather seats. I knew it was her car because the license plate read GUCCI.

The valet attendant tapped my window to get my attention. He opened my door and took my keys, and another escort opened the door and walked me in. I was ready for my day of pampering. This place was full of rich women with big diamonds and designer handbags. Today I was one of them, hanging out at the S-P-A.

"Yes, I'm meeting Megan Cole," I expressed in my rich, arrogant voice. The lady escorted me to a dim, candle-lit waiting area. The scent of the aroma-therapy candle was divine. I glanced at the room. There was a place card in a brass frame, located in

the middle of the cocktail table, which read COLE PARTY. I was impressed. To the right of us there was a crystal pitcher of ice water filled with lemons, oranges, and limes.

I greeted Megan and Kelly with hugs. "This is nice, Megan," I said, pouring a glass of water.

"Only the best for me and my girls," Megan rejoiced.

"Here, Kelly." I handed her a bag before taking a seat on the suede sofa.

"So, girl, tell us about the proposal," Kelly ordered eagerly.

"The next day, after the slumber party, Victor took me on a carriage ride. The driver gave me a box wrapped in pink glossy wrapping paper, topped with a light-green bow. He told me not to open it until after the ride. The package was the size of a hatbox, so I didn't think anything. When we completed the ride, as the horse and carriage were trotting off, I noticed a banner on the back of the carriage. It read MEGAN, I LOVE YOU. WILL YOU MARRY ME?"

She ran in place. "I peeped down at the box in my hand and I tore into it. There was a ring inside and keys to my new 2004 BMW 525."

"I saw that bad baby outside with the Gucci license plate."

"Isn't it lovely? I'm finally a real diva with an updated BMW," Megan said as she peeped in Kelly's bag.

"What's in the bag, Shelby?" Kelly asked as she fumbled with the bag I had given her.

Kelly's eyes were gaping as she opened the bag and removed the tissue paper. "A Gucci purse,

thank you." Kelly jumped in her seat. "I have never owned a real designer purse, only fake flea market duplicates. Thank you so much, darling."

"You're welcome. Thank your boss too. He paid big bucks for it."

"Blair and I received Gucci key chains, and she gets a purse," Megan hissed, staring at herself in the mirrored table.

I blew a kiss at Megan. "I love you too, baby. Stop being so selfish. You have a hundred Gucci purses."

The escort reentered the room with Blair and four cream robes. She issued a room to each one of us. Then she directed us to the dressing area.

Blair shouted from her dressing room. "I have to take off all my clothes?"

We all answered in unison. "Yes, silly."

One female and three male masseuses entered the Cole Party waiting room. I wasn't letting a woman rub on my body, so I leaped in front of the first man I saw. "I'm ready."

Then Blair came out. "Oh, baby. I have to have a man."

Kelly was the last one out. "I don't have a problem with a woman."

All of us were seated on clear, warm mattresses for our hydrotherapy massages. The girls didn't know it, but Megan was paying, so I could get the works. The man pulled down my towel and began to work magic. His hands were miraculous. He massaged the oils into my skin as I lay on my stomach. I forgot about all my problems. Hell, I fell asleep.

When I awoke, I asked for a leg and full bikini

wax. Megan said she got them all the time because Victor loved it. Hell, I was in a new relationship and I was willing to try anything. Plus, I wanted to go swimming and I couldn't have wild hairs hanging out. I hated to see women at the beach with big Afros peeping out between their legs.

I pointed to my vagina. "I want it all off. A Brazilian wax, please."

I proceeded out of the massage room feeling rejuvenated. The essence of the oils covered my tan body. My soft skin was glistening. *I am reborn. A new creature. A new character. A diva.*

The escort spoke. "Ladies, follow me to the pedicure spa."

Blair hit my arm. "Damn, Shelby and Megan. What took you two so long?"

The four of us followed.

"Kelly and I were through twenty minutes ago."

"I have special needs, since I have a new man."

Kelly spun around. "Are you sexing Dexter? I know he's not always playing golf. You two spend a lot of time together."

I lied, "I'm not having sex with Dexter yet, but I will be soon."

"There is no need to have a man with a big dick if you're not going to screw him," Kelly said, waving her finger side to side.

Blair tapped my shoulder. "I saw you two on the dance floor at the party."

I smacked my lips. "I saw you and Sapphire too."

"Yeah, girl, what's up with that?"

"Sapphire is bisexual," Blair replied.

"No joke," Kelly said, bopping Blair on the forehead.

Blair began to speak, "Sapphire has a crush on me. She said she started to tongue-kiss me the night of Bryan's birthday in front of everybody. She's trying to turn me out, but I'm all about dick. Bryan and I are considering marriage in the future. There is nothing a woman can do for me."

Blair chuckled then looked at Shelby. "Sapphire said she used to have a crush on you in high school, but you had too much mouth and attitude."

A look of detest covered my face. "That nasty ho wanted my man, and I threatened to kick her ass. That's why she doesn't like me."

Blair put her hand up. "I'm going to spank you. You're cursing again. You told us to remind you."

"Don't try to change the subject. I told you I was on a ho stroll. I curse and do whatever else I want. Now what's up with you?"

Megan opened her mouth. "Blair, we were starting to think you were gay."

Blair stuck her middle finger up at me and Megan. "That's the one sin I will never commit. I can't see myself nibbling on another's woman cat or vice versa."

I squinted. "Just be careful, because the girl is desperate and sick. I've diagnosed her as bi-polar."

The girls sang, "She will, Mother Shelby."

LUST TWENTY-THREE

It was seven o'clock on the dot and Dexter was at my house with dinner. Every Thursday he cooked or bought something for us to eat. Tonight I was eager to see him. I had some news that just couldn't wait and I didn't want to discuss it over the phone. The bell barely rang once before I snatched the door open. I had been looking out the window since ten minutes before seven awaiting his visit.

"Sit down," I said impatiently, brushing a dry kiss on his cheek, escorting him to the kitchen table.

"You're acting weird. Are you pregnant?" Dexter asked, rubbing his forehead.

I rubbed my stomach. A tear rolled down my red cheek. I looked down. I didn't respond.

Dexter rubbed his hands through my hair. "Baby, it's okay. Talk to me."

I lifted my head and stared into his light brown eyes. "I went to the doctor today." Another tear

crept out. "You said you loved me," I whimpered, "and that if I was pregnant you'd take care of me."

Dexter embraced my hands. "Yeah, baby. I meant that." He kissed my wet cheek. "I love you."

I put my fingernail in my mouth. "Will you still love me when I tell you what I'm about to tell you?"

"Yes," Dexter said quickly, growing impatient.

"I'm not pregnant," I blurted out with the biggest smirk.

I'd never been so happy in my life when the doctor gave me my results. I just knew my life was over and I'd end up another statistic. However, a part of me—an exceptionally small part—would have loved to carry Dexter's seed. But the way I felt, we had plenty of time to make babies after I finished school and we were married.

"You know what? You are so dramatic," he replied, and handed me a warm bag of food. "I told you, you weren't pregnant, but you were so paranoid and worried."

"I know. I was scared."

Dexter touched my cheek. A somber picture painted his face. "I kind of wanted to have a shorty by you. A beautiful daughter who looked just like you. We could've named her Savannah," he articulated softly, "after my grandmother that passed away." Dexter snickered. "I'm going to get you pregnant one day. Except, when I do, you'll be Mrs. JeanPierre."

I blushed, loving every word I was hearing. I kissed his hand. "I love you so much."

He beamed with joy. "I love you too, with all your drama."

"Speaking of drama, I have more news for you. The doctor said I have no STD's and no HIV. So I guess you were telling the truth."

Dexter waved me off. "The only condom that has ever broken has been with you. Explain that shit to me. And I've fuck . . ."

I looked at Dexter. "And you've fucked some hoes in your life. . . . Is that what you were going to say?"

"What I'm saying is, I have safe sex. I went raw in you, but that's it. I keep my shit covered. You the only one."

"Well, I have the birth control patch for backup, since we can't seem to keep condoms from breaking."

Dexter giggled and went on to say that I was the reason the condom broke. He said I was too wild in New Orleans.

Dexter smiled. "Let's eat. Bryan told me about this rib joint on 159th Street in Markham. Let me know how it tastes." He gazed at me intently.

I opened the bag. There were slabs of ribs, rib tips, hot links, French fries, coleslaw, and a slim Zales box. I opened the box. A gold diamond tennis bracelet was inside. I was so excited. I reached to kiss Dexter.

"Thank you."

Dexter reached to put the bracelet on my wrist.

"Kelly told me you wanted a new tennis bracelet."

I smiled frantically as he clasped the bracelet shut. "It's three carats. I wanted this. It's much bigger than my other tennis bracelet. You are so

sweet. I'll have to thank Kelly too. I didn't think she ever paid any attention to what I liked. I've always wanted a man who would be attentive to my needs and desires."

Dexter laughed. "Here I am. I'm ready to do anything and everything to please you. My job is to make you happy. If I can make you smile and laugh, then I've accomplished my goal."

I loved the way the ribs were slapped on top of the fries and drenched with barbecue sauce.

"If Bryan recommended the place, I knew it would be good."

Dexter placed a fry in my mouth.

Then I tasted the ribs. They were delicious. I wiped my mouth and swallowed. "I don't want you to think I'm keeping any secrets. Guess who came by this morning?"

"Max already told me he came by. He's pissed off too. I'm going to tell my boy what's up."

"No," I yelled out.

"Why?" Dexter asked.

"He'll kill me. Let's wait a while," I pleaded.

"He wouldn't kill you. If I told Max how I felt about you, he'd give us his blessing. You haven't given him a chance. That's my best friend, and I can't live like this. I have to be honest with my boy."

I turned my head away. "Please wait." I sighed.

Dexter turned my face back to his. He kissed the barbecue sauce off my lips.

He paused. "Anything for you."

We walked upstairs to my bedroom.

"I have something for you too. I keep on forgetting to give this to you."

Dexter turned the television on and sat down on my bed. I passed him a big bag. He opened it. "You didn't. These shoes were over four hundred dollars." He picked them up and touched the leather. "I love them."

I flopped down next to him, and he planted kisses on my neck and ear.

Minutes later, his whole demeanor changed.

I clutched his hands. "What's wrong?"

His eyes focused on the chair in my room. His expression displayed rage. I had never seen him look so mad before. "Did you sleep with Max last night? He told me you did."

I turned my head quick. "Hell no," I shouted.

He walked to my dresser. Dexter told me he didn't believe Max, until he noticed the male boxers in my chair and the diamond-studded earring on my dresser.

"Shelby, your ears aren't pierced, and Max has that same earring," Dexter said, brushing me off.

My heart began to flutter. "Baby, those are Joel's belongings. He slept in my room the other night when I was with you."

Dexter pulled me close to his body. "Don't lie to me, baby."

I caressed his hand. "I would never lie to you. I thought we were better than this. Don't you trust me?"

He whispered, "Yes, I trust you. I trust you too much. Girl, you just make me crazy."

"I see," I sighed.

I reassured Dexter that I loved him and I would never jeopardize our relationship.

I looked up at him. "I'm crazy too. I'm crazy in love with you."

He gazed into my eyes. "I love you too, Shelby. I love you more than you realize. I love you so much, I feel like a little bitch sometimes."

I stood on my tiptoes and reached my arms around his neck and our lips met. He hugged my small waist and caressed my bottom as our tongues explored each other's mouth. Dexter carried me to my bed, and we made love.

LUST TWENTY-FOUR

A s I sat in class, my mind drifted. There was no way I was packing up and moving to California. I'd probably stay in Chicago when I finished medical school. I couldn't give my all to a man who wasn't my husband.

Dr. Myru approached me. "Well, Shelby, you'll be done soon. Have you applied for any jobs?"

I looked down. "Not yet," I replied.

"I may be able to help you out. I have connections in Louisiana. That's if you want to move," Dr. Myru suggested.

My eyes brightened. Dexter's hometown, which would be nice if he was there. "What about New Orleans?"

"I have connections at Tulane, West Jefferson, Charity Hospital, and Earl K. Long in Baton Rouge. Just let me know."

"Thank you. I will."

"Oh, what time are you meeting Megan? She told me you guys were going shopping for dresses."

"I'm meeting her in the train station when I leave here," I said.

Dr. Myru handed me his platinum American Express card. "Tell her to knock herself out."

I took the card and put it in my purse. "Thank you. You shouldn't have. I won't buy too much." I laughed. "I'll give it to Megan. She'll be thrilled. I bet she'll buy another pair of shoes."

While walking rapidly toward the train, my cell phone rang.

"Hey, sweetie, just giving you the four-one-one. Max and Bryan are having a surprise going away party for Dexter at the Kat's Meow next Thursday night. By any chance, have you told Max about you and Dexter?" Blair asked.

I was so tired of people asking if I told Max yet. I was through with Max, so I really didn't see what the big deal was. It wasn't like Max and I were dating exclusively.

"Stay out my business," I replied, with attitude. "It's over between Max and me. And Dexter is moving to California, so it doesn't matter."

"Girl, Dexter is only going to be in California for a second. He is certainly moving back to Chi-town."

"Cool, if he does or doesn't . . . Blair, I'll be at the party."

"Good. We can hang tight. The girls are coming too. Max won't bother . . ." The roaring sound of the train drowned out her last sentence.

"Blair," I yelled. The phone went dead as I walked down the cement stairs leading to the subway. I took a quick look at the spray-painted graffiti

on the cement wall, which read SHELIA LOVES RALPH. I was in love again and I felt like telling everyone in world, except Max.

I slid my ticket in the machine and twisted through the steel bars. I glanced around looking for Megan. I noticed four guys wearing baggy pants with their hats cocked to the right, standing around shooting dice. I strapped my purse strap across my chest, hoping no one would notice my paranoid behavior.

I discovered Megan. She was wearing her beautiful one-carat diamond *M* necklace, platinum diamond engagement ring, two three-carat diamond tennis bracelets, and was carrying her large red Gucci purse. Megan knew better, looking like a Beverly Hills queen in the subway. She didn't see me, so I decided to sneak up on her. I walked briskly in her direction.

Before I could make it to her, I noticed one of the guys in baggy pants running up behind her. I yelled out, "Megan, run."

She didn't hear me. I dashed toward her with high speed.

The man snatched her purse. Then he reached for her neck.

Megan swung around real fast.

The guy pointed to his belt. "Give me your necklace," he barked.

"You're not getting shit. Give me back my damn purse. That's a two-thousand-dollar purse," Megan screeched.

The guy grabbed her waist and put his hand over her mouth. "Shut up, bitch."

Tears streamed down Megan's face, but her cries were muffled.

I was terrified. I rambled in my purse as I ran. I screamed, "Help."

Looking around, there was no cop in sight. My heart started beating extremely fast. I was afraid he was going to harm her. I looked for my cell phone, and that was when I located my pepper spray. I pulled the safety notch out.

The man didn't see me. He was too busy wrestling with Megan. She wasn't letting him have her necklace.

I was so scared that, without thinking, I snuck up behind the punk and squirted the pepper spray in the corner of his eyes. The fool fell and let out an earsplitting cry. I looked down at his face. He couldn't have been older than sixteen. I sprayed him again directly in both of his eyes. He rumbled on the ground, not able to move his hands to comfort his face.

Megan snatched her purse from his shocked hands. After that she took the heel of her shoe and stomped the guy in his stomach. The noise "UUMM" came from his mouth.

"You piece of trash," she hollered.

The train was roaring in, and silver and blue sparks were flying from the rails. We ran as fast as we could to catch the train. I peeped back, but the man still hadn't gotten up. The doors slid open and people hurried through. We entered the train and scurried through each car quickly.

The train took off. We stood in one place, holding onto the steel bars above our heads.

"Thank you," Megan shrieked as we hugged each other.

"You better give the next thief all of your stuff," I teased.

"Girl, I wasn't giving up my thousand-dollar necklace and my Gucci purse. I had five hundred dollars in my purse and credit cards." Megan laughed nervously as she looked for her hand sanitizer.

I handed her Dr. Myru's credit card. "Your honey told me to give this to you. Material things come and go. They can be replaced, but your life can't. Are you okay?" I asked.

"Yes. Remember, I was mugged on the subway last year, and I promised I would never let another poor motherfucker steal anything else I worked hard to get," Megan lectured, rubbing her hands with the clear gel.

"Well, let's just thank God that we're both okay."

One tear dropped out of Megan's left eye. "Shelby, thank you for having my back."

"Now let's go find you a wedding dress," I said, trying to change things to a more cheerful mood.

LUST TWENTY-FIVE

It was Thursday night and the Kat's Meow sign was lit up with neon purple lights. I arrived early. There was no way I was missing my man's going-away party. I knew I would feel awkward with Max being there, but I was willing to make some sacrifices, even if it meant embarrassment and being put on "front street."

I walked in the dark place, painted in purple and orange. It was very retro-looking. The wall lamps had orange lights. In the Kitty Lounge, purple velvet couches were lined up against the wall. Behind each sofa were huge, round aquariums built into the panel. There were also round mirror cocktail tables in front of each sofa. Rotating silver disco balls were hanging down from the ceiling, centered in the middle of each table.

I sat at the bar, which was decorated in black with purple velvet trimming, studying the fish as they swam around in the huge square customized aquarium.

My purse vibrated from my cell phone. "Hello," I answered.

"Hey, sweetie. I'll be over late tonight. Max and I are going out," Dexter informed me.

"Okay. I'm going out too."

"With who?"

"Blair and Kelly."

"See you around eleven," he said, unruffled.

I looked at the receiver of the phone. "You'll be back that soon?"

"Yes, I can't stay away from you that long. I want to spend all the time I have left with you. There isn't a thing in the streets for me."

"I love you," I whispered.

"I love you too."

I spotted Blair, Bryan, and Sapphire sitting at a sofa way in the back of the room. My hot pink, low-cut dress clung to my body as I pranced to the back. I took a seat next to Blair and crossed my legs, which were fully exposed by the two slits in my dress.

"I'm glad you came," Blair said, grinning.

"Well, I was in the neighborhood," I said, sounding like I just rehearsed the line.

"Hey, Shelby," Bryan said while extending his hand. "Max will be so happy to see you."

Blair interrupted, "Not!"

We shared a smile.

Bryan looked shocked. "So you and my boy broke up? He didn't tell me that."

I laughed softly. "Yes, I ended things with the *pimp player*."

"Would you ladies like a drink?" Bryan asked.

"Sprite," I answered promptly.

"What?" Blair asked, alarmed by my drink request.

"Blair, I don't drink anymore," I replied hastily.

"Whatever. You change with the wind. One minute you're saved, the next minute you're not. The cycle continues. Baby, bring me an apple martini."

"Make that two," Sapphire said, holding up two fingers. "Shelby is what you call a backslider," Sapphire said boldly.

I breathed heavily and let out a dry laugh. "I'm not drinking because of school. And, yes, I'm still a Christian. But I'm not practicing now. I'm what the preachers call a chameleon Christian. I blend in with my environment." I giggled as I watched Bryan walk to the bar.

Sapphire rose quickly, wiggling her tight, short, blue spandex skirt down. "Bryan, I'm coming with you. I'll help you carry those drinks," she said in a prissy voice.

"She's disgusting," I squealed.

"Shelby, don't start. Sapphire is cool," Blair voiced, proudly.

"I just get bad vibes from her, and it has nothing to do with her liking Sebastian or dating Joel in the past," I admitted.

Before Blair could respond, Kelly greeted us with a drink in her hand. "Are you two talking about that stank ho?" she slurred.

"Of course. Ms. Goodie doesn't like her," Blair mocked.

"I don't either. The bitch thinks she looks better than me," Kelly exclaimed. Then she took a sip from her drink.

"Honey, everything isn't always about you," Blair said.

"Well, you better watch her around your man," Kelly stuttered.

"I'm not worried about Sapphire. She likes women," Blair testified nonchalantly.

"And men." Kelly pushed her chest up. "Huhh. If she is really gay, I know she would've come on to me by now," Kelly bragged, stammering over her words.

I interrupted. "Lush, everybody doesn't want you."

"Miss Holy, don't be jealous, because she doesn't want you anymore," Kelly expressed amusingly.

"What are you drinking?" I inquired.

"Gin and juice, of course. Don't act like you don't know my drink. Gin makes you sin, all night long," Kelly bawled as she swirled her hips.

"You better watch yourself," I lectured.

"I don't plan on being an alcoholic. I know how to control myself. This is just my fourth drink tonight, bitch. Go have a baby if you want to boss someone around."

"Bitch, you were 'Ned-the-Wino' drunk when you came. How did you get here anyway?" Blair asked Kelly amusingly.

"Kevin dropped me off."

Blair gazed at her. "Why didn't he come in?"

Kelly puckered her lips. "Darling, I party alone. You know I don't like Kevin. He just gives me a free place to live." Kelly changed the subject. "Well, is Megan coming?"

"I don't know," Blair replied.

Kelly made a noise as if she was clearing her throat. "That rich bitch spends all her time with that short-ass African."

Blair turned to Kelly and gestured for her to have a seat on the sofa. "Shut up. You must have had a pint of gin before you came here."

Kelly nodded, smacked her lips, and plopped down on the sofa. "Of course. I am a bartender; I drink for free all day and night."

Blair turned to me, shaking her head. "Please prescribe an anti-psychotic for your girl. Anyway, Megan told me you guys were attacked in the subway."

"Yeah, it was a pretty scary moment, but we did what we had to do," I said nervously.

Blair covered her mouth with her hand. Then she pointed at two girls who were standing across the room. "Look, aren't those the girls who were at Bryan's party?"

Kelly cackled loudly, "Those whores come to the shop all the time, smelling up Dexter and Max's ass."

"Yes. That's the bitch I busted Max with in front of the barbershop, the other one is Dexter's old girlfriend," I explained.

Kelly smacked her fist against the palm of her hand. "We oughta cut them bitches up."

I rolled my eyes at Kelly. She was drunk, talking out of her mind. I didn't know why Kevin let her come out in her condition. The new job at Gentlemen's Touch did nothing to help her drinking problem. An alcoholic had no business working as a bartender.

"Come on, y'all, let's slash 'em up," Kelly slurred.

"Please, I wouldn't dare fight over a man," I pronounced arrogantly.

Blair grunted, "You wanted to fight that little nerd girl Persia over Sebastian."

"Don't remind me. I was a young fool back in the day. Hell, I was one the other day. Joel and I saw her, and I started to whip her ass again."

Blair remembered everything. She was always bringing up the past. I was ashamed of my past behavior. I couldn't believe I let Sebastian, out of all people, make an ass out of me.

Blair snapped her fingers in my face. "Bryan and Max think Dexter hooked back up with some ex-girlfriend in New Orleans. I overheard them talking about a mark he had on his neck when he came back from his New Orleans trip. I wanted to tell them, 'If you only knew.' They were saying how funny he has been acting now and how he hardly hangs out. I don't know what Dexter has told them, but they are in the dark."

I couldn't stop laughing as I listened to Blair, watching Bryan and Sapphire advancing in our direction with the drinks.

"Sapphire is so thoughtful. Nobody else bothered to help my man, but she did," Blair stated, licking her tongue out smugly.

"Why did you pierce your tongue? Sapphire has you doing some wild things. I can deal with your different hair colors and styles every week, even the crazy nail designs, but I can't get with the tongue-piercing."

"Chill out, chick. They can hear you."

Bryan and Sapphire were standing right in our

face, so I smiled and thanked Bryan for my drink. Sapphire thanked Bryan also. Then she and Kelly walked to the other side of the lounge.

"Sapphire seems to be a really nice girl," Bryan shared.

I shook my head, wondering what was really going on between her and Blair.

"I don't care what Shelby thinks about Sapphire, she's still my girl. The girl really supported me with some personal issues. I was on the verge of having a nervous breakdown. We complement one another. It doesn't matter that she's gay. I know eventually, one day, she's going to turn her life around. She's changing now. I notice something different about her each day. She prays with my child, and she reads the Bible to him," Blair confessed.

I wasn't in the mood to hear any more testimony about Sapphire, so I excused myself. "I'm going next door to the movie room."

Bryan looked at me. "Shelby, bring me back four hotdogs and some nachos."

"I can't carry all of that. I'll get Kelly and Sapphire to help me," I said as Blair handed me twenty dollars.

The movie room was painted in black and was bustling with activity. There was a bar across one end of the room and a movie screen at the other. They even had popcorn, hotdogs, and nachos. I looked at the movie seats, which had long bar tables across the front of the chairs. I was impressed. It reminded me of the desks in huge college auditorium classes. There were small round cocktail tables and chairs located around the front of the

screen. People were getting their drink on while watching *Dolomite* play on the huge movie screen. I took a seat at the bar next to the girls.

"They only show old-school, black movies," Sapphire volunteered to tell me.

"Hi, Sapphire. I'm sorry for not speaking to you earlier," I said.

"I'm sorry too. I avoided looking at you on purpose because you're always avoiding me," she said.

"I can be a bitch sometimes," I admitted.

Sapphire giggled. "I know. I don't want you, if that's what you're worried about."

Kelly put her drink down and smirked. "Well, since we're being honest, why don't you want me?"

"Please, Kelly. We are too much alike. The blind can't lead the blind," Sapphire replied.

Kelly caressed her breast. "Okay, that's cool."

"Anyway, I'd have to kick your ass about all those men," Sapphire said, laughing, almost falling off the stool.

"I need another gin and juice," Kelly informed the bartender.

I looked at the bartender. "I think she's had enough. Give me four hotdogs and some nachos with cheese and jalapeños."

The bartender looked at me in disbelief. "I see you're a hungry little lady."

I smirked. "The food is for my friend."

Sapphire glimpsed at me. "You must be talking about Bryan. He is a fat, greedy-ass bastard. He comes by Blair's house and eats up all the damn food. We can't keep groceries because of his gluttonous ass."

Minutes later, Blair stepped in the room. "Come

on, girls. Max just called. They're on their way in," Blair said joyfully.

I handed Blair the hotdogs then seized Kelly's hand, and we followed Blair back to the other side. We sat at our VIP sofa near the entrance of the lounge. Kelly sprawled her body down and rested her head on the armrest.

I glared across the room. The place was over-flowing with all types of men. I snuck a quick peek at Kandace, Dexter's sister. I didn't want her to see me. She was sitting near the back of the room with her man. Kandace only knew me as Dexter's woman. She had no idea I used to date Max, and I wanted to keep it that way. The room was packed. If I kept my distance, she wouldn't notice me. I just prayed she didn't ask Dexter about me in front of Max.

The two guys stepped in. Max pranced in first, looking as if he was going to a prom. Dexter walked in behind him.

"Surprise," everyone shouted.

He turned his head, twisting his body around to see if they were yelling at someone else.

Dexter threw his arms out. "For me?"

My baby was looking good. I did an entire body check on him. He wore what looked like a black linen Ralph Lauren suit and his black Gucci shoes I bought him in New Orleans. Underneath his jacket, he wore a fitted tan shirt, which displayed every muscle bulge in his chest. He caught my eye as well as the eye of almost every other single woman in the place. I noticed their gawking eyes the minute my sweetheart walked into the room.

I looked at Dexter and mouthed, "I love you." I

knew he would keep our affair on the down low tonight. There was no way he was going to start any confusion with Max. As for me, there was no need to tell Max, since it was over between us and Dexter was leaving next week.

Bryan, Max, and Dexter huddled in a circle and embraced one another.

"We're going to miss you, brotha," the boys sincerely expressed.

"Give us a round of Amstel Lights and three shots of Courvoisier," Max yelled to the bartender.

They retired to the sofa next to ours. The bartender brought back three bottled beers and three shots.

"Attention. Attention. Can a starving man get some food in this place? Just kidding. Max has an announcement," Bryan yelled.

"I would like to announce a toast to Dexter, who is my boy, my brother, and my best friend. I wish you well with your dreams, goals, and endeavors in life. You deserve the world, and I love you, man."

Following Max's speech, the crowd swarmed in on Dexter to wish him well. I tracked his every move with my eyes.

Kandace and her friend were two of the last people to greet Dexter. After she congratulated him, I saw Dexter directing her my way. "Hey, Shelby. What am I going to do without my brother?" she said sadly. Then she embraced me. "Please continue to visit, just not at two in the morning." She chuckled.

"Oh, Kandace, these are my friends, Blair, Kelly, and Sapphire."

Blair gave me an astounding stare. Indeed, I

frightened myself when I introduced Sapphire as my friend.

"Nice meeting you, ladies," Kandace replied.

"The feeling is mutual," Sapphire retorted eagerly.

"Look who's walking up to Dexter," Blair instigated.

It was Joy, Dexter's funky little ex-girlfriend. I felt a twinge in my heart; jealousy was setting in.

Blair looked at me. "Don't get up, Shelby."

I rose anyway.

"I thought you didn't fight over men," Blair taunted.

I sauntered directly toward them.

"Somebody grab that crazy rascal," Blair screeched, shaking Kelly's body.

Kelly sprung up out of her stupor and passed me up. She dashed for Dexter, almost pushing the girl out of the way. "Honey, let's go," she bellowed, seizing his hand.

Joy waved. "Congratulations, Dex."

"Thank you," Kelly answered before he could.

I looked back at Blair. "What is that bimbo doing?" is what I think she asked, but I couldn't hear clearly from that far distance.

Dexter seized Kelly's hand and followed her.

I was right behind them, headed to the movie lounge. Kelly's arm firmly wrapped itself around Dexter's waist, as if she was staking her "claim," but winked at me. They headed to a dark area in the movie room. I could see Dexter grinning as Kelly whispered in his ear. I smiled knowing my girl had my back.

Blair sprinted past me and reached out to grab

Kelly away from Dexter, but noticed Kelly escorting Dexter directly to a table for me and him to sit at.

"Here you go," Kelly spoke with flushed cheeks. She turned to Blair and looked down at her hand like it was trash. "What are you doing?"

"Oh. I . . . I . . . was . . ." Blair mumbled speechlessly.

"You dirty bitch. You thought I was sneaking off with Dexter," Kelly verbalized in an angry tone.

"Well, hell, yeah," Blair clamored.

"I wouldn't do that to my friend. I can see that man is her soul mate. I helped get them together. And, besides, we don't have the same taste in men," Kelly expressed defensively.

Blair looked at Kelly and noticed the anger and hurt displayed in her face.

"Everyone is capable of changing. Blair, you out of all people should know that," Kelly said nervously, almost in tears.

Blair held Kelly in her arms. "I'm sorry."

Kelly rushed off. "I just need to be alone."

Blair followed her. I wanted to chase after her, but I wanted to be with my man too.

Dexter touched my back. I turned around slowly. He caressed my lips with his passionate kisses. My salty tears almost drowned us. I started to tremble uncontrollably. My heart ached. I gasped for breath.

He stopped kissing me and wiped my tears away with his hands. "What's wrong, sweetheart?"

"I'm going to miss you," I cried, not believing I was breaking down in front of Dexter. I had held

my tears in for weeks, and today my emotions exploded.

"Baby, I'm going to miss you too. I don't know what I'm going to do without you, but this isn't the end," Dexter moaned.

Too many emotions were roaring inside of me, and we were in a public place. I pushed Dexter away. "Go back next door and mingle with your guests. We'll talk later." I tried hard to shift my emotions.

He didn't argue. "I want to be with you tonight," he said, while kissing me on the cheek.

I watched Dexter walk next door. Then I wiped my face and reapplied more spice gold lipstick. I was truly in love with Dexter. We had a spiritual connection. I didn't love him based upon false promises, because he made none. He was spontaneous, caring, and giving. He put me first in every aspect of his life. Dexter was the man I had dreamed about. We were destined to be together, and I was willing to wait for him.

I toddled back into the Kitty Lounge and sat at the first sofa available. Then I looked around the room in search of Kelly and Blair, but they were nowhere to be seen. Shortly, I spotted Sapphire at a sofa snuggled up with a red-haired woman.

"Hi, darling, why are you sitting here alone?" Max asked in a flirty tone.

I turned around, taking my eyes off of Sapphire and her new lover. "What is it to you?" I replied, annoyed by his audacious behavior.

"I really want to make things right."

"Make things right by being a good friend. We just weren't meant to be lovers," I voiced sternly.

"Shelby, I won't stop trying until you're all mine again."

"Max, that won't happen."

Max clutched my hand and kissed it. "You my baby. I will always love you."

"Stop, Max." I pulled my hand away.

"Shelby, you are the woman I plan to marry."

"Oh, really? So you ho around and do what you want to do and then you want to settle down with someone like me? Why lead people on if you can't be faithful to them?"

"Hell, somebody else might snatch them up," Max stated.

"Well, Max, I'm not the same naive little girl you got over on in the past. I've been snatched up."

"When? By who?" Max asked, nudging me.

"While you were out playing games and pimping whores. And don't worry about by who." I glanced over at Dexter. He was drinking another beer.

"Would you like another drink?" Max asked.

"Sure. A virgin cranberry splash," I said anxiously to get Max away from me.

As soon as Max strutted off to the bar, I heard a whisper in my ear. "What were you and your little boyfriend fussing about? Looked like things got heated up," Dexter said.

I pulled his suit jacket. "Were you jealous? I like it when you're jealous, baby."

"Never that." He smoothly walked away with Bryan.

"Come on, man. Let's get another beer," Bryan urged him.

Minutes later, Max returned. "Here you go," he said, handing me the drink.

"Thank you," I replied.

"So where were we?"

I told him we weren't anywhere. I made it clear that there was no way we were getting back together. "I'm celibate," I shouted unexpectedly.

"Yeah, yeah . . . you been celibate. That's good. That's exactly how I want my woman to be," Max boasted.

"What?"

"You need to be sex-free until we get married." Max laughed quietly.

"You really should've made a career out of your humor," I teased.

A woman marched up to us. "Are you going to talk to her all evening?" She looked at Max annoyingly. Then she gave me a gaze that could kill.

I placed my hand out, gesturing to Max. Then I spoke to her in a very composed manner. "Wait, Nakia. Isn't your name Nakia?"

She rolled her eyes and nodded.

I continued. "Max and I are just friends. I'm no threat to you anymore," I said, emphasizing *anymore*.

Max ignored what I said. He had no mercy. "Look, Nakia I'm talking to Shelby right now. When I get a second, I'll come handle you. Don't ever interrupt one of my conversations again," he said then shoved her off.

She caught her balance and apologized, "Okay, baby, I'm sorry."

I was astonished. Nakia frolicked off. I don't know what I was thinking, but Max was surely controlling and violent. I'm glad I didn't go back to the way I was. Max would be pimping me and beat-

ing my ass too. "Max, go talk to your woman, you're blocking my action," I sneered. "But thanks for the drink." I strutted off toward Sapphire.

Max caught up with me and yanked my arm. "Shelby, we still need to talk."

"I don't think so," I replied casually, pulling out of his grasp and hurriedly walking away.

I stood in front of Sapphire. "Sapphire, where are Blair and Kelly?" I repeated my statement a little louder. "Sapphire, I said, 'Where are Blair and Kelly?'"

She was too busy. Her lips were wrapped around the red-haired girl's ear, yet she managed to mumble, "I have no idea."

"How are you getting home?" I asked politely.

Sapphire answered abruptly, "I don't know. I'll ride with Bryan and Blair."

"Alrighty," I murmured, feeling like a fool. Sapphire wasn't paying any attention to me. The red-haired woman looked like she was going to get her groove on. I bet the two planned to head straight to the motel. Sapphire waved, with her head buried in the girl's neck. Then I flounced away.

"Pretty in pink, how are you doing? I've been watching you all night. What's your name?" a handsome man asked.

"I'm Kelly," I replied, for the fun of it.

"Can I have your number?" he asked.

"Sure," I stated swiftly and gave him Kelly's name and cell number.

"Kelly, can we go out?" he questioned.

"Just call me. What's your name?" I asked, as if I was interested.

"I'm Milton," he said seductively.

The golden-brown brother was fine. I was having fun flirting with him. He gave me something to do, since I was at the party alone. "Brother, your body is off the hook."

Suddenly, I was caught off guard by someone grabbing my waist from behind. A hard object chafed against my backside. I was aroused instantly. The masculine smell of the violator's cologne didn't make things any better, as tingling sensations vibrated throughout my body. I only knew one man who made me feel that way at just the smell of him, and that was Dexter.

Dexter enclosed his lips around my neck and sucked. I moaned, enjoying every split second.

"What's up, Dexter?" Milton said with a huge grin, interrupting our enticing moment. "I'm sorry, Dexter. I didn't know this beautiful woman was for you."

"What's up, Milt? It's all good. I just need to check my woman," he stated enthusiastically.

"See ya later, Kelly," Milton goaded.

I laughed silently and waved.

"Kelly?"

"I gave him Kelly's number. Just a little game I was playing."

Dexter embraced me tenderly. "I can't leave you alone for one second. Don't be making me jealous around here. I'll tear this motherfucker up."

I tried to squirm loose from his touch. "Max might see us."

"Girl, you were just letting me kiss you. Furthermore, fuck Max. I want the world to know I love you," Dexter roared.

I kissed Dexter's lips lightly in an attempt to

quiet him down. "Honey, there's a proper way to do things. We don't need to expose our relationship here."

"You're right. That's what I love about you. You always keep me in line."

"Go wrap things up so we can go get freaky."

"That what I'm talking about. I'm going to tell everyone good-bye," Dexter said, gesturing toward the bar.

"Shelby, what are you and Dex doing later on?" Kandace asked as she approached me. "I'm not coming home tonight, so the house is free," she joked.

She startled me, so it took time for me to answer her. "Your brother is a little buzzed, so that would be great."

"Girl, Max is drunk too, but then again that's nothing new. I saw him and his girl Nakia snuggled up together in the movie lounge.

She walked me to the front of the club. "Shelby, I've been meaning to ask you about your friend. He is so damn cute."

"Who?" I asked, stunned by her boldness.

"That fine *brotha* that is always dropping you off. I just knew he'd be here with you tonight," she exclaimed.

"Oh, Joel. I don't know where he is. I should've brought him with me because I hardly know anyone here," I explained.

"Tell him I asked about him," she said as she walked away.

I wandered to the movie area, still looking for Blair and Kelly. I found Kelly, all the way in the

back of the theater with her head down on the table, asleep.

I touched her shoulder. Kelly didn't move. "Are you okay?"

She looked up after a few seconds. Her eyeliner was smudged, her eyes wet and red.

"Is there something bothering you?" I asked, kneeling down next to her.

Kelly put her head down as more tears streamed down her face.

I clutched her. "Let's get out of here."

I located Dexter. "I'm going to take Kelly home. I'll meet you later."

"Is Kelly okay?" he asked.

I hunched my shoulders and kissed him quickly.

"What's wrong?" I asked Kelly as we sat in my car.

She didn't reply. I didn't know where we were going, but I had to find out what was bothering her.

"Would you like some coffee to help sober you up?"

She nodded.

I started the car and veered into traffic. I turned on the radio and Whitney Houston's song, "Miracle," played. I found the words relaxing. "*How can you throw away a miracle.*"

Kelly looked at me and started to cry.

"My singing isn't that bad, is it?"

"I . . . I . . ." More tears flowed down her face.

I had never seen strong, bold, outspoken Kelly cry this much. She was fine earlier, but then again she was loaded and now her high was gone, leav-

ing her depressed and sober to deal with her problem.

"Let me pull into Dunkin Donuts on Fifty-third
and Kentwood. It looks empty."

We found a cozy table in the back and ordered
two cappuccinos.

Kelly took a deep breath. "Shelby, this morning
I found out I have cancer."

"Oh, Kelly." I exhaled noisily. "You acted like
you were fine in the club."

"That's because I was drunk. I drank a quart of
gin before I came to the party. I drank until I was
numb." She blew her nose. "My entire uterus has
to be removed. The doctor found cancer cells all
over my uterus."

"Baby, I'm here for you," I said with tears in my
eyes.

Kelly laughed a little. After that, she closed her
eyes tight. "Girl, do you know how many babies
I've killed?" she whimpered.

"We all make mistakes. Your sin is no different
than anyone else's sins," I stated, trying to uplift
her spirits, remembering the Word I still had in
me.

"Shelby, you don't understand. I want to get
married one day. I want to have a house and kids.
Now, I might die." She wailed.

I reached to embrace her body. "We can get
through this. Cancer doesn't mean death anymore. My father has been in remission for over
twenty years."

"I'm scared. I feel bad. I haven't been a good
person or friend to any of y'all. If I die today, I'd
probably go to hell," she moaned.

"Kelly, repent and get your life together. If they take your uterus out, the cancer is gone."

Kelly smiled faintly. "I want to live. I promise I'll never hurt anyone of you again. I didn't mean to ignore you when you were with Sebastian, but I was hurting. He took you away from me. We were always together, and I felt that you abandoned me. You were all I had when my father died."

"I'm sorry. I didn't realize I was pushing you out of my life. Please forgive me for being so selfish. I'm here for you now. I'll never abandon you again," I expressed lovingly.

"Dance with My Father" by Luther Vandross played on the intercom in the donut shop. Kelly put her hands over her ears and moved her head from left to right. "This is a beautiful song, but I hate it. They need to change the song. Change the fucking song," she screamed. "My daddy is dead. How am I supposed to dance with him if he's gone?"

The worker in the donut shop looked our way. I mouthed that everything was okay, pulling Kelly's hands from her ears.

"I know you've been through a lot, and I know you have never dealt with your father's death. It's okay to cry. You need to grieve. Let it all out."

Kelly opened her mouth, but no words came out. Only moans. She put her head down and sobbed in her hands more. "Daddy, Daddy, I miss you. I love you. I never got a chance to say goodbye." She wept hysterically. "Who's going to love me like you did? Who's going to give me unconditional love? You were my everything, my best friend."

My eyes became watery as Kelly pounded her fist on the table.

"You were my world, my king. You were the only man who loved me." She howled.

I couldn't hold back my tears. Tears covered my face. "Baby, it's okay. Let it out," I yelled.

She continued to cry uncontrollably, while pounding her fist on the table. "Daddy, why did you have to leave me? Lord, why did You take away my sunshine? My sunshine is gone. My sunshine is gone. Daddy, I love you. Come back to me. I need you. I need you."

She continued, "Lord, I don't want to die too. I know you took my daddy for a reason. I'm just asking You to give me another chance at life. I'm going to do right. Please save and forgive me for all of the sins I've committed. Lord, I will change if You heal me."

I held Kelly tight. "Let's go. In the name of Jesus, everything is going to be okay."

Kelly sighed heavily. "You can drop me off at my mother's house. I need to tell her about my cancer."

LUST TWENTY-SIX

I arrived at Dexter's house late that night. The minute I stepped in the door, he swept me off my feet and carried me up the stairs. He pulled my dress off immediately and my panties down, sooner than I could speak. He lifted my body up and placed me on his shoulders, exposing my treasure to his face. He supported my back on the wall and began demolishing my inner recesses.

His spontaneity took me away, heightening the moment. My head swiveled as I enjoyed the act. His tongue moved in and out vivaciously. I held onto his head as his long tongue explored my insides. I jolted as my hand hit the wall, causing his clock to fall to the ground.

After several minutes had passed, Dexter put me down. "I'll be back." He returned with a condom on.

I opened my legs wide and touched myself. "Touch this. Look at how plump it is."

"I know how plump it is. I tasted it. Spread your legs open wider."

"Okay, but touch it first. See how plump it is."

He touched my pulsating, plump pussy. "God, Shelby, it's so moist and fat. Lay back and take this dick."

"Give it to me, daddy," I murmured lightly, as I obeyed his command, allowing his body to nestle between my legs.

"I'm going to give you all of this," Dexter said passionately.

I took all of him in as he thrust in and out of me at a steady flow. My toes contracted, and I began to giggle uncontrollably. "Baby, I love it," I screamed.

My body trembled, legs jerked, and vagina throbbed as the locomotion of Dexter's thrusting sped up. He was working his body like a porn movie on fast forward. "You are amaz . . . ing," I stuttered, unable to speak clearly from all of the excitement swirling up in me.

The whole adventure was tantalizing. I hadn't experienced so many orgasms in my life. He was in rare form. The alcohol had turned him into the Energizer Bunny because he kept going, going, and going.

"Baby, I can't keep up with you," I protested, almost out of breath as I gyrated in slow, mechanical movements.

"Just lay back and let me do all the work," he answered back, traveling further inside of me and quickening up his pace.

I was happy when he finally crumpled, because my body was depleted of energy. I thought about what my mother always said, "Don't let a man eat you. That makes you weak and fragile." She wasn't lying. I couldn't walk to the bathroom. Dexter had

to bring the washcloth to the bed. Moments later, my eyes shut of exhaustion.

The morning came quickly as the bright waves of the sun glared through the blinds. I looked over at Dexter. He was still asleep.

After I finished showering, I put on one of his T-shirts and I ran some bath water for him.

"Hey, girl," Kandace said in a chipper tone.

I jumped because she scared the hell out of me. "Good morning," I said startled. I turned the water off and walked downstairs with Kandace.

"Want some coffee and toast?" she asked.

"Sure," I replied. I sat at the table, and she began making the coffee and toast.

"You guys must've had a wild night. It's already nine o'clock. That's late for you two."

"Yes, our night was perfect," I said with the biggest grin ever.

"I'm glad yours was. I'm ready to dump my loser. He is such a nerd. He doesn't want to have sex, and I'm ready. I've been a virgin for too long."

"That's good. Stay a virgin until you get married," I said strongly.

Kandace put the coffee and toast on the table. "Humm . . . I know you and my brother are getting busy. You don't come here at two in the morning for nothing," she said sarcastically.

"You're right. We are having sex, but it's wrong. If I could do it all over again, I would wait until I'm married. We are sinning. Our lovemaking is cursed. After each act, I have to repent, and I feel bad about having to constantly repent. When you're a virgin,

you are in God's favor. You are pure. You don't have to worry about getting pregnant or catching venereal diseases. Premarital sex brings problems into relationships."

Kandace looked puzzled.

I winked at her. "You can't miss what you've never had. If you stay a virgin, you will be worry-free."

We heard shuffling sounds coming from upstairs.

"I guess your man is up," Kandace stated.

I took a bite of my toast, not wanting to appear anxious. I was looking forward to bathing Dexter. "Do me a favor; call me before you decide to have sex. I'll give you a hundred reasons not to."

Kandace smiled. "Thank you, Shelby."

I took another bite of my toast and fled up the stairs.

Dexter was so damn sexy. He was piddling around his room in his boxers.

"Good morning, my love." I greeted him with a kiss and a hug. We stayed embraced for a while. Dexter hugged me tight.

I noticed one tear rolling down his right brown eye. "I love you with all my heart," he whispered into my left ear.

"I love you too," I said hoarsely. I was on the verge of breaking down in tears again. "I can't cry again," I repeated to myself several times.

"Hey, you, I ran your bath water," I whispered seductively. I took his hand, led him to the bathroom, and pulled his boxers off. He entered the hot water filled with bubbles. Then I caressed his back and wiped it in a circular motion. Next, I lo-

cated my favorite part of his body. My hand moved up and down the familiar part.

Dexter looked at me. "You ready for round two?"

I gave him a dirty look. "Don't start. I'm still sore from last night."

"Baby, don't say that. You can't be serious."

I shook my head, letting Dexter know I was very serious. I smiled and touched his shoulder. "And you're going to help me be good. Hell, messing around with you, I won't be able to go to school in the morning."

"Shelby, Shelby, someone wants to talk to you," Kandace yelled from downstairs.

I looked crazed as I trampled down the stairs, leaving my man's penis standing straight up.

"Hello," I answered, wondering who the hell was calling me at Dexter's house.

"What are you doing over there?"

"I was talking to Kandace," I answered swiftly. "What do you want?"

"I was calling for Dexter," he replied.

"Well, he's taking a bath."

"Kandace told me. Can I come see you tonight?" he questioned.

"No," I said firmly. Then I hung up the phone.

"Max is such a flirt. The boy is nosy too," Kandace voiced in response to my conversation with Max.

I walked into the bathroom.

"I know that was Max. He saw your car in front of my house. How many people have a silver car with *Shelby 5* on it?" Dexter said.

"You're right. That fool was trying to see what

he could find out. He probably asked Kandace if I was over here," I commented, trying to convince myself.

"None of that matters," Dexter said as he pulled my head toward his and caught my mouth with his soft lips.

My tongue was in bondage like a hostage. I loved every lap his tongue ran in my mouth. My mind was gone. I was on cloud nine.

"Put your feet in the tub," he beckoned.

I pulled my socks off and placed my feet in the warm water. I sat on the edge of the tub facing him. My neon pink toenails gleamed in the water.

Dexter picked my left foot up and sucked my big toe. I was wet, instantly. After that, he moved to my other toes. I let out a light sigh.

When he was done with my toes, he pulled my panties off. He spread my legs open while I sat on the edge of the tub. Then he made love to my wet, hot spot with his mouth.

LUST TWENTY-SEVEN

On my way home from school I picked up my cell phone to call Blair.

"Hey, what happened to you and Kelly Thursday night?" she asked, her voice full of concern.

I said slowly, "I've been meaning to call you. Kelly has cancer."

Blair blurted out, "Whaa . . . What?"

I pulled my car over and tried to regain my composure. I didn't want Blair to hear the fear in my voice.

I coughed to clear my throat. "She's going to be okay. They're removing her uterus. She doesn't have to have any chemotherapy or radiation."

"Good. She'll be one hundred percent cured?" Blair asked.

I paused for a slight second. "That's what her doctor told her," I said, trying not to cry.

Blair didn't say one word. She heaved a heavy sigh, "But . . . Kelly can't have kids? Oh my God, she wanted a house full of children."

"Yes, three of them, Journee, Justus, and Jordan," I said, remembering our dreams as teenagers.

I informed Blair that Kelly's surgery would take place on Thursday.

"I'll be there, and she can stay with me until she recuperates," Blair asserted.

"She can stay with me," I intercepted.

"Please . . . Joel stays with you."

"You have a child and a roommate," I reminded her.

"Okay, Mother Shelby," Blair said, mocking me.

"Anyway, Kelly was my friend first. I introduced you to her," I stated in a childish way, before ending our conversation.

When I walked into my front door, I felt drained. My body ached from all the sex on Thursday, and my mind throbbed due to all the information I'd processed. I climbed up the stairs, anxiously wanting to jump into my bed.

I crossed the threshold of my bedroom door, only to find Joel in my bed again. "Joel, get out of my bed," I screamed.

Joel was lying in my bed butt naked. His huge black erect penis was yelling, "Look at me." His stuff was all over my room.

"Your belongings are all over the place. You had my man mad at me the other day. Get out of my bed," I ranted, swinging his dirty shirt at him.

He took his time getting out of my bed. Then he glided slowly to the chair, grabbed his boxers, and put them on. He had no shame. I could see why. The boy had an incredible body.

"Did you have a bitch in my bed?" I yelled out.

"Naw, you know better. I was relaxing. What's up with that *bitch* word?"

"Yeah, yeah, I'm working on the cursing. It takes time. I'm tired. I'm going to take a nap. Dexter should be coming over tonight, so don't pop in on us tomorrow, because my baby leaves Friday. And Kelly will be staying with us next week. So clean the room that you are supposed to be sleeping in. You'll have to hit the couch."

"I'll be downstairs," he snapped back.

After he closed my bedroom door, I took all my clothes off and drifted off to sleep.

As I was lying on top of my comforter face down, I heard my front door open and close. Then I heard footsteps coming up the plush stairs. My bedroom door creaked open. I felt a soft delicate kiss on the back of my neck. Then kisses were placed up and down my back. I swung as I opened my eyes. My nude body was exposed. I was startled and shocked.

He caught my hand and kissed it. "Did I scare you?"

"Yes, you did," I said dryly, still a little drowsy.

Dexter kissed my lips and looked at my body. "I see you were waiting on me."

His erection bulged out. "I wish you wouldn't tempt me. Go put on a turtleneck and some baggy jeans." I grabbed him by the waist. "You worked pretty late today. How was business?"

"The shop is really picking up. I just hired your girl Brooklyn, and the guys love her. She'll be as good as Kelly in a minute. Kelly brings that cash in."

I sat up with a surprised expression on my face. I

couldn't believe Kelly was bringing in so much revenue. I hated to tell him the dollars were going to stop due to Kelly's illness.

He wiped his forehead. "I just left the golf course. I'm beat."

"You're giving all your time and money to Cherry Hills Country Club."

"Baby, it's walking distance from your condo."

Dexter kissed my cheek with his wet, succulent lips. I wanted to melt. His touches were so erotic, a peck on the cheek lit my fire. The kiss made me instantly forget about his lust for golf. I held Dexter's hands and cherished the feel of his skin.

I became saddened at the thought of being away from him. "I can't believe you're leaving."

"Yes, I'll be in California in a few days, but it isn't the end. I'll be done with the Air Force after I complete these few months. While I'm there, I'm going to locate a site for our new location. Be happy, we are finally becoming a franchise. That's enough about me and the business," he reported gleefully.

"As long as you have your business, I know you're coming back."

"If I didn't have a business here, I'd come back for you. I'm going to make you my wife. You're the woman I've been searching for all my life, but it's going to be hard not seeing your lovely face every day," Dexter said softly.

I was feeling mushy inside. I didn't want to feel sad, so I changed the subject. "Was Max at the shop? Did he ask why I was at your house the other morning?" I asked, trying to sound unconcerned.

"No, he didn't mention you. You are such a

paranoid person. Are you a schizophrenic?" he said playfully.

Two knocks banged at my door. "Come in," I yelled.

Dexter rushed, trying to cover my body with the comforter, before Joel stepped into the room.

Joel pranced into my room as if he owned the place. His bare buff chest was exposed. "Shelby, I'm getting ready to go to work." Joel walked to my dresser and picked up his wallet. Then he stuffed it in his back pocket.

Dexter recognized his familiarity with my bedroom.

"Cool. Don't forget Kelly will be staying here for a while," I reminded Joel.

"What's up, Dex?" he said, raising his fist in the air.

"I can't call it," Dexter replied, with a perturbed look.

After Joel closed the door, I pulled off the sheets. I wanted to tell Dexter that Joel sees me naked all the time. When I looked at the expression on his face, I decided against that.

When Dexter heard the front door close, he started, "You two are a little too close."

"Who? Joel? We are only friends," I said defensively.

Dexter stood up. Then he looked down at me. "You in this bitch naked and shit. Nigga walks up in here with his shirt off, swolled up like 50 Cent . . . What? Y'all trying to play me? I ain't down for all the game-playing and bullshit."

"What? You don't trust me? I gave you a key. Do you think I would risk you walking in on us?"

"What am I supposed to think?" he said, sounding frustrated.

I sat up in the bed after I realized he was serious. My heart started to beat fast. I had never seen Dexter so mad before. "Well, I don't have time for your insecurities," I screamed.

"You must be fucking him," Dexter shouted.

I paused for a moment. That comment stung. It felt as if I had been punched in the stomach. I couldn't believe Dexter thought I'd do something like that. I thought about the statement again. Since I did mess around with him, knowing he was Max's best friend, did he respect me, or was I just another whore in his book? Was the truth finally coming out?

"What? I have never slept with Joel. How could you say that?"

"Easy. Look at the damn picture. You have two bedrooms in this motherfucka and his shit is always in your room."

"Don't you trust me? You told me you loved me. Nothing is going on between Joel and me," I pleaded.

I tried to grab his hand, but Dexter brushed me off swiftly as he stood up and walked toward the hallway.

"You know what? If you ain't fucking him, I'm going to give y'all the opportunity to. I'm out this motherfucka," he roared.

"You can't be serious. Stop tripping. Nothing happened," I pleaded.

A frustrated Dexter replied, "Even if ain't nothing happened, you got that charge anyway. I'm a man, and I deserve respect around this bitch."

The tears were brewing inside of me. I wanted to get on my knees and beg him to stay, but I refused to submit to him. I wasn't going to let him see me break down, so my cool side stepped in. He was being ghetto with me; therefore, it was only fitting that I return the favor.

"Bitch, give me my damn key. I don't want you to walk in on Joel and me fucking," I shouted.

Dexter gave me a heated look. "I got you bitch," he mumbled. "Take your muthafucking key." Dexter lightly placed the key on my dresser and walked down the stairs.

When I heard the door slam, I closed my eyes tight. My face tensed up. I couldn't control my tears. I loved Dexter, but I wasn't going into another depression. I stomped down the stairs and placed the double lock on the door. Then I stared out the window, hoping he would return.

Bookstore, Community Book Center, B's Books and More, CandaceK, RAWSISTAZ, Tee C. Royal, Mary B. Morrison, Mark Anthony, Anthony Carr, Naleighna Kai, Diane Andrews, Victoria Christopher Murray, Gayle Jackson Sloan, Tina Brooks McKinney, J.J. Michael, Corliss Martin, J.L. Woodson, Candice Dow, Andrea Blackstone, Michael McKenzie, Ivory Toldsen, Naija, Java Weathersby, C.J. Domino, Kiffany Dugger, and all my readers.

know I act like a rude, distant, selfish *B* sometimes, but I really cherish our friendship and everything you do for me. By the way, thank you for lunch yesterday."

"You're welcome and I love you too. I'll be there in twenty minutes," I uttered with a smile.

"Megan is picking me up. Go get Blair," Kelly informed me before hanging up.

I agreed to pick up Blair and wished her well.

I thought about Dexter. I hadn't heard from him since he walked out on me. A part of me wanted to call, but there was no turning back. I dressed quickly to keep my mind off of him. Putting on a pink jogging suit with the pink letter *S* shirt and white-and-pink Nike tennis shoes, I pulled my hair back into a ponytail. A grin lurked across my face as I dressed. I was pleased to hear Kelly talking so rationally. She was stepping out on faith, and I was proud of her.

There is hope for my girl and me too, *I thought.*

"Sapphire, Sapphire, wake up. I need you to watch Blairson while I'm gone," Blair expressed angrily as I stood waiting in her living room.

"Where is Blairson?" I heard Sapphire ask Blair in a sleepy voice.

"He's in his bedroom," Blair said, with plenty of attitude.

"What is your problem, Blair?" Sapphire asked calmly.

"You have responsibility here. You are Blairson's paid nanny. I haven't heard from you since Thursday night."

"I was taking care of some personal business."

"If you're going to stay in my house, you're going to have to be a little more professional. Let me know if you can't keep my child."

Then Blair exited the room and headed to meet me in the living room. Her blouse was open, and she was nowhere close to being ready.

I have to be on time for Kelly's surgery. Blair, you are pissing me off. Hurry up, I repeated to myself, not wanting to cause a scene.

Sapphire walked into the room with nothing on. Her black short hair was dazzling. It looked like she had just left the beauty shop. The pencil curls were nice and neat, and the back was tapered to perfection. She stood in the doorway for a few seconds watching Blair dress. Sapphire fondled her clit-piercing then she quietly walked toward Blair, never acknowledging my presence. She touched Blair's neck. "Is something else bothering you? I've stayed away from home without calling before."

Blair lashed out. "Look, trick. Bryan told me you left with a woman. I don't like you being so carefree when you have obligations here."

"I'm grown. How I live my life is my business. I asked you if you wanted to be with me. You refused," Sapphire shouted.

"Wait one minute, dyke. I told you I wasn't down with women. I love men, men with big dicks and hairy balls. I'm talking about your obligations to take care of my son," Blair bellowed, buttoning up her shirt.

"Yeah, I like dick too, every now and then, but it's nothing like the sweet touch of a woman," Sapphire

said seductively, while pushing her nude breasts against Blair's face and winking her eye at me.

I quickly turned my head and buried my face in the March issue of *Essence*.

Blair stood up. Her hands were clenched into tight fists. "Bitch, I will kill you if you ever push up on me again."

Sapphire licked her own nipples. "Blair, I can please you. I want to make you feel like no man has ever made you feel. Let me make love to you."

I almost fell out of my seat. They were cutting up, and evidently some unresolved emotions were being revealed.

Blair raised her hands in the air and sighed gently. Then she took a seat next to me on the sofa, her demeanor changing drastically. "Sapphire, I have a lot on my plate. I don't want to argue. Just be here to take care of my son and be careful when you're out in the streets. I love you like a sister, and I don't want anything to happen to you," Blair expressed calmly as she placed her shoes on.

Sapphire kneeled down in front of us. She pushed Blair's long micro braids out of her face and kissed her on the forehead lightly. "I still love you, and I don't care who knows it," Sapphire confessed, taking a quick glance at me and rolling her eyes.

I sat there speechless, not believing everything, yet antsy about getting to Kelly's surgery on time.

"Blair, I hate to break up this party, but we have to get going. They'll be taking Kelly to surgery soon."

Blair picked up her pack of cigarettes from the cocktail table and pulled one out. Sapphire reached for the lighter and lit the end of the cigarette for

Blair. Blair quickly inhaled and blew the smoke into Sapphire's face.

"You know I don't go both ways. So if you can't respect that you need to move," Blair announced sternly then motioned for me to get up so we could leave. "And, Shelby, before you start I don't want to hear any of your I-told-you-so lectures. I'd appreciate if none of this leaves my house," Blair barked as we exited her front door.

Blair and I walked into the hospital waiting area. Megan was sitting in the blue padded chair, looking into her mirror.

"Did they take her back?" I asked anxiously.

"Yeah, they said it should take about an hour," Megan answered, taking a break from staring at herself in her mirror.

"I hope they get it all," Blair said.

"They will. This surgery is typically very successful. She'll be discharged in two or three days," Megan replied, applying black mascara on her eyelashes. "Why didn't Sapphire come?"

I looked at Blair, wanting to tell Megan all about her and Sapphire's drama, but decided not to when I saw the evil expression on Blair's face.

"She had to babysit," Blair explained hurriedly.

Megan continued putting on her make-up, not giving the reply much thought.

"Was my baby nervous?" Blair asked.

"No. She was very strong. Kelly is a fighter," Megan answered back.

Kelly's fragile little mother, Estelle, waddled in.

She looked buzzed as usual, and you could smell the booze. "How are you tramps doing?" she slurred.

"We're fine," we replied simultaneously.

What I really wanted to say was, *We're fine, you skinny white drunk.*

"So, Shelby, Kelly tells me she's staying at your house?"

"Yes, she is."

"I can take care of my child," she said with a French accent and plenty of attitude.

"You can?" I said as if I was talking to someone in nursery school.

"Yes, darling, I think that would be more appropriate," she verbalized in a manner a queen would.

"Well, tell your daughter that," I said politely.

She looked at the three of us like we were trash. "You sluts have ruined my daughter. She wouldn't be in this predicament if she had left you black girls and all of those big-dick black boys alone."

Blair jumped up. "Excuse me."

I was about to curse Miss Smirnoff out too. We were taught to respect our elders, but this woman was completely out of order.

Megan gestured to us with her finger in front of her mouth. *Shhh.*

Blair sat down slowly. It was hard, but Blair and I kept quiet until Estelle left the waiting room.

After the commotion died down, I dozed off in the waiting room chair. I dreamed about Dexter, imagining the two of us back together again and happy. We were walking on the beach barefoot, holding hands and talking about our future together as husband and wife.

Suddenly, I sat straight up in my chair, rubbing my stiff neck. "Oh my God," I yelled.

"Are you okay?" Megan asked, stunned by my abruptness.

"Yeah, I'm fine. Just had a bad dream about Max killing me for dating Dexter."

A deep grin appeared on Megan's shiny gloss-covered lips. She quickly dismissed my statement with a sway of her hand.

"Well, Kelly's surgery was a success. Her mother is in the recovery room with her," Megan announced.

"I'm glad. I was worried about her," I admitted.

"You seem to have other things on your mind too. Max killing you?"

"I told you I had a nightmare about Max," I snickered.

"Girl, please. We've been friends most of our lives. What's up with you?"

"Well, Dexter and I ended things on bad terms. It doesn't hurt like I thought it would," I said, trying hard to make myself believe it.

"Shelby, what happened?" Megan asked.

"He thinks Joel and I are sleeping together. He flipped. I have never heard him act as ghetto as Max before," I stated with worry written all over my face.

"I bet you loved that thug behavior when it exploded on you," Megan joked.

I came clean. "Actually it was very arousing, until I realized he was serious. I wanted to run after him, but my pride wouldn't let me."

"You did well. The old Shelby would've chased him down like a hunting dog." Megan chuckled.

"I'm trying. I believe in destiny. If God wants us to be together then we shall meet again," I said softly. "He leaves tomorrow. I was supposed to take him."

"That's right. Never love a man more than he loves you." Megan laughed with a sneaky little smirk on her face. "So did you do the do with Joel?"

"I see you're full of humor. Seriously, you know I would never sleep with Joel. He's like a brother to me. Dexter is just very jealous."

"Shelby, I have to side with Dexter. I know you wouldn't do anything with Joel, but most men wouldn't believe that. You two are very close, and it looks suspicious. You should've set some boundaries with Joel when you and Dexter started getting serious. Dexter didn't feel respected," Megan argued.

"You are right," I replied somberly.

As much as it hurt, I had to admit Megan was right. If the tables were turned, I would've felt very uncomfortable if Kandace was Dexter's best friend, and not his sister. I didn't think I would've ever gotten serious with him. I would always wonder if they were messing around on the side.

Blair had a huge smile on her face as she ran to Megan and me. She was so happy, she was shaking.

"Kelly is okay."

"Megan told me," I answered quickly.

"No, she's okay. They didn't find cancer anywhere else. She is cancer-free," Blair cheered.

"Can we go see her?" I asked gleefully.

"Follow me. Hopefully frail Estelle the bitch from hell is gone," Blair clowned.

Megan and I laughed aloud. "We hope so."

I smirked. "Her mother is a sick noodle. I think she had a mental problem before she started killing her brain with heroin and liquor."

A brown finger pressed the up button on the elevator, before my hand could reach it.

"Hello, ladies. How's my baby?" Kevin questioned.

Blair and I looked at each other.

"Damn. Do they still go together?" Blair whispered.

The information flowed out of my mouth. "She's gonna be okay."

"You two look surprised to see me. Miss Swanson told me to come," Kevin said with a false sense of security.

He knew what we thought of him. He was a wimpy man that urinated in the bed. Kelly despised him. She cheated on him time after time and felt no remorse. He busted her one time. She had another man in his bed, and he still didn't put her out.

We all stepped into the elevator. Silence covered the air. I pressed the number seven and watched the elevator travel up at a slow pace. The elevator opened with a loud beeping sound. And Kevin put his hand on the door, letting all of us exit the elevator before him.

We entered Kelly's room. She was sitting up in the bed with an enormous grin covering her face, not looking like she just had major surgery. "Thank God. I'm healed. He gets all the glory," she cried.

Kevin walked up to Kelly and whispered, "I want

you to come home with me. I'm going to take care of you."

Kelly laughed then she raised her arm in the air. "I will not dwell in hell. I can't live with you in sin. We aren't married. I'm not the same Kelly. Hallelujah. The Holy Spirit has set me free." She closed her eyes. "I asked God to grant me peace. He said, 'Yes, if you come to Me.' I am with Jesus now. I can't see you anymore."

I was happy for Kelly's renewed faith, but she was acting crazy. I couldn't believe how lively she was after going through surgery. I guess the anesthesia hadn't worn off yet.

Kevin was dumbfounded. He held her hand and spoke timidly. "Baby, let's talk when you get better."

"That won't be necessary. Flee from me, devil. Now get out of here," she screamed like a woman in the mental ward.

Kevin rushed out, without saying bye.

The minute he hit the threshold, Kelly busted out laughing. She laughed so hard she started crying. "Ohhh. Ouch." She snorted.

"Were you pulling his leg?" I asked.

Kelly shook her head.

"Girl, I thought you had lost it too. You should go to Hollywood," Megan suggested, standing at the sink washing her hands.

"I'm thinking about it, seriously. I have always wanted to be an actress," she expressed.

"Follow your dreams, while you're young," Blair said.

Kelly grinned. "I could be the next Halle Berry

since we're both biracial. Hmmmm. I hope I got rid of Kevin. I can't deal with him. He doesn't take charge. I need a leader, a man who can be the head of his house."

"Halle Berry, please, take it easy. Let those stitches heal. Get your rest," Nurse Megan ordered then whispered in our ears, "Kelly needs her rest; it's time for us to go."

"We are getting ready to go," Blair and Megan stated, hugging Kelly.

I walked up and hugged Kelly tightly. She embraced me back and spoke softly into my ear. "I'm going to go home with my momma. She's tripping for me to move back home with her, and she needs me."

I thought about Estelle, her frail frame, wrinkled skin, and the marks that lined her arm. Instantly, I started feeling a little sorry for her. She had a drug and alcohol addiction that was hard to conquer.

"I think that's a good idea. She doesn't need to be alone." I nodded, agreeing with Kelly's decision to move back home.

I leaped in my car and pulled my purse from under the seat. I opened my purse and pulled out my cell phone. I scrolled to *missed calls*. Dexter's number was nowhere to be found. I guess he was serious. He was leaving without a good-bye? The one man I loved with all of my heart was going away. The pain hurt more than losing Sebastian. I wanted to cry until I had no more tears left, but I was determined to push on and not wallow in self-pity.

"Joel was there for me when I went through this

with Sebastian," I recited aloud as I dialed his cell. The phone rang three times and I grew paranoid. I needed to talk to him so he could tell me everything would be okay.

When he finally picked up on the fourth ring, I perked up. I told him all about Dexter leaving me and how it was his fault.

"Look, Shelby, I'm not going through this drama with you again. He was leaving anyway, and that long distance love never works," he said with no emotion.

I wanted to hang up on his insensitive ass, but he was right.

"You're right. That's what I keep on telling myself." I paused. "Please help me get over him. Take me out, let's do something fun," I begged, feeling hopeless and lonely.

"I can do more than take you out. And I will. You'll see. Wait until I get home," Joel replied in an intimate voice, before hanging up.

LUST TWENTY-NINE

The sun was gone, dusk had fallen, and the love of my life had vanished. It was early Saturday morning. My Friday had been slept away. I had only gotten up to use the bathroom. It was now three in the morning, and still no word from Dexter.

And Joel wasn't any better. He'd promised to come home to cheer me up, but I hadn't seen him either.

I lay in my bed with my eyes wide open, staring at the ceiling, unable to sleep anymore. I was occupied with thoughts of Dexter, wondering what he was doing, thinking where did I go wrong.

Unexpectedly, around four in the morning, I heard my front door open then close. I didn't budge as I anxiously awaited the love of my life. His footsteps were distinctive and loud as usual and they echoed up the stairs.

The bedroom door opened slowly. A smirk skated across my lips. Only one man entered my room with those mannerisms. I wanted to greet

him with a smile and warm kisses, but my body was
too weak to respond or even turn toward the door.

He pulled my leg which was dangling out of the
bed. "Wake up, girl."

When I heard that well-known voice my stomach
dropped. Insides fluttered. Suddenly, reality stepped
in, and I remembered him giving me my key back.
My eyes filled up with fluid. Disappointment sprayed
my body. "Joel, what do you want?" I screamed.

He looked at my disheveled appearance. "What
the hell is wrong with you?"

I swung my hair out of my face. Then I looked
away from his stare. "I thought you were Dexter," I
cried.

"Duh. Didn't you tell me it was over? The boy's
plane left Friday morning."

"I didn't really think it was over. I thought
maybe he decided to stay and . . ." I sighed softly.

"And sweep you away. What fairy tale have you
been reading? I'm not having a pity party with you.
Put some clothes on. Fix yourself up. You didn't
do anything wrong." He rubbed my back. "I'll take
you out to eat tomorrow. I promised to make you
feel better, and I will."

I continued crying. "But I love him."

"If he can't understand that we're just friends,
you don't need him anyway. An envious brotha will
kill you. Don't you watch the news? All these over-
jealous men killing their girlfriends, it's a good
thing you found out before it was too late," Joel
said, trying to convince me.

I rested in the bed. My mind processed what
Joel said, but my mouth remained closed.

"Turn over," he ordered.

I did what he told me to do. I was too tired to argue.

Joel sat on my butt. He placed his hands on my shoulders and began massaging them. Then he jumped off me and blasted downstairs.

Joel returned several seconds later. He resumed massaging my shoulders with warm massage oil that he had heated in the microwave.

My eyes fluttered, feeling his large erection on my butt. "J-o-e-l," I yelped.

He moved to my back, kneading all of the tension knots out.

I turned my head, looked deep into Joel's eyes and saw the lust, but I ignored it. I was too caught up in the moment. The feeling was mesmerizing. I couldn't stop him. His hands felt like magic, and hell, my body deserved special attention.

Special Thanks

Ashley Augustine (helping me name characters, especially Shelby) Damatia Gipson, Nichole Morgan, Irma Jean Bickham (sex scenes), Choretta & Tony Burns (continuous encouragement and love), Carey Yazeed (believing in me), Mr. & Mrs. Landris Tobias, David Bruce Alexander, Stanley Griffin, Warren Tobias, Karyn Sullivan, Martha Edwina LeBlanc, Kathleen Tate, Zshoan Williams, Arnold Williams, Aunt Mae Bell, Connie Stallings (spiritual mentor), Carla Norton, Alvin Norton, Chris Gipson, Derrick Clark, Don Patrick LeDuff (they love Sapphire), Patricia Smith, Chad Cooper, Corey Cooper, Shelton Slack, Sarita & Samuel Slack, Kathleen Fontenette (my biggest fan), Monique Abraham, Pamela Rodgers, Karshieka Graves, Louis Thomas, Michelle Thomas (I added more sex), Mr. & Mrs. Mark Butler (Talmar), Editha Brown (oldest friend), Janelle Allen, Sharon Underwood, Aneathria Winfield Major, Edmund Carey, Kimberly Decker (book cover model), Marcus Talbert (book cover model), Melissa Robertson (book cover photographer), Dreama Lee-Woldman, Omni, Shay Ashford, Mr. & Mrs. Curtis Jackson, Lynel Washington, Kevin Maxie, Tillis DeVaughn, Renetta Cobbing, Dawn Epting, Warren Shells, Stephanie Brooks, Rita Scott, Monica Lange, Lydia Rogers, Michelle Stansbury, FMC North Foster crew, Weathersbee Design, Literary Ladies Book Club (my true sisters), Reading & Reflecting Book Club, Passion4Reading Book Club, APOOO Book Club, Simply Sisters Book Club, Reflections Bookstore, Roots

cause the poorly built homes resembled wooden shacks. Goats and pigs frolicked through the streets. Trash was everywhere, including old car tires and mattresses thrown in the front yards of many homes. Clothes were also hanging to dry, outside on ropes. This wasn't what I pictured. The nice little brochure didn't reveal any of this.

LUST THIRTY-NINE

The resort was exquisite and I was relieved. There was a waterfall at the entrance with palm trees surrounding it. The lobby was outside under a glass atrium, and cocktail bars were located all around the lobby. Bob Marley's music played through the speakers.

I looked at the golf course and spotted Dexter instantly. It looked like he was trying to show Patrick, Bryan's cousin from Mississippi, how to play. My heart fluttered enthusiastically. I couldn't believe we were at the same place at the same time. I was delighted. I couldn't wait to get in my bathing suit and prance around in front of him.

"I'm staying with you and Kelly tonight," Blair publicized.

"Yes, we don't want you two ruining your vows by sleeping together the night before," Kelly stated.

Everyone was getting used to the new Kelly, so they ignored her.

Megan pointed to Kelly. "Don't go there. My fi-

ancé and I are sharing a room," Megan said before Kelly got around to sacking her out.

"Why not? You're already living in sin," Kelly replied.

"Shelby, get Mother Theresa," Megan yelled.

I grabbed Kelly's arm and walked toward the lobby chairs.

Megan yelled out to Kelly, "Actually, Victor and I aren't sinning. We are already married. Do you think my husband, a man of God, would live in sin? We were married months ago. Our huge, glamorous wedding will be held in August."

We all remained silent, stunned by Megan's statement. Feelings of hurt submerged my body. Why didn't Megan tell us? We were supposed to be best friends.

"Congratulations, you two," I said after a long pause, finally feeling happy that Megan and Victor did things the right way.

"Congratulations," the others said one by one.

"We can't check in until later. So I scheduled for us to meet with the wedding coordinator now," Blair tried explaining to the stunned group.

Megan faced Blair. "That whore just turned holy yesterday. Now she's condemning everyone else."

"Just lock the nun up in the room. I liked her better when she was buck wild. I know we made more money at the bar because of her," Max joked.

"She just needs to stop judging everyone since she's saved. You can't judge people from the outside because you don't know what's going on inside. We have all changed to some extent, and all

of us are working toward getting our lives together. I don't know about you, Max," Megan stated.

Max stared at Megan and threw his hands out. "You're judging me now. Why do you hate me?"

Megan's gold bangle bracelets jingled as she pointed to Max. "You made me hate you. Why were you such an angry, mean child?"

Max hit his forehead. "We were young. Boys acted mean when they liked someone. I had a little crush on you. I thought you were cute. Don't tell me you're still upset about me teasing you and pushing your face in the dirt." Max chuckled.

Megan didn't crack a smile. She was serious. She went off. "Yes, I am still mad. You made my childhood miserable. You were cruel. You are a male chauvinist. By the way, the curl made my hair fall out. You knew I wasn't bald-headed. And where the hell is my Michael Jackson button you stole? I hate you."

I saw that Megan was upset, so I marched over to comfort her. "Megan, are you okay? We were only kids. You know how cruel kids can be. Get over it."

"You are crazy. He teased you about your grand-father being an alcoholic and you continue to talk to him," Megan ranted. She looked at Max with hurt in her eyes. "We never teased you about your aunt being on crack."

Max looked shocked. He looked away.

I had to put my two cents in. "We were young, and children tease. Megan, you can't live in the past. We came from the same neighborhood. You've known Max and me for sixteen years. Let's

overcome these childhood obstacles that keep on crossing our paths."

Max walked up to Megan. His speech was slow and genuine. "Megan, I'm sorry for hurting you." Then he stuck his hand out for a handshake.

Megan didn't move. Victor stepped up and nudged her on the shoulder. Her feet remained planted to the ground.

"I think Sister Kelly and I need to give you a sermon on forgiveness," I said with a smile.

Megan hurried up and grabbed Max's hand. She hugged him too.

We all laughed.

"See, that's why you can't take black folks nowhere. We always have to have some kind of altercation." Blair giggled.

As we waited for the wedding coordinator, the men grew restless.

"I'm going to get a drink and some food since it's free. I'm going to eat until I pop." Bryan chuckled.

Blair pointed to the golf course. "I think I see Dexter and Patrick playing golf."

Bryan glanced that way. "That sure is them. I'm going to grab something to eat first."

Max checked out the bar and grinned at all the liquor. "I'm going to get a drink."

Victor followed him.

"I'll come get you when the coordinator arrives," Blair stated.

* * *

"Where are the fellas? I can't believe you two aren't with your men?" I teased Blair and Megan.

"They're coming. Dexter arrived, so they're chilling with him," Blair said nonchalantly.

"No, they're not." I glanced over at the bar.

Victor and Max were chatting away. Max had his cognac in his hand, and Victor had a root beer.

I peeped at the golf course. A mesmerizing spirit inundated my soul with thoughts of Dexter. I was crying inside, and my breathing was erratic as my eyes studied every movement Dexter made. He was still beautiful as the day he stormed out of my house.

"What ya looking at? If it's meant to be, God will see to it that it is so. Don't pick your own man. Let God choose for you," Kelly stated, nearly scaring me to death.

"Thank you. I needed that because you know I'm dying to speak to him," I admitted.

Blair uttered, "Don't speak to him. He's walking over here now. Let him approach you."

"That's right. Be a lady. Let a man come to you. Furthermore, there are too many rich men out here to worry about one," Megan pointed out.

"Guys, the coordinator's here," Blair screamed.

Kelly peered at Blair. "Stop being so ghetto. You don't have to yell that loud."

Megan touched the coordinator's shoulder. "Excuse me, can you make an announcement for us? We would appreciate it very much."

We jumped into the coordinator's long golf cart and headed toward the part of the resort where the wedding was going to take place. I didn't look behind me. This time I was taking my girls' advice

about not speaking to Dexter. And he hadn't mumbled a word to me either.

The wedding site was located near the ocean, by the cottages. The view was extraordinary. The cottages were almost sitting in the pure blue water, and the view of the green mountains was eye-catching.

"Attention. Let's take our places. Who are the best man and maid of honor?" the coordinator announced.

Blair addressed her, "They all are."

The coordinator went over the instructions for the wedding very briefly and started preparing for the wedding, which was going to be held the next day.

"The formal restaurant is reserved for our rehearsal dinner in an hour," Blair announced.

"Do we have to dress up?" I asked.

"No, we'll be the only people in there," she answered.

Dexter didn't look at me the whole time, and I couldn't believe he didn't speak either. I wanted to run up to him and pour my heart out, but I wasn't playing the fool again. "He walked out on me," I kept mumbling to myself.

The rehearsal dinner ended quickly, and the gang was ready to have some fun.

"Man, we gotta go out. I see too many naked females running around this place to stand idle," Patrick said, like a horny teenager.

"They are also having a wet T-shirt contest in the sports bar tonight," Dexter mentioned.

Max walked up to me. "Do you need me to do anything for you before I leave?"

"No. Thank you for all your help. I really appreciate your kindness."

Max mouthed, "You're welcome," and sprinted off, trying to catch up with the guys who had walked away and were now in a huddle.

"We can go on the beach and watch those Jamaican men eat fire," I said.

"Sounds cool. I'm done with the club scene anyway," Blair acclaimed.

"I need a drink if I'm going to be hanging with you squares." Megan chuckled.

"Get me a piña colada," Blair called out.

"Pretty ladies, y'awl be married, mon?" one of the workers asked.

Blair pointed to Kelly and I. "Those two are single."

"Do you believe in Jesus? If you do, we can talk about Jesus all night long," Kelly attested.

The man trotted away quickly.

"That's right. Preach, sister," I said as we settled on the beach to watch the fire show.

The men parked themselves at the resort's sports bar, and when we returned from the fire show they were still in there chatting away. Dexter sat at the end, next to a group of women. The women were dressed in flimsy swimsuits that left nothing to the imagination. Megan, Blair, Kelly, and I sat at a round cocktail a few feet from the ladies.

"I'll have Hennessy with a splash of Coke on the rocks," Max requested to the bartender.

"You changed your drink up a little?" Dexter asked.

"Man, you know they don't serve Courvoisier

for free. I always get a splash of Coke with Hennessy, every once in a while."

The rest of the fellas were drinking Red Stripe, the Jamaican beer.

One of the attractive women tapped Dexter on the shoulder then whispered in his ear.

"Which one?" he yelled out, full of energy.

She pointed to Max.

Dexter nudged Max. "This fine-ass female would like to holla at ya."

Max looked at the woman. "Baby, I'm about to get married."

Max's reply shocked me. Now who was he marrying? I really wanted to know.

"What's up, Max? You've been hanging pretty low," Dexter pried.

Bryan added his part to the conversation. "Man, Max is after Shelby again. I saw him trying to work his way back in. That's a sweet girl, and my baby, Blair, thinks highly of her. You should've never messed up, Max."

Dexter gave a phony laugh. "Yeah, Max."

"You're right, man. It's time for me to change. I'm sick of lying and cheating. I can't keep up with the game-playing anymore. I'm getting older, and I want a good woman who cares about me. I want a woman I can build something with. I'm thinking about retiring my player cards," Max rambled loud enough for me to hear.

Victor donated to the conversation like I wasn't in the same room. "Shelby is about to become a psychiatrist too."

The fellas laughed and kept on sipping their drinks.

Dexter looked at Max's used-to-be-gangster face. I think he noticed the hurt in Max's face. We had been deceitful and sneaky. I was supposed to be Max's childhood friend and girl, and Dexter was his best friend. A part of me felt bad. Max had changed. He wasn't the same hard, cold person.

Dexter pounded his fist on Max's back lightly and lowered his tone, permitting me to hear nothing. Whatever it was, it left Max dumbfounded and frozen. They had to be discussing me.

I excused myself and escaped to the darkness outside near the waterfall surrounded by palms and other greenery in the lounging area.

Max and Dexter walked out of the bar moments later. Dexter had Max in a headlock embrace. Just my luck. The two people I was trying my best to avoid were in close proximity to me again. They couldn't see me. I was wearing a straw hat, and my back was toward them. I could hear everything they said, loud and clear.

"Man, I've missed you. Do you realize we've never been separated this long since we've been friends?" Max testified.

"I need to come all the way clean about some shit," Dexter said, his voice sounding like he was backing up.

"I know. You told me already. I'm cool with you hollering at Shelby while I was tripping," Max said, shunning Dexter off.

"No, I left some things out. I didn't tell you that things got really serious between the two of us."

I peeped at the two of them and saw Max's facial expression turn to a frown.

"Like what? What you trying to say, player?"

"Shelby and I made love," Dexter confessed.

My heart dropped. I couldn't believe this was happening. My head sank down. I started to pray.

"Wait a minute . . . You backstabbing mother-fucka, you said the two of you just went out a couple of times," Max screeched.

"I'm sorry, I wasn't honest with you. I care for Shelby a great deal. We made love several times, but it wasn't just sex. We connected. I wouldn't even tell you all of this if I didn't love her," Dexter sighed.

Max became enraged. "Love her?"

Dexter put his hand on his eyebrows. "Dog, I'm sorry. I fell in love with her."

"You two motherfuckas played me. She never gave me the pussy. But yo' bitch ass hit it."

"You're not listening. It wasn't about the sex. The two of us had a spiritual connection. I'm in love with Shelby," Dexter tried explaining in a rational manner.

The words inspired me; there was hope. He felt the same way I did.

But Max was infuriated. He wasn't trying to listen. "Love? Spiritual connection? What the fuck is spiritual about fucking my woman? You knew how I felt about Shelby. I treasured her. She was mine."

"Yours? What? You treated her like shit. She was never yours. You were too busy chasing other bitches. You didn't realize you had a good thing. I saw what you had, so I treated her like a lady is supposed to be treated," Dexter shouted.

I heard rapid movements and then a splash. I glanced over my shoulder and saw liquid running from Dexter's head down to his face.

"You need to cool off, lover boy."

Dexter punched Max in the chest. "You weren't treating her right. You were too busy fucking them stupid-ass ducks," Dexter yelled.

Max lost his balance, but managed not to fall. "We were supposed to be boys. Tight like brothers." Max slapped his chest with his fist. Then his arm extended, and he punched Dexter in the jaw.

Dexter's head turned. He charged at Max.

Before Dexter's fist could connect with Max's left eye, a Jamaican resort worker flew in between the two. "Mon, can't we just all get along? Isn't that what you guys say in America?"

Max shrugged his shoulders and walked off. "Fuck you, Dex!"

Dexter didn't acknowledge Max's statement. He just walked away with blood dripping from his mouth.

LUST FORTY

The sun gleamed across the sky. The birds chirped a beautiful melody, and the clear, blue ocean waves danced to the occasion. The white canopy tent was set up on the beach, and Blair's wedding was about to begin at seven in the morning. Blair was always unique. She was determined to be different with her morning wedding.

White calla lilies trailed the homemade aisle. The men were standing in their white suits near the gazebo, waiting for the ceremony to begin.

Bryan stood inside of the gazebo and started singing Brian McKnight's lyrics. *"Lying alone in my room, don't know what I'm going to do."*

I proceeded down the aisle barefoot with a red and white flower in my hair. All of us were wearing Robert Cavalli's white, slinky, silk jersey halter dresses, sassily adorned with a ruffled hem and a lace-up "peek-a-boo" slit that traced the curves of our respective waists. The breeze from the ocean traveled up my white dress as I glided down the aisle holding one single red calla lily. My sandy

brown hair was micro braided with silky weave, and I didn't know how to act as I strutted down the aisle like an American top model. Max greeted me when I made it halfway down the aisle, and tears drifted out of my eyes.

Bryan continued singing, *"Just can't stop thinking about the way you make me feel inside."*

Megan followed me smoothly. Her black hair was micro braided too, and it was very attractive on her. She swung her long hair to the side when Patrick stepped up to escort her the rest of the way.

Kelly pranced down the aisle last. Her long braided hair was unprocessed, and the ends were full of body as the breeze from the ocean flowed through it.

"Could you fall in love with me?" Bryan's voice was radiant. He sounded just like Brian McKnight. When I closed my eyes, I couldn't tell the difference.

I opened my eyes wide and gazed at Dexter as he escorted Kelly the rest of the way down the aisle. I searched his mouth hard for any remnants of the fight with Max, but found no scratches or bruises. Dexter was striking, a handsome man that I wanted desperately. My heart longed for him. He was the missing magic puzzle piece that I needed to make my life complete. Tears of sadness rolled down my face, and I couldn't stop them.

When the song was complete, the six of us stood around the gazebo. Bryan took the cordless microphone and moved to the bottom of the gazebo. He kneeled on one knee in front of the gazebo to ser-

enade Blair. He sang "This Very Moment" by KC & JoJo.

"I can't believe it's true. I'm standing here in front of you and you are here with me."

Blair moved gracefully down the aisle like a princess. She was so happy, and her dress was beautiful. Blair never did anything traditional. Her dress was a red sleeveless, form-fitting halter dress, with sprinklings of crystals highlighting the bust line, waist, and legs. The train of the dress was long, laced in crystals. The edge of the train spelled out in crystal, BLAIR AND BRYAN FOREVER. Her long, black, wavy hair was radiant. She had her hazel contacts in too. She looked like a black Delta Barbie doll in all of her red.

We all glanced at each other and winked. I couldn't get over us being in white and the queen in red. Blair was representing her sorority colors, even on her wedding day.

"You look so beautiful," I whispered with watery eyes.

Bryan looked into her eyes and sang deeper. Blair's father wiped her tears with his handkerchief as they stood in front of the gazebo.

I tried to pull myself together, but it was so hard. So many emotions were stirring.

If I had just stopped Dexter, maybe the two of us would be married today. Lord, being with him was so easy.

"Who gives this bride away?" the preacher asked.

"I do," Blair's father said firmly.

Bryan stepped up to greet Blair, and the two walked up the stairs onto the gazebo.

The preacher started his sermon. Blair's long

black hair shined as the bright sun cast down on it. The breeze from the ocean blew her hair elegantly as she waited to be Mrs. Bryan Cooper.

The two exchanged rings and vows.

"I now pronounce you man and wife," the preacher announced.

Blair and Bryan kissed immediately. She held on tight to Bryan's head as she forced her tongue down his throat.

The reception followed the ceremony in the white canopy tent. There were four small round cocktail tables draped in white linen with ice sculptures of doves in the center of each one. The bridal party tables formed in the shape of a *U*. The bride and groom's table was in front.

I had to sit next to Max during the entire reception, per the coordinator. I didn't mind, because he hadn't said much to me the whole morning. He didn't even speak to Dexter, but then again, Dexter wasn't speaking to anyone. He hadn't looked my way, which was cool with me, because I didn't know if I could control my feelings.

"The wedding party to the floor," the DJ announced.

We danced to the song "Love" by Musiq.

Max wasn't himself. He barely touched me as we pranced across the floor.

"Are you mad at me?" I whispered into his ear.

He just nodded his head yes, offering no other explanation.

Max and I sat at our table with no words spoken. He sipped on his alcoholic beverage, and I longed

for Dexter. When the silence became unbearable, I decided to mess with Max to spice things up. "What are you drinking this early in the morning? Liquor?"

Max jumped back and looked at me as if I was stupid. "This is Jamaica; you can drink all day long for free. Why not liquor?"

I got defensive. "What's wrong with you?"

"Shelby, what's up with you? You're the one who cried the entire wedding."

"I just get emotional at weddings," I answered abruptly.

"We all do, but that's not what I'm talking about." He paused. Then he put his drink down. "Were you in love with Dexter?"

I looked away.

He held my hand. "Baby, I need to know," he said softly.

I started crying uncontrollably, sniveling and blubbering like a five-year-old. "Why?"

"Shelby, tell me the truth."

"What are you talking about? Dexter and I had nothing. Do you see him talking to me?" I answered roughly.

"Cut the act, Shelby. Ya boy and I had a fight last night. He told me everything, that he loved you and that the two of you made love. I know you don't make love to just anyone."

I couldn't speak. I knew about the fight. Yes, I'd seen and heard everything they said.

Max moved his chair closer to me. "I'll respect you more if you're honest with me."

I mouthed very low. "Yes, it's true. We made love because I loved him." My stomach trembled. I cov-

ered my eyes with my hands, not wanting anyone
to see me.

Max held me close. "Don't cry. He appreciated
you, and I didn't at that time. I wasn't ready to
commit, but now I realize what I was missing and
searching for is right in front of my eyes."

I moved my hands, not believing what I was
hearing. I had noticed a change in Max, but I didn't
think it was this drastic.

"Max, I've changed in the past couple of
months. I renewed my faith as a Christian. I can't
live like I was living. I won't make love to another
man until I am his wife. I'm not going to play
around with foreplay either, because lust is a sin . . .
I know you could never be true to that."

Max exhaled softly, "I respect you for being honest with me. I've changed too. I plan on doing
things right this time around."

"Are you serious?" I asked, shocked by this new
character.

"Yes, very. I have always loved you. Don't get me
wrong. I am pissed, but I wasn't honest with you either. And what goes around comes around." He
rubbed my back. "Why don't you go back to your
room and think about everything?"

LUST FORTY-ONE

The lovely reception was over at ten, and I still had the entire day to myself. Kelly and I went back to the room. Blair and her husband retired to their oceanside cottage. Victor and Megan also checked into a cottage on the beach. I had no man, so I decided to tour the resort and lay out on the beach in my swim suit.

I was so glad Kelly wanted to take a nap because I needed to be alone. My soul needed to be searched. I changed quickly, wrapped a skirt around my waist, and toddled to the door. I looked back and noticed Kelly's Bible on the dresser, so I tossed it in my bag. It had to be a sign from God.

The crystal-clear water splashed onto the shore. The white sand drifted with each movement. I sashayed barefoot through the pure sand with my cute pink sandals in my hand. The hot sand adored my bright crimson red polished toes. A shady plantain tree alerted me with its island attraction, so I took a seat next to it. I spread my beach towel out and had a seat.

I rubbed tanning oil all over my body, put black sunglasses on, and a straw hat. I gazed out into the ocean. The scenery was breathtaking. I felt instant serenity when I closed my eyes and took deep breaths. The breeze from the waves purified my thoughts, as it rushed across my face. This was truly paradise.

I opened my bag, pulled out Kelly's Bible, and started to read. Shortly after, the noise from a jet ski distracted me. I looked out in the ocean, and a man was riding on the jet ski, while two girls were standing in the water, up to their knees, waiting for their turn. He finally stopped to let them ride. The smaller woman got on first, and he assisted the big girl on next. The two sat on the jet ski proudly. The minute they pulled off, the machine flipped over. I couldn't stop laughing. The girls were drenched. I didn't want them to hear me laughing, so I chuckled without smiling.

"What's so funny?" a voice asked from behind me.

I turned around slowly. I couldn't believe my eyes. I needed to move very quickly because my eyes were enjoying the view of the man that stood behind me.

"I need to be reading the Bible with you. Can I sit down beside you?" he asked.

"Sure," I replied, not wanting to be rude.

"So what were you laughing at?" he asked again.

"The two girls in the water flipped over," I answered, still laughing.

He looked in the water. "That must have been a sight."

"Yes, it surely was." I giggled.

"My name is Carlos Ricardo Diamante, and I'm from Orlando, Florida."

"She's Shelby Lynn Tate, and she's from Chicago, Illinois," a seductive voice answered for me.

I was bewildered as I looked up at the man standing before me. He was standing in his white suit, barefoot, with his pants rolled up.

Dexter seized my hand, sweeping me up. I left everything lying in the sand as we soared along the shore hand in hand. Just like my dream.

"I like your hair. Braids look good on you, and I see you're wearing the sunglasses I bought you. I thought you would've thrown them away when you tossed me out of your life."

I chuckled lightly, too prideful to speak the words my heart was crying out.

We journeyed to the edge of the ocean. The waves flowed over the top of our feet.

Dexter halted. He faced me and held my hand firmly. "When I left, I left my heart with you. I know you're the one, because I haven't been with anyone sexually since we separated. I tried to pull myself together and I couldn't. . . . Girl, I got baptized again because of you. I prayed for God to make me whole again, but my prayers remained unanswered. I'm incomplete without you in my life. My faith has been confirmed, and I'm ready to do things right."

He closed his eyes gently as tears rolled down his face. "I love you and I can't live without you. I ran out on you without giving you a chance to explain. Baby, please forgive me for not trusting you. Can you find the strength to give me one more chance? I promise I will never leave you again."

I exhaled sharply. I glanced away from his stare. I let go of his hand. I started to speak, but nothing came out.

I opened my mouth. "I can't . . ."

"Is it Max?" he asked.

I sprinted away instantaneously, not looking back.

NO MORE LUST

"Grab your swimsuits and enjoy your last day of Jamaica. Bryan and Blair Cooper's wedding party is heading to Dunn River Falls," the activity director broadcast over the loudspeaker around two. Kelly and I rushed to the lobby, wanting to savor our final day in paradise.

"Hey, strangers," Kelly and I said, staring at Victor and Megan.

Blair was busy running her mouth with her family.

Max moved toward me. "Are we sitting together?"

I directed my eyes to Kelly. "Yeah, we can sit next to each other if Kelly doesn't mind."

I looked for Dexter, but he was nowhere to be found. Guilt shadowed my conscience as I thought about how I rejected him and ran off.

"Are you okay?" Max asked as he kissed my cheek.

"Yeah, I'm just ready to see this Dunn River Falls," I said excitedly.

The bus stopped in a small town at the entrance of a stream of multicolored huts that branched up into the hills. Tourists were out shopping for souvenirs in the huts. We exited the bus, the girls flocked together, and the men followed behind us.

"Pretty ladies, come see what I have."

"No, come to me, I have cheaper prices than her."

"Big spender, buy your lady this dress. Cute, huh?"

People were coming out of the huts from everywhere, trying to sell us merchandise. I felt like I was being attacked.

A man with long, thick, brown dreadlocks approached Victor. "Hey, man, you want to buy some smoke? It's good stuff."

"No, I don't smoke. I'm a man of God."

"Man of God, my ass. You Americans smoke lots of marijuana. Always coming here looking for it."

We quickly walked past the man, trying to ignore him.

"The tour guide said we can buy surf shoes here or rent some at the place."

"Blair, we all need to buy some. I'm not sticking my feet in used shoes," Megan responded.

Kelly walked over to an older woman. "Do you have surf shoes?"

"Come see. What sizes? Just twelve of your dollars."

The woman next door rushed into the hut. She grabbed Blair's hand. "Don't buy from that old bitch. She steal all my customers. I sell to you. You have shoes from me for nine of your dollars."

"Well, shit, let's follow her. You can't beat nine

dollars. That's what I'm talking about," Blair shouted.

Kelly didn't move. "I'm not buying from that cursing woman. This old lady needs the money."

"Come, let Hunky Joe stay. You buy from me."

I stayed with Kelly, and so did everyone else, except Bryan and Blair. I was in no mood to be bothered with the feisty Jamaican woman.

Max walked off after he purchased his surf shoes. Blair and I didn't venture far. We walked two huts down to where a man was carving wood pictures and sculptures, while Megan and Victor journeyed up the maze of shops.

"Sexy lady, come. He can carve you whatever you want."

"I have to have that nude sculpture. Can you carve my name and Jamaica 2004 into the bottom of that one?"

Blair pointed to the carving of two people making love. "Please carve the names Bryan and Blair into that sculpture."

I looked around for Kelly. "Don't let Kelly see my sculpture. She'll fuss at me about the nudity."

Kelly walked up behind me. "Shelby, there is nothing wrong with nudity. This is a beautiful piece of art. God created our bodies."

While standing at the bus waiting for everyone to return, we couldn't help but laugh when we saw Victor struggling with Megan's things. Megan had a new straw hat on and a straw bag with her name on it in green and pink. My girl had to represent her sorority, no matter what.

Max walked up with a bottle of Appleton Jamaican rum.

"Where did you find rum?" Bryan asked, rubbing his huge belly.

"Don't worry about it. I got hook-ups. I thought about you, man," Max said, passing Bryan a rum cake.

Dunn River Falls was gorgeous. It was a tall, steep cliff along the ocean, with waterfalls running down it.

"I know we aren't climbing this?" I yelled out to Blair.

"Girl, live a little," she said, giving me the eye.

The tour guide directed us to the bottom of the cliff, which was surrounded by sand. He extended his dark hands, which were holding surfer shoes. "The shoes will stop you from slipping on the rocks. Everyone has to have on a pair," he announced, handing the shoes to people who didn't have any.

Everyone put the shoes on their feet before marching in line.

"Hold hands. Don't let go of the person's hand next to you," he shouted over the running water.

The voyage began with Kelly and me at the end of the link. I placed my foot on the rocks as Max led me up higher. Kelly grasped my other hand as she followed me nervously up the steep cliff.

The rocks were wet and slippery. We took a quick look up at the top of the cliff and saw people tripping over the huge rocks.

"Are they adding water to the waterfall?"

Kelly smirked. "No, silly. It's raining. Look up at the sky."

We climbed up far above the ground. I peeked down. I grasped Max and Kelly's hands tightly. The

rain was intensifying the climb. I could barely see in front of me. The rain flooded my face. I glanced up. More water streamed down my face. The climb was steep and quite scary. My paranoia set in when I looked down and noticed how high we were.

"This is crazy," I told Kelly as we held hands tight and moved further up the cliff.

It appeared we were reaching a plateau. There was a deep part of the cliff resembling a Jacuzzi. The waterfall was directly over it. As people reached the plateau, the tour guide would make them jump into the pool of water then he would snap a picture of them.

The chain stopped moving. I felt at ease because I saw the flat land.

I nudged Max. "Get them to move up some."

I saw Blair and Bryan standing still by the plateau. Bryan took the tour guide's microphone and started singing another Brian McKnight song to Blair. My heart dropped. He was so romantic. I couldn't see that well, but I could hear the sound of his sweet voice.

Max peered down at me. "That boy loves Brian McKnight."

"I want to see," I yelled to Max again.

The link moved up. We reached the plateau. Bryan sang from the rock above us. Blair smiled. I looked up and waved at her, almost slipping into the water, but Kelly held me up.

Bryan stopped singing and listened to the voice near him.

"Shelby Denise Tate, I love you. I'm not letting you slip away again. Without you, my life is meaningless. I can't live another minute without you.

I'm stepping out on faith. Please be my wife? Will you marry me, Shelby Tate? Right here, right now."

My heart fluttered expeditiously. I almost fainted. I was momentarily speechless; however, I did find strength to answer.

"Yes," I screamed.

Bryan continued to sing the rest of Brian Mc-Knight's song. *"Let me tell you for the rest of my life, I'll be true . . . And let me tell you this evening; and the rest of my days and nights belong to you . . ."*

I was shaking as I looked up at Max. He winked his eye. I let go of Kelly's hand. She kissed me on my cheek and gestured for me to move up the cliff. Max reached for me. We stood side by side. He closed his eyes, embraced me tightly, and delicately placed a kiss on my forehead.

My body was quivering as he handed me to my husband-to-be, who was standing near the waterfall with a huge diamond wedding ring. I draped my arms around my true love's body, wondering how and when all of this took place.

The tour guide took his microphone from Bryan and passed it up to Victor. My eyes glared down at Max one last time. I searched his face for animosity, but I only found a smile filled with genuine joy. At that moment, I knew Dexter and I had Max's blessing.

"We are gathered here today to celebrate the marriage of Shelby Tate and Dexter JeanPierre. Do you promise to honor, respect, and cherish each other to the day that you die?"

We answered on key, "We do."

Kelly winked at me. "This is all of God."

Dexter placed the ring on my finger, with tears in his eyes; I started to cry too.

Megan looked down at me with watery eyes. She mouthed, "Your wedding rings are bigger than ours." She passed a ring to me. It was the one from Tiffany & Co., the same one I said would be for my husband should I ever get married.

I placed the ring on Dexter's finger. It slipped right on. I cried tears of joy and thought Kelly, Blair, and Megan must have collaborated with Dexter to pull this one off. Then I thought about it again. It had to be God.

"I now pronounce you Mr. and Mrs. Dexter JeanPierre."

Dexter captured me with his masculine arms. I held onto him with all that I had. I wasn't letting him go this time. We fixed our eyes on each other and kissed under the waterfalls in the rain.

The End.

About the Author

The author was born and raised in Chicago, Illinois. She received her master's degree from Tulane University in New Orleans. LeBlanc is a wife, mother, professional, and writer. At this time she is working on the sequel to *Characters of Lust*, entitled *Taste of Lust*, which is expected to be released winter 2008.

the perfect backdrop against her round breasts. Firm and sweet like two ripe peaches dipped in baker's chocolate. They are a little more than a handful, and greatly appreciated. Touching her makes me feel like I've finally found peace on earth, and there is no feeling in the world greater than that.

Right now her eyes are closed, and her bottom lip is tightly tucked between her teeth. From my viewpoint, between her wide-spread legs, I can see the beginnings of yet another orgasm playing across her angelic face. These are the moments that make it all worthwhile. Her perfectly arched eyebrows go into a deep frown, and her eyelids flutter slightly. When her head falls back I know she's about to explode.

I move up on my knees so that we are pelvis to pelvis. Both of us are dripping wet from the humidity and the situation. Her legs are up on my shoulders, and her hands are cupping my breasts. I can't tell where her skin begins or where mine ends. As I look down at her, and watch her face go through way too many emotions I smile a little bit. She always did love the dick, and since we've been together she's never had to go without it. Especially since the one I have never goes down.

I'm pushing her tool into her soft folds inch by inch as if it were really a part of me, and her body is alive. I say "her tool" because it belongs to her, and I just enjoy using it on her. Her hip-length dreads seem to wrap us in a cocoon of coconut oil and sweat, body heat and moisture, soft moans and teardrops, pleasure and pain, until we seem-

My Little Secret

BY ANNA J.

Ask Yourself

Ask yourself a question . . . have you ever had a session of love making, do you want me? Have you ever been to heaven?
—*Raheem DeVaughn*

February 9th, 2007

She feels like melted chocolate on my finger-tips. The same color from the top of her head to the very tips of her feet. Her nipples are two shades darker than the rest of her, and they make her skin

LUST THIRTY

A week had gone by. I missed Dexter, but I had to go on with my life. I only dragged around the house for two days and that was it. After that, I kept on going. I attended school daily and did exactly what Joel told me to do. Focused on fixing everything up that I didn't like.

I got my nails done on Monday, hair done on Tuesday, and a pedicure on Wednesday. With my busy schedule, I didn't have time to think about Dexter. I was beginning to spend my student loan funds on myself, and with Joel living with me, I had a lot more money to splurge.

So when Megan asked me to go shopping with her after class one day I obliged. We hit all the premium high-end stores on Michigan Avenue's Gold Coast. It felt good to pretend for one day. A high that only a woman would appreciate, shopping with the rich and elite.

I bought an extravagant black cocktail dress from Neiman Marcus and some designer BCBG Max Azria jeans. Megan insisted that every girl needed

one classy dress and one pair of good two-hundred-dollar jeans. I also purchased three pair of shoes from Bloomingdale's. All of that courtesy of Sallie Mae. I'd worry about the cost when I graduated.

"Shelby, we have to stop at Tiffany. I have to get Victor a ring."

When we walked in the jewelry store, Megan pointed to a platinum band.

"Do you like this band? It's five hundred dollars."

I frowned. "It doesn't have any diamonds." I pointed to an 18K gold ring with ten diamonds. "This is the ring I would get my husband. Isn't it nice?"

"It sure is, but Victor doesn't like flashy rings. Although I wish he did."

"Can I see that ring?"

The woman handed the ring to me.

I picked it up and examined it closely. A somber expression covered my face. The ring would've looked so good on Dexter. I whined to Megan.

"We aren't having that shit. Get over it. There are too many other brothers out here." She pointed to the diamond necklaces. "Now let's look at something for you. Diamonds always make me feel better," she professed, pulling my arm to the diamond necklace display case.

Later that evening, as promised, Joel took me to the Signature Room restaurant which was located on the ninety-fifth floor of the John Hancock building, directly across from the Water Tower. The ambiance of the place was incomparable to

any place I'd ever been in my life. The sweeping view of the city of Chicago, the elegant wood designs, and the art decor interior created an inviting and intimate atmosphere.

We drank expensive wine, listened to live jazz, and ate the finest cuisine Chicago had to offer. The evening was amazing, and Joel was on his best behavior, showing me a side of him that I didn't know existed. He was refined, conservative, polite, and incredibly generous. The whole night was spent catering to me, satisfying my every desire, making me feel whole again—self-confident, beautiful, happy, and strikingly sexy.

LUST THIRTY-ONE

Two months passed since the day Dexter walked out on me. It was now November. The days were shorter and the cold was here for a while. Joel and I laid on my bed watching *Girlfriends* on UPN. Joel turned his head away from the television and looked at me momentarily.

I caught his glimpse. "What?" I questioned, wondering what he found so amusing.

"Do you still want me to do that?" Joel asked nervously.

"Do what?"

"You know," he said softly with raised eyebrows.

"What?" I asked, not believing he was saying what I thought he was saying. "Are you serious?" I stared into his deep brown eyes for confirmation.

"Yeah, come sit on my face."

That was all he had to say. I hadn't been with a man since Dexter, and I'd grown accustomed to having my vagina licked. As a matter of fact, I was obsessed with oral sex, an addict of some sort. So, without hesitation, I rolled to his side of the bed,

pulled my panties off, lifted my nightshirt up, and squatted down on his face. This was done in seconds. There was no time for regrets or changing of minds. I was determined to hold him to his word.

Joel's thick, salivating tongue invaded my warm, throbbing pussyhole. He lashed his tongue in and out with great expertise, reaching every crevice that housed any source of sensation, licking me from front to back. He freely devoured my vagina and anus, driving me wild. My body loved him for it too, as it rode his face like a brand-new Porsche, bouncing about on his bumpy turf and increasing speed with every shift change. Juices flowed freely down Joel's mouth, showing I had missed the touch of a man. Emotions were stirring, and romantic thoughts of Dexter and I flooded my mind as I sprang back and forward on Joel's face, only harder and faster this time, utilizing his tongue for sex and imagining him being Dexter.

Joel, still unaware of my deceitfulness, continued pleasing me. Like the little engine that could, he was trying his best to make me cum with his magical mouth. He put his hands under my thighs and lifted my body up and down on his tongue in a supernatural way.

"I think I can . . . I think I can . . . I think I can't. . ." I repeated to myself as the pressure built up inside of me, ready to burst out like steam from a locomotive. My legs trembled uncontrollably, toes pointed out, and body convulsed. I couldn't contain the beast that roared inside of me to be released. "Oh. Oh . . . Oh, shit. Oh, shit," I screamed like an uncivilized being, experiencing orgasm after orgasm with no breaks in between.

I wanted to call Preston up myself and personally thank him for the FYI on Joel. He had definitely hooked me up with the best pussy-eater in the world. My best friend had skills, talents I wish I had known about when I broke up with Sebastian. An expertise that would have made me forget about any man, except Dexter. Joel was incredible with his tongue; better than Dexter, I had to admit, but I didn't love him.

Guilt dashed across my conscience. How could I let my best friend perform oral sex on me when I was still in love Dexter? I had moved further and further away from God. Now a selfish person resided in me—an individual only interested in satisfying self. The same thing I'd accused Kelly of being. The main reason I despised her in the past.

The next day, Joel and I acted as if nothing had happened. The guilt I felt after our act had moved on; escaped and settled itself on some other lost soul.

"I'm going to work," I said nonchalantly.

"Be careful. It snowed last night," Joel warned me.

I put on my coat, wrapped my scarf around my face, and placed my leather gloves on. When I walked outside, the cold, brisk, dry air swept my breath away. The white frost expelled from my mouth each time I took a breath. The snow was almost up to my knees in the grass. I backtracked to the sidewalk and dusted the light, fluffy snow off my pants with my gloves as I stomped my feet to shake the rest of the flakes off.

The sidewalk looked freshly shoveled. I assumed Joel cleaned the walkway last night when he was working down his erection. He did appear a little upset when I didn't return the favor, but there was no way I was putting any part of him in my mouth. That was just an act I couldn't perform. It was a pleasure I'd leave for the man I married.

I glanced at my car, which was covered with snow. I opened the trunk and took out my snow scraper. I eased in through the front door, put my key into the ignition, and turned on the engine. The heat blew on high from the night before, toasting my insides but doing nothing for the frosted windows. I changed the gauge to defrost, to help melt the ice. However, the snow was too thick, and a little woman-power was needed. I exhaled noisily, opened and closed the car door, and began scraping the snow and ice off all of the windows, except the two side back windows. When I was finished, I placed the scraper back in the trunk.

My stiff, frigid body crumbled in the front seat of my car, thawing out as the warm heat greeted me. It made my red cheeks and cold toes pleased. The leather riding boots I was wearing were only for fashion because my toes were ice cold, even with two pairs of socks on. I was freezing my butt off in Chicago, while Dexter was enjoying warm, sunny California.

I turned the radio on immediately, trying to keep my mind clear and not think about Dexter. Warm melodies and lyrics of love echoed throughout the car. Without hesitation, I changed the sta-

tion to hip-hop and joined in with the Geto Boys as they rapped to "My Mind Playing Tricks on Me."

"Yeah, your mind is playing tricks on you all right," I heard a male voice state, simultaneously opening my door, which was unlocked. He grabbed my legs and yanked.

I couldn't believe someone was trying to pull me out of my car. My hands were hanging on to the steering wheel firmly, refusing to be snatched back into the cold air.

The masked perpetrator was persistent in his attempt, but not too aggressive.

"Joel, stop playing. I'm going to be late for school," I pleaded, pushing his hands off of my legs.

However, the light-colored masculine hands didn't belong to Joel.

Terror embodied me. Paranoia swept across my soul. I couldn't see the stranger's face. Hysteria settled in. "Who are you? Leave me the fuck alone!" I wiggled my legs fiercely, but the attacker's grasp was firm. "Help," I screamed.

The man laughed loudly.

I turned my head around, kicking like a mad woman, pulling my gloves off, ready to fight back. I swung my arm around, and my fingernails attacked the stalker's face through the black knit skull cap. I felt his slimy skin under my nails.

He shrieked, dropped my legs, grabbed his face and pulled the hat off. His hands lightly stroked his cheeks. "You fucked my face up."

My lips poked out, and I was breathing hard, trying to regain my composure. He was enraged. He snatched my wrist. "I heard you have a new man."

"Are you crazy? I haven't seen you in months. What are you talking about? We aren't together anymore," I yelled.

He held both of my wrists tightly and kissed me on the neck. "I want you back. I miss what we had."

I jerked my arm out of his grasp and punched him in the eye. "You psycho motherfucker."

He looked at me shockingly. "Shelby, who have you been hanging out with? I've never heard you curse like this. I see you've gotten a bit feisty. I like it . . ."

I looked at him with a hard, steady gaze. "You don't know me anymore, and I don't know you. But I tell you what, you better not ever touch me again."

He lowered his voice. "I'm sorry. Can we talk peacefully?"

I turned my head. "Bitch, you tried to attack me. There is nothing to talk about. It's over. We're finished. I don't love you. We broke up over a year ago. What? Are you a stalker now?"

"I thought you wanted to be my wife. You were supposed to be the mother of my kids. Remember Amber and Caleb?"

I hissed, "Boy, I was young and dumb back in the day. I wouldn't dare marry you nor have a kid by you. You have big balls. I'm not the same person you messed over. I'm a mature woman, not that young, naïve little girl you remember. I would never get back with you. I've been with a real man. I know what true love is now."

Sebastian rubbed his knuckle and showed me his hands. "This is how you treat me? I almost got frost bite shoveling your snow this morning."

"And that makes you a damn fool. Fuck you," I shouted, as I placed one leg into my car.

He looked at me with the evil eye. I thought he was getting ready to hit me. Instead, he walked away.

As he was walking toward his car he hollered, "I was your first. You cried over me for many nights. Don't come crying back to me, Shelby."

"Sebastian, I would never come running back to you!"

LUST THIRTY-TWO

I entered the county hospital hurriedly, rushing expeditiously before all of my performances of yesterday caught up with me. "You let your best friend go down on you," I mumbled, rushing down the dingy hallways to make it to class on time. I bumped into a woman, not paying attention to where I was going. My mind was still defrosting the turmoil with Joel and the beat-down I nearly received from Sebastian.

"Hi, Miss Tate," a lady called out from behind me.

I turned around curtly to hear who owned the friendly voice. Shock plastered my body. I couldn't believe my eyes. It was Sydney. I had managed to dodge her since our incident on the phone, not wanting her to know that I was the other woman Max was seeing.

"Hi. How are you?" I froze anxiously, avoiding direct eye contact with her.

She was beaming. "Let's see. I'm going to Chicago State in January. I left my child's father

last month. He doesn't know where I am, which is a blessing. Therefore, as you can see, I'm doing better. I've come a long way from wanting to die to fighting to live."

Sydney had made so much progress, finally leaving Max and moving on with her life, and I was proud of her. She wasn't the same weak vessel I'd observed in the suicidal group months ago. Seeing her transformation just filled my heart with joy.

My eyes met with hers. "I am so proud of you. Finish school and never let a man stop you from achieving your goals."

"I won't. I'm on my way to an empowering group now. Are you training in any this semester?"

"No," I answered, not caring anymore if she noticed my voice.

"Nice seeing you, Shelby," she said with a slight smirk.

"You too. I'm running late," I said while rushing off, instantly dismissing her sneer.

"Please, don't tell Max you saw me," she blurted out, stopping me in motion.

I closed my eyes and took a deep breath. She knew who I was. I wanted to start running to avoid our controversial conversation. But I remained calm, turning around slowly to meet face to face with "the baby mama" of Max. We met each other halfway and took a seat in the waiting area.

"When I found out you were the same Sydney, I had my supervisor change my group for ethical reasons," I confessed.

"I knew you were the same Shelby when you called our house. I never forget a voice. I remembered your name from high school. One day I saw

him wearing a gold rope chain with a name plate on it, SHELBY, big as day in block letters. Max has always loved you. You know he still has that chain," she said with so much sincerity.

"Sydney, please understand. I never knew he was seeing you. When I found out a few months ago, I ended things because, really and truly, I never loved Max in an intimate way. I loved him as a friend. A childhood friend I shared history with. So please don't be mad."

"I'm not mad. You were only one of the many women Max has had affairs with. Max is just a dog constantly searching for a new bone, and I'm not putting up with it anymore. I wanted to kill him, but I realized I had a child to take care of. I'm growing stronger daily with the help of God and these support groups," she reported.

With the help of God, those words pierced my skin. God was someone I hadn't conversed with lately. Someone who was always there for me and who pulled me out of any and all drama I experienced. But yet, I'd abandoned him to do my own thing.

Lord, I need You. My life is escalating down. Talk to me again.

"I'm happy for you. Keep on praying, and God will see you through all of your trials and tribulations," I replied after a long pause. "But please don't let Max know I know who you are."

"I won't. I'm hiding from him. He'll just beg me to come back home, and I can't go back," she said nervously.

"How's the pregnancy?"

A tear crawled down her cheek. "I had a miscarriage."

I expressed my sympathy by touching the small of her back. "I'm sorry to hear that."

She started to cry. "The Lord knows best. That's where I got the courage to leave Max. The stress in our dysfunctional relationship cost me my unborn child. I had to leave. I had to leave," she groaned.

I reached out and hugged her tight. Her body vibrated, heaving in and out. Tears streamed down her face and moistened my neck. I was going to be late for class, but I couldn't leave her in that condition. Dr. Myru would understand, and if not, I'd have Megan help him see things my way.

It was four-thirty and it was already dark. However, the falling snowflakes made it look a little brighter. I couldn't stop thinking about Sydney. Max really put her through a lot. I jumped in my car and headed south. I decided to sit in traffic on the Dan Ryan to avoid the snowed-in side streets. The expressways were always clear and free from snow, but it took the city trucks a lifetime to clear local streets and pour salt on the roads.

While sitting in traffic, I checked my messages on my cell phone. Checking my messages was a daily task, hoping one day Dexter would decide to call. I sighed. There were no messages from Dexter, nor any incoming long-distance calls. However, I noticed Max called. What did he want? I hadn't heard from him since Dexter's going-away party almost three months ago. Sydney must have told Max she ran into me at the hospital.

"What the hell?" I stated hypothetically as I hur-

ried to return his call. I spoke into the phone, "Hello, Max."

"Hello, Shelby. Why don't you come fly with me to Cali to visit Dexter?"

"What?" I exclaimed. He totally caught me off guard. I couldn't believe Dexter told him about us. I was speechless.

"Max, don't call me anymore," I replied and hung up the phone.

Before I could think about what happened, my phone rang. Max shouted into the receiver, "You are bogus. Dexter told me what went on between you two. That was some ho-ass shit you pulled, straight out-of-character for you. I expected more out of you."

I didn't utter a word. He was right. I expected more out of myself. I had fallen down flights of stairs. Had lost my priceless soul, traded it in for lust. I had given my body, soul, and mind to a man that was not my husband. I remained silent.

"What the hell do you have to say?" he demanded.

I addressed him in a low tone, wanting desperately to hurt his arrogant ass. "It's true. I was messing around with Dexter."

Actually, I was attracted to him the first day I saw him in the club. I tried to fight the feelings I had for him, but each time I'd see him, the emotion grew stronger. So when Max decided to cheat, I followed my heart to fulfill my own selfish lust and to hurt him. To finally prove to him that he wasn't so slick and smart. To steal the one person he considered a best friend, a deceitful rendezvous he'd never forget.

"Did you screw him?" he interrogated me, sounding a little wounded.

"Whatever he told you happened, happened," I stated casually, cheering inside.

"I asked you."

"And I've told you . . . Are we done having this conversation?" I scoffed.

Max giggled. "Thanks for hooking my boy up until he was able to get to his main girl in Cali."

"No problem. You're very welcome," I said sarcastically.

I heard anger in Max's voice. "I'm gonna ask you again. Did he get your panties down? You didn't let me hit it. Did my boy get the ass? Yeah, that *busta* put all those passion marks on your neck."

"I'm not discussing my business with you. Furthermore, how can you be mad when you were screwing everything with a hole? You fucked Sapphire and Nakia in that threesome."

"You're right. You got me. By the way, you still owe me some pussy from that night at the Ritz," Max snickered before hanging up.

Max was a stupid man. He could be so sweet and then turn into a devil, with no warning. His words burned my soul, "*Main girl in Cali.*" I was furious. I couldn't believe Dexter played me. Max knew how to upset me. I was livid. The one person I claimed as my soul mate, the love of my life, was a fake.

I wanted to look him up and curse him out for playing with my heart even though he knew all I had been through. I thought about giving Kandace a call, to quiz her about his woman in California, but she wouldn't tell. After that, I thought

about getting Joel to call her and get the scoop, but he would unquestionably hit that, especially when he found out she was a virgin. I decided against it. If Dexter played me, it was good while it lasted. There was no sense in me being angry with yesterday's issues like I was with Sebastian. It was finally time to grow up.

LUST THIRTY-THREE

I made it home after sitting in traffic over two hours. When I arrived home, Joel was gone. He was always busy working overtime, so I didn't complain. I wasn't too sure how we'd interact with one another, since our innocent friendship had turned into an intimate relationship. I sat in the middle of the floor and pulled my boots and socks off, rubbing my cold red toes, trying to warm them up, continuously thinking about how chaotic my life had become.

A series of knocks planted themselves on my front door. I rose up to see who was at the door. Looked out of the small brass peephole. It was Blair and her son, Blairson. Blair had blonde hair today, and it was flowing down her back.

I opened the door swiftly. "Girl, come on in out of the cold." I picked up Blairson and carried him in. She had him wrapped like a zombie in his blue snowsuit. "Hey, Pooh," I said, giggling in his face as I took his layers of clothes off.

Blair swung her hair, trying to shake the snow out. Her long, manicured nails had gold and black designs with diamonds painted on them.

"I like your nails."

Then she showed me her other hand. She had a huge rock on her ring finger, a marquis. She put her head back. "Bryan proposed," Blair screamed.

"Blair, that's great. You and Megan should do a double ceremony."

"No, honey. We are getting married in April," she said in a sassy way.

"How are we going to plan a wedding in less than three months?"

"One word. Jamaica," she gloated.

"Come on. Let's go to the kitchen. Sit down," I said anxiously. I picked up Blairson and sat him on the sofa. I turned to channel eleven so he could watch *Sesame Street.*

"It's time for me to get my act together. I'll be thirty before you know it. I need to stop acting like I'm eighteen. Bryan is the one. He's a businessman, and I'm all about business," Blair said, smacking her lips.

"I'm really happy for you," I said with little feeling. I was jealous. Dexter and I were supposed to be engaged. Now Megan and Blair were going to be brides.

I guess I'll be a bridesmaid for the rest of my life. Kelly and I will be the only two single ones left, and she will probably get married before me.

"Is Kelly coming?" I asked.

"I don't know if the 'good sister' is coming. She says it depends on how her money is flowing. She's

not working for your boys anymore, and you know her church secretary job doesn't pay that much," Blair reported.

Blair pulled her cigarettes out of her purse. I gave her the look.

"You know I don't allow smoking in my house," I sneered.

"That's exactly why I don't come over here." Blair laughed.

"You need to stop smoking anyway. Smoking kills. And it hurts us non-smokers more. Like your child," I preached.

"I'm working on that, along with other issues. When you stop cursing, I'll stop smoking," Blair said quickly.

"You got a deal," I said.

I wanted to ask Blair if Bryan spoke with Dexter, but I didn't, remembering my vow to not be like I was when I was with Sebastian.

"I have to get rid of Sapphire. I'm not down with that lesbian, bisexual shit around Blairson. At first, it was cool. But after the way she came on to me the day of Kelly's surgery, she has to go," Blair said forcefully.

"I was just beginning to like her."

"I don't know what's been up with her. I had to put Blairson in daycare. She hardly ever comes home and when she does, she's out of it."

"She's probably on drugs."

"Yeah, I know that. Which one?"

I got up and boiled some milk to make cocoa. Then I opened the cabinet and pulled out the graham cracker box. I gave Blair one graham

cracker to give to her son. She walked down the three steps.

Blairson grabbed the cracker quickly. "Tank you," he murmured.

Blair came back to the kitchen talking. "Bottom-line, she has to go. I even think she hit on Bryan. He won't tell me, but I think she tried to steal my man."

"Blair, are you sure she didn't hit on you?" I said, poking my index finger through my left hand which was formed in a circle. "You seem terrified when you talk about her. Don't do something you'll regret for the rest of your life."

"Shelby, I am not gay. Nothing happened between us, believe me. I'm just starting to feel very uncomfortable around her. I'm scared."

"Blair, you are a big woman. Kick her ass if she tries anything."

"I told you I'm worried about her messing with Bryan. Hell, I can defend myself, but I don't trust her around my man. I can't live with a bitch I don't trust. I'm putting her out ASAP. Now, let's drop the discussion. Your mind wanders too much."

"Cool. Would you like some cocoa?"

"Godiva? Yes. Treat me like the rich and famous. You and Megan need to stop with all the high-priced goodies. You really need to since you don't have a rich man or a job," Blair teased.

"That hurt. I'll have a rich man one day and a job."

When the milk was hot, I poured it in and stirred the cocoa in our cups.

"How is Dexter?" Blair asked then sipped her

cocoa. "Damn. This is good," she said, wiping the foam from her lip.

"Still haven't heard from him," I said unhappily.

"I'm sure you will," Blair professed. "He'll be in my wedding."

I smirked as I sipped my cocoa, just thinking about a chance to see Dexter again.

"Where is Joel's sexy ass at? I'd love to slam him one good time before I get married. I don't know how you sit up in here with him all day and not reap the benefits," Blair said.

"Easy. I don't look at him like that," I lied.

"Son," Blair called out.

"Un-huh . . ." Blairson yelped.

"It's time to go," Blair announced loudly. Blair-son crawled off the couch and headed toward Blair. "Come on, pooky pooh."

I lifted my lazy body from the kitchen chair and strolled to the closet. I handed Blair their coats. "How much are our tickets?"

"It's four hundred for our guests for the four days. That includes accommodations, roundtrip airfare, transports to and from the resort," Blair said, shaking her hand.

"That's a good deal. How did you get that hook-up?"

"Through my job," Blair bragged.

We stood at the front door.

"I'll be there. Megan said they have plenty of men on those resorts, so I might be able to find me a fella," I joked.

I opened the door, and Blair walked out with her son in her arms.

"Congratulations, again."

* * *

The next day the aroma of grilled onions hit me as I opened my front door. I peeked in the kitchen.

"I have your favorite," Joel announced.

I looked on the counter. There were two brown paper bags with grease spots on them, and a pizza box. My mouth flew wide open. "Maxwell Polish sausages and pizza from Italian Fiesta," I said surprised.

"I was on Ninety-fifth Street today," Joel remarked.

I pulled down a paper plate from the cabinet and took a seat at the table with Joel. I removed the Polish sausage and fries out of the brown paper bag and placed them on my plate. The Polish sausage was covered with grilled onions and two hot peppers were on top. I squeezed the pepper juice on my fries and sausage. Joel placed a slice of pizza on my plate. The Italian sausage was falling off the pizza. I placed the cheesy Italian sausage pizza in my mouth, which was oozing with mozzarella cheese. After that, I bit into my Polish sausage; onions fell everywhere.

"The ghetto has the best food," Joel said with food in his mouth.

I nodded my head in agreement. "They sure do."

My body retired on the sofa, and Joel caved in on the love seat.

"You know I shouldn't go to sleep after eating all that food," I said between yawns.

Joel reached his arm out.

I knew what that meant. It was on. I joined him on the sofa. He pulled my panties off with his teeth and lifted me on his face. His tongue wasted no time piercing the inside of my tunnel. It lashed about, tantalizing my clit. I was overcome with pleasure as I bounced in a circular motion on top of his face.

"Oh Joel, this feels so good. Dexter doesn't have anything on you," I yelled excitedly, gawking at his dark chocolate, oversized penis, which was standing straight up like a sergeant in the military.

My mouth began to water. He was pleasing me orally and orgasms were coming in pairs.

Couldn't I return the favor? He's not your husband. No telling where and who his dick has been in. But how can I let him give me pleasure and not reciprocate the act? Easy, you don't love him like that.

Thoughts of riding his extensive dark chocolate delicacy clouded my mind. I inched toward it, wanting to plunge down and fulfill the craving inside of me.

Joel sat me on his stomach and nudged me toward his penis. My sweet nectar covered his six-pack.

"Shelby, get on top of me and ride it. Once you get some of this you'll forget all about Dexter."

I backed up like a crawfish. "If we have sex, our friendship will never be the same."

"What?" Joel said abruptly and stopped. "Girl, put your panties on. I'm through."

"Okay," I stated nonchalantly, reaching for my underwear.

"You can't be teasing a brotha."

"Whatever," I said. The area between my thighs quivered, longing to be satisfied.

Joel snatched my panties out of my hand. "Girl, you know I love you. Come on. Sit back on my face. I'ma hook you up."

I leaped onto Joel's mouth, and he wasted no time re-attacking my insides.

"Thank you," I muttered as he gulped down my juices.

"Cum in my face again," he mumbled between licks.

"Ooh! Ahh! Don't stop," I yelped as Joel bench pressed me on top of his mouth.

Joel's juicy, thick tongue glided to the crack of my bottom, which was sitting in front of his face. I thought I would faint as he rotated in and around my anus.

"I'm going to cum," I moaned, while pinning my body to his face. I experienced multiple orgasms by the time our escapade ended.

LUST THIRTY-FOUR

It was February. The cold wind was lashing out rapidly as the foamy waves busted out of the ice and swayed forcefully against the rocks. The heat from the sun beamed down on Joel and I as we sat in his car enjoying the view of the lake. I gazed out and then I closed my eyes.

Joel positioned his seat all the way back. "Sit on my face," he said seductively.

I followed his demand promptly and on cue. I stripped down and frantically planted my bottom down on his face and gyrated my hips like a belly dancer. The sprinkles of water from the waves splashed the front window of the car and Joel dashed in and out of me. He passionately demolished my insides until I reached my climax, moaning and jerking for him to stop.

After we finished our lustful act, I told him I wanted to go out and watch the waves burst out of the ice. I knew he thought I was crazy, but Joel smiled, grabbed my hand, and we exited the car anyway. We walked on the huge rocks, and he

threw little stones into the frozen lake. The more he threw, the more the ice cracked.

The wind was whipping our bodies. So we hurried back to the car to warm up. Joel opened the passenger door and let me in. He sat in the driver's seat as we gazed out at the lake. The oldies played. The moment was so right.

Joel wrapped his arm around me. I turned to him. He caressed my lips with his mouth. Then his tongue entered. I kissed him back.

When I realized what was happening, I pulled away. "We can't do this," I said.

"Shelby, I love you," he replied.

"What?" I asked, stunned by his confession. "We're friends. I didn't feel anything when I kissed you," I tried to explain.

"I felt plenty. I have always wanted you," Joel expressed passionately.

"What are you saying? You're scaring me. We can't take this any further," I demanded.

"So it's okay for me to please you?" he said assertively, before placing his key in the ignition.

"No. I should've never let you do that to me," I cried.

"Shelby, I did it because I love you," he said sincerely.

"Joel, listen to me. Lovers come and go. But we will always be friends," I pleaded, trying to erase some of the guilt I felt for leading him on. Tears formed and I began to pray silently.

Lord, I'm coming home. This is it. I'm tired of this sinful, hectic life. Please forgive me. Allow me to be Your child again. I can't live like this. I repent in the mighty name of Jesus. Father, I will not have sex again until I

am married. I mean it this time. I rededicate my life to You.

"Don't trip. I'm not hearing what you're saying. For three months, I was eating your pussy. You were straight-up pimping me like a paid ho. You couldn't even hook me up with a wet whistle or a hand job," he muttered. His fist beat down on the steering wheel.

"I'm sorry," I said softly.

LUST THIRTY-FIVE

I spent Valentine's Day with Kelly. The two of us spent our evening chaperoning the children at her church on an ice skating trip. We went downtown to the Daley Plaza. The rink was outside and very beautiful. The kids skated outside all bundled up with their heavy coats, scarves, hats, and gloves. The lovely snow covered their garments and the rink, making the occasion a picturesque moment. Blairson banged on the window, wanting to go out and skate, as Kelly and I sat inside the warm waiting area watching the kids from afar.

As I looked at the lovely winter atmosphere, I fell into a deep trance. Kelly didn't have a man by choice, and I didn't. Joel decided to get serious with Chloe, so he spent very little time at my house, and things were never the same after our escapade at the lake. As for Dexter, he never called after the night he walked out on me. Max and Sebastian hadn't dialed my number either, and that was a wrap for the men in my life. The only man I needed and counted on was Jesus.

Kelly looked at me intensely while I was sitting reevaluating my life.

"What's going on in that head of yours?" she asked.

"Just thinking about all the problems I've had with men," I replied.

"You do you know how much I've repented?" Kelly responded. She went on to explain how she had to let things go in the worldly life. Kelly was deep into her religion. She knew the Word. She spent five hours a day studying her Bible in isolation. "Shelby, I had to do all or nothing. I was too far gone. You haven't done much," she said, trying to console me.

"That's what you think. I do my dirt on the down low. I slept with Dexter. That sin was sooo . . . good," I groaned.

"Down low? Fool, we all knew you were slam-dunking Dexter. It was all in your face. You were too happy, and so was he," Kelly disclosed.

"Girl, I even used Joel. He was eating me out almost every day," I confessed.

"What? I didn't expect that one. Joel is like your brother."

I shook my head. "He was the bomb."

We laughed.

Then Kelly got serious. "That's just like having sex."

"No, it's not. There are no feelings attached. No penetration, and you can't get pregnant," I said, defending my wrongful act.

"The best thing to do is to pray daily. Ask God to show up and give you guidance. Don't have any type of physical contact with a man that may lead

to sexual intercourse or oral sex in your case. And, remember, if you lust, you've already committed the sin as if you had sex," Kelly preached.

"I'll just go on with my plan to save myself for my husband," I stated firmly, really meaning it this time.

"That's easy to say, Shelby. Avoiding lust requires discipline. Read your bible. Start with 1 John 2:15-17."

"I know anything I put before God is a lust. Sexual intercourse and oral sex, lusting for a man or woman, smoking, cursing, drinking, gambling, stealing, overeating, overspending, sports, and the list goes on," I recited, putting an end to my silly beliefs.

"You should join my spiritual ministries group. You'll learn so much, and you'll stay in line. Our group is going to see *The Passion of Christ* tomorrow because we're doing a series on it."

"I'll think about that. If I would have stayed with my church group, I never would have strayed away. The church is the foundation, and I needed my fellow sisters and brothers to help me turn back to God. But I stayed away from them. I went nowhere near church folks."

"Well, thank God you're back." Kelly applauded and hugged me tight.

"I'm glad you welcomed me into your church home," I said, patting Kelly's back.

We unlocked embraces and promised to be there for one another. "You have to read your Bible daily to keep up with the Word. And keep me uplifted," Kelly told me, a huge grin on her face.

"I will," I confessed, returning a loyal gaze.

"Stop me if you see me going down that destructive road again."

"Now, Shelby, you know I will. I'm radical with the Word." Kelly motioned for Blairson to agree with her. "By the way, are you going to Blair's wedding?"

"Of course, I wouldn't miss it. That's why I volunteered to watch Blairson today. She's doing her last-minute details." I beamed joyfully.

"I'm praying about it. There might be too much temptation. All those men and unlimited drinks."

"I told you I'm here for you. I'll keep you in line. We are sisters, sisters in Christ," I spoke openly, making gestures with my hand. "And don't tell me it's a sin to have a little drink or look at men?" I asked, thinking she was being ridiculous.

"For me, yes. You never had a problem with drinking. I can't have one drink. Just like I couldn't have one man. What's a sin for me may not be one for you. Your sin seems to be oral sex. That's mine too, though. Anything to do with sex is mine. Music is a sin if it makes you lust over someone. That's mine too. I've had so many lovers. When I listen to music, I reminisce about where I was at, at that time. Don't listen to me, though. Read and interpret the Bible. If you want to stop cursing, start reading Proverbs. It talks about controlling your anger and a lot more important stuff."

Kelly was really impressing me. She had gained so much knowledge in the past few months. She cut everything out, including the clubs and listening to regular music. I was happy. She was finally doing something with her life. She was even going

back to school to become a minister. Kelly also watched Blairson during the day for Blair, who'd kicked Sapphire out.

I grinned. "I love the new you."

She returned my smile. "That's because the selfish hellion is gone. Now, you see Jesus in me."

LUST THIRTY-SIX

"Just two more days until the wedding. I can't believe you're getting married before me," Megan announced.

Kelly, Blair, and I were at Megan's house rehearsing last-minute details for the wedding.

"The lady just finished my dress yesterday," Blair said with a look of relief on her face.

"Can we see it?" I asked.

"Put it on. Put it on," Kelly cried out.

"No, it's a surprise," Blair said.

Megan laughed. "Yeah, we know how you do it. That dress is probably off the chain, ghetto-fabulous. You have to be seen. What crazy thing are you doing with your hair?"

Blair swung her braids. "Excuse me, 'material girl,' if I'm too ghetto for you. If you really want to know, I'm dyeing my hair black. It will not be dyed blonde or red on my special day, but I am getting that long, wavy weave."

"Blair, I don't think you're ghetto. You do all the things I wish I had the nerves to do. You're your

own woman, and you have your own unique style. I like to see what new styles you come up with. I've never done anything wild and crazy, except dating two friends," I answered hastily, not wanting to tell the girls about the Joel story. Kelly and I winked because she was the only one who knew.

"That's it? I wish we all could be like you," Blair said sarcastically.

"Let's all get micro braids," Megan said enthusiastically, changing the subject.

"We only have two days left," Kelly reminded us.

"We can get it done in Jamaica a day before the wedding. They do it at the resort spa, and it doesn't take long," Megan insisted.

Kelly and I said okay. I had never braided my hair before, and I was down for a change.

"So when is your big date, Megan?" Kelly asked.

"You forgot? It's in August, the date he proposed. How did you forget?" Megan asked, shaking her index finger.

"The Lord has been working on me. I am trying not to remember anything about my past," Kelly confessed.

I got very quiet. I hadn't asked this question, but I needed to know.

"Is Dexter still coming?" I asked timidly.

"He sure is," Blair announced gleefully.

"I'm making you two walk together. Kelly will be with Max, and Megan will be with Bryan's cousin, Patrick."

"I can't be with Max. That's too much lust. You know I'm weak for dark-skinned men," Kelly shouted, acting silly.

"Well, sister, you better stay in Jamaica. I hear it

is full of rich, sexy, dark men just waiting for some American *gina*," Megan remarked.

Kelly laughed. "I'll be prayed up before the wedding."

"I don't know how I'm going to react when I see Dexter. I still love him," I sighed.

"Bryan said he hasn't gotten married yet," Blair conveyed in a soothing manner.

I pursed my lips together. "Max told me Dexter had a girlfriend in California."

"Please. Misery loves company. Shelby, he'll tell you anything to get you back with him. That fool is obsessed with revenge," Megan lectured.

"Get your mind off of Dexter. You'll start lusting when you see him. You can't go back to sin," Kelly uttered.

"I'm not. Dexter and I are over. I just dread seeing him after all this time."

Kelly put the sign of the cross up. "You and Megan are tainting my Christian sister."

Blair joked, "Look, Mother Theresa, you hush, or I'll steal your Bible. Shelby needs to walk with the man she loves. Life is too short."

LUST THIRTY-SEVEN

T he doorbell gave a chiming sound. I rushed
down the stairs.

The limo is here, and I'm not ready.

I searched everywhere for my purse.

Joel answered the door. A short, long-headed,
but nice-looking, older black man wearing a check-
ered blue-and-black "soul brother" suit greeted him.

"Airway Limousine Service, I'm here to pick up
Shelby Tate."

Joel picked up my suitcases, which were near
the door, and handed them to the driver. After
that, Joel reached in the closet and handed me my
purse. "Here's the purse you were looking for." He
embraced me.

I hadn't felt the touch of his body in months. A
part of me was aroused, but I knew it was only lust.
I rambled to myself silently, *Shelby, control yourself.
Lust is a sin. Lust is a sin.*

"Have a safe trip. Make sure you enjoy yourself.
I should be a married man and all moved out by
the time you get back."

I wanted to tell Joel that I thought he was making the worst mistake in his life by marrying Chloe, but I knew he would take it the wrong way. I actually blamed myself. I think I pushed him into her arms when I rejected his love.

"Tell the truth. Why are you really marrying Chloe? You call her ghetto and you never bring her around. Joel, why are you doing this?"

"Because I can't have you. You are the one true love of my life."

I could have slapped Joel for launching all of this on me as I was leaving out the door. Was he willing to ruin his life to prove a point to me? The man was trying to force me to make a decision at that very moment. But, then again, I asked him, not really expecting him to tell the truth.

Joel stared away from me. He sighed in a low voice, "I don't want to be alone."

When he said those six words, "I don't want to be alone," I was mesmerized. Suddenly, I understood the reason why many men settle for less. He answered the question to why men cheat. If Joel couldn't have me, he would marry anyone to fill a void in his life, even a hood rat. Chloe loved him, and that was all that mattered to him. She would cater to his ego, and he would continue to lust for me, the one true love of his life.

"I'll try to have a good time, if Sister Kelly doesn't monitor my every move." I giggled to break up our intense conversation.

Joel looked at me and licked his lips softly. "I love you, Shelby, and I'll meet you in Jamaica if you change your mind about us."

I answered earnestly, "Joel, we can't be more than friends."

Joel touched my hand delicately. His face showed an expression of distress, but no words followed his expression. I was done counseling Joel because I wasn't getting anywhere with him. He was determined to have me, and I didn't want to be had. There was only one thing to do and that was to wish him well.

"I've hurt you too much. What we did was a huge mistake. Enjoy your life with Chloe and your son. They need you."

I gave Joel a hug and a light kiss on the cheek as I walked out of the house.

"I'm Bobby J. Right this way."

Kelly, Megan, Victor, and Blair were already in the limousine waiting for me.

"The next stop is on Eighty-seventh Street," Blair yelled out.

Kelly saw the confusion in my eyes. "Are you okay?"

"I'm fine. It's nothing a little vacation won't fix."

"We weren't born yesterday. What happened between you and Joel?" Kelly asked.

"Joel?" Blair boldly asked.

"I knew something was up between you two."

Kelly waved her hands at Blair. She mumbled, "You are so late. That's old."

I sighed. "He's moving out and marrying Chloe, if I won't be with him."

Blair's eyes widened. "Good, that brother is fine. Give him some play."

Kelly looked at Blair and then at me. "He is try-

ing to tempt you. You should've made him move out months ago. You knew that boy was in love with you."

Maybe I did know Joel was in love with me, but that wasn't the point. I wanted my friend back. It upset me that I was about to lose a great friend; however, I realized our friendship really ended months ago, that night at Lake Michigan. When romance hits a friendship, the relationship is never the same. The bond between Joel and I was gone.

"When are your parents coming?" I asked, trying to change the subject.

"They're catching a red-eye flight tonight," Blair replied.

It was daylight by the time the limousine arrived at Bryan's house. The driver opened the door and let Max and Bryan in. I was praying Max wouldn't sit in the empty seat next to me.

"What's up, folks?" Bryan said while entering the car.

I gazed out the window as the rain beat across it.

Max followed him and sat down right next to me. He didn't look at me or say anything, and I did the same.

I gazed out the window, preoccupied with the large falling raindrops and the thunder.

Bryan had a huge tray of croissant breakfast sandwiches in his hand. "Have some. Wait—let my wife get hers first. I like how that sounds, baby," he said, kissing Blair on her cheek. "Yes, *my wife,*" Bryan said, nodding his head.

Kelly laughed, while hitting Bryan's shoulder. "Bryan, we can always count on you bringing the

food. That boy is a trip. He snuck twenty pieces of hot wings into the Keith Sweat concert."

Silence struck the limousine; the booming sounds of thunder made the only noise. Bryan stopped chewing. We all stopped chewing, except Max. Our eyes and mouth froze in place.

I slowly turned my head toward Kelly.

"What?" She laughed nervously.

Blair closed her eyes. "You are the big-lip chick that put that disgusting raggedy heart mark on Bryan's neck at the Keith Sweat concert." Then she laughed hysterically.

We looked at Blair as if she was insane.

Bryan exhaled deeply. "Are you alright, baby? I'm sorry, I love you."

Blair preached calmly, "What did I tell you that night? I told you it was cool. You haven't given me any reason not to trust you since that incident. It doesn't matter that it was my friend. That was the old Kelly, the devil version of her. I know nothing like that will happen again. Our relationship was new back then. That was the past. We are two different people today."

Blair hugged Bryan, and then she embraced Kelly. "I love both of you cheating dogs."

Kelly kissed Blair. "I love you too, and I'm so sorry for what the devil made me do. I was waiting for Bryan to tell you."

Blair was so calm, sincere, and mature. She didn't let anything bother her anymore. I admired how she handled the situation, because it took a real woman to say the things she said.

Max looked at me and cleared his throat. "How have you been, Shelby?"

"Fine," I replied softly.

I looked around. Megan was all in Victor's face and the newlyweds-to-be were deep in conversation. I glimpsed at Kelly then at Max, hoping Kelly would cram the Bible down his throat the entire trip.

Max whispered in my ear, "I would still like to be friends."

"I never stopped being your friend. You were upset with me," I explained maturely.

"Yes, I was. You know I wasn't going to talk to you anymore. You and Dexter betrayed me. I know you guys never had sex, but it still hurt. He knew how I felt about you," Max expressed sincerely.

"I'm sorry," I sighed deeply. In fact I was happy that Dexter hadn't told Max about us. It appeared he was clueless about the sexual affair Dexter and I had. My baby had remained loyal to me.

"Are you seeing anyone?" Max asked.

"No. I'm saving myself for the right man," I expressed openly.

"What happened to us? This could have been you and me getting married," Max joked.

"We're getting along. Let's not ruin things by talking about the past."

Max held my hand gently. "You're right. The future is all that matters."

LUST THIRTY-EIGHT

The airport was a madhouse. The weather was terrible. It was still raining dreadfully hard, and people were driving crazy. Cars lined up everywhere, and the police were writing tickets. The driver dropped us off near the curb. We handed him a forty-dollar tip, and he emptied our luggage out of the trunk and sped off. Max grabbed my suitcase, and we headed to the check-in counter. I was so grateful for Max. I hated carrying bags, and boy, did I have a lot. Not as many as Megan, who had five Gucci suitcases.

We had a non-stop flight to Jamaica, but airport security was no joke. Bryan was checked thoroughly; they thought he had something hidden in his belly as they searched his entire body. He had to pull off his shoes too. None of us complained, as we were grateful for the security. It really showed America's concern for our lives.

Blair made all of our arrangements, so of course, Max, Kelly, and I sat together. Max lifted

our carry-on luggage into the overhead compartment and allowed us to enter the seats first. "I want
to sit near the window," Kelly requested.

Max and I honored her request.

The plane took off and Kelly started to pray.
"Heavenly Father, I come to You in the name of
Jesus, asking that you protect us as we fly. Dear
God, watch over us, protect us, and let nothing
harm us. In Jesus' name, we pray."

We had our heads bowed in agreement. I was
nervous. I hadn't ridden on a plane in over three
years, since the September 11 deadly disaster.

The plane reached its altitude, and my anxiety
level decreased. I think Max was anxious too because he ordered a shot of Courvoisier the minute
the attendant came.

"Would you two like drinks?" Max asked politely.

"No. We don't drink anymore," Kelly answered
for the both of us.

"You don't drink, Kelly? You were always down-
ing drinks at the bar. Dexter and I had to get on
your case all the time about drinking on the job."
Max giggled, peering over me, talking to Kelly.

"I am saved now. Thank you very much. That's
why I quit. Too much temptation," Kelly shouted.

I sat in my seat snickering. Kelly turned her
back away from me, picked up her bible, and
started to read.

Max gazed into my eyes. "I really miss being
around you."

"Really," I said, not wanting to listen to his pick-
up line.

"I'm serious. I really enjoy your company," he
expressed sincerely.

I acknowledged his comment. "I'm glad we can talk like friends."

The plane started bumping. "Ladies and gentlemen, please fasten your seatbelts. We are experiencing turbulence," the attendant announced.

I grabbed Max's shoulder.

He wrapped his arm around me. "It's okay," he assured me.

My nerves were wearing thin. I started tapping my foot fast and praying.

"We are going through some bad weather. You can expect more turbulence," the pilot announced this time.

"Kelly, please read to me," I begged, inching closer to her.

"You are such a baby." Kelly reached in her bag and passed me another Bible.

I held the Bible in my hand, closed my eyes and shook my legs uncontrollably. "Jesus, please watch over me. Give me strength, Father," I mumbled. I started to read the New Testament, beginning with Matthew.

We experienced a sudden drop.

"What was that?" I screamed.

The pilot spoke again, "Flight attendants to your seats. Fasten your seatbelts."

Kelly grabbed my hand. "Cast your worries upon Him and He shall grant you peace. In the name of Jesus, I rebuke fear. Lord, we have too much living to do. Give her strength."

Max held my other hand. I didn't say a word. My body was shivering.

Megan tapped on the back of my chair. "You need a valium?"

I sniffed anxiously. "Do you have one in your purse?"

"Give that fool some Prozac," Blair shouted in front of us.

Bryan pouted. "Man, I need to eat. They were just about to serve us before the pilot made them sit down. Does anyone have a snack? Peanuts? Popcorn? Chips? Candy bar? Tic Tac? Anything?"

"Max, give her a swig of that cognac. It may knock her out," Blair said.

I was shaking. "Will it calm me down?"

Max looked down at his glass as if he didn't want to share. "If you drink enough."

Kelly tapped the bible. "She doesn't need that. Talk to Jesus, girl."

I started reading Matthew again. The plane lowered its altitude again. It was dark outside, and the rain was beating down on the window. Lightning flashed. I breathed heavily, but I continued reading.

Max wrapped his arm around me tightly. I could hear his heart pounding. I think he was more terrified than I was. The entire plane was silent.

The turbulence stopped. "Thank you, Jesus," I yelled.

"Oh ye of little faith, the Lord said we were going to be okay. You're acting like the disciples when they were on the boat with Jesus and the boat started rocking. Have faith," Kelly summoned me.

"Shelby, I can't believe you're acting like you've never flown before," Megan whispered from the back.

I didn't utter a word. I was too busy praising God silently.

As we were landing in Jamaica, I looked over Kelly's head, trying to see the beautiful mountains and the sparkling blue ocean from the plane. This place was like a dream come true.

After exiting the plane, we were bombarded by Customs.

"I thought we didn't have to show our identification if we had a passport," Blair argued.

"Just give them the shit," Megan cursed.

As we walked toward the door, a man approached us. "Hey, mon, I carry your items to the van," he said with a strong Jamaican accent.

"That's okay, we have help," I replied politely.

He jabbered something and walked off quickly. The men had all of our suitcases except Kelly's and she'd only brought one. She wasn't a diva anymore, so she packed light.

"The people are very rude, so don't be alarmed," Megan warned us. This was her third time coming to Jamaica. Ms. Gucci had been everywhere.

The closer we walked to the door, the hotter it became.

"Need a ride, mon? Come ride in my taxi? I have air condition," another driver rambled on.

"No, no, sweety," Blair said, while reaching for her cigarettes.

When we made it outside, I thought I would faint as the blazing sun shocked my eyes. I had to locate my Gucci sunglasses that Dexter bought me to withstand the bright ball of flame.

The area around the airport looked like a flea market. It seemed like everyone was trying to hustle. The taxis were really advocating their business. The men were walking up to people at the same time, begging them to ride in their taxi. People were even trying to charge tourists to ride in their raggedy old cars. There wasn't a new-model car anywhere.

Blair lit her cigarette.

"Put that out, now. I've told you I don't want my wife to be smoking," Bryan said assertively. He took the cigarette and the box from her hand and gave them both to a guy who was outside begging for money.

Blair didn't say a word. She kissed him and kept on walking. Blair loved it when her man took charge.

"There's the shuttle for our resort," Blair pointed out.

We took a seat on the shuttle.

"Kelly, I'm sitting next to the window this time."

"I don't think so."

"Max, can I sit next to the window?"

Max moved over. "Sure, Shelby, you can ride all the way to Negril next to me."

My eyes stayed glued to the window as the shuttle bus traveled down a two-lane road. I looked up at the beautiful homes nestled in the mountains. As we traveled down farther, out of the city limits, I couldn't see anything but trees of the jungle.

The bus picked up speed down the dusty road, clouding my view. When the air was clear, I looked in amazement as we traveled through a small town. The community appeared to be impoverished be-

captive. I'm practically screaming and begging her to stop, and just when I think I'm about to check out of here, she lets my clit go.

I take a few more minutes to get my head together, allowing her to pull me into her and rub my back. Moments like this make it all worthwhile. We lay like that for a while longer, listening to each other breathe, and much to my dismay, she slides my head from where it was resting on her arm and gets up out of the bed.

I don't say a word. I just lie on the bed and watch her get dressed. I swear, everything she does is so graceful, like there's a rhythm riding behind it. Pretty soon she is dressed and standing beside the bed, looking down at me. She smiles and I smile back, not worried, because she promised me our lover's day, and that's only a week away.

"So, Valentine's Day belongs to me, right?" I ask her again just to be certain.

"Yes, it belongs to you."

We kiss one last time, and I can still taste my honey on her lips. She already knows the routine, locking the bottom lock behind her. Just thinking about her makes me so horny, and I pick up her favorite toy to finish the job. Five more days, and it'll be on again.

erect nipples, making them harder than before, until her hands warm them back up again.

She knows when I can't take anymore, and she rubs and caresses me until I am begging her to kiss my lips. I can see her smile through half-closed eyelids, and she does what I requested. Dipping her head down between my legs, she kisses my lips just as I asked, using her tongue to part them so that she can taste my clit. My body goes into mini-convulsions on contact, and I am fighting a battle to not cum that I never win.

"Valentine's Day belongs to us, right?" I ask her again between moans. I need her to be here. V-Day is for lovers, and her and her husband haven't been that in ages. I deserve it . . . I deserve her. I just don't want this to be a repeat of Christmas or New Year's Eve.

"Yes, it's yours," she says between kisses on my thigh and sticking her tongue inside of me. Two of her fingers have found their way inside of my tight walls, and my pelvic area automatically bounces up and down on her hand as my orgasm approaches.

"Tell me you love me," I say to her as my breathing becomes raspy. Fire is spreading across my legs and working its way up to the pit of my stomach. I need her to tell me before I explode.

"I love you," she says, and at the moment she places her tongue in my slit, I release my honey all over her tongue.

It feels like I am on the Tea Cup ride at the amusement park, as my orgasm jerks my body uncontrollably, and it feels like the room is spinning. She is sucking and slurping my clit, while the weight of her body holds the bottom half of me

Valentine's Day is fast approaching, and I have a wonderful evening planned for the two of us. She already promised me that her husband wouldn't be an issue because he'll be out of town that weekend. And besides all that they haven't celebrated Cupid's day since the year after they were married, so I didn't even think twice about it. After seven years it should be over for them anyway.

"It's your turn now," she says to me in a husky, lust-filled voice, and I can't wait for her to take control.

The ultimate pleasure is giving pleasure . . . and, man, does it feel good both ways. She starts by rubbing her oil-slicked hands over the front of my body, taking extra time around my sensitive nipples, before bringing her hands down across my flat stomach. I've since then removed the strap-on dildo, and am completely naked under her hands.

I can still feel her sweat on my skin, and I can still taste her on my lips. Closing my eyes I enjoy the sensual massage that I'm being treated to. After two years of us making love it's still good and gets better every time.

She likes to take her time covering every inch of my body, and I enjoy letting her. She skips past my love box, and starts at my feet, massaging my legs from the toes up. When she gets to my pleasure point, her fingertips graze the smooth, hairless skin there, quickly teasing me before she heads back down and does the same thing with my other limb. My legs are spread apart and lying flat on the bed with her in between, relaxing my body with ease. A cool breeze from the cracked window blows across the room every so often, caressing my

like a vise. She moans louder, and I kick the toy up a notch to medium, much to her delight. Removing my mouth from her clit, I rotate between flicking my wet tongue across it to heat it, and blowing my breath on it to cool it, bringing her to yet another screaming orgasm, followed by strings of "I love you" and "Please don't stop."

Torturing her body slowly, I continue to stimulate her clit, pushing her toy in and out of her on a constant rhythm. When she lifts her legs to her chest, I take the opportunity to let the ears on the rabbit toy that we are using do their job on her clit while my tongue find their way to her chocolate ass. I bite one cheek at a time, replacing it with wet kisses, afterwards sliding my tongue in between to taste her there. Her body squirming underneath me lets me know I've hit the jackpot, and I fuck her with my tongue there also.

She's moaning, telling me in a loud whisper that she can't take it anymore. That's my cue to turn the toy up high. The buzzing from the toy matches that of the radio, and with her moans and my pants mixed in, we sound like a well-rehearsed orchestra singing a symphony of passion. I allow her to buck against my face while I keep up with the rhythm of the toy, her juice oozing out the sides and forming a puddle under her ass. I'm loving it.

She moans and shakes until the feeling in the pit of her stomach subsides and she is able to breathe at a normal rate. My lips taste salty-sweet from kissing her body while she tries to get her head together, rubbing the sides of my body up and down in a lazy motion.

ingly burst into an inferno of hot-like-fire ecstasy. Our chocolate skin is searing to the touch, and we melt into each other becoming one. I can't tell where hers begins . . . I can't tell where mine ends.

She smiles . . . her eyes are still closed, and she's still shaking from the intensity. I take this opportunity to taste her lips, and to lick the salty sweetness from the side of her neck. My hands begin to explore, and my tongue encircles her dark nipples. She arches her back when my full lips close around her nipple and I begin to suck softly as if she's feeding me life from within her soul.

Her hands find their way to my head and become tangled in my soft locks, identical to hers but not as long. I push into her deep, and grind softly against her clit in search of her "J-spot" because it belongs to me, Jada. She speaks my name so soft that I barely heard her. I know she wants me to take what she so willingly gave me, and I want to hear her beg for it.

I start to pull back slowly, and I can feel her body tightening up trying to keep me from moving. One of many soft moans is heard over the low hum of the clock radio that sits next to our bed. I hear slight snatches of Raheem DeVaughn singing about being in heaven, and I'm almost certain he wrote that song for me and my lady.

I open her lips up so that I can have full view of her sensitive pearl. Her body quakes with anticipation from the feel of my warm breath touching it, my mouth just mere inches away. I blow cool air on her stiff clit, causing her to tense up briefly, her hands taking hold of my head, trying to pull me

closer. At this point my mouth is so close to her all I would have to do is twitch my lips to make contact, but I don't . . . I want her to beg for it.

My index finger is making small circles against my own clit, my honey sticky between my legs. The ultimate pleasure is giving pleasure, and I've experienced that on both accounts. My baby can't wait anymore, and her soft pants are turning into low moans. I stick my tongue out, and her clit gladly kisses me back.

Her body responds by releasing a syrupy-sweet slickness that I lap up until it's all gone, fucking her with my tongue the way she likes it. I hold her legs up and out to intensify her orgasm because I know she can't handle it that way.

"Does your husband do you like this?" I ask between licks. Before she could answer I wrap my full lips around her clit and suck her into my mouth, swirling my tongue around her hardened bud, causing her body to shake.

Snatching a second toy from the side of the bed, I take one hand to part her lips, and I ease her favorite toy (the rabbit) inside of her. Wishing that the strap-on I was wearing was a real dick so that I could feel her pulsate, I turn the toy on low at first, wanting her to receive the ultimate pleasure. In the dark room the glow-in-the-dark toy is lit brightly, the light disappearing inside of her when I push it all the way in.

The head of the curved toy turns in a slow circle while the pearl beads jump around on the inside, hitting up against her smooth walls during insertion. When I push the toy in she pushes her pelvis up to receive it, my mouth latched onto her clit